Marcy

D1519198

Sharon Manea

Marcy
by Sharon Manea

Printed in the United States of America.

ISBN 9781498450553

www.xulonpress.com

TABLE OF CONTENTS

Thanks Be to God...

...for all those who helped and encouraged me in writing this book.

Lisa & Lori – the first ones who read *Marcy*. Indeed, they read it chapter by chapter as I got them done and even acted excited about getting the next 'installment'. Thanks for not only encouraging me, but also being kind enough to correct me when you saw something amiss.

Jeff – a rather prolific author – You inspired me to write and publish.

Debbie – thank you painstakingly going through the manuscript on several occasions to find the mistakes. And for being biggest pusher when I got bogged down. I think I can truly say that without you, *Marcy* wouldn't be on the market.

Sarah – Thank you for being my 'I'm not quite happy with this, but I can't think how to fix it, can you give me a suggestion?' go-to person. I'm also grateful for your artistic abilities.

Daddy – thanks for reading 'one word at a time'! I love you!

And of course there is my husband – thank you for your patience, for putting up with me and for demonstrating God's faithfulness and love to me. I love you, too!

Chapter 1

BARING HEARTS

*H*am.

Again.

Marcy Kelman sat on the sagging, green vinyl couch in the break room, nibbling on her sandwich.

At least this time she attempted to add a little variety to her lunch. Putting the ham on a French roll, spread with a mixture of Neufchatel and crushed pineapples wasn't bad, but it was still ham. Cooking for one wasn't very appealing and she had gotten into the bad habit of picking up whatever was on sale at the grocery store, just eating that until it was gone, and then starting over with a new sale. It wasn't a healthy way to eat, she knew, but it was easier. She had gotten too much ham though. The deli person had misunderstood what she had said, and given her twice what she had asked for. Instead of correcting the mistake, she just bought it. And now she was eating it and eating it...

She'd been having it for lunch and supper every day for the last several days and now she even started to have it for breakfast. Yuck. Even less appetizing was eating it in the break room with its tastelessly painted walls the color of fading daffodils. A row of old metal lockers spray painted in a pattern of primary colors lined one wall and part of another. Marcy assumed it was supposed to be cheerful, but to her it only succeeded to look chintzy.

The hand-written notes in magic marker and posters of food ads – taped none too carefully – to the walls only added to the "back room" look. The grocery store's public areas always looked bright, clean, and appealing. Marcy often wondered why the break room couldn't look that way, too. *"At least,"* she thought, *"we could have one of those newer pop machines with the modern graphics."* She was sure that the break room vending machines qualified as antiques. But they were the ugly, drab-colored boxy things, not the cute ones people collected.

Some of the cashiers and stockers were on their break at the same time. They sat on mismatched chairs around the wobbly, chipped tables trying to squeeze as much talking in the half hour break as possible. Some of them were close friends with each other and involved in each other's personal lives.

Working part-time in the office limited Marcy's interaction on the job and although she'd gone to school with some of her co-workers, she felt she never quite fit with the crowd with whom she had her breaks and hadn't become close with any of them. Sometimes she would sit and talk with them, but today she wasn't in the mood to join the conversation and was only half listening. The talk today seemed to be mostly gossip. She was contemplating pitching the ham sandwich and buying an apple when a name caught her attention.

Apparently Ryan Robinson was back in town, still single and had gotten a good job that a mutual friend or acquaintance was hoping to get via promotion. The conversation was littered with crude language, derogatory comments and defamation of the job usurper and his family.

Marcy was glad that her break was over, she had heard enough. She had heard that Ryan had been wild in college, but this gossip didn't sound like him or his family.

Growing up next door to the Robinsons since she was five, she and her older brother, Mark, had become close friends with Ryan. Mark was two years Marcy's senior and Ryan fit right in the middle. She and Mark practically regarded him as another brother. He seemed to feel the same way about them. He never, (well, hardly ever,) made her feel she was a pest and included her in many of his boyhood games. Marcy could even talk him into playing 'Store' and 'House' with her, as long as his other friends didn't find out.

As she and Ryan got older, they became each other's confidants. Sharing secrets, dreams and wishes, even though their interests changed as did their other friends. Marcy never felt like they were 'girlfriend and boyfriend', but definitely best friends.

Neither she nor Ryan were very good at writing letters. So Marcy had mostly kept up to date on Ryan through his parents until she went to college. She started to get busier with her studies, and didn't see Mr. and Mrs. Robinson as much. When her parents sold the house and moved to Sheridan, Marcy rented a small house so she could stay in Lakeland Grove. It would be easier to keep her part time job and finish her courses. She was nearer to the college and her job, but her home was clear across town from the Robinsons. After a bit, she hardly saw or talked to the old neighbors and Ryan occupied very little time in her thought life.

Marcy went back to work, wishing she had left to go buy the apple instead of eavesdropping. Gossiping had always been distasteful to her, so why did she listen in today? And why didn't she try to defend Mr. Robinson? Because she didn't have the facts, she excused herself. Feeling dissatisfied and irritable the rest of the day, she was glad when it was time to go home.

Marcy put all her energy into throwing the clay on the wheel. It was a good way for her to vent frustration and rid herself of stress. This was her real work, what she went to school to learn to do. She made pottery. It didn't bring in enough money to totally support her, but she loved it. She sold pieces out of several different craft consignment shops, and also to quite a number of those artsy-trendy stores. Picking up direct sales from people wanting place settings and matching completer sets for gifts also added to her income. Her sales area was growing, too. Just last week she had sold to *La CleAires*, a chain that had several boutiques not only in this state, but also in the neighboring state.

Marcy's studio was in her home. One of the reasons she chose this house was for the enclosed porch in the back that could be heated in the winter. It made a great place to work, providing plenty of room and natural light. It also had a small set of cabinets with a counter top and a utility sink. The small basement was good storage for extra materials and overflowing pottery. She didn't own a kiln, but had an agreement with the local high school to use theirs whenever it didn't interfere with their schedule. Marcy paid them for the use of it. Pottery was one of last art teacher's weak areas, so Marcy was often called on to be a guest teacher when the classes were studying pottery. This didn't hurt Marcy's budget, and almost made up for the money she spent renting their kiln.

Today she was forming a pitcher for a dish set. She already had the place settings done, and only had three items left of the completer set. The wedding wasn't for another month yet. She was well ahead of schedule. This customer wanted it in Marcy's favorite color – cobalt blue.

She was just finished centering the lump and was beginning to shape it, when her front door bell rang. Drats! She looked down at her clothes; a raggedy pair of cutoffs and a faded oversized T-shirt. Water and clay were the only things decorating her attire. Being a potter wasn't a particularly neat job. She did choose to wipe her hands on a rag instead of her pants or shirt, as was her usual custom. She caught a glimpse of her reflection in the window. Her brown hair was starting to fall out of its restraining clip. She hastily released the clip and tried to recapture it into a loose bun at the back of her head. It didn't look much better than it had. Oh, well. Whoever it was would have to take her as she was.

The bell ringer was Dave Lewis, a manager and friend at the grocery store. She went out with him from time to time. Nothing was serious on her part. She didn't remember planning anything with him tonight. So what brought him over? His smile faded as she opened the door and he got a full look at her.

"You look a mess!"

"Thanks, Dave. You look nice yourself, as always." Dave was a nice looking guy. He had a trim figure – it wasn't muscular or athletic, but there weren't any 'love handles' either. That was because he was always doing something; it seemed like it was hard for him to sit still and relax. Of course that was probably one of the reasons he advanced to assistant store manager rather quickly. Marcy pictured him as one of those little boys that kept his mom on her toes, and made her cherish his short nap times. He always seemed to look tidy: shirts pressed and tucked neatly, tie in place and never loose, glasses always clean. His short curly blonde hair never seemed to get out of place, either, not even in foul weather. She often wondered if it was because it was curly and short, or if he used spray to keep it that way. Even when he helped unload trucks, he still kept his neat appearance.

"What are you doing to get that way?" he asked in a hesitant voice. The look on his face reminded Marcy of a little kid feeling squeamish about touching a frog for the first time.

"I'm in the middle of throwing a pitcher. You'll have to come on back to the studio and visit, I can't really stop now." She led the way to the back, picking up a chair on the way so he could sit. Dave grabbed some paper towels from the sink and wiped off the chair before he did. He watched her as she started the wheel again and took up forming the clay where she got interrupted. He looked a bit uncomfortable as he looked around.

"It's kind of dirty back here, isn't it?"

"Clay is dirt, Dave. Things tend to get dirty when you work with dirt."

"Why don't you quit and work at the store full time? I know that they'd love to have you. And so would I." He looked at her expectantly.

"I like doing this." She didn't want to add that she didn't particularly like working at the store, and the only reason she did was that it helped pay the bills.

He wrinkled his nose, "You like getting messy?"

"I like making pottery. Getting messy just happens to come with the territory. Besides, I'm starting to get more business. So... what brings you over tonight? I didn't think we were going out, were we?"

"Can we go in the living room and talk?"

"Nope, sorry. If you want to talk, it'll have to be in here, I'm in the middle of this piece. It's part of an order that I'm doing for a wedding present. Would you like something to drink?"

"Is there any beer left?"

"I've got tea, juice, lemonade, milk and pop. The beer's gone, sorry."

He shook his head, "No thanks."

"So, what did you want to talk about?"

"You're kind of curt tonight. Did I make a mistake coming over without notice? Do you want me to go?"

Marcy sighed, and looked at him apologetically. She wasn't very good at hiding her feelings. "I'm sorry, Dave. It's nothing you did. When I get going on the wheel, it's like I get into a rhythm or something, and sometimes it's hard to get it back if it gets interrupted. But that isn't your fault and I shouldn't take it out on you."

"You were kind of irritable this afternoon after your break. So what happened to make you cranky? Is something the matter?"

"Ham."

"*Ham?*"

"Yeah, I had yet another ham sandwich; of which I'm getting sick, and it wasn't very satisfying."

Dave grinned, "How much ham do you have left? I'll be sure to inform the cashiers not to let you buy any more, if this is how ham affects you."

Marcy chuckled. Every once in a while Dave could be relaxing to be around. It looked like tonight could be one of those times.

"Are you sure it was just the ham that made you cranky? Or could it be that you over-heard Jeanette and the others talking about Ryan Robinson?"

Maybe this wouldn't be one of those times, after all. Marcy looked up from her work and fastened her eyes on his, waiting for an explanation.

"Jeanette said that they forgot you were sitting on the couch where you could hear them talking at the table. She said that they had been talking about Ryan moving back in the area, and that what they said wasn't the most flattering. Jeanette thought that you two used to be good friends. *Very* good friends. Is that what changed your demeanor?"

Marcy gave the pitcher her attention before she answered. "Ryan and I grew up together. We were next-door neighbors. We were buddies and he was more like my brother than anything else. I haven't seen him in over ten years though, and we haven't communicated. His coming back to the area was a surprise to me."

"So how does his coming back make you feel?"

"Make me feel?" Marcy tipped her head and gave her shoulders a quick shrug. "Curious mostly. What is this, Dave? I feel like you're trying to psycho-analyze me. And don't give me any of that nonsense about maintaining good relations between the employees. That's not why you came here." She really didn't want to talk about Ryan Robinson's return to the area. She didn't know exactly how she felt, other than curious, or why she felt like she did – and that made her feel irritable. One thing was for sure, she wasn't going to try to figure it out with Dave. Marcy stopped the wheel. She couldn't work anymore. She'd have to cover it and hope that she could get back to it before it dried out.

Dave looked sheepish. This wasn't how he had meant the conversation to go. He had just wanted to spend some time with her and see if he could subtly ascertain where he stood. It didn't look like he was going to be able to.

"Jeanette said that he's still available, and that she thought that you used to have feelings for each other. I was wondering if that was true."

"Why?"

"Why?" He hadn't expected her to ask that. She was certainly direct tonight, and it looked as if she expected him to be also.

"Yes, why."

Dave hedged. He wasn't sure how Marcy felt about him, although he was pretty sure how he felt about her. He didn't want to bare his heart until he was more certain of hers. "Well, because... because I wondered if that would break us up."

"Break us up? We're not going together. Sure, we go out once in a while, but that doesn't make us an item. We have a platonic relationship."

He was pretty sure of her feelings now. Dave looked down at the floor, and light dawned for Marcy.

"Don't we, Dave?" she asked him quietly, hesitantly. She didn't mean to hurt him. Dave stood up and paced to the window. He absentmindedly ran his finger over the frame, wiping off the dust.

"I don't know, do we? I know we don't keep steady company or anything, but you don't go out with anyone else. So, I guess that I thought that meant there was hope for me." His guts were spilled, and he sounded hurt.

Something turned over in her stomach and Marcy couldn't respond right then. She never dreamed that was the kind of relationship Dave was wanting. She must have missed some clues, somewhere. When she didn't respond, he stepped over to where she sat at the wheel. He took her by the arms and brought her to her feet. For a moment he searched her eyes to see if there was any hope for him there. Seeing confusion and concern for him, he pulled her into his arms and kissed her. Kisses from him had always been sweet good-night kisses on the cheek. This one asked questions.

"Is there any hope for me, Marcy?"

Marcy stood in his arms for a minute, unsure what to say or do next. She sighed and gently pushed him away from her. Dave stepped back and leaned against the wall, shoulders sagging. He looked dejected and her heart went out to him.

"Dave, I didn't know. I had no idea. It's not that I don't like you; it's just that I don't like you like *that*. You're a good friend, Dave, and I didn't ever mean to lead you on. I don't want to hurt you, but I don't want to get into a serious relationship now. I can't. I'm not satisfied with my life. I'm not sure where I'm headed with it, and I feel discontented, restless."

"Maybe you just need to settle into a good stable relationship – one with security." Dave hinted.

"That would be unfair to you. What would happen if we got married and I still felt discontented two years later? That would make for an unhappy relationship and a lot of hurt feelings. And I don't believe in divorce. I know it sounds old fashioned, but marriage is 'forever-after, till-death-us-do-part' with me."

Dave pleaded, "Can't we at least try, Marcy? Isn't there even a chance? Maybe you could eventually learn to like me as more than..."

Marcy's gentle head shaking stopped his coaxing. She didn't want to hurt him, but she didn't want to leave room for misunderstanding, either. She spoke quietly.

"Please be my friend, Dave. Please don't force my hand."

There was a long silence as he searched her face for any glimmer of hope. Resignation finally settled in and Dave sighed. He gave her a sad little smile.

"I could use a drink. Want to go for one with me?"

Marcy chuckled and pointed to the area where her hands had rested against his chest. "I don't know – you're pretty messy."

Dave looked where she indicated and sighed dramatically. "Women! They'll mess you up."

"Don't worry, it'll wash out. Tell you what – I can't work anymore tonight. I think there's a half-way decent movie on TV. Why don't I clean up and you pop some popcorn to go with the movie?"

They sat together on the couch watching a comedy and talking about unimportant things, trying to keep the rest of the evening light. Dave seemed to be trying to make their relationship be as just friends, and Marcy was trying not to do anything else that might give him false hope. She didn't want to hurt his feelings any more than she already had. He helped her clean up the little bit of the mess there was from the snacks, then went home without a kiss, but not before Marcy promised to go out with him Saturday evening, "Just as friends."

Chapter 2

GALLANT KNIGHT

*M*arcy stretched as she got up from her small kitchen table to put her breakfast dishes in the sink. The windows were open, letting in the out-of-doors. The morning was one of those beautiful early-summer Saturdays. There had been a thunderstorm and a hard rain the day before, but this morning the sun was out. The storm front had brought cooler temperatures and the rain had settled the dust and washed everything off, leaving the day smelling fresh. Marcy glanced at her studio, and thought about the work out there that she should probably do, but the day was just too beautiful to have to stay inside. She opted for riding her bike on the errands she had to run. That would get her out of the house and would help her feel like she hadn't totally wasted the day if she did the errands and besides, she needed some exercise.

She had a lot of time before her date tonight. Taking the "scenic route" – as she called any variance from the regular and shortest way to wherever she was going – took her quite far out of her way onto Cobblewood, one of the last two 'real' boulevards in Lakeland Grove. Cobblewood was one of the loveliest streets in town. It was lined with mature trees that reached out across the divided road to meet the trees lining the meridian, making one feel as if they were driving through a tunnel. She neared the neighborhood that she thought was the best of all, the oldest part of town. Part of the street still had stretches of brick like the original construction. She loved the huge two story houses, laced with the gingerbread that decorated the porches and eaves. Mark was born in one of these regal houses (quite by accident, thanks to a freaky late March blizzard.)

Marcy slowed as she approached her all-time favorite house. It was a huge two story that sat on a corner lot. The attic had windows on all sides and Marcy always thought that it could be turned into a great playroom. It wasn't just a square house; there were lots of corners to tuck things into. There was a large porch in the front that wrapped half way around the right side; just right for a porch swing and maybe a table and a couple of chairs. There was another porch in the back. Marcy couldn't see it as well because of a large tree and some shrubbery that obstructed her view. The yard looked rather plain and Marcy always wondered why someone didn't do more with the landscaping.

Marcy resumed her pace as she passed the house and reflected on why she had come all the way out here today. She hadn't been in this neighborhood on purpose in years, and never on her bike. This certainly was the wrong direction to the stores and usually if she wanted just scenery, she would take the river road to the park outside of town. Could it be that she was giving in to the curiosity that had been piqued at lunch the other day? Shame on her! But she was here now, and what was she thinking? What was she going to do? She didn't have to stop. She could just ride on by. No one would ever know the difference, but what if someone was out and saw her? Mrs. Robinson would be hurt if she knew Marcy was in the neighborhood and hadn't stopped. She felt embarrassed, since she hadn't been there for so long. Yet, how could she gracefully stop in, what reason could she give?

"Hi! I just heard some girls gossiping at lunch the other day, and I thought that I'd pop in and see if it any of it was true."

Not hardly.

Marcy didn't slow down her pace as she had neared the Robinson home. If anything, she sped up due to her quandary. Maybe if she looked like she was actually on her way to somewhere, instead of just meandering, wasting a beautiful Saturday morning... Good grief, she felt like a teenager, out after curfew with no right to be there. *These are public roads, anybody can be on them, you ninny! For crying out loud, Marcy, act your age!*" So why was her heart thumping hard enough that she could feel it above the jarring of the bike on the brick pavement?

She first saw the house in which she grew up. Good, Mr. and Mrs. Sheffler, the 'new' owners of over eight years now, were still keeping it up and it looked in as good of shape as when they moved in. Better, maybe, because they were semi-retired, and according to Mrs. Sheffler, Mr. Sheffler's favorite thing to do was to "putter around, fixing things before they were broken." He had already started compiling a list of things before they had decided to buy it. Marcy secretly thought that one of the reasons they ended up buying the house was not that it was a sound, well-built house, but that there were lots of minor things that could be fixed after they bought it, thereby keeping Mr. Sheffler occupied for quite a while. Dad's business hadn't given him the time to keep on top of things like he would have liked to do himself. And Mark could no longer help because he had gotten married. He had also settled about 300 miles away to the neighboring state, close to his new wife's family, and also a lucrative job with his father-in-law's business.

The Shefflers had added a short picket fence, about thigh high, and he was out in the yard painting it white. Part of it was still the color of new wood. The reasons for the new fence were rolling about, playing with each other a few yards behind him – two small, fluffy puppies. Mr. Sheffler was painting the part of the fence nearest to the driveway. The Robinson's drive was only a narrow strip of grass away from the Sheffler's.

There was a dark blue sedan being unloaded in the Robinson driveway. Mr. Sheffler was apparently talking to the person unloading the car, because he seemed to be doing more gesturing with his paint brush than applying paint.

To Marcy's chagrin, as she got nearer, the puppies came running to the fence and started yapping. Mr. Sheffler stopped talking and turned to see why the dogs were making such a fuss. When he saw the bike rider, he raised his hand in a friendly wave. Marcy did not slow her pace; she had decided that she was not going to stop, but she couldn't be unfriendly and so raised her hand to wave back. That was a mistake.

As she raised her hand, her front wheel ran across the man-hole cover, still wet from the rain. The handle bars jerked as it hit the rough bricks, also still slick from the rain. Her upraised hand slammed back down on the handle bar and grabbed at the brakes. She vaguely heard someone call out to be careful, but it was too late. She skidded closer towards the edge of the road, unable to regain control of the bike. The curb grabbed the front tire, halting it abruptly, causing the rear end to whip around, where it then grabbed the back tire. With both tires firmly in its grasp, Marcy was neatly ejected sideways from her mount. A concrete sidewalk was conveniently located only a few feet from the curb. That would have been Marcy's destination, had not a tree been firmly planted between the two. It caught Marcy in her midsection, wrapping her around its trunk, so that she could more easily slide down it to the mud and damp grass at its feet.

Ryan Robinson turned from his car to see why Mr. Sheffler had stopped in the middle of his sentence. He was just in time to watch a scene from his boyhood days being replayed in front of him – only this time the bike rider was bigger and so was the tree trunk. Ryan dropped his boxes and sprinted to the person lying on the ground. Mr. Sheffler crossed the fence with great finesse for one of his age, and arrived at almost the same time as Ryan.

Marcy just laid there with her eyes closed for a minute, fighting to get back the wind that had been knocked out of her. She heard the men approach and felt a hand lift off the bike helmet that had been knocked askew. Opening her eyes she looked up into two pairs of blue eyes; one older, duller, and showing great concern. The other younger, brighter, and... laughing at her!

"Well, well! Great performances do bear repeating! I'm glad at least that this time you chose to wear a helmet!"

Mr. Sheffler looked askance at Ryan. "This is no time for levity, young man! She could be seriously hurt!" He couldn't see the humor because he didn't understand that this whole scene was a repeat of the day the Robinsons first moved into their home when Marcy was five. She had been learning to ride her bike then. What was her excuse, now?

The smile fell off Ryan's face and he became concerned at once. "Are you hurt, Marcy?"

She struggled to sit up and two pairs of hands tried to help her. "I think the injury to my pride is fatal, but other than that, I don't think there's much damage." She half grinned realizing how humorous it looked to Ryan, but wishing at the same time that she could crawl into a hole and pretend this whole thing never happened.

"Come on, Dearie," Mr. Sheffler said. "Let's get you cleaned up, and check you over to make sure."

Marcy looked down at herself for the first time. What a mess! Not only did she have mud and grass stains on her shorts and shirt, but there were tears from the rough bark of the tree. The skin on her upper legs and on her arms had taken some abuse from the slide down the trunk, too, and they were scraped and bleeding. The helmet had slipped down partially covering her face when she got thrown from the bicycle, otherwise her face probably would have more damage to it also. As it was, there was just a bit of a scratch on the side of her jaw and chin. As she stood up, there was a sharp pain in her ribs on the side that took most of the impact. Marcy winced.

"Do you think she needs to go to the doctor?" Mr. Sheffler asked Ryan. "Are you sure you're alright?"

Marcy nodded, "I think that the shock is wearing off and I'm started to feel the effects, is all."

"Well, come on in the house. Let's get those scrapes cleaned up. I think that Mom has some clothes you can borrow."

As they started towards the house, Marcy started to ache all over and feel light-headed.

She hesitated by the porch, "Listen, could I just call a cab? I think I really just want to go right home. I'll clean up there."

Mr. Sheffler looked at Marcy and then at Ryan. "I think that you ought to get her to a doctor. I think she's looking a little peaked. That was a pretty hard fall! I'd take her in, but my wife has the car."

"No, please. I'll be fine. I just need to call a cab." Marcy was beginning to feel even more embarrassed. She hated when people made fusses over her.

Ryan looked at her thoughtfully with his lips scrunched to one side, as if he were trying to read how she was really feeling. "Tell you what... I'll drive you to where you need to go. Just let me take that last load of stuff in the house." He reached over to open the front car door for Marcy to get in. She hesitated.

"A cab would be fine, really. That's a lot of trouble for you, and besides, I'll get the inside of your car messed up."

For an answer, he walked around to the other side of the car, and dug in one of the boxes that he had dropped earlier. He came around again and handed her a big towel.

"You can sit on this, if that will make you feel better." When Marcy just stared, he spread it on the car seat. "It's an old one, I promise."

Mr. Sheffler, still holding one of Marcy's arms, propelled her to the car. "I think that you'd better, Dearie. You'll get where you're going faster than if you wait for a cab."

He helped Marcy in and shut the door. Ryan just put the boxes on the porch and asked Mr. Sheffler to let his folks know what happened if they should get back before he did. They backed out of the drive, and Marcy gave him her address. He looked at her amused, with raised eyebrows and chuckled. She looked back at him sideways.

"What's so funny?"

"You live quite a distance from here. You must still really like to ride bikes!"

Marcy nodded. "I don't get to do it as much as I used to, though."

Ryan chuckled again. "That might be a blessing in disguise!"

"Ha ha." She leaned her head back on the seat and closed her eyes. The sharp pain in her side was there every time she took a breath now, and she was beginning to feel nauseous. What a mess her curiosity had gotten her into! Why did she always have to try to find things out for herself? Why was she always so clumsy? She wanted nothing more than to soak in a hot bath to relieve the aches, and then crawl into bed until she felt better.

To crawl into bed until... when? She had better feel better fast. Dave was supposed to pick her up at six. He had reminded her about this date practically every time he saw her since Wednesday night. He said he had tickets to somewhere, she couldn't remember where. She had agreed to go out tonight, not because she particularly wanted too, but because she couldn't bear to hurt his feeling again. He assured her that it was just as friends, but Thursday and Friday had felt strained from Wednesday. She suspected that he was going to try to ease her into a more serious relationship. Dave wasn't pushy, but neither did he easily give up trying. Would he understand if she called him? He'd probably have to come over and see for himself, and then when he did, he'd probably insist on staying to play nursemaid to her. Dave was one of the last people that she would want in that role. He'd probably take the opportunity to point out that she really needed him.

Marcy gave a little groan and winced at those disturbing thoughts, forgetting that she wasn't alone. Ryan had just been letting her rest and didn't require her to carry on a conversation. He heard the groan and gave her a probative look. She was still resting her head against the seat with her eyes closed. She was holding her side and her face seemed to be paler than it had been. He made a detour. Marcy was still wrestling about the problem with Dave and wishing she'd never gotten up this morning, so she was unaware that he had pulled into the town's small hospital.

She opened her eyes when the car stopped and she felt Ryan get out of the car. He came around and opened the door.

"This isn't home! Why are we stopping?"

"We're at the emergency room. Come on, I'll help you out."

Marcy focused on her surroundings to confirm what he said.

"Oh no! Please, just let me go home. I just need to soak in a tub and rest a bit. Really – I'll be fine!" she begged, and tried to pull the car door closed again.

Ryan didn't relinquish his hold on the door and continued to stand there, waiting for her to get out.

"I told you that I would take you where you needed to go and I've been watching you. I decided that Mr. Sheffler was right. Now either get out on your own accord, or I'll go in and get some orderlies to get you out. Your choice."

He stood with his hand out to help her. She looked at him a moment, trying to decide if he would push it and really make a scene. He looked pretty determined, and she didn't feel up to the fight. Slowly she extended her hand for his help.

"You haven't changed much, still bossy and insisting on your own way."

Ryan didn't reply, just smiled and laughed at her with his eyes. Marcy got out of the car like an ancient old lady. Pain was evident on her face as she eased out of the car.

"Would you like me to carry you?"

"No!" Marcy snapped.

"I see you haven't changed much, either. Still grouchy when you can't have your way," he teased.

Marcy shot him a dark look.

Ryan chuckled.

"Marcy! What happened to you this time, girl?" The receptionist greeted Marcy as they approached the desk. She and Kandy had gotten to know each other through Marcy's many trips to the emergency room and had become close friends since. Dumb things kept happening to her; nothing ever erious, just bad enough to require attention. And dumb. Like two months ago when she missed the bottom step at work, spraining her ankle. Glenn, a burly looking stock boy was just getting off work and offered to take her in that time. Luckily, he drove a pick-up truck so Marcy's bike would make it home with her. If these things had to happen, why couldn't they happen during her doctor's regular office hours?

"I fell off my bike."

Kandy eyed Marcy's good looking escort and quickly looked to see if there was a wedding ring. "Is this the gallant knight that rescued you? Take it from me, Marcy, this one's a lot better than the last one. Your taste in rescuers is improving!"

Marcy's face grew hot. "For crying out loud, Kandy! He's just a neighbor that I grew up with. He's more like my abductor."

Ryan laughed outright. Kandy raised questioning eyes at Marcy's ungracious response. Marcy's face got hotter. One of the things that Kandy liked about Marcy was her ability to laugh at herself and see the funny side. This was out of character.

"I take it you didn't want to come in. I guess I'd better get you in a room and looked at before you walk out again!"

"Don't worry, she'll stay."

Kandy thought he sounded confident.

Marcy thought he sounded cocky.

Marcy fumed silently as she followed Kandy back to the examination room and waited for the doctor to see her. Not only did she feel embarrassed for making such a spectacle of herself, but she felt humiliated for seeming to be so ungrateful for the help and kindness shown her. And that infuriated her. It was a good thing Ryan wasn't in the room with her, she felt like kicking him in the shins like she did when she was little.

The doctor escorted Marcy to the waiting room. Ryan rose when they entered and walked over to meet them.

"There are no broken bones, but see that she takes it easy and gets some rest. No heavy lifting for a bit. No riding bicycles 'till those ribs are better, either."

"See, I told you that I didn't need to come in and that I'd be fine. I just needed a hot bath and..."

"Young lady," the doctor scolded, "It's a good thing that he did bring you in. Those ribs could've been just as easily broken as bruised. And as for your arms and legs, a hot bath wouldn't have cleaned them out, and you could've gotten a serious infection. Now obey my instructions and don't begrudge him doing the right thing."

The doctor addressed Ryan, "You *are* the one that's going to be taking her home, right? Good. We gave her some medicine for the pain and also something to help her sleep, she should start to feel the effects in about half an hour, don't let her drive. Get this prescription filled on your way. We had to clean out some debris from those scrapes. This will help fight any infection that might try to develop."

Once again Marcy was humiliated. She dropped her head. She couldn't trust herself to talk or look at either of the two men. She felt like crying and was afraid she would if she had to do either. The medicine they had given her to help the pain in her body was working, but not on the painful emotions. How could such a beautiful morning turn into such a rotten day!

She waited until Ryan had finished receiving the instructions from the doctor, and then silently walked out to the waiting car. Ryan helped her in the car and drove her home without saying a word. Not even when he stopped at the pharmacy did they speak. She simply held out her hand for the prescription, he gave it to her, and then helped her out of the car. He followed her inside, waited with her for it to be filled and paid for, and then helped her back into the car. Marcy never once got the feeling that he was angry with her, or that his feelings were hurt because she was so ungrateful and therefore sulking. He seemed to sense that she was feeling miserable, emotionally as well as physically, and was trying to help her feel better. And that made the lump in her throat bigger.

At her house, he took the keys and unlocked the door for her. As if it were the normal thing to do, he stepped inside after her. He followed her into the kitchen and watched her take a pill. She walked into the bedroom and shut the door. She could hear him in the kitchen as she changed into her pajamas. It sounded like he was looking for something. Why did he come inside in the first place, and why was he still here?

"Well I'm not going to go out and ask him, he came in on his own and he can just leave on his own. What made him think he had the right to assume he could come in anyway?" she groused.

She hadn't seen him in almost ten years, and yet by the events of today, it would seem like their friendship was old hat. He took the events of the day in stride, as if driving her home or taking her into the emergency room was a common occurrence. He didn't act like it was unusual that she would just happen to be riding by on her bike. He didn't even ask what-in-the-world she was doing clear out in his neighborhood. He seemed so... so... Marcy struggled to find the word.

She pulled back the covers on her bed and got under them. The medicine they gave her to help her sleep was starting to take effect and she was getting drowsy. She fluffed her pillow and tried to get comfortable.

Comfortable! That was it. He seemed so comfortable. He was comfortable with himself and others. She felt comfortable with him, too, kind of like a lost old shoe that just got found. It almost felt like their friendship could pick up where it got left off without having to be broken in all over again.

There was a soft tap at her door, and Marcy raised herself up on one elbow as Ryan opened it. He had a plate with a sandwich on it and a glass of milk.

"It's after lunch time and I thought that you might be hungry," he spoke softly as if again he were trying to make her feel better.

Marcy shook her head no that she wasn't hungry, and tried to smile that she appreciated it though. He moved over to the night stand by the bed and set the food down next to her.

"You might want it later," he said in explanation. "It's peanut butter and pickle."

Definitely a comfortable old shoe.

He remembered her favorite childhood sandwich. She wanted to thank him and tried to smile, but couldn't look at him. With eyes closed, all she could manage was a nod in acknowledgement. He stood there for a moment, looking at her, not sure what to do. She felt him kneel down beside the bed. He laid his hand on her head and his voice was close and incredibly tender when he spoke.

"Marcy... I'm sorry."

What did he have to be sorry for? He went to a lot of trouble trying to help. She ended up taking a big chunk of his morning and part of his afternoon. He was sure to have better things to do than wait upon an ungracious idiot. She was the one that should say she was sorry. She wanted to explain and thank him for all his help. But all that managed to come out was an unintelligible mutter, muffled by the pillow. He sighed and gave her shoulder a pat.

"I'll leave you alone, Spitfire." Still gentle.

She felt him stand up and heard him walk to the door.

"I'll check in on you later, okay?"

Evidently he wasn't expecting her to say "No, it wasn't okay," because he didn't wait for a response. Quietly he shut the bedroom door and let himself out. He certainly wasn't acting like the unethical scoundrel she heard described at the store. She hadn't really pictured what a reunion with Ryan would be like, but if she had, it definitely wouldn't have been like this one.

Chapter 3

GOOD-LOOKIN'-IN-AN-APRON

Marcy didn't want to wake up, and she wished that whoever was banging would quit. She turned over and put the pillow over her head. It didn't help. She could still hear the banging. Why was anyone banging, anyway? Marcy started to come out of the fog of the drug induced sleep. It sounded like someone was pounding at her front door. She couldn't think who it could be, and wished they would go away. They didn't. In fact now the banger was calling her name. It sounded like Dave. But it couldn't be – he always rang the doorbell.

Marcy's mind snapped alert. Dave! She forgot to call him! What time was it? 6:10. Marcy groaned. He was here to take her out.

She got out of bed and threw on the kimono that she used for a bath robe. She crossed the living room, hoping that he wasn't too angry. As she opened the front door, Dave's face went from that of determination, to surprise and then to frustration. The hand that was holding a package wrapped in florist paper looking suspiciously like flowers, dropped to his side.

"What took you so long to answer the door? Why aren't you ready, yet? The concert starts at 7:30."

"I'm sorry. I was sleeping. Are those for me?" she indicated the flowers by his side. "Why didn't you ring the doorbell?"

"Of course these are for you! I did ring the bell, I but after a while I thought that it might not be working, so I started knocking." Dave handed Marcy the flowers, then reached over and gave the bell a test push. It still worked.

"Wow, that pill the hospital gave me must have really knocked me out. I didn't hear the bell at all... What concert is it?"

"What pill? Why were you at the hospital? You're not sick are you?"

"The hospital gave me a pill to help me rest. I'm not sick; I just lost control of my bike and wrapped myself around a tree. I went in to see if anything was broken."

"The concert in Sheridan. Remember, I told you that I got tickets for the orchestra." Dave noticed the scratches on her face. "Was anything broken?"

"No, I just got scraped up and bruised my ribs. If I hurry, we should have time to still make it."

"Are you up to going? We could just stay in if you want."

Marcy didn't really feel like going out, but the option of staying in with Dave was less acceptable. It would be easier to keep the relationship "just friends" in public. "No, I don't want you to waste the tickets. Besides, I like orchestras. It isn't like listening is a physical activity. I'll be fine."

"Well, if you're sure... Hurry and get ready then. I'll call and change our reservations at the restaurant."

As Dave moved to use the phone, Marcy handed him the flowers and went to the bedroom. She sighed as she got ready – it was going to be a late night. When she sat down on the edge of the bed to put on her nylons, she noticed the sandwich still sitting there. She smiled. Peanut butter and pickle; she hadn't had one in a long time. Her stomach growled – she hadn't had anything to eat since the bowl of cereal early this morning. She picked it up and took a bite. It was a bit dry from sitting out, but it still brought back pleasant memories. She took a swallow of milk to wash down the sandwich. Yuck. The milk was too warm for her tastes. Oh well, she'd just have to wait until supper.

Marcy had been planning to wear an evening dress, but that would leave her arms bare. It wouldn't bother her, but it might bother other people. She decided on her long, slinky, black skirt and an equally slinky, but simple, creamy blouse. The blouse had loose fitting, long, sleeves that would hide the bandages on her arms. She left her hair down, curled and soft, to help cover the scrapes on her face. Adding a facetted, black glass bead necklace, she felt dressed fine enough for the concert.

Dave must have thought so, too. His eyes lit up when she emerged from the bedroom. He had arranged the flowers in a vase he had found and set them in the middle of the coffee table where Marcy could see them often. Marcy noticed what they were for the first time – a dozen long stemmed red roses with Baby's Breath. They were beautiful. Her mouth almost fell open. She looked at him with a question in her eyes.

"Thank you, Dave. They're gorgeous... But why?"

He smiled sheepishly and shrugged. "Are you sure you don't want to stay in?"

Marcy rolled her eyes and smiled. "Come on, Dave, I hate being late."

Dave held the door open for her and gave a gallant bow as she passed through. As he ushered Marcy to his car, neither one of them noticed that a blue sedan was coming to a stop across the street.

As Ryan got closer to Marcy's house, he saw an extra car in the driveway. Maybe she already had enough company and he shouldn't bother her. He would just stop in for a brief moment, just to make sure she was doing okay. He wouldn't stay long, but his mother would require some kind of report. She had been quite concerned when he filled her in on his day. She even sent some food over in case Marcy wasn't up to cooking.

As he pulled up to the curb opposite her house, he watched another man in a suit, bow at the door. Interesting. When he stopped, this other man was escorting Marcy to the extra car. She must be feeling better. She was dressed up and she looked really nice, even from across the street. He had remembered that she was cute when she was young and pretty through her teenage years. Now she was beautiful. He had seen that this morning even through the mud and blood. Ryan watched as Marcy was helped into the car and they drove off.

He had been hoping to do some catching up tonight, and renew their friendship if she had felt up to it. It would be nice to have a friend in town after he'd been gone for so many years. It looked like she felt up to his visit, but he hadn't considered she might be going out.

When he saw her fall off her bike that morning, it felt to him like he had stepped back in time. From the first day he met her when he was six, he felt like he needed to protect her. The Robinson's were just moving in and Ryan was helping his Dad unload the moving truck in the driveway. Marcy had just learned to ride her bike recently, and thought that she would try to tackle the rough brick road in front instead of staying on the smooth sidewalk. She lost control when she hit the manhole that time, too. She wasn't going as fast but her head received the brunt of the impact and since there were no helmets then, she knocked herself out. Ryan had sniggered at the sight, and it was his father that reprimanded him instead of Mr. Sheffler. It was then that he took the responsibility to be her protector. They became chums very quickly.

In grade school they walked to and from school together. He protected her from playground bullies, she cheered for him in playground games and later in sports. In high school she continued to be his greatest fan, attending as many of his games as she could. She tried out for cheerleading so she could go to more. And he consoled her when she didn't make the squad.

When he was a senior and she a junior, Marcy had a crush on Danny, a popular junior. She was thrilled when he asked her to the prom. Ryan had overheard Danny talking about the plans he had for her and some other derogatory remarks in the locker room the day before the dance. Ryan walked over to him with a determined look, grabbed him by the shirt front, and pinned him against the lockers. Ryan let Danny know what he would do to him if he carried out his plans, or if he even heard him say anything like that about her again, and warned him that he'd better never raise a finger to hurt her.

Ryan went to the prom with his date. He caught a glimpse of Danny with a group of his friends, but didn't see Marcy. When he got home, he found out that Marcy had been stood up. Danny hadn't called or said anything, just left her waiting. Marcy cried all weekend. Ryan tried to tell her what a cad he was without revealing the locker room scene. It didn't seem to help.

Monday, he caught up to Danny at the lunch hour. Ryan let him know, in no uncertain terms, that he didn't like the fact that he'd hurt Marcy's feelings and insisted that he ask her out again. Danny sneered and Ryan threw the first punch. Ryan received a black eye and a week of detentions for his effort, but Danny asked Marcy out. She turned him down flat and chose to help Ryan serve his detentions.

It hadn't occurred to him that someone else might have taken over his old role, that she might have a boyfriend or maybe even be married. He was pretty sure that she wasn't married as there had been no ring on her finger, and then there was that comment from the ER receptionist. A boyfriend, however was another matter. Well, why wouldn't she have one? There was certainly nothing wrong with her looks. She used to have a wonderful personality, too. Ryan chuckled, remembering that morning; she really hadn't been at her best.

He told himself that he had come out here just to check on her and get reacquainted. For some reason he felt disappointed that she was going out with another man. He sighed and looked at the casserole getting cold on the seat beside him. He might as well get back to his parents' house and finish unpacking.

It had been quite late when Dave brought Marcy home. He seemed to want to linger over dinner after the concert, and then he came inside when he brought her to the door. He had taken his time leaving, and Marcy couldn't bring herself to just ask outright for him to leave. He had been so solicitously kind and considerate, almost overly so, trying to make sure everything was just right. As the night progressed, she could see that he wasn't content to have their relationship be on a 'friends only' terms. It didn't feel like he was trying to force her, just merely trying to present himself differently, hoping it would help Marcy see him in a different light.

It was almost noon when Marcy woke up the next morning. She groaned as she forced herself to get out of bed. The pain medication had long worn off, and now she felt stiff and sore on top of that.

She padded her way into the kitchen looking forward to a light breakfast and then a long soak in a hot tub. She opened the fridge trying to decide if she should have a bagel or cereal. She reached for the orange juice. Whatever she had, she'd start with this. She just finished pouring herself a glass when the doorbell rang. Marcy groaned inwardly. She was hoping to have the day to herself.

"Hi!" It was Dave's smiling face that greeted her. He had a six pack of beer dangling from his hand. Marcy opened the door further to let him in.

"You almost look like a repeat of yesterday, except that I know that I didn't wake you up because you've got a glass of orange juice in your hand," he teased as he took in the tousled hair and bathrobe. "Did I catch you in the middle of breakfast?"

"No, I was just going to make it. And then I was going to soak in a hot bath. I'm all stiff from yesterday." She added the last, hoping he would take a hint.

"Tell you what, why don't you let me make breakfast for you while you take your bath."

"I was going to soak a lo-o-ong time. I'm real stiff."

"All the more reason for me to cook your breakfast. I bet you didn't know that I'm a pretty good cook, did you. And you can soak as long as you like."

"That's a lot to ask of you. I'll be fine, really."

"It's no trouble at all. I'd love to cook for you!"

It didn't look as though he were going to take a hint. "Dave..."

His voice softened. "I was having such a wonderful time last night that I forgot that you probably weren't really up to going out in the first place. I felt like such a cad when I remembered. Won't you let me make it up to you?"

"Dave..."

He raised both hands to stop her next sentence. "Just friends."

Marcy sighed and nodded. Dave gave her a quick but gentle squeeze then turned her towards the bathroom.

"Now go soak till you turn into a prune. I know where the kitchen is, and I'll find whatever I need. Just give me a holler a couple of minutes before you get out."

The soak in the tub wasn't as relaxing as Marcy had hoped. Therefore it wasn't as long. She let Dave know she was getting out after only 20 minutes. The door was locked but she still felt uncomfortable with Dave being in the house while she was bathing, especially now that she knew how he felt. Just as she was dressing, she heard the doorbell ring again. Now who?

Dave called out that he'd get it and heard him open it. Marcy emerged immediately from the bathroom. It was Kandy. Marcy was actually glad to see her.

"You were pretty banged up yesterday, so I came over to see how you were doing and to see if you need any help with the bandages on your arms." Kandy eyed Dave in one of Marcy's aprons, holding a dish towel, and took in Marcy in her pajamas, Kimono and damp hair. "But it looks to me like you've got help already."

Marcy coaxed Kandy into the house. "Come on in, I can use your help with the bandages. And you're in time for breakfast. Dave was just making it. If you've already had breakfast, consider it lunch."

"Are you sure that's okay? I mean…"

"Oh sure! It is fine really, isn't it Dave… See, its fine! Oh silly me! Where are my manners? Kandy, this is Dave Lewis. Dave, Kandy Caine."

Dave looked at Marcy to see if she was joking. He had acquiesced, but his voice and expression didn't say he liked the idea.

Kandy thought Marcy seemed to be uptight. And since she was Marcy's friend, not Dave's, she decided to stay. She laughed to ease some tension and pretended like he was questioning her name.

"My name is a product of my parent's strange sense of humor. They just thought that I was so-o-o-o sweet when I was born. I'm looking for a husband so I can change it," she joked, "But I had to refuse three previous offers from Mr. Corn, Mr. Apple, and Mr. Kisses."

Marcy giggled. Dave didn't. He turned and headed back to the kitchen. "Breakfast will be ready in about 15 minutes. I'll put another place on the table."

Kandy followed Marcy into the bedroom and shut the door behind her. Marcy slumped down on the bed. Kandy stood, arms akimbo studying her friend.

"Are you alright?"

"Yeah." Marcy reached over to the night stand for the bandages the hospital sent home.

Kandy sat down on the bed and started dressing her injured arms.

"Okay, so talk to me… You came in yesterday on the arm of 'Gallant Knight', and your snappiness suggested that he was not 'just a neighbor'. Today I come over and 'Mr.-Good-Lookin'-in-an-Apron-'Cuz-He's-Making-Breakfast' greets me at the door. You say you're okay, but you're wound up tighter than a drum and practically force me to stay and eat. So what's going on?"

Marcy gave Kandy a weak smile. She needed to talk to someone and her parents were on vacation in Hawaii. Marcy took a deep breath and let it out again. She trusted Kandy, and she was certainly easy to talk to.

"First of all, Gallant Knight is Ryan Robinson. I did live next door to him. We were best buddies growing up. We kind of drifted our separate ways after high school. He went to university in a different state, and we lost track of each other. When I fell off my bike in front of his parents' house yesterday, it was the first time I'd seen him in over ten years. And it had been almost as long since I'd talked to him."

"What were you doing in front of his parents' house?"

"I'm not sure. I think it was mostly curiosity. Wednesday when I was on break, I overheard someone say that he was moving back to the area."

"So why were you so grouchy?"

"I don't know. When I heard them gossiping and that he was moving in with his folks, I felt... I don't know how I felt, or why I felt what I felt. Then to wreck my bike and make a complete fool of myself..." Marcy trailed off and shrugged.

Marcy didn't need help with the bandages on her legs, but Kandy did them anyway. And Marcy let her. It felt good to get the events of the last several days off her chest.

"So now tell me about Dave Lewis out there."

"Dave is the assistant manager where I work. Wednesday, one of the cashiers told him that Ryan and I had been *really* good friends, if you know what I mean. So he came over to find out. That's when I found out that he didn't think of me in the same way that I thought of him. I had no idea. We'd joke around at the store together, and sometimes we'd go somewhere or he'd come over here. It wasn't that often, and it never felt like a date."

"Are those gorgeous roses I saw in the living room from him?"

Marcy nodded and sighed.

"Did you tell him how you feel?"

"Uh-huh. He seemed to understand, but ever since Wednesday he's been treating me differently. Last night he took me out, and it was the first time he acted like he was actually dating me. I wouldn't have gone but he really is nice. And he seemed so hurt when I let him know how I felt that I didn't have the heart to turn him down. That's when he brought the roses."

"What's he doing here this morning? You didn't let him stay over, did you?"

35

"No! He just came over about 45 minutes ago. I tried to let him know that I didn't want him, but he didn't take the hint and insisted that I go ahead and soak while he made breakfast. He said he wanted to make up for keeping me out so late."

"Maybe you didn't do it good enough."

"Didn't do what good enough?"

"Tell him how you feel."

"I told him bluntly, Kandy. He keeps saying, 'Just friends.' I think he's just trying to change my mind."

A knock sounded at the door. "Breakfast is ready, ladies."

"Coming!"

Marcy quickly slipped into shorts and a T-shirt.

Dave had certainly found whatever he needed for the kitchen. The table, sporting her favorite dishware, was complete with tablecloth, napkins and a single rose in the center. As Dave was putting the last things on the table, Kandy caught Marcy's eye and gave a low whistle. Marcy closed her eyes and gave her head a shake in reply. Dave held their chairs for them as they sat. The breakfast he served was not the light fare Marcy was going to fix.

"The table's beautiful, Dave, and the food smells wonderful, too."

"I'll say! How much do you charge? Maybe I can hire you!"

Kandy's presence and sense of humor kept the conversation light and safe. Breakfast was pleasant. Kandy watched and listened to Dave, sizing him up without seeming to.

Kandy leaned back in her chair and patted her stomach. "Boy that was great! I haven't had a breakfast like that in a long time! Are you sure you're not for hire?"

"That was wonderful, Dave. I never knew you were so handy in the kitchen."

Dave looked straight in Marcy's eyes. "There are a lot of other things you don't know about me, yet, Marcy."

"Dave..."

"Hey, kid," interrupted Kandy, "Why don't you go relax in the living room. Remember the doctor's orders; you're supposed to rest those ribs. The chef here and I will clean up, okay?" Kandy stood up, "It shouldn't take too long, 'cuz he didn't make much of a mess."

Marcy hesitated.

"Get going, now! We'll be fine!"

Kandy shooed her out of the kitchen. Marcy didn't get a chance to see how Dave was reacting to this. He seemed to have loosened up a bit as the meal progressed. She stretched out in the recliner, wishing she could stretch out on her bed. It seemed odd just sitting there while Dave and Kandy were washing her dishes in her kitchen. She closed her eyes and listened to their banter. Kandy was easy going and liked to tease. She seemed to be able to draw people out and help them relax. She was doing a fine job with Dave. He was teasing Kandy back.

Marcy dozed off and didn't hear when the dishes were done. Dave and Kandy sat and talked on the couch while she slept.

About an hour later she woke up with a gasp and start. She'd been dreaming that she was jousting on her bike against an apron wielding a pancake flipper. Just as she got close to the apron, something hit her bike and she fell off.

"Goodness, Marcy! You okay? You startled us!"

"I was just dreaming, I guess."

"Must've been some dream."

"I dreamt that I fell off my bike." Marcy rubbed her eyes. "How long have I been asleep? I didn't mean to doze off. That was pretty rude of me."

"You've only been asleep about an hour. And personally I enjoyed watching you." That was from Dave.

"Think nothing of it. Dave and I have been having a fine time getting to know each other. If you want to go back to sleep again, I won't object."

Marcy giggled, got up and stretched. "I need a drink of water. Do either of you want anything?"

"I wouldn't mind a beer, Marcy."

"That sounds fine for me, too."

Marcy handed Dave his opened drink. "Where's Kandy?"

Dave indicated the direction of the bathroom, but before Marcy could set Kandy's drink down, the doorbell rang.

Marcy answered the door still holding Kandy's beer.

"Hi, dear! I heard about your accident and thought I'd bring a casserole by and see how you were doing." It was Mrs. Robinson.

Marcy was too stunned to say anything, and didn't even think to invite her in. Mrs. Robinson took in Marcy's hair, disheveled from her snooze, the open beer in her hand, and the uncomfortable look on her face. From the doorway she could see the young man on her couch. When Marcy didn't say anything, Mrs. Robinson started to apologize.

"I didn't mean to come at a bad time, I can't stay long. I insisted that my son run me by on the way to the mall, he's out in the car waiting for me now."

Marcy didn't need to look at the car to know who that was. Mr. and Mrs. Robinson only had one child. But she looked anyway and could see Ryan waiting behind the wheel. Apparently he was watching the proceedings at the door, because when Marcy looked over, he gave a little wave and smiled. She lifted her hand that wasn't on the door knob to wave back. It was then she realized that she was still holding the open beer and quickly lowered it again. She felt flustered. It embarrassed her that Mrs. Robinson saw her with an alcoholic beverage, and put it behind her back. Silly, she knew.

The Robinsons didn't drink. Not only were they faithful church attendees, but also active. Mrs. Robinson had taught Sunday school for years, and Marcy wouldn't be surprised if she still did. Mr. Robinson had been an elder. Marcy's parents weren't against church but they tended to go only on Christmas, Easter, and a few other occasions. It was the Robinsons that invited Marcy to church with them every Sunday. Her parents allowed her to go about once or twice a month. When she was little she looked forward to hearing the Bible stories. When she was a teen her attendance, albeit irregular, had become a habit, and she enjoyed the youth group's social activities. She had gotten out of the habit of going after she moved.

Marcy found her voice at last.

"No, you didn't come at a bad time. We were just... I was... I'm surprised to see you here, that's all. It's just that it's been a long time. That was sweet of you to bring a casserole, you didn't have to, you know."

"I know, but I wanted to. After I heard about your mishap, I realized how much I've missed our little chats, and this seemed like a good excuse."

"Oh."

Mrs. Robinson could see that Marcy was very uncomfortable, and making her feel that way had not been her intention in coming. She held out the dish for Marcy to take. Marcy thanked her and accepted it with the hand that had been holding the door knob.

"I need to go. Don't worry about the dish, I've got plenty, so don't feel in a hurry to return it." Mrs. Robinson smiled warmly. "Please stop in for a visit sometime." She reached up a soft, gentle hand and patted Marcy's cheek. "I've missed you, dear. We've all missed you."

Marcy just nodded and lowered her head. Mrs. Robinson turned and walked back to the car. Marcy watched as they backed out and drove away. The sight of Marcy standing in the doorway pulled on the mother's-heart within her, and a little prayer for Marcy left her lips and went heavenward.

Marcy turned and shut the door when she heard Kandy come from the bathroom.

"Who was that, more company? My, but you're popular!"

"That was Mr. Shefflers' neighbor."

"Who's Mr. Sheffler?"

"Mr. Sheffler helped me when I fell off my bike yesterday."

Something sounded funny to Kandy, but she wasn't going to pursue it with Dave sitting on the couch, so she let it drop. Marcy handed Kandy her drink and stuck the casserole in the refrigerator.

Kandy and Dave had settled back into a discussion and Marcy joined them. She didn't contribute much because her mind was in a whirl. Why had she been so uncomfortable? Why didn't she just tell Kandy that it was Mrs. Robinson? Why had she been afraid that Mrs. Robinson was going to mention Ryan's name? What was wrong with her lately, anyway?

After a bit, Dave got up to leave. He had to work the late shift tonight. Kandy got up too, claiming she hadn't realized how late it was. She had to work, as well. She had walked over and hoped she would get home in time now to get ready. Dave kindly offered her a lift home, and she accepted. Marcy thanked Kandy for coming over, and thanked Dave for the wonderful breakfast again. She watched them as they walked to Dave's car. She shut the door and sighed as they pulled away. She was alone again – finally.

Mrs. Robinson patted her son's arm as they pulled away from Marcy's home. "Maybe you were right, dear." she said. "It was probably better that you didn't go to the door, too. I don't think she was happy to see me there, either."

Ryan's only response was a nod.

She looked at him quizzically. "So how did you know this?"

"Was there a blonde guy with her?"

"Yes... he was sitting on the couch. Why?"

"The car in the drive was the same one that they left in last night." Ryan paused. He wasn't sure how to put into words what he was thinking.

Mrs. Robinson just waited. She knew he'd finish explaining in his own time.

"Last night when I stopped by to see how she was doing, I came just in time to see her leave in the car that was parked in front of her house just now. She wasn't leaving alone, and they both were very dressed up. It was obvious by his actions that they were going out." Again Ryan stopped.

"So... why did you think you couldn't just stop in as a concerned friend? It's not as if you were trying to horn in on his territory."

Ryan chuckled at his mother's cliché.

"I know, but yesterday when I took her into the hospital, it seemed as if she was upset that I did."

Mrs. Robinson smiled, "Ryan, surely you haven't forgotten why she was nicknamed Spitfire. She was probably embarrassed for falling and you know how she hates to be embarrassed."

No, Ryan hadn't forgotten. He almost reached down and rubbed his shin just thinking about it. She often had accidents that would cause her embarrassment. She got upset with herself when this happened. It made her even madder if Ryan knew she was embarrassed.

One hot day when they had gotten home from grammar school, her mom had two glasses of ice cold cherry-flavored soft drink waiting for them. They were standing at the counter drinking it, when Mrs. Kelman asked Marcy about something that happened in school. Marcy was about to take a drink, but instead, decided to answer her mother first. That was fine, except that she forgot to stop tipping the glass when she turned her head, and ended up spilling the red drink all over the front of her white blouse. Her mother just shook her head and said, "Oh, Marcy."

Ryan had learned not to laugh, so he quickly looked down to hide his mirth, and tried to keep from smiling. He felt Marcy's embarrassment and looked up in concern. He met her eyes and she knew that he knew that she was embarrassed. She quickly kicked his shin. Mrs. Kelman reprimanded her. Marcy felt embarrassed for her actions. She looked at Ryan to apologize and again she knew that he knew. This time she got his other shin and ran up the stairs to her room. Since things like that seemed to happen often to her, Ryan's shins got kicked quite a lot. Marcy had outgrown kicking by the time she got to junior high, and by high school, she had started to learn to be able to laugh at herself. Ryan wondered briefly if she had reverted to pre-high school days.

"I know, but it seemed like it was more than that. It was if she really hated me being there, as if she were ashamed of me or something."

"Surely not."

"When the ER receptionist inquired about me bringing her in, I was 'just a neighbor that she grew up with.' Not Ryan, not a friend: just a neighbor. Then, when we left the hospital she just quit talking to me. She didn't say a word, not even when I dropped her off. Not even thank you."

"Is that why you helped her, to have her say thanks?"

Ryan sighed. "No, Mom, and it doesn't hurt my feelings or anything either. It just seemed as if she didn't want to see me. She just didn't seem like the Marcy we knew. You remember how tender towards other people's feelings she was. Even when she was angry, she always felt badly if she thought she might have hurt them."

"Maybe she isn't the Marcy we knew. We haven't seen her in a long time, dear. A lot could have happened. We'll have to pray for her. I'm ashamed to say that I'd quit praying for her like I should."

"I know." He was ashamed of himself, too. "I haven't either."

"Well then!" He mother's voice perked up, "We'll make her our prayer project. We'll turn her over to our Father, okay?"

Ryan smiled at his mother and nodded.

Chapter 4

DANBURY'S

Marcy's week fell into her normal routine. She was very productive in her studio and completed the wedding order. She also produced a number of very good pieces that should bring a good price. The boutiques should be able to sell them easily.

At work, a few co-workers made comments about her and Dave's new relationship. So it wasn't just her imagination that he was acting more a suitor then a friend. She tried to avoid him without being obvious. She was glad they didn't always work the same hours.

On Friday of that week, as she was pulling into the parking lot going to work, she saw Kandy just leaving the store. Kandy had a bit of a smile on her face and looked lost in thought. It wasn't until Marcy was close enough to almost touch her, and called her name twice, that Kandy responded.

"I bet your thoughts are worth more than a penny today! Boy, were you deep in them. Wanna share? Or is it private?"

Kandy looked a bit uncomfortable and then smiled. "You're right; I had a lot on my mind. What are you doing here?"

Marcy laughed. "I work here, remember?"

"I know that. What I meant was, I didn't expect to have the privilege of running into you, I thought you started later on Thursdays."

"I do. I just came in early in hopes that I could get my job done and get off earlier."

"Ahh... got a date?"

"No, I need to go to the high school and use the kiln. They like it better if I get there earlier during the summer, so they can close up on time."

Kandy shuffled a bit. Marcy thought it a bit odd of her usually forthright friend.

"Uh... Tell me Marcy, how's it been going with Dave?"

"Going with Dave?" Marcy repeated.

"Yeah. Does he definitely understand your feelings, yet?"

"I wish. I keep telling him, and he keeps saying it's just friends, but he doesn't act like it. Some of the cashiers have made comments, so I know that it must be obvious that he doesn't."

"He must think an awfully lot of you. It seems to me he could make some girl a great husband."

"He probably would at that, Kandy. I think that he's very nice, but I don't think that girl ought to be me."

"I don't know, Marcy. I think that I would think it over if I were you. From what I saw last Sunday, he seems to care for you a great deal. He's kind, considerate, has a good personality... good men are getting harder to find these days, you know."

"Kandy! Are you my friend or not?"

"Yes, I am! I'm trying to keep you from making a mistake, that's all!"

"Well what kind of wife would I be, if I don't love him? Would that be fair to him?"

"Think about it, is all I'm saying. Although, if I were you, I'd snatch him up before someone else did."

Marcy was starting to get irritated with this line of talk. Was Kandy actually trying to push her to Dave?

"Well, if you think that, why don't you snatch him up?"

Kandy's face fell. "It's you he's smitten with."

"I'm sorry, Kandy," said a contrite Marcy. "I didn't mean to snap. Please don't push me to him. I just don't feel that way about him."

"I'm sorry, too. I just don't understand why you don't." Kandy gave Marcy a quick hug. "Friends?"

"Of course."

Marcy spent a good deal of the morning thinking about her encounter with Kandy. Dave asked her out that Saturday and she turned him down. She turned him down the following week, too.

A week after Marcy had the encounter with Kandy she had the day off at the grocery store. Marcy decided to go into Sheridan and call on a number of shops that sold her products. She would collect from the consignment shops and restock them and the boutiques. Marcy had her car loaded with wares. She didn't like to go about trying to get new outlets, although she knew that it was necessary if she was going to build her business. Once relationships with the shop owners were established, though, she liked going back. Then she felt more like she was going to visit friends than conducting business. She wasn't trying to get new contacts this time, so she looked forward to the day.

By 11:00 Marcy had the northern half of her route done. She stopped for a quick lunch then headed for the southern half. Her next stop was *Danbury's*, an upscale store that sold the wares of several artists. Mr. Danbury carried some pictures and sculptures, but his store specialized in handmade "usable" items, as he referred to them. He carried original clothing pieces, ranging from unique bead or painted artwork on T-shirts and blouses, to hand-woven tunics and purses, to original design evening wear. He also carried one-of-a-kind items for the home in ceramics, wood, metals, and glass. Marcy's ceramics were a big part of *Danbury's* kitchen wares inventory.

Marcy enjoyed going to *Danbury's* more than any of the other shops in which she sold wares. It was mostly because of Mr. Danbury, himself. He was a jovial, rotund, absent-minded professor type that sported square Benjamin Franklin glasses half-way down his nose. His silver hair always looked a little mussed and like it needed cutting. Marcy never saw him in a full suit, but he always wore a vest which matched his pants, with a pocket watch that rested in his shirt pocket while being firmly attached by a fob to his top vest button. His tie was usually loose and his shirt sleeves rolled up to his elbows.

Mr. Danbury always met with Marcy on the floor. She was never told to go to the back, giving her the feeling that he never was too busy to see her. Sometimes she found it hard to tear herself away from his friendly conversations. He always enquired after her, as if he really cared what went on in her life. Marcy thought that one of the reasons he was so successful in his business was that he treated everybody that came in as a personal friend and not just a possible sale.

Today he greeted her with, "And how are you today, Miss Kelman?"

"Oh, I'm fine."

"And what is 'fine' today? Are you healthy and happy?"

Marcy smiled and nodded.

"You weren't healthy just recently, I see." He reached up a finger to the pink marks that were temporarily decorating her chin and tipped his head back to better see through his glasses. "What happened to you?"

She heard the bells on the door announce another customer, and the sales lady inquire if she could help. The man responded that he was just browsing, so Marcy didn't feel like she would keep Mr. Danbury from other duties and told him briefly about the bike accident.

"So you're healing well, and not working too hard, yes?"

"No." Marcy giggled.

"Is your hobby at the grocery store going well?" He always referred to the store as her hobby, since she had mentioned once that she felt like the ceramics was her real job.

"Yes, it is. How's your hobby these days?"

"It is very good. And I want to show you a piece from my real job that I think you will like. But, Marcy, first I have another question."

"Okay, shoot."

"I want to tell you that I like orchestra music very much and that I attended a fine concert shortly back. I thought that I saw my favorite supplier there on the arm of a very nice looking young man. Was I right?"

Marcy tried to appear neutral, although her insides were telling her she didn't want to talk about it. Why was her social life such a big concern lately? "I was there, and I thought that it was very good, too. Where were you sitting? I didn't see you. Were you with someone?" She tried to steer the conversation elsewhere.

"Maybe someone was occupying your thoughts and you weren't looking for an old man. Tell me, Marcy; is this a new love in your life?" Mr. Danbury was certainly personal today and hard to side-track.

"Well, everyone seems to think that it is, or should be anyway."

"What about you?"

She wanted to say, "Mind your own business", but instead just shrugged.

"I could easily tell from the look on his face how he felt. But yours was harder to read."

Marcy sighed. "Mr. Danbury, Dave is very nice, and I like him a lot. People, including my closest friend, think that I ought to snatch him up... Now, would you like to show me your latest piece? Or should I show you mine?"

"Forgive my nosiness. Please indulge me one bit of advice: Other people don't walk in your shoes; so don't get into something just because *they* think it's right. You need to know in your heart." Mr. Danbury smiled and patted her cheek. "You're a sweet girl... Now, let me show you my window."

Marcy smiled and followed him to the corner where he had a display of stained glass pieces, glad to change the conversation. This was Mr. Danbury's 'real job.' He made a large assortment of beautiful items. Fruit bowls, lamp shades, jewelry, and jewelry boxes were just a few. Today he had a front door window to show her. It was absolutely gorgeous. It depicted a country scene in great detail, complete with appropriate wildlife. Mr. Danbury was quite an artist in his own right.

Ryan walked into *Danbury's* hoping to find a birthday present for his mother. It was tomorrow and he didn't even have an idea what to get yet. Maybe he could find something here or at least get an idea. As he started to browse, he became aware of the conversation between a young woman and older gentleman towards the back of the store. She seemed to be relating an incident that rang familiar to Ryan's ears. Her voice sounded familiar, too. Ryan could only see the back of her, but when the gentleman said her name, it left no doubt who she was. He found himself listening to the conversation. The store was not very large, and therefore one could hear without trying. Ryan told himself to concentrate on his mother's present but continually found himself paying attention to Marcy.

She sounded uneasy with the conversation about her social life. It didn't appear that Marcy felt strongly attracted to this Dave. Why should he feel pleasure at that thought? Ryan half listened as she talked to Mr.

Danbury about the stained glass work, and then as she showed him the pieces she had. She was very friendly, knowledgeable and poised.

Ryan had been considering a pair of ceramic candle holders for his mother. The sales lady was showing him that it was designed to hold a flower arrangement also. She cinched the sale when the she pointed out that "the young lady talking to Mr. Danbury is the creator of these lovely pieces", and that "you can always tell her work by the stamp." She had turned the piece over and was showing him Marcy's unique signature stamp on the bottom, when Mr. Danbury and Marcy walked over to the display with her work.

Ryan looked up when he heard Marcy's voice on the other side of the display. It was apparent her attention was on showing Mr. Danbury how one of her new pieces worked with one already on display. She hadn't realized Ryan was the customer that had come in the door earlier. Ryan waited for a pause in the conversation before smiling and saying hi. Marcy was still smiling from her conversation with Mr. Danbury as she looked up to see what pleasant voice had greeted her. Her smile slowly slid from her face as she recognized Ryan.

"So these items are your handiwork?" he asked when she didn't respond. His grin hadn't left its spot between the two deep etches on his cheeks. The smile wrinkles also held their place at the corners of his eyes.

Marcy still couldn't find her voice. The memory of her behavior on that awful Saturday suddenly sprang up to haunt her.

"They are very good, too! She does excellent work, wouldn't you say?" Mr. Danbury saw Marcy's discomfiture and stepped in. She fumbled with the piece in her hand and dropped it. "And they don't break very easily either!" he chuckled as he and Marcy both bent over at the same time to pick it up and bumped heads.

Ryan's smile widened and he turned to the sales lady. "I'll take these. Would you wrap them for me? Thanks." He turned back to Marcy and Mr. Danbury.

"What are you doing here?" Marcy's voice was back, but it came out almost harsh. Mr. Danbury was surprised at her response and looked at Ryan as if the reason could be found with him. A hurt look crossed Ryan's face and then turned quickly into a question. Marcy instantly felt badly. "I, um... I'm sorry... I didn't mean... I meant... what brings you here?"

Marcy had lost her poise and was trying to regain it. He'd try to help her. He smiled gently and nodded. "I was shopping for a birthday present for Mom."

Marcy quickly searched for and recalled the dates needed in her mind, "That's right; it's tomorrow, isn't it?"

"Yes it is! She doesn't care much for parties, but we are having a few friends over to help celebrate."

"Did you find anything for her yet?"

"Yes I did, as a matter of fact. It's being wrapped now."

"Oh."

"If you selected something from this display, you made an excellent choice! Miss Kelman's wares sell very well here!" Mr. Danbury inserted. He motioned toward the back counter. "She has brought me more today. Shall we pack you up, my girl?" He guided Marcy by the elbow to where they had left her things, an obvious ending to the exchange. Ryan walked over to the counter where the present was being wrapped and waited. Mr. Danbury looked to make sure Ryan wasn't within earshot, then leaned towards her and whispered, "Does that man bother you?"

Marcy grimaced and shook her head. Why was she acting like an idiot again? "No, he doesn't bother me. We used to be good friends. I haven't seen him in a long time. He's fine, really, it's me. He helped me when I had the bike accident." Marcy whispered back.

Mr. Danbury straightened up and bobbed his head sagely. "I see."

Ryan just finished paying for his purchase as Marcy finished her business and they both reached the front door together. Ryan opened the door for Marcy, and Mr. Danbury called good-by to her. She turned her head to tell him good-by also, and to thank Ryan for holding the door. She walked into the doorpost. She was carrying a box in front of her, and thankfully it was less than half full, because the impact caused her to drop the box. Marcy's face flamed red and she kept her head down as she stooped to pick up the pottery. Mr. Danbury rushed over to help pick it up and examine it.

"That door," stated Mr. Danbury as if it had been at fault. "I should have done something with it a long time ago. It is way too narrow for comfort. Maybe I will replace it and put in a door that has a beautiful window. Maybe one of my works, yes? Ah, here..." he held up a broken plate to mourn and the door was forgotten.

Mr. Danbury clucked and hmmm'ed as he worked. Ryan was silent. She forced herself to not look at him.

The pottery was wrapped well, and most of it was undamaged. Mr. Danbury and Ryan stood as she put the last piece back in the box.

"There," said Mr. Danbury as if consoling a child, "That wasn't as bad as it could have been, only one plate lost."

Marcy stood up, looked at his kind face and gave a weak smile. He patted her on the back and squeezed her shoulder. She started to bend down to pick up the box.

"May I carry that to your car for you?" Ryan asked softly.

Marcy nodded and this time she was the one to hold the door. She gave a small wave to Mr. Danbury, but couldn't bring herself to look at Ryan. She knew she'd have to though, and she had to apologize for her behavior, too. That was the least she owed him. She remained silent as she led him to her station wagon, opened the tailgate and watched him place the box in the car.

She watched as Ryan shut the door and turned to face her. Marcy squared her shoulders, took a deep breath and let it out again. She opened her mouth to speak, hoping it would come out right.

"Ryan, I need to apologize to you. I've acted abominably. You've been kind and helpful, and I've been surly and ungrateful. Please forgive me. I don't know what you must think." her voice trailed off as she became lost for words.

"I'm glad."

Marcy's head came up and she looked him directly in the eyes for the first time since she left him at the display. What was in them? Merriment? But that wasn't all, there was something else, but she wasn't sure what. His response threw her off guard.

"Glad?" she repeated stupidly.

"Uh-huh. I'm glad that you've out-grown kicking, I left my shin guards at home." The blue eyes were filled with mirth now.

Marcy's face flamed red once again. At this moment, she wished she hadn't out-grown it. The cad! It had been hard enough to apologize and now he reminded her of other embarrassing moments from the past. Ryan gave a short chuckle. Her eyes threw darts at him, while her fists clenched and unclenched, not knowing what to do next.

When he saw she was nonplussed, his voice was contrite. "Marcy, I'm sorry. I didn't mean to make you angry." He smiled. "I accept your apology. Will you accept mine?"

The fight left Marcy and her eyes dropped to his shoes. She nodded.

"I haven't eaten yet and still have time before I need to get back to work. I was wondering if you would allow me to take you to lunch."

She looked up to read his face. "I've already eaten, and I have the rest of my route to run, I'm sorry." He looked genuinely disappointed as he studied her face for a moment.

"Could I take you some other time, then?"

She gave him a smile and nodded. "Some other time."

As he opened the driver's door for her, Marcy wished she hadn't stopped for lunch. After she pulled out of the space, and started to drive off, she glanced in her rear view mirror. He was standing there watching her drive away. Her heart did a little flip flop.

Chapter 5

PRAYER IN THE BURGER PLACE

Dave came into the office just as Marcy sat back in her chair, raised her arms and stretched. The only other person present was a high school girl sitting at Dave's desk filling out new-hire paperwork for her new after school job. He snuck up behind Marcy and poked her in the ribs. She shrieked in surprise and slammed her arms down to her sides. At Marcy's outcry, the girl at Dave's desk jumped, jerking her hand. Her hand hit a coffee mug, still half full of coffee. The coffee mug knocked a pile of price lists onto the floor and followed after them. The mug broke and the papers got soaked with creamed coffee.

The girl looked at Marcy, horrified. "I'm sorry."

Marcy looked at Dave. "Now look what you've done."

"Rats! I wasn't done with my coffee, yet."

"You've scared the new help. How will we ever keep them if you do things like that?"

"New help is easy to come by," he smiled and winked at the girl, "It was that perfect cup of coffee that's elusive."

The girl smiled back at Dave, relieved, and bent down to clean up the mess.

"No, no. Just leave it. He made the mess and he'll clean it up," Marcy instructed.

Dave stepped over and started picking up the papers. "That's right. Hurry and fill out those papers. It looks as if Marcy here will be leaving us real soon and maybe you'd like her position."

The girl looked to see if this was still in fun or not. She saw the twinkle in Dave's eye and the laugh on Marcy's face, decided it was play, giggled, and turned back to her papers. Marcy found some paper towels to help with the mess.

Dave certainly was in a light-hearted mood today. Usually messes bothered him. Of course he wasn't usually the one to cause the messes. But poking her in the ribs wasn't like him either. After she had turned him down last Saturday, he seemed a bit out of sorts Monday. Of course she didn't see him Tuesday because that had been her day off. Since Wednesday, he hadn't really spoken to her a great deal. He was friendly when he did, but he wasn't acting the suitor that he had the week before. But today... He'd been in a good mood, almost silly, often teasing her.

"Hey, Marcy – I have the afternoon off tomorrow, and I was thinking about taking in the early show of the new movie that just came out. Wanna see it with me?"

Marcy swiveled her chair sideways to the desk to better look at him. "Oh, Dave, I'm sorry. I do want to see it. In fact I am going to see it tomorrow with Kandy. We already made plans last night." Marcy was happy now that she let Kandy talk her into it for tomorrow evening. She really didn't want to go with Dave like a date, and this helped her to keep her afternoon free without hurting his feelings. She had a lot of work to do to restock her inventory. She had sold almost all of it the last time she had run her route.

Dave scrunched his lips in and out, studying Marcy. "Would you mind me tagging along? Going to a movie by myself is no fun. And two girls are better than no one. Or are you going to be doing foo-foo things, too?"

Marcy giggled, "Foo-foo things?"

"Yeah, you know – girl things. Getting hair done, shopping, getting a manicure... foo-foo things that guys don't like to do together. Although you know..." he changed the tone of his voice and held out his hand to examine his nails, "Ah could stahnd to hahve mah nails done, too. Don't you think? What color do you see me in?" Marcy giggled as Dave batted his eyes at her.

"Dave, you're awful!"

Dave grinned. "What makes me awful, because I want to go to the movie with you instead of by myself, or because I need my nails done?"

Dave dropped down in front of her with his hands on the arms of her chair. "Please, Marcy, please let me go with you! I promise I'll behave! I promise! Please, can I, huh, can I? Please?" His voice was joking but there was something serious in his eyes.

Marcy rolled her eyes at his antics. "Alright Davy, I'll check with Aunt Kandy to see if it's okay with her. But you have to promise to be good." She had turned him down twice, maybe going as a threesome would be okay.

As Dave stood up, he gave her a loud popping kiss on the mouth. "Thanks Mom, I'll do my best to be good!" He gave her a wink and left the room whistling. Marcy shook her head and turned back to her work.

"Is he your boyfriend?"

Marcy had forgotten the girl at the desk, and blushed. "No, we're just friends."

"I wish I had a 'friend' like that!"

Marcy was up with the birds the next morning. She was a morning person and early riser by nature, but today she was up earlier than usual. It was supposed to be a hot day. The sun in the studio's windows made it hard to keep cool even with the air conditioner, so she wanted to get an early start and beat the heat. If she got a lot accomplished, she wouldn't feel guilty stopping early.

Hair braided in a single short braid, donned in her usual work clothes of raggedy cut-offs and oversized T-shirt, Marcy had several pieces already drying on the metal shelves by 11:00. She had just enough clay left for one more soup bowl before she would have to mix more. She placed the lump of clay in the middle of her wheel and gave the heavy fly wheel a kick to get it going. She no sooner got it up to speed than the doorbell announced a visitor. Marcy let out a sigh of frustration. It better not be Dave, he knew that she had a lot of work she wanted to get done today.

She tromped through the house, wiping her hands on her T-shirt as if it were a towel. She opened the door with a jerk, intending to give Dave a piece of her mind. "Listen, it's not 6:30 yet, and I..."

"Hi! Delivery for Marcy Kelman?" It was Ryan's smiling face that greeted her and not Dave's. He took in her wrinkled, wet, and dirty shirt. "If you would like, I'll go away and bring it back at 6:30."

The cloud lifted from Marcy's face and she smiled then. "No. You're fine. I was expecting that you were someone else."

"I'm glad I'm not! I prefer the welcoming smile than what looked like a possible tongue lashing."

Marcy grimaced. "So what did you mean, 'delivery'?"

Ryan motioned to his car in the drive. I brought back something that we thought you might be missing. She looked at the trunk and saw her bike sticking out, keeping the lid from shutting. She had almost forgotten about it. She hadn't gotten a desire to go riding in the last few weeks.

Marcy followed him to the car. "Thank you. I didn't expect you to bring it. You didn't need to."

"You're welcome. I know you didn't, but I wanted to." He sat it down in front of her. "Mr. Sheffler fixed some of the things that were damaged."

Marcy peered at the bike. She hadn't even considered that it might have gotten wrecked. It looked better than before she fell. "That was sweet of him! He shouldn't have done that!"

"Well, you know Mr. Sheffler. He likes to fix things. I think he got a great kick out of it. It was something different than what he normally works on."

Marcy opened the garage door for Ryan.

"I'll have to repay him for his trouble."

Ryan shut the garage door and wiped his brow. The day was definitely heating up. His brown hair was stuck to his forehead where it fell. He pushed it back running his fingers through his hair trying to get it to stay. There was an uncomfortable pause while Marcy was trying to decide what to do next.

"Uh... Ryan... I really am sorry for the way I acted. I... um... I don't know why... It wasn't exactly how I would have chosen to re-establish a rela..., um, a friendship." She felt irritated with herself for stumbling so. What had happened to the comfortable-old-shoe feeling she had felt at first? She looked up to search Ryan's face. She found a look of understanding.

"I already told you last time that I accepted your apology. You're forgiven. So now, Spitfire, how about if we start over. Okay, chum?" Ryan chucked her on the arm and Marcy nodded and smiled at him.

"Would you like to come in for something to drink?"

"Well, actually I was hoping this would be some other time."

Marcy's brows furrowed. "Some other time?"

"At *Danbury's* you said that I could take you to lunch 'some other time'. I was hoping this was then."

Marcy looked down at her frowsy appearance, debating. She needed to work, but she really wanted to go with Ryan, too.

"If you're too busy, I'll understand. I know that you didn't expect me, I didn't call or anything. Don't worry about how you look; I wasn't planning on anywhere fancy." He opened his arms indicating his attire. He too, was in cut offs and a T-shirt.

Even if Marcy didn't have clay all over her, she wouldn't look as good as he did. "I am working. I guess that I still have to eat though. I can't be gone too long and I'll still have to change."

"I'll keep it as short as you want, but please don't dress up."

"Why don't you come on in? You're welcome to have something cool to drink while I clean up."

Ryan helped himself to some lemonade while Marcy changed. He hadn't really looked around when he was here before, other than for things in the kitchen. The house was a small, older home. The door to the kitchen was straight back from the front entrance to the house. Almost straight through the kitchen was another door, Ryan guessed it led to the back porch. The door was shut and the yellow gingham curtain was closed that hung over its window. Her kitchen (which was almost as big as the living room,) was a cheerful white and lemon yellow. A number of pottery pieces setting out were being used as canisters and to hold utensils. They added a cobalt blue accent to the cozy kitchen. Ryan noticed a bowl holding fruit in the middle of the kitchen table was blue stained glass. It sat directly beneath a Tiffany lamp done in blues with yellow irises. These obviously came from *Danbury's*.

Her living room was in neutral colors and tastefully accented with pillows and some of Marcy's more unusual pieces. He noticed the vase on the coffee table with the roses in it. They needed to be thrown out. Petals were falling off and they drooped terribly. Ryan pondered why she hadn't pitched them yet. Was it because of sentimental reasons? If so, who gave them to her?

Ryan let Marcy choose the restaurant and she chose the local burger place. She observed Ryan from the booth while he ordered the food. There was something different about him than when they were kids. He was older and more mature, sure, but it wasn't something that years alone would have put there.

She watched, making a mental list, trying to figure out what it was. He wasn't of a particularly tall stature, being only a half a head taller than she, but he seemed tall. It was probably because he stood straight, and had an air of confidence about himself, not from vain pride or arrogance, but from quiet self-assurance. She watched as he allowed two elderly women that came in behind him to step in front of him. They tittered their appreciation, patting him on the arm as they stepped in front.

Kind and courteous.

His kindness to the ladies reminded Marcy how he always opened the doors, allowing her to go first.

A gentleman.

He helped her in and out of the car, too.

Helpful.

Two high-school girls in the line next to him looked at him shyly. He smiled at them and spoke something that made them smile and nod.

He was friendly, too.

His line moved ahead and he stepped forward. One of the girls whispered something to the other. They both looked him over from head to toe, and then turned to each other, putting their heads together, giggling.

He was definitely good looking.

He walked back to the booth with their tray of food, smiling at Marcy as he came.

Add 'cheerful' to his list of attributes.

These qualities weren't different about him; he'd always had these qualities to one degree or another. They seemed accentuated now, though. He would have made his Boy Scout leader proud. Except that he was never in Boy Scouts. Marcy chuckled to herself picturing him in a Boy Scout uniform with a sash loaded with badges.

"What's so funny?" He placed the tray on the table and slid into the booth across from her. Marcy felt as if she got caught with her hand in the cookie jar.

"Oh, nothing really, it was just an amusing thought. It wouldn't be funny if you didn't know the surrounding stuff. It was one of those things where you would've had to have been there." She tried to be flippant and squash the guilty feelings.

"Been where?"

"In my thoughts, following my line of thinking."

"Was I?"

"Were you what?"

"In your thoughts." His eyes seemed to already know the truth and teased.

Marcy blushed. Ryan laughed. Strike *'kind'* off the list. She started to retract her hand that was lying on the table, trying to pull away physically as well as emotionally. Ryan reached out and took the hand before it got away and gave it a little squeeze.

"I'm hoping I was, you know."

Put *'kind'* back on the list and add *'understanding'* with it.

Marcy, returning an appreciative smile, became aware of the hand that was holding hers. It was strong, warm, and she liked the feel of it. Marcy nodded in response to his apology. Ryan squeezed her hand again.

"Shall we?"

Marcy thought he meant 'shall we eat' and so nodded again. He didn't let go of her hand as she expected, instead, he started praying over the food.

Out loud.

There in public.

Marcy's head snapped up in surprise. His head was bowed and his eyes closed. He didn't notice that he was embarrassing her by this display. She felt like everybody was watching him, and then realized that it probably appeared that she was praying with him. Marcy squirmed. The prayer was quite short, but to Marcy it took forever. She knew his parents prayed over their meals. She didn't remember them doing it out loud in public though. She was all for praying over food; she even did it once in a while herself. But in public? And over a fast food hamburger, for Pete's sake!

Ryan looked up when he was done and caught Marcy staring at him with a look of annoyance. Disappointment and concern covered the happy light in his eyes and he busied himself with the food. Now why should she feel she was wrong for being annoyed? He was the one making a spectacle of himself, not her. Marcy didn't like the way she was feeling now. Guilty. Again. And he caused it. She unwrapped her sandwich with a vengeance. She glanced up at him. He was still preoccupied with the food. She let a little sigh escape. Still – for some reason, she liked being with him.

Ryan's heart was saddened by her reaction to his prayer. Would she have reacted like that in high school? Of course he wouldn't have prayed like that when she was in high school. He hadn't been Christian when they had parted company over ten years ago. Maybe she didn't realize he was one now. He had forgotten for a minute that their lives had taken different paths. He had just assumed that she became a Christian because he had. When the Kelmans had moved, the Robinsons influence was removed from Marcy's life. He knew that his parents had lost contact with Marcy just as he had done. There might not have been anyone left to encourage her and help her come to know the Savior. Her parents probably wouldn't have done this. They had let Marcy attend church with the Robinsons as she was growing up because it was a nice social thing to do, as long as she didn't get fanatical about it. They had viewed the Robinson's as nice people that probably took this church thing a little too seriously. He needed to be a friend and a witness. He sent up a short prayer, silently this time.

Ryan took a drink and cleared his throat. "So, do you have plans to own your own shop?"

Marcy was grateful that he started the conversation about something neutral. The silence was becoming uncomfortable for her, but she didn't know what to say to break it.

"I'd like to, yes. But at this point, my ceramics don't bring in quite enough to live on."

Ryan drew her out, getting her to talk about her work and her dreams. Ryan was a good listener and knew the right questions to ask. Marcy started to relax. He saw that she was still fun and easy to talk and laugh with. He tried to guide the conversation to her social life, but she wasn't inclined to talk about that and he didn't push it.

He looked down at his watch, and started to collect the sandwich wrappers. "We'd better go. I didn't mean to keep you so long." *Considerate.*

Marcy looked at her watch, too. She was shocked at the time. It felt as though they had only been talking for a few minutes and she was disappointed that lunch was over.

Ryan walked her to her door when they got back to her house. "This was nice."

"Yes it was. I enjoyed it. Thank you." Marcy smiled.

"We'll have to do it again sometime. Only next time, I get to pick the restaurant, and we won't wear cut-offs." He smiled and started to turn to leave.

"Uh... would, um... would you like to come in for a bit?"

Ryan stopped and looked at her questioningly. Why did she hope that he'd come in? Marcy felt stupid for asking now, because she had already told him that she had a lot to do. And she had just invited him in as if she didn't. What was she doing?

"You don't have to, I just wondered if you'd like to. You must have other things that you need to do."

Ryan smiled at her back-peddling. "I don't have any pressing matters, and I would love to stay and visit, but I don't want to keep you from your work."

"I... well ..."

Ryan chuckled, "I'll come back." He chucked her under the chin with his finger and walked to the car. He gave her a short wave as he pulled out of her drive. Marcy sighed and went in the house to get back to the work she no longer felt like doing.

Marcy had finished the soup bowl that she had started and mixed another batch of clay, but the thought of sitting at the wheel throwing more plates and bowls was a dreary one. She decided to glaze the bisque ware instead, but found herself doing more daydreaming than glazing. Her heart hadn't been in her work since Ryan left. So when her doorbell rang again at 4:00, this time she didn't mind the interruption. Maybe it was Ryan again. He said he'd come back, but hadn't said when. Her heart lightened at the thought.

It was Dave.

"Thought I'd come early and scare something up to eat before we go. You can keep working while I get it ready. Doesn't that sound good? It would be an efficient use of your time."

"I'm glazing."

"Yeah? So?"

"So... that means I'm working in the kitchen and that my stuff is spread all over the table."

"Oh that won't bother me. I won't need the table, and I don't mind if you watch me work." He smiled and wiggled his eyebrows at her Groucho fashion.

Marcy shrugged and walked into the kitchen. Why was she feeling irritated at Dave? She felt like he was intruding on her privacy. The phone rang and Marcy answered.

"Hi, Marcy, Kandy here!"

"Hi, Kandy. What's up?"

"Um... I have to cancel the movie."

"Oh, Kandy, I was looking forward to going with you. Are you sure?"

"Yep. Another friend asked if I would do a favor for him, and I told him I would. He wasn't sure when that would be, and he didn't find out until after I made plans with you. He's counting on me and I like to keep my promises. So I have to cancel with you. I hope you understand."

"Of course I do. I'm just disappointed."

"Maybe another time?"

"Of course."

When Marcy hung up from talking to Kandy, disappointment was written on her face. Dave could hear it in her voice and continued to rummage for something to eat.

"That was Kandy. She can't go tonight."

"I'm sorry. Does this mean you don't want to go either?"

"No, I'll go. I feel like getting out and doing something. This afternoon was kind of a drag."

"Well I am glad that you prefer my company to a draggy afternoon, anyway."

"I'm sorry. I didn't mean it to sound like that."

You're forgiven." Dave peered into the refrigerator, "Your stock is running low, Marcy."

"I know. I haven't done my shopping yet."

Dave opened a container to see if it was promising. A putrid odor rising from the greenish meat assaulted his nose.

"Oh yuck! Phew! What is this?!" He quickly shut the container.

Marcy smiled at his reaction. "It's ham. I just couldn't force myself to eat the rest of it."

Dave threw the whole thing in the garbage.

"Hey! Don't throw the container away!" Marcy protested.

"I'll buy you another one. Why didn't you throw it out sooner?"

"Well I didn't want to throw it away when it was still good, but I just couldn't eat it. Then I forgot about it. And well..."

"There's not really much to work with in here. And I have an idea. How about you go change, and we'll catch an early movie. The crowd won't be as big, and then we'll pick up something to eat afterwards. How's that sound?"

Marcy agreed to the plans and went to change. Dave sat down in the living room to wait for Marcy and noticed the roses and promptly got up, threw them away and cleaned up the mess they had made. He wondered why she still had them. A smile came to his face; maybe she kept them for sentimental reasons and he meant something to her after all. He relaxed in the recliner, pleased with himself. His plans were working pretty well so far.

The movie was a comedy and it helped to lighten Marcy's mood considerably. Dave was glad to see the change.

Instead of taking her out to eat, he pulled into a grocery store parking lot.

"What are we doing here, you nut!"

"I told you that we'd pick up something to eat. Did I say where?"

"No," she laughed. "This isn't even our store, though."

"If I go into 'our' store, as you so fondly called it, someone will stop me for something about work. I don't want to work tonight. Besides, it doesn't hurt to scout out the competition. So, what would you like for supper?"

They walked in and Marcy pushed the cart while Dave shopped. He had some of the previous day's goofiness still hanging on. Shopping with

Dave was actually fun tonight. Dave was encouraged by her laughter. She seemed to have let down her guard and accepted him as her escort, no longer holding him at arm's length as she had been. Dave laughed and joked throughout the store often grabbing her hand or throwing an arm across her shoulders.

Instead of taking Marcy back to her home, Dave took her to his apartment to fix their supper. Marcy had been to Dave's place before, and she never felt very comfortable, always a bit nervous like she couldn't relax. It was decorated tastefully, but it lacked a sense of warmth and hominess. The lines were all clean and crisp. To Marcy they looked aseptic and severe. She felt she had to be very careful not to touch anything. Everything was always in place and always immaculate. The couch even looked stern to Marcy. "Sit in the middle of me. Sit up straight, don't slouch. Don't lean on the arms, don't scrunch my pillows and don't even think about putting your feet up. Not on me or my associate the coffee table."

Marcy sat in the kitchen and visited while Dave prepared supper. The kitchen was no more relaxing than the living room. Nothing sat out on the counter tops, no coffee pot, no canisters, and no paper towels. The refrigerator didn't even have a magnet on it. If a stranger were to walk into the kitchen, they'd have to open the cabinet doors to tell that anyone lived here. A mess wasn't even made while Dave cooked.

Dave sensed that Marcy wasn't as relaxed as she had been, and so after supper, drove her home. He asked if he could come in for a cup of coffee, and Marcy assented. Dave was careful to keep the conversation light. He'd play the game her way and show her that he could be whatever she needed him to be: A caretaker, provider, friend and companion, and then when he thought that the time was right, a lover. Ever since he had revealed his feelings for Marcy, he wanted her more than ever. He would be patient, though, he didn't want to blow it and tonight she was responding well to 'playful companion'.

Marcy was just about to trounce Dave at a hand of cards when her phone rang. The phone was closest to Dave, so he answered. It was Ryan. Marcy couldn't read the look on his face as he handed her the phone. Dave watched her as she talked.

"Hello? Oh hi! No, you aren't... Yeah, I'm sure... Uh, well, I was planning to visit my parents tomorrow morning. I haven't seen them since they got back from their vacation this week... Hawaii... I'm sure they have a ton of pictures... Supper at 6:00 sounds fine. I should be back by then... Should I bring anything?... Okay, if she's sure... Tell her I said thank you for the invitation... Bye!" Marcy handed the phone back to Dave to hang up.

"Ryan? As in Robinson?"

Did his voice hold a bit of jealousy? A red flag went up for Marcy.

"Yes... how did you know it was Ryan?" Marcy countered, trying to feel Dave out. Dave sensed he needed to be careful to not blow it.

His voice took on a playful tone. "Hello, this is Ryan. Is Marcy there?" He paused and smiled at her. "He gave me a pretty good hint."

Marcy laughed. "Yes, Ryan as in Robinson. Why?"

"No reason, really. Curiosity, I guess. I'm about ready to go out, are you?"

"To go out?"

Dave held up his hand of cards and waved them at her. Marcy giggled and picked hers up.

"So he's really back in town, huh?"

"Yep, and he's really staying with his parents. He called because his mom wanted to know if I'd go to church with them in the morning and stay for dinner."

"Church?" Dave smirked.

"Yes. Church." Marcy bristled, "I used to go with them when I was growing up."

"Hey, hey. Don't get mad!" Dave put up his hands as if to ward her off. "I just thought that it was funny. You said you hadn't seen them in how many years, and then out of the blue they call up and invite you to church of all places."

"They didn't just call up out of the blue. I've seen Ryan a couple of times and once at *Danbury's* when I was restocking. He was there looking for a birthday present for his mom and I told him to tell her Happy Birthday. I'm sure he told her. Mrs. Robinson is very nice and I guess she took that as a sign to get reacquainted. She's like that."

"You've seen Ryan a couple of times?"

"I've run into him, Dave, nothing planned, I promise."

"Are you picking up your friendship where you left off?"

"Why do I feel like I'm getting the third degree?"

Dave almost blew it, too nosey.

"Because, my dear Marcy, you don't play well when you get ruffled." He laid down his cards and beamed at Marcy, "Gin."

Marcy looked at Dave askance. Was he trying to cover up or was he really trying to throw her off guard? He certainly seemed to be delighted in his win. Dave looked at his watch, sat back and stretched.

"I guess that I can go home now. We would've had to play another round if I'd lost. So you're lucky that I can sidetrack you so easily!"

Marcy laughed and threw her cards at him. Maybe he was just sidetracking her. She walked him to the door and stepped outside.

"Thank you for the evening, Dave. It was fun."

Marcy thought that she saw something cross Dave's eyes, but wasn't sure. Dave hesitated before responding. She looked lovely and he wanted more than anything to take her in his arms. He held himself in check. Not yet.

"I had fun, too. 'Night Marcy."

Marcy smiled as she watched him go to the car. He hadn't even tried to kiss her – maybe he was going to be 'just a friend' after all.

Chapter 6

SPERK THE JERK AND A SUNSET

arcy's parents lived in the new townhome complex in Sheridan. It was very modern and offered many extras, including a security gate with guard. All of the homes were identical, in shape and color, making it hard for Marcy to remember exactly which one belonged to her parents. They weren't just square buildings, but had nice lines with layered roofs and dormer windows. They stood in pairs lining the streets, with their double-wide garages standing out like sentinels, separating and keeping watch over the recessed entrances.

The landscaping matched the town homes: tasteful, neat, precise, and identical. Stray flowers weren't allowed out of their specifically designed location and a bush dare not have a shaggy haircut. Even the trees were selected for their shape. There were no sprawling limbs to provide shade beyond the tree's predetermined boundary of shade giving. Grass, in the tiny yards, was cut all to the same height, and was mowed regularly whether it looked like it was needed or not.

There weren't very many children that lived there. Marcy very rarely saw any playing on the playground equipment that was located in the center of the complex along with an indoor pool and meeting room. The playground was kept as immaculate as the complex grounds.

She often wondered how her parents could leave the wonderful home on Cobblewood, where no two houses were the same, for one of these.

Marcy knew that her dad liked the fact that grounds keeping and building maintenance were taken care of by the HOA fees. He never really enjoyed doing these chores and didn't begrudge the money that he spent to let someone else handle it. Marcy thought to herself that Dave would love a place like this.

The security guard at the gate had buzzed her folks for permission to let Marcy come in, so her Mom was standing in the driveway watching expectantly for her as she pulled up.

Her mom was petite in form, only coming up to about Marcy's shoulder. She kept her hair just long enough to be able to pull it back into a chignon. Marcy couldn't remember her mother ever having her hair another way except for when she let it down to sleep. Even if she was sick, she pulled it back. The only thing she changed about her hair was the color, and that was in effort to keep it the same. She said she didn't feel old enough to be getting grey hair yet so she dyed it the brown color of her younger days. The style of her hair set off the delicate lines of her face, bringing out the beauty of her eyes. As Marcy was growing up, she often heard her dad say that he married her mom so he could keep the jewels. This had confused Marcy, never seeing any jewels. One day she finally asked if she could see them. Her dad took her by the hand and led her over to where her mom was sitting.

"There," he said, pointing to her mom's eyes. "Aren't those the most beautiful jewels you've ever seen?" Her mom was beaming up at her husband, and Marcy could see the love pouring out. There was never any question about the love they had for each other.

Her dad was inside, sitting on the couch reading the paper, waiting for Marcy to come in. He seemed to be just the opposite of his wife in personality. Where Mrs. Kelman was flighty and seemed to run on nervous energy, Mr. Kelman was steady; he never seemed to get ruffled, but just calmly thought things through.

Marcy had a delightful visit with her folks. Mrs. Kelman had started logging their trip in pictures from the time they got to the airport in Sheridan until they returned to the airport in Sheridan. This amounted to photo album page after photo album page of pictures and Marcy got to see them all and hear the story behind each one.

They had also brought home souvenirs, a couple of which were for her. Marcy received typical Hawaiian tourist souvenirs from her dad. Not so from her mom. Her mom brought her a small stack of business cards wrapped with a green rubber band. A part of them were held together with a paper clip. Marcy looked at her mom questioningly. "Thanks, Mom. What are these?"

Her mom smiled indulgently. "They're business cards, sweetheart."

"I know they're business cards, Mom. I want to know what they're for, why you gave them to me."

"Well, I just was thinking of you while we were over there, and how much I thought you would've loved it. We visited many shops that sold pottery, which brought you to mind even more. So I just got business cards from the owners! They're wrapped in a *green* rubber band to remind you to *go* visit them whenever you go to Hawaii. The ones in the paper clip are for the ones that are consignment shops. Remember green for 'go there' and *cah*-lip for '*con*-signment'. I thought that your work is just as good as any I saw there. See, here, I brought you back a piece to show you a sample of the things they sell."

She placed a tall, faceted vase in Marcy's lap. It was a pinkish cream color with a crackled glaze. "Now see, you do every bit as good as that. And the prices they ask! Not only that, but whoever makes some of them, must run out of ideas and get stuck in a rut. This had several others just like it. Some of them were painted different colors, but their shapes were the same. I think that your work would sell well there, sweetie."

Something struck Marcy that this was a product of mass production and not an island original. She turned it over. Sure enough, "Made in China" was imprinted on the bottom. She smiled at her mom. There was no doubt in Marcy's mind that her parents supported her efforts in pottery. Her mom didn't seem to understand it, but she was certainly supportive. Marcy giggled at the thought of adding Hawaii to her route.

As she was leaving to go home, her dad gave her a hug and whispered. "When you decide to expand to Hawaii, Spitfire, I'd like to apply for the sales position that would cover that route." Marcy chuckled and kissed her dad's cheek. "You'd probably get it seeing as you have an 'in' with the boss."

As Marcy was driving home from her parent's, she became more and more nervous about going over to the Robinson's for supper. She almost felt like she was going out on her first date. What should she wear? Would she say or do something dumb? How should she fix her hair? What do Mr. and Mrs. Robinson think of her? Was this Ryan's idea or his parents? Maybe she should cancel.

"Marcy, girl – snap out of it! You're just going over for supper. You've known these people all your life! They are just friends with whom you're going to get reacquainted! Now get a hold of yourself! You're acting like a teenager!" she verbally reprimanded herself to take control of her emotions. Her emotions didn't obey very well, they just took another tack.

Why was she feeling so shy and nervous about going to the Robinson's? She really enjoyed the visit with Ryan, in spite of his embarrassing prayer. She had felt tongue tied at first, but then relaxed. He was easy to be with. That's why she had asked him to come in, even when she knew she had a lot to do. She remembered the way he watched her leave *Danbury's* and how her heart reacted so strangely. She had caught herself thinking about him quite a bit ever since then. She remembered the feel of her hand in his as he held it while he prayed. It wasn't like holding her brother's hand either. Or Dave's for that matter. She had liked it. *A lot.*

That wasn't how you were supposed to think about a brother, and that's basically what he'd been to her most of her life. But that's not how she was feeling towards him now. She'd definitely have to squelch those feelings. They made her feel guilty and that's why she felt shy and nervous about going. She didn't like feeling guilty, and if she was going to get the feelings under control, she shouldn't give them opportunity to grow. What if he should find out? What if something she said or did, gave it away? She made up her mind – when she got home, she was going to call and cancel.

She arrived home about twenty minutes before she would have to leave to make it to the Robinson's on time. Marcy dropped her stuff on the coffee table, wondering what was different in the living room, as she made her way to the kitchen. She took down the phone book from the top of the refrigerator and sat down at the table with the phone. She just found the Robinson's phone number and was about to dial when the doorbell chimed. Marcy glanced at the clock as she went to answer the door. She ought to call as soon as she could to give them as much notice as possible. She wasn't quite sure what she would say if they asked for a specific reason. She hoped they wouldn't.

"Ryan! What are you doing here?" Again, she greeted him ungraciously.

"Hello yourself. It's nice to see you again, too." Again, he smiled in return.

"I'm, ah, sorry. I'm just surprised that you're here. I'm supposed to be at your folks in just a little bit."

"I know. I was in the area, picking up a couple of last minute things at the store for Mom. I thought I'd swing by and see if you'd like a ride."

"Oh... I... um, that was thoughtful of you, but you didn't need too, really."

"I know... but I wanted to. Besides," his eyes teased her, "if I came to pick you up, it'd be harder for you to change your mind about coming over."

A blush started to creep up Marcy's face. Ryan noticed it and glanced over to the kitchen. He could see the phone book open next to the phone on the table. He raised his eyebrows in speculation. He had just been teasing, but was she about to call and cancel? She obviously was a bit uncomfortable that he was here.

"So," he said in a still teasing manner, "would you allow me to take you, or do you want me to waste the trip?"

Marcy couldn't look him in the eyes. Did she have the courage to tell him that she had decided not to go, since she had to do it face to face? "How would I get home?" She stalled, trying to decide.

"Well, there are three options. One, you could walk back. Two, we could stick your bike in the trunk and you could peddle back. And three, I could drive you back. My personal favorite is number three."

Marcy smiled tremulously and looked up at him. She'd have to go, she didn't have the guts. "I need to change. I won't take long. Could I get you something to drink while you wait?"

"Thanks. You go ahead and change, if I want anything, I can find it."

Marcy nodded and went to her room. Ryan was curious. He went into the kitchen and looked at the phone book. Sure enough, it was still open to the page that had their name listed. He walked back to the living room and sat on the couch to wait. The dead flowers were gone. Ryan smiled to himself.

Marcy came out in just a few minutes. She heaved a sigh and squared her shoulders, "Okay, I'm ready."

Ryan stood up and searched her face. She said that as if she had steeled herself to do something she dreaded. She looked like it, too. "Is everything okay? You don't have to go if you really would rather not."

Was she that obvious? "No, I'm fine really. Let's go."

Ryan crossed to the door and opened it for Marcy. He waited beside her as she locked the house and put the key back in her purse. Walking to the car in silence, she kept her head down. She was not the confident person she appeared to be with Mr. Danbury. Yesterday she seemed at ease and acted as though she welcomed his company. What was bothering her tonight? As he opened the car door for her, he hesitated. She looked up then, questioning the reason for the pause. His eyes reassured her, as if he could tell what she was thinking.

"Marcy, we don't bite; we promise not to eat you for supper."

Marcy mentally berated herself for the way she was acting. She had to quit letting her emotions get the best of her. She had to put her feelings to the side.

Ryan kept the conversation cheerful and light, joking and teasing. So by the time they arrived at his house, Marcy was feeling more relaxed. She had a genuine smile on her face as they pulled into the drive.

She entered the house and paused just inside the doorway. Familiarities rushed upon her, bidding her memories to awaken. Each room with its own personality, its own unique sounds and feelings evoked childhood memories of happiness and contentment, love and acceptance, and a few lessons learned.

The runner on the dark wooden floor in front of her led to a set of double doors. These were heavy all-wood pocket doors with carved fleur-de-lis to match the French doors leading to the sitting room on her right. Though normally closed, they were open now, and Marcy could see into the formal dining room. Like the wood trim and floors, the table, chairs, china cabinet and buffet were all of dark wood. There was a modest chandelier that hung over the center of the table which sat in the middle of an area rug. In the left wall, at the far end of the table, was a tall double window that was adorned with creamy lace curtains. The walls were wall-papered with a subtly shaded floral pattern on a creamy background. The table was set beautifully.

Marcy had eaten many meals with the Robinsons, but they were in the kitchen where the family usually ate. She could remember only once eating in the formal dining room. She was eleven and was dressed in her very best dress and Ryan wore a suit. She didn't remember the occasion, but she remembered thinking that the guests must have been very special and that it was a special occasion. She was so nervous about the possibility of spilling on herself, or worse, the lace tablecloth, thereby causing an embarrassment to the Robinsons, that she could hardly even eat.

Marcy closed her eyes and took a deep breath. There were wonderful aromas drifting from the kitchen, but those weren't what Marcy noticed first. The Robinson's house had its own special perfume that Marcy loved. To Marcy, it was the house's own unique signature. The smell was a mixture of things. She could detect the scent of the wood soap and oil that Mrs. Robinson used to keep the wood looking so rich, and she recognized the soft scent of Mrs. Robinson's cologne. But there were still other things that mingled with these that Marcy couldn't discern. The fragrance they made together was pleasant and soothing.

Mrs. Robinson came through the dining room doors with a welcoming smile on her face and her arms out-stretched to greet Marcy. Marcy had always received hugs from the elder Robinsons when she came over. It was the standard way of greeting guests at this house. Her family had always been close, but they weren't 'huggy' like this family. She often observed Ryan giving and getting hugs from his parents as they were growing up. Marcy had given and gotten a pretty big share from them also. She used to love it, but now she felt a little awkward. Apparently Mrs. Robinson didn't; her hug was just as warm and welcoming as Marcy remembered.

"I'm so glad that you came, dear. I feel just awful that I let things slip so."

"Thank you for having me. I should have kept in touch better, too."

"Why don't you go on into the living room and relax. I just have a couple of things left to do, and then it will be ready to eat. Ryan, did you get the things I needed?"

Ryan nodded, held up a sack, wagging it at his mom. "Where's Dad?"

"He's upstairs, dear, he'll be down in just a minute."

"Is there anything I can do to help you?" Marcy inquired.

"Everything is under control, and it's almost ready."

"I hope you didn't put yourself out on my account."

Mrs. Robinson squeezed Marcy's shoulders as she led her through the dining room. "I don't feel that I did, and if you feel that I did, just remember that I wanted to. You're special to us and I hope we help you feel that way."

Marcy smiled a confirmation at Mrs. Robinson. She had always felt like she was special to them, it seemed they looked forward to her company and they enjoyed her presence in their lives.

Marcy walked into the living room with Ryan. Not much had changed there, either. "They must be content with their lives," Marcy mused. Her mom always seemed to be redecorating something, buying new or rearranging furniture. Time had stopped at the Robinson's. They weren't boring people, with no impetus – on the contrary. It was just that they were satisfied with their material possessions, and if it was still good, why change? It gave a stable, secure feeling.

Marcy heard Mr. Robinson come into the room and turned to greet him. He, too, embraced Marcy.

"Well, here you finally are! I was beginning to wonder if we'd ever get to see you again. Ryan told us about your mishap in the front yard. Let me look at you." He held her back to look her over. "Hmm... you seem to be healing up fine." He held up her left arm and peered at it through the reading glasses that were a fairly permanent fixture on his face. He tapped at the pink lines with his index finger. "These don't look like they will leave scars." Marcy only came up to his shoulders, so he had to tilt his head down quite far to look into her eyes over the top of the spectacles. Mr. Robinson's eyes twinkled at her. "So that manhole still throws you, hmm?"

Marcy grinned at him.

"And did Ryan laugh at you this time, too?"

"Uh... well, not really. He was very helpful. He did far more than what was expected of him."

Mr. Robinson stepped back and looked at Ryan, smiling. "Far more, hmm... He's a good man, isn't he?" Mr. Robinson loved his son; Marcy could see it in his eyes. There was more than just love there, she could tell that he was pleased with Ryan and respected him, too.

Mrs. Robinson called them in for supper. Mr. Robinson tucked Marcy's hand into the crook of his arm and escorted her to the dinner table. Marcy was seated between Ryan and his father. The Robinsons bowed their heads and took hands to give thanks for the meal, as was their usual custom. Marcy followed suit. Mr. Robinson's prayer didn't surprise her like Ryan's had, but it still made her feel funny for some reason unknown to her.

"What a difference between my parents and his," Marcy mused to herself. Mr. and Mrs. Robinson were older than her parents by a number of years. They had wanted children sooner, and had tried, but Ryan didn't come along until they were both in their mid-30's. The Kelmans had married young, barely out of high school. Mark was a surprise, showing up only a year and a half after they were married. Marcy surprised them, too, two and a half years later, and neither one of them twenty-five yet.

Her mom was the one that did the talking in the family. Buzzing around from subject to subject, it wouldn't be uncommon for her mother to change to a totally different subject in the middle of a sentence. Marcy was used to her mother doing this, but it would still disconcert her at times.

Her father was 'the silent type' making a statement only when necessary or when there was no one else saying anything and he thought he had an interesting comment. He was usually reading a newspaper or something, even at the table, so he often wasn't tuned in to the conversation, anyway.

No one was reading at this table or watching TV. Meal times were family times here, and they always had been as far as Marcy could remember. The Robinsons shared conversations with each other, often asking the others their opinion and listening to what they had to say. Conversation flowed naturally from one subject to another, not jerking with sudden starts and stops. The four of them had a pleasant time catching up on the lost years. Ryan said very little during the meal today, just interspersing comments here and there. Mr. and Mrs. Robinson split their side of the conversation about equally.

Marcy had always thought Mrs. Robinson was beautiful. She had large, brown eyes, that always 'understood' and her short hair was a salt 'n pepper, with more salt than pepper. Marcy never thought of it as grey, but as silver. She had asked her once why she didn't dye it to cover the grey like her mom did. She had smiled and squeezed Marcy. "Because," she explained, "the splendor of the young is their strength, and the splendor of the old is their grey head. It's my crown of beauty that God let me have for living for Him."

Marcy could easily see Mrs. Robinson with a crown. She was more than physically beautiful, Marcy always thought of her as regal. Never snooty, though. She had a quiet grace about her. It was that same quality of self-assurance that Ryan had. Mr. Robinson had it, too.

Mr. Robinson was losing most of his 'crown', but it didn't seem to bother him in the least. He was getting just a hint of love-handles, but was by no means paunchy. Ryan had gotten his blue eyes from his father. They always seemed to twinkle and be full of fun. Smile wrinkles attested to this and the same long creases bracketed his smile, also.

Mrs. Robinson had fixed Marcy's favorite dishes, from the meat to the dessert. Everything was delicious and Marcy ate far more than she should have. It was then that she remembered the casserole dish that she was going to bring back. She apologized that she had neglected to return it for so long.

"That's quite all right, dear, I told you that I wasn't in any hurry. You can bring it the next time you come."

Mr. Robinson sat back in his chair and patted his stomach. "As always, my dear, the meal was wonderful. Thank you so much for all the work you put into it. Maybe I should get up and get some exercise."

Everyone helped to clear the table and wash the little bit of dishes that didn't fit in the dishwasher. As Marcy was helping Mrs. Robinson put some things away in the buffet, she noticed the flower and candle holders that Ryan had purchased at Danbury's. She almost said something about them, not recognizing her own work in use. There were very attractive silk arrangements with a long tapered candle in them, which complimented the decor of the dining room.

"You do lovely work, dear. I love those holders. They are quite unique and are just the perfect thing to set off this mirror and buffet. When Ryan told me that you made them, they became even more special."

"Thank you. But I think that the arrangements you put in them are even nicer. I'm glad that you like them. I didn't realize Ryan had purchased them."

"He seems to be fond of your work, dear. Did you notice the pitcher on my counter? He brought that home just last week."

Marcy peered through the kitchen door that stood open. She hadn't noticed the pitcher that was holding a spray of dried flowers earlier.

Mr. Robinson sauntered over to the two women, drying his hands on a towel. He looked at his watch and then at his wife. "It's getting to be that time, dear. Do you still want to go?"

"Oh, I'm sorry. I didn't mean to keep you from something."

"You're not keeping us from anything, dear. We're having a special speaker at church tonight and we thought we would like to hear him. Would you like to go with us?"

Mr. Robinson explained further. "He has attended our church for quite some time. He felt like the Lord called him to the ministry. He just graduated from a Bible School and is going to be getting his own church not a great distance from here. Our pastor invited him back to give his first message since he graduated."

Ryan came up just then and joined in the conversation. "You might remember him. I don't think that he was too far ahead of you in school – maybe in Mark's class. Geoffrey Sperks."

Marcy's eye widened. "Geoff Sperks, otherwise known as 'Sperk the Jerk'?" She hadn't known him personally, but she had heard of him. He was in Mark's class, but his reputation had filtered down. He was probably the rowdiest kid in the school until he graduated. Her parents had said that he had come by it naturally, his father had been in and out of prison, and his mother drank to excess. Geoffrey often came to school un-bathed and in the same clothes all week long. He started drinking and challenging the law when he was in seventh grade. It had been a wonder that he had graduated and not ended up in jail himself.

"Yep, you remember. Only now, he's not 'Sperk the Jerk.'"

"It's marvelous what the Lord can do with a life that's yielded to Him, dear." Mrs. Robinson patted Marcy's arm. "We'd be glad to have you come with us."

"We sure would, it would seem like old times. But if you would rather not, that's okay, too." Mr. Robison added.

Marcy got that uncomfortable feeling again. She really didn't want to go, but didn't want to offend these gracious people either. She looked down to her clothes as a possible excuse to get out of going.

"You're dressed fine, and you didn't even spill on yourself." Ryan offered. Then he added with a chuckle, "And maybe if we promise not to talk, they'll let us sit together!"

Marcy grinned and rolled her eyes. Mr. Robinson shook his head at his son. Mrs. Robinson just said, "Oh Ryan."

Marcy decided to go to church with them. She didn't want to keep Ryan from being able to go, how long could church take anyway? Besides, her curiosity was piqued about Geoffrey Sperks.

The Robinson's sat in approximately the same place as they did all those years ago, three or four rows from the front on the right-hand side of the center aisle. Marcy was the first in, followed by Ryan, then Mrs. Robinson with Mr. Robinson next to the aisle.

The singing was spirited and upbeat at the beginning and then turned softer and worshipful toward the end. Marcy couldn't carry a tune in the proverbial bucket, so she sang quietly. She enjoyed listening to the people singing around her. Ryan surprised Marcy by harmonizing beautifully, she hadn't remembered this. He must have been a late bloomer in this area, because the last she remembered, his parents had teased both of them about making joyful noises together.

She looked at Ryan to communicate her surprise and approval. She shouldn't have bothered; Ryan seemed oblivious to those around him. He was totally caught up in the singing. She looked past him to his parents. They too, were caught up in the worship. She tried to look around at others without being obvious. Most of the others she could see also had looks on their faces of something that Marcy couldn't define. She suddenly felt like she was missing out on something. Something everyone else knew about except her. This made her uncomfortable.

Mr. Robinson was now an usher, and when the offering was taken shortly after the song service, he helped to pass the plate. Marcy hadn't planned on coming to church and had brought no money. She felt even more uncomfortable when she let it pass her by without contributing.

She settled into the padded pew, pressing herself down and back, as if she could make herself smaller by that action. She was beginning to wish she hadn't come at all. She glanced at her watch. Marcy was surprised at the relatively short time they had been there. It seemed like it was at least twice as long.

Geoffrey Sperks was introduced, and that piqued Marcy's interest for a while. He wasn't anything like what Marcy had pictured. She wouldn't have recognized him, had they met on the street. There was very little about him that would suggest he was the same guy that was in his senior picture or that he'd had the reputation that he'd had. Marcy listened for a while to his message. It was interesting, but she got distracted by things around her.

There was a cute baby two rows in front of her, making faces and blowing bubbles as he peered over his mother's shoulder. It must be a good baby, Marcy thought, it didn't get cranky the whole time. Sitting down the pew from her were two kids about five years old who were playing finger games with each other. They were being good and not making any noise, but the movements of their hands caught Marcy's eye. Marcy noticed the plants in the sanctuary. They looked quite healthy. She wondered if a professional plant company came in and cared for them, or if there was someone in the church with a knack for plants. Maybe they were artificial. She tried to notice things about them that would give her a clue. The lighting inside the sanctuary certainly would support live plants. On both side walls were a series of tall narrow windows that started at the back and continued to the front. They were not stained glass, but let in natural light.

Ryan shifted in the pew beside her and draped his arm across the pew behind her. She looked at him. He was watching the speaker and had a smile on his face. Again, she looked down the row at Mr. and Mrs. Robinson. They seemed to be very attentive to what Geoffrey Sperks was saying, too. Again that feeling of missing out on something crept in. Marcy chided herself for letting her thoughts meander, and now she wondered if she had missed something important. Ryan felt Marcy's eyes on him and turned to look at her.

"Does my arm being there bother you?" he whispered.

Marcy shook her head no, but maybe that wasn't altogether true. His question made her very aware of his arm. She felt its warmth and imagined its comfort. She had this urge to scoot closer to him and snuggle under his arm, laying her head on his shoulder. Maybe that would help dispel her odd feeling of being left out. Would he wrap it around her shoulder and hold her close to him?

"Marcy! Shame on you! You're in church! Get a grip on yourself!" Her conscience scolded and now there was a battle going on in her mind. Part of it was very aware of Ryan's closeness and the other part was scolding her for thinking those thoughts in church of all places. Marcy looked at Ryan out of the corner of her eye to see if he noticed this battle that was

very loud to her. Good, he seemed unaware. She would be mortified if he knew her thoughts.

Soon the service was over, and people filed into the aisles. The Robinsons greeted a lot of people and chatted with quite a few of them. Not wanting Marcy to feel left out, they introduced her to them. All Marcy wanted was to get out of there. Her confused feelings were making her feel agitated. She had missed more than half the sermon because of her errant thoughts, and desperately hoped they weren't going to discuss the message on the way home. It had been their custom to do so in the past, and it wasn't likely that it had changed.

They did discuss it on the way home, but mercifully didn't ask Marcy her opinion. When they got back to their house, they invited Marcy in for "just a little bite of pie." Marcy declined the invitation claiming she was still full from supper. She received more hugs and warm invitations to please come back again. She didn't have to wait for an invitation, she was welcome anytime. Ryan drove her home, but not directly. Marcy had been silent until he missed the turn at the usual place.

"Where're you going?"

"I'm kidnapping you."

Marcy giggled. "Serious. Where're we headed?"

"I thought that I would take the scenic route, and try to catch one of the greatest shows around. I'm glad you didn't want to go in for pie, or we would have missed it altogether. As it is, we'll just barely make it."

Marcy looked at him puzzled. "What are you talking about?"

Ryan looked at her with mock horror. "Don't tell me you don't remember! How could you forget the sunsets over the lake?!"

Marcy leaned her head back on the seat. Yes, she remembered. Before they were old enough to drive, sometimes on Friday evenings, they and maybe some of their friends would peddle their bikes to the park. They would goof around, taking trails or skipping rocks across the water. They always stayed to watch the sunset before they would go back home. It always seemed to have a calming effect on the group and they would settle down for the night.

After Ryan had gotten his car every once in a while they would go in the middle of the week on a spur of the moment. Marcy still enjoyed going out to watch, but it wasn't as much fun to go alone. It was a moment that you shared with someone else.

Ryan turned onto the river road that led to the entrance of the park. Neither one of them spoke. They didn't need to as it was a comfortable silence. The park service had built a shelter at the edge of the lake with three porch swings overlooking it. There was an older couple enjoying the view from one of them. Marcy and Ryan sat down in the far one and pushed off, setting the swing into its soothing motion. They sat on opposite ends of the swing and neither one spoke as they watched the reflections on the water.

The frogs and night bugs took up the song as the sun and water finished their duet. The other couple left, but neither Ryan nor Marcy made a move to follow suit. Ryan wanted to talk to Marcy about the church service and was having trouble knowing how to bring it up. He had sensed that she was ill at ease, and suspected that was the main reason she hadn't come in for pie afterwards. She seemed to relax again on the way home and still seemed to be so. Marcy opened the conversation first, with questions that had nagged at her since she heard the gossip in the break room.

"Why did you move back in with your folks?"

Ryan smiled at her bluntness. "I got a job in Sheridan."

"I know, but why move in with your folks, why not get an apartment in Sheridan? It would've been closer to your job. Isn't it hard after you've been on your own so long?"

"Well, it would've been closer, yes. And there are adjustments to make. But they invited me when they found out that I'd gotten the position with *Krenshaw, Bixby, & Barnes*. I thought that it would be a burden on them, especially after they got used to their privacy, but they seemed to really want me to. I pay them rent to help with the extra expense, but it still isn't as much as a place in Sheridan, so it saves me money, too. I try to help them around the house with things, even though they don't seem to need it."

Marcy was silent.

"The biggest reason I think, is because Lakeland Grove feels like home, not Sheridan. I already know people here."

"So why did you move back in the first place? I thought that you had a good job where you were."

"I guess that I missed you."

Marcy turned her head to look to see if he was teasing. He grinned at her.

"I got homesick. I didn't really have any close friends. I wanted family, not just acquaintances, and a home, not just an impersonal apartment.

There was no family there. And some things are more important than making a lot of money."

"So how did you get the job in Sheridan?"

"I'd wanted a job closer to Lakeland Grove for quite a while. My parents knew about it and kept an ear out for me. When the position at *Krenshaw, Bixby & Barnes* opened up, Dad told me about it. It didn't pay as well as my current job, so I wasn't sure if it was for me or not. The more I prayed about it, though, the more I felt like I should apply, and so I did."

It irritated Marcy that he brought up praying about the job. She prayed on occasion, she hadn't totally forgotten things that she had learned in Sunday School. But praying about whether one should take a job or not seemed a bit much. Weren't you supposed to weigh the pros and cons and decide from there? "Did your dad have an 'in' over there or something? A lot of people wanted that job, I heard."

Ryan chuckled, "No, he didn't have an 'in' over there. He just happened to be in the barber shop at the same time as the guy was that was leaving that position. Barber shops are a lot like beauty shops, you know. Men talk to their barbers like ladies talk to their hairdressers. We have an advantage, though."

Ryan stopped and Marcy took the bait. "What's that?"

"We talk about useful things. Also we don't sit under noisy hair dryers, so we can hear what everyone else is talking about. "

Marcy threw the twig at him that she was playing with as they sat.

"I heard that it was a toss-up between you and Bob Deckner as to who got the job. What edge did you have to beat him out of it?"

Marcy's voice carried a hint of derisiveness to it. Ryan didn't answer for a bit, pondering what was lying beneath the question. He had met Bob Deckner on occasion at work. He seemed to be a rather negative sort that carried a chip on his shoulder. He didn't have a very good work record and blamed others for his mistakes. As far Ryan knew, Bob wasn't even considered as a candidate. Marcy probably didn't know him personally, as he lived in a town on the other side of Sheridan. He had relatives that lived in Lakeland Grove, though. Maybe there was a connection there. He chose his answer carefully.

"I don't know who all applied for the job. I simply gave them my résumé and prayed for favor. God answered my prayers."

Marcy stood up. She had wanted to ask him about the incident in college, too, but she had the idea that it would lead back to God. She didn't want to talk about God. She didn't like to feel guilty and that's what she felt when Ryan mentioned God. Ryan sighed and stood up, too. The conversation wasn't exactly what he'd intended. Marcy stood next to the railing looking out over the lake. He moved up beside her to better see her face. She didn't have to say anything; Ryan could see and feel her agitation.

Ryan picked up Marcy's hand that was resting on the railing. "Thank you for sharing the sunset with me, Marcy. It's been a long time since I'd been here. I missed it."

Marcy didn't look at him, but just nodded. She didn't trust herself to speak. His hand was doing funny things to her insides. How could he irritate her one minute, and stir up butterflies inside her, the next?

It was completely dark out now, and the meager light from the quarter moon didn't do much to help light the way to the car. The small parking lot had one light, but its influence didn't reach past the edge of it. Ryan tucked Marcy's hand in the crook of his arm and gave it a pat. The same gesture his father had used to escort her to the table, earlier. She hadn't reacted the same way to Mr. Robinson. Ryan guided her through the darkness and back to the car. Marcy walked closer to him than was necessary. If Ryan noticed, he never let on.

Chapter 7

ANGRY SUITOR

*A*s Ryan approached Marcy's home, Marcy sat up straighter and tried to distinguish who it was that was sitting on the step of her front porch. Her porch light was off and they were still too far away to see much but a shape. The car parked across the street was under a street lamp. She recognized it as belonging to Dave. Marcy glanced at the car clock. It was almost eleven. It was kind of late for him to be at her house, she wondered if anything was wrong. As Ryan pulled into the drive, Marcy saw the long box that was lying beside him. A florist box. Marcy sighed. She really didn't want to have to deal with Dave. He didn't look especially pleased. Why was he here? She hadn't invited him to wait for her.

Ryan didn't hear her sigh. To him it was obvious that the man on Marcy's step was a suitor, and right now, he was miffed at being kept waiting. Maybe it would be better if he didn't walk her to the door. It struck him as odd that she hadn't said anything about meeting someone. Maybe she had forgotten.

Ryan didn't turn the car off, but got out and opened her door to give her a hand getting out.

"Thank you for the evening, Marcy."

"Aren't you going to turn the car off?"

"I thought that it would be better if I left. I'm sorry I kept you out so late. I hope I didn't mess anything up for you."

Marcy's grip tightened on his hand. "But you've got to stay! I'm mean, you don't need to leave!"

Ryan studied Marcy's face. Maybe she wasn't expecting the man on her porch. His presence seemed to cause consternation on Marcy's part. When Ryan wasn't immediately forthcoming with a response, Marcy felt compelled to come up with a good reason for him to stay a bit.

"You've got to come in... umm... for... you've got to come in for your mother's baking dish!" Marcy was relieved to find a suitable reason to delay his departure, glad now that she had forgotten the dish earlier.

Ryan reached through the passenger side and turned off the car, then escorted Marcy to her waiting guest. Dave stood and watched as they approached the porch. Marcy fumbled in her purse for her house keys. Ryan held out his hand and she gave him the keys without a word. Marcy looked up as they got to the porch.

"Hi, Dave. What are you doing here?"

"I'm waiting for you. What does it look like?"

Ryan unlocked the door and reached in to turn on the lights. This Dave person was clearly upset. He observed the exchange quietly.

"Why?" Marcy's single word was clipped, making it a demand rather than a request.

"Why?!" Dave sputtered.

"Yes. Why. We didn't have anything scheduled for this evening. And you knew that I was invited out for supper. You were there when I accepted the invitation that was issued." Marcy seemed in control now; her voice didn't quiver slightly as it had done when she told him he needed to stay. She was certainly direct. Her posture was ramrod stiff. 'Spitfire' was still appropriate. Marcy's hands caught Ryan's attention. Ah, this was a facade. She was twisting her purse strap unmercifully. He wondered if Dave noticed. Apparently not, he was too busy frowning at Ryan and questioning Marcy.

"Suppers don't usually take this long."

"We went to church afterwards."

"And it just got out?"

Marcy's eyes narrowed. "No. Mr. and Mrs. Robinson invited me in for pie after church. We talked."

Ryan didn't miss the prevarication. Marcy evidently didn't want him to know they had spent time alone at the park. He must be the jealous type. He was acting like it now.

"You must have had a lot to talk about."

"What is this, Dave, an interrogation? You're the one that should be answering questions. Why are you here?"

"I was waiting for you to get back from supper."

"So?"

Ryan reached over and gently took the purse from Marcy's hands; rescuing the strap before she broke it. She let him take it from her without a question or a glance. Her eyes were boring into Dave. Dave was watching Ryan. Ryan was glad he wasn't Dave.

"So I thought I'd come over and keep you company afterwards."

"How long have you been waiting?"

Dave glanced at his watch, "About two hours."

"Two hours? Two hours! If I had known you were going to come over, I would have told you not to bother."

Dave glowered as he watched Ryan drop Marcy's keys back in her purse. "I brought you something."

"What."

Ryan slipped the purse strap back over her shoulder. Dave sizzled at the supposed insinuation of intimacy.

"Well, are you going to introduce us or not?"

Marcy 'hmmph'ed and adjusted the purse strap. "I suppose. Dave, this is Ryan Robinson, we grew up together. Ryan, this is Dave Lewis, the assistant store manager where I work," Marcy widened her eyes at Dave, "Just a friend."

Ryan extended his hand to Dave.

Dave scowled at Ryan and ignored the hand, shoving the box at Marcy. "They're to replace the other ones."

Marcy opened the box; more roses of course. "Dave, you didn't have to do that, the other ones are just fine."

Dave was exasperated. "Marcy! The other ones are dead!" He pushed her door open further. "I threw them out yesterday!" Marcy looked puzzled. Dave took her by the arm and propelled her into the living room. He made an exaggerated gesture towards the spot on the coffee table where the dead roses had been residing.

"So that was what was different about my living room!" Marcy mused out loud. "I knew there was something different, but I couldn't figure out what it was."

Ryan headed into the kitchen for a glass of water. He didn't want one, but it was a good excuse to move further into the house. He was near enough to know what was going on, and to have his presence felt, but not so close that it was threatening.

It was also a good way to hide the smile that was tugging at his mouth. Marcy never had paid much attention to things that she didn't deem important. Evidently those roses hadn't been important.

"I'm sorry, Dave. I guess that I'm not very observant some times." Marcy was aware that the rose business probably hurt his feelings, and that wasn't her goal. She just wanted him to leave.

"You're not very observant about a lot of things, Marcy." His voice was angry. Marcy's shoulders drooped and she dropped her eyes. Dave's voice stayed angry but not as harsh. "Sometimes I wonder how you've made it through life this far."

"Thank you for the flowers. It was very kind of you. I'm sorry I wasted your time." Marcy didn't look up, but Ryan could tell it was a definite dismissal. Dave glanced at Ryan who was leaning against the kitchen door frame, observing.

"Marcy, can we talk a minute?" he glanced at Ryan again. "Privately?"

Ryan waited to take his cue from Marcy.

"I think that it would be best if you left now, Dave."

"Marcy, please..."

Marcy looked up at Dave then, her voice, quiet, but firm. "Good night, Dave."

Dave turned on his heels and strode out the door. He didn't shut the door behind him, afraid that he might slam it if he did. Marcy walked over to the door and shut it. She waited there until she heard his tires squeal away.

She walked past Ryan into the kitchen. Her posture had returned to ramrod stiff and her fists were clenched. The vase that her mom brought from Hawaii was sitting on the counter. She picked it up, shoved it under the faucet, filling it with water. She jerked open a drawer, retrieved a knife and slammed it shut again. Ryan now leaned against the kitchen side of the door frame, watching Marcy. He couldn't tell if Marcy remembered if he was there or not. She was clearly agitated, the facade gone. Her actions as she cut the rose stems and jammed them in the vase were forceful and tight.

"Would you like to talk?"

Marcy didn't respond, she just kept cutting and jamming. The vase was too little to hold a dozen roses. Her effort to cram the seventh rose into the opening was futile. That didn't help her mood.

Ryan stepped up behind her and removed the knife and rose from her hands. She curled her hands into fists again. He could feel her stiff form trembling as she just stood there facing the sink. Dave and the roses weren't the only things she'd been hard on. Ryan noticed the drops of blood on her hands where the roses had pricked her. He reached over and tore a paper towel from the roll.

"Here," he said, opening her fists. She took the towel from him and wiped her hands. This action seemed to calm her down. He could feel some of her anger dissipate.

"I'm sorry," her voice was barely above a whisper.

Ryan wrapped his arm across her shoulders and gave them a gentle squeeze. "Would you like to talk?" His voice was gentle beside her ear.

His nearness woke up the butterflies that had been active in her stomach when he took her hand at the park. They must not have felt equal to their task, because they woke up friends.

She hadn't stopped trembling and Ryan felt her start to stiffen again. He took a small step back and turned her to face him. His hands slid down her arms to pick up her hands that had fallen stiffly to her side. The friends woke up more friends.

"Marcy, are you okay?"

She nodded stiffly. He tried to peer into her eyes but couldn't. She stared at the fourth button on his shirt, her jaw clenched. She could not look at him. She couldn't stand there like an imbecile, either. She pushed him away from her gently. "Thank you for coming in. I'm sorry that I put you into an uncomfortable spot." She still stared at the fourth button.

"Did I do something wrong?" He sounded puzzled.

Marcy closed her eyes and shook her head. "No, you did nothing wrong." *"I'm the one doing things wrong,"* her thoughts accused her.

Ryan crooked his finger under Marcy's chin and tipped her chin up so he could look into her eyes. Marcy kept her eyes closed and held her breath. She sent up a panicked prayer for help. What would he think of her if her eyes gave her away? She heard him sigh and his hands move back to her shoulders.

"Marcy, look at me." Ryan's voice was firm. He squeezed her shoulders. "Are you afraid of that guy? Does he... does he abuse you?"

God answered that prayer. His question took her aback, her eyes flew open. When they connected with his, they registered surprise. His were a mixture of concern, confusion, and another emotion that she couldn't discern. She let her breath out all at once. Her shoulders slumped under his hands, and she raised a hand to rub her forehead as if by that action, she could clear her mind. "No. He doesn't abuse me."

Ryan turned her shoulders, and guided her to the couch. She sat in a corner facing the middle, and clutched a big throw pillow in front of her. She appeared to need a little space, so he tactfully sat in the opposite corner. He watched her play with the tassel on the edge of the pillow, waiting for her to compose herself. She took a deep breath.

"Dave doesn't abuse me and I've never been afraid that he would. The reason I wanted you to come in was because Dave can be hard to get rid of sometimes. You being here helped a lot. I know that it wasn't exactly pleasant and I appreciate it a lot." Marcy paused, still playing with the tassel. Ryan had the distinct feeling that there was more to the episode that just took place.

"It didn't appear that my being here helped all that much."

"It did. He can be very persistent, and persuasive. Sometimes I know that he's trying to manipulate me, but I don't know how to stop it." Marcy stopped and looked up at Ryan. "I think that I'm giving you a very horrible picture of Dave. He's nice. Really he is. He's usually a lot of fun. We've been friends for quite a while. It's just that lately we've been having... conflicts in our relationship. And I don't know how to straighten it out. Sometimes I think that everything is okay, and then other times..." Marcy paused and shrugged.

"Let me guess – you want a platonic relationship and he wants more."

Marcy grimaced and nodded. "I tried to talk to Kandy. Do you remember the receptionist in ER?"

Ryan nodded.

"I tried to solicit her help, and at first she seemed to understand my feelings. But I think he 'wowed' her as she would put it – she seems to have gone over to his side. Every time I see her, she talks about how wonderful

Dave is and how he's too good to let go. Now they're both trying to change my mind about him. I don't know how to make myself clearer." Marcy paused and sighed.

"You said he's the assistant store manager. Does that make him your boss?"

Marcy nodded.

"Are you concerned about your job in any way?"

Marcy shook her head. "No, Dave's not like that. I guess it does make it harder since we work together and I see him all the time. The hardest thing is that I never know how he's going to be from day to day. He didn't use to be like that. Now one day he'll be sullen, then the next day he's not sullen, but doesn't talk to me. The day after, he's extra friendly, and then he goes back to sullen. Sometimes he calls to see if he can come over or if we can go out. Then poof! Like tonight, it seems like he thinks he owns me. He shows up unexpectedly with the attitude that I should be available for him and accountable for my whereabouts! Last night he was so easy to be with, I thought that he finally understood, even after he answered your phone call. I just feel so frustrated!" Marcy was getting stirred up again. Again she rubbed her forehead as if to clear her head. When she spoke again her voice was calmer and it was almost as if she were thinking out loud.

"It's not that big of a deal really. I just got so angry! Between Dave and Kandy, and you and God... I guess that I just feel like I've been on an emotional roller coaster this last month!"

Ryan wondered about her reference to him and God. It sounded like it slipped out and that she wasn't even aware that she said it. He didn't feel that he should ask. "Have you told anyone else these feelings?"

Marcy shook her head and shrugged, "Who was there to tell? Kandy and Dave are my best friends, and going to them didn't work. Mom and Dad were in Hawaii, and even if I tried talking to Mom – you know how she is – I don't think that she'd hear half of what I say, and wouldn't understand the other half. Everything got pent up and you got the brunt of its release. I'm sorry. You must think I'm loony tunes." Marcy could feel the tears burning at the backs of her eyes. She willed them to not fall.

Ryan smiled at her. "Is there anything I can do to help?"

"You've done above and beyond the call of duty already. Just listening to me rant and rave helped tremendously. Thank you." Marcy stood up. "I'd better let you go. I'm sure you had no intention of staying out so late.

I know that you have to get up early to go to work. I didn't mean to take up so much of your time."

Ryan stood up to leave, and Marcy moved towards the door.

"I really do appreciate you. I can't tell you how much you helped. Thank you."

"Are you going to be okay, now?" he asked.

Marcy nodded.

"Sure?"

She gave him a tremulous smile. A thought unbidden crossed her mind and he saw the smile fade and trepidation enter her eyes. "You seem to catch me at my worst." Her eyes begged him to believe her.

Ryan sighed and pulled her to him. One of his hands rubbed her back comfortingly. His voice quietly reassured her. "I know, Spitfire. I know... Don't worry." He gave her back a comforting pat and let her go.

He turned back halfway through the door. He reached up and stroked her cheek with the back of his finger. "Sleep tight." Then he left and Marcy watched him drive away.

She had forgotten to give him the baking dish.

Ryan drove away from Marcy's home, and this time he was the one that checked the rear view mirror. Marcy was standing in the doorway watching him leave. He wanted to go back and spend more time getting to know her again. It didn't matter to him how late it was. Even though he enjoyed the time at his parent's and at church, he was glad when he was able to be alone with her. He really had wanted to talk to her about her relationship with the Lord; he cared deeply for her soul. The lake could have been a good place to talk, but it had not been a wise choice.

It was during one of their sunset watches that Ryan had looked at Marcy differently for the first time. It was towards the end of her sophomore year and his junior year. She had been in a school play along with the girl Ryan had been seeing. They had both been major players, with Marcy taking the role of the villainess, and his girlfriend was the good guy's lawyer. They both played their parts very well, and when Ryan watched the play, he found himself taking Marcy's part and feeling upset with his girlfriend for accusing Marcy's character. He felt silly when the play was done for having those feelings. Yet he had a hard time shaking them. He broke up with the girl a couple of days after the performance.

Later that week a bunch of them went to the park. He and Marcy and a couple of other friends were sitting on the pier, tossing rocks into the lake. Marcy was next to Ryan, and he had to look past her to watch the sunset. The fading light and the breeze played on her hair, and Ryan found himself hardly able to take his eyes off her. He still laughed and joked with the others but had felt detached.

After they left the park and had dropped off the last person, Ryan was going to reveal his feelings to Marcy. He had just decided how to introduce the subject when Marcy started talking first. On an adjoining section of the pier there had been another couple that they both knew. They had been acting like Ryan wanted to act with Marcy that evening.

"Did you see the way they were carrying on? I thought it was disgusting! They'd known each other for a long time. In fact she told me that they were just friends, just last week! And now look at them, all goo-goo eyed over each other! Like they never knew the other existed before. I don't think that it can happen that way. How could you trust someone that changes feelings so fast, anyway? I'm glad you're not like that."

Ryan squelched his feelings and kept a tight lid on them, glad he hadn't said anything. He didn't date anyone else for quite a while. There were plenty of girls in high school that would be glad to have Ryan's attentions. Although he allowed himself to be distracted and took some of them out, he never made 'goo-goo eyes' at them. There had been no one else that he enjoyed sharing sunsets with as much as Marcy.

When he shared this sunset with her, he was reminded of that one that had been special to him. It was hard to keep his eyes off of her again. He had wanted to do more than pick up her hand and guide her to the car.

When he pulled up to Marcy's house and saw Dave on her porch step, it had irked him. He was glad when Marcy had wanted him to stay. Then when Dave had grabbed Marcy's elbow and pulled her into the living room, he wanted to throttle the scoundrel and teach him 'how a good man treats a lady'. And he probably would have if it hadn't taken him by surprise and Dave released her arm so quickly. It had pleased him immensely when he realized that the roses meant nothing to Marcy. He felt fiercely protective when Marcy was so upset and he considered that Dave might have hurt her.

Ryan hadn't wanted to sit so far from her on the couch to talk with her. And when he hugged her, he hadn't wanted to let her go. He liked the way she felt in his arms. He liked the smell of her hair and its softness against his cheek. He wanted to do more than just hug her. Could she hear his heart pounding when he held her to him? What would she have done if he had kissed her? Would she have rejected him? Had she trembled the second time he held her?

When he turned in the doorway to say good night, he thought he had detected something in her eyes that might indicate she had feelings other than that of a friend or sister. Could he be right? Ryan's heart raced at the thought. Could that be why she often seemed nervous with him? Maybe she was having some of these same feelings for him and she wasn't sure what to do with them. Was that the reason for her emotional roller coaster reference to him and God?

And God.

Scriptures about resisting temptation and bringing thoughts into captivity popped unbidden into his mind. His wandering and not-so-godly thoughts came screeching to a halt. The realization of the path his errant thoughts were taking, hit him with almost a physical blow.

"No!" he said out loud, "I will not go against what I believe and know to be right!"

His obedience to his Heavenly Father (who knew best) and Marcy's eternal life were his first priorities, not his hormones. When he got home, he opened his Bible to re-establish his heart.

Chapter 8

TRICKED

Marcy yawned as she walked into the kitchen the next morning. Not only had it been late when she had gotten to bed, but she had been unable to sleep when she got there. As she reached for a glass, she noticed the roses still lying in the sink from the night before. They looked pitiful since she had failed to put them in water. She gathered them up and cleaned up the mess.

Ryan had been so gentle as he took the rose and knife from her. The memory of being in the circle of his arms awakened the feeling of last night and her heart started racing again. Marcy sighed. She doubted if he felt like she did. It certainly hadn't seemed so. He hadn't held her any too long. His parents had given her longer hugs on different occasions when she was upset. He seemed to care about her, but in the same way he had always cared about her as they were growing up. Like a brother.

The six roses left in the vase weren't very good, either. She had been quite rough on them and most of the stems were broken towards the bloom. She doubted if she would keep them even if they had been okay. They just would have reminded her of Dave's actions last night. Marcy sighed as she threw them in the trash. What a waste of money and roses.

Marcy looked at her watch. Drats! She was running late. She would just barely have time for a quick shower and a glass of juice. She drank the juice on the way to the shower.

As she got into the bathroom, she looked into the mirror and groaned. There were dark circles under her eyes. She wished she didn't have to work at the store today. Not just because she was tired, but because Dave was going to be there. She did not look forward to having contact with him today after last night. Chances are he would be testy. He would undoubtedly notice her eyes and know she hadn't slept much. He would probably assume that Ryan had stayed late and that would put him in even a testier mood than he was bound to be already.

Marcy hadn't needed to fret about seeing Dave. He had called in sick. The next day Marcy was off. When Marcy went in on Wednesday, it was Dave's day off.

Marcy sat at a corner table to eat her lunch. Half way through her break, Jeanette sat down across from her. Marcy wasn't overly fond of her. She guessed that Jeanette was in her forties, but it was hard to tell, she didn't keep up her appearances very well. Marcy knew that she wasn't married now. She had made references to her 'ex' in the same manner that she made references to a lot of things – crass and vulgar. She liked to gossip and if there wasn't anything apparent to gossip about, she tried to find something. This trait often made her the creator of rumors, many of which weren't pleasant. Marcy usually tried to avoid her, but she didn't see any way now without being blatantly rude.

"So... How are you today?"

"Fine."

"You didn't look real 'fine' Monday. D'you have a bad night?"

"I was tired Monday, but I'm not today."

"Dave wasn't in a very good mood yesterday; do you know what was wrong with him?"

"Nope."

"I thought that maybe you would since you two are so close."

"I don't. Maybe he still wasn't feeling up to par from being sick on Monday."

"I worked the evening shift Sunday." Jeanette paused to see if she could get Marcy's interest up. Marcy just took another bite of her sandwich. "Dave left the store about eight o'clock. He seemed to be pretty chipper. Then a little before midnight, he came back in for something. He was a totally different man. This time his face was like a storm cloud. Then

Monday he calls in sick. Somehow I didn't get the feeling that he was really sick... If you know what I mean."

Marcy still didn't reply, just finished her sandwich.

"There was a cute little thing that came in the store yesterday. She didn't seem real int'rested in shopping, but spent quite a little time talking to Dave. I couldn't hear what they were sayin', but Dave was real int'rested in whatever it was."

Again, Marcy didn't reply.

"Do you know who she is?"

"Nope. Whoever she is though, if Dave's interests lay that way, I hope she's nice. Dave is a nice guy and we're good friends. So I hope he finds someone nice. I gotta go, my lunch is over." Marcy stood up to leave. "Have a nice day, Jeanette."

Marcy was glad for the excuse to end the conversation. Marcy tried to keep her mind on her work, but it kept drifting back to what Jeanette said about Dave talking to another girl. Maybe that was the answer. Get Dave interested in someone else. Maybe she could find out who it was and play matchmaker.

Thursday, Dave was at the store, and in quite a dour mood. He didn't talk to Marcy except when necessary, for which she was thankful. She was friendly to him, but she didn't really know what to say to him other than work related things. She was sorry that their friendship was going through a rocky time, but she didn't feel obligated to apologize for Sunday evening. The day crept by slowly. She was sure Jeanette was trying to figure something out. Marcy was glad that she didn't have to work on the floor with her. It was bad enough being under her scrutiny the few times she came into the office. She had checked when the lunch breaks were and avoided the time when Jeanette was sure to be there.

Friday was better. Dave was in a slightly better mood. He went out for lunch and when he came back his mood was even more improved. At the end of the day he timed his leaving with Marcy's.

"Did you ride your bike, today?"

"No, it was already too hot when I left, and it wasn't supposed to get any better."

"Oh... where did you park?"

"Around the side toward the end."

"May I walk you to your car? I'm parked over that way."

"Sure."

Dave was silent and pensive until they got to her car.

"Marcy... I want to apologize to you for Sunday. I had no right to act like I did. Will you forgive me?"

"Yes, I forgive you."

"No hard feelings?"

"No hard feelings."

"I've never seen you so angry. I thought maybe I'd overstepped the bounds."

Marcy wanted to say that he did, but seeing how hard it seemed for Dave to approach her, she cushioned her answer. "You're usually fun to be with and I like you. I want to be your *friend*, Dave. Please understand that."

Dave let out a sigh and gave her a quick hug. "Thanks."

"You're welcome." Marcy opened her door and got in. Dave stepped back and watched her back out of the parking spot.

That evening Kandy called to see if Marcy wanted to come over to watch a movie with her. Or better yet, if she could go to Marcy's. Her DVD player wasn't working like it should and she didn't want it to eat the rented DVD. Marcy thought that sounded like fun. Just after Kandy got there Dave called to see if he might come over to watch TV with her.

"Well," Marcy hesitated, "Kandy just got here. We were going to watch a movie that she rented."

"What are you watching?"

Marcy told him the title, and Dave thought that it sounded good.

Kandy heard Marcy and asked if it was Dave. Marcy shook her head yes, and Kandy said that if he wanted to come over it was fine with her. Marcy wished Kandy hadn't heard. Now there wasn't any reason for him not to come, so she told him okay. They popped corn and chatted while they waited for Dave to get there. About fifteen minutes after Dave's call, Kandy's beeper went off.

Marcy watched as she called the number on her pager and spoke briefly to whoever it was. Kandy's face looked disappointed, and Marcy questioned her.

Kandy shrugged. "Duty calls. It looks like I have to go."

"Oh Kandy. Tonight? Now?"

"Sorry."

"But the movie and the popcorn! Dave's coming over!"

Kandy grinned. "I'll leave the movie, and Dave can help you eat the popcorn."

"But Kandy..."

"Hey kid, I'd rather stay, believe me. But I've gotta go." Kandy saw the panicky look on Marcy's face. "Marcy... it's not the end of the world."

"I know. It's not that, it's just that..." She didn't get to finish her sentence, for the doorbell rang at that moment. She sighed and opened the door for Dave. Kandy picked up her purse and headed out.

"You leaving?"

"Duty called."

"Oh. Sorry to hear that." Dave didn't look sorry.

"'Night, Marcy. Dave."

"'Night." Marcy watched her walk to her car, and then closed the door.

Dave had walked into the kitchen and got a beer that was still in Marcy's refrigerator, saw the popcorn and took it into the living room. He sat in the recliner. Marcy put the DVD in and sat on the couch. They watched the previews for other movies, and Dave realized that it was hard for both of them to reach the popcorn so he moved next to Marcy on the couch, kind of slouching in the corner. About a half hour into the movie, he shifted positions and straightened up, moving closer to Marcy. Marcy looked at him out of the side of her eyes, but he did not look suspicious. Later he shifted again. The bowl of popcorn was empty, so he removed it from his lap and placed it on the coffee table. When he sat back, he draped his arms across the back of the couch. Again Marcy looked at him suspiciously, but he seemed innocent. He didn't move again for a while and Marcy got caught up in the movie. It was a moving story with a sad ending. Marcy started sniffing a little past half-way through the movie. By the time the ending got there, Dave had to give her his handkerchief for all the tears.

"I'm sorry. It's silly I know, because it's just a movie, and not real. I just can't help it, I always cry over sad movies," she sniffed.

Dave lowered his arm to drape it around Marcy's shoulder, and drew her to him. "It's okay. My mom use to do the same thing. In fact she still does."

Marcy sat sniveling into the handkerchief trying to pull herself together, she didn't even notice Dave's arm. Dave sat quietly examining her face.

"You're cute when you cry."

"Yeah, sure," she sniffed again.

Dave reached across and turned her face towards him. His eyes turned soft as he took in the red nose. Her wet lashes accentuated her eyes that were large and dewy. Her mind was still clouded from the emotion of the movie.

"You are," he said it as if to convince her then bent his head and kissed her tenderly.

Reality crept back, pushing the clouds out. Marcy put her hand up to push Dave away. "Dave, don't. You know..."

He pulled her in tighter to himself, cutting off her sentence with another kiss. This one was more insistent, much more.

"Dave! Stop it!" Marcy pushed him back harder and tried to get up. Dave let her go and Marcy stood up. "I think you need to leave now."

Dave stood up, too. "Marcy, I'm sorry. I didn't mean to scare you." He looked at Marcy for the forgiveness she had so easily given earlier that day. There was none.

"I don't know why you did that, Dave. You know that is not how I want our relationship to be or how I feel about you," Marcy scolded.

"But it *is* how *I* feel about you." He was hurt, and he was starting to get angry. "What about how *I* want the relationship to be? What about *my* feelings? Do I always have to trick you to be alone with you?"

"Trick me?" Marcy was suspicious.

Dave pretended not to hear; that had slipped out unintentionally. "It's like you keep me at a distance lately."

"I don't want to lead you on and get your hopes up."

"Too late. My hopes were already up."

"But I didn't know that! What do you mean 'trick me'?" Marcy's ire was beginning to show.

Dave squirmed. "It's that Robinson, isn't it? He's why you won't give me a chance."

"He has nothing to do with our relationship. Now answer my question. What did you mean when you said 'trick me'?" Dave didn't answer. He stood there looking trapped. "Did you trick me tonight?" Now Marcy's dander was up. She marched to the phone and dialed Kandy's number.

Kandy answered. Marcy slammed down the receiver without answering. She turned back to Dave, irate. "Was that a trick last Saturday, too?

Dave didn't answer.

"Get out."

"Marcy..."

"Get out!" Her eyes spit darts at him.

"It wasn't her idea, it was mine. I..."

"I don't want to hear it, Dave." Marcy punched the eject button on the DVD player and with trembling hands, snapped the DVD back in its case. She shoved it at Dave. "You can take this back to Kandy. Tell her I said 'Thanks for being my friend." Marcy jerked the front door open. "Now get out."

Dave sighed, took the DVD, and walked out the door with his head down. Marcy slammed the door after him.

Marcy paced around her apartment for a little bit. It was dark out, or else she would go for a bike ride to let off some steam. She looked at the clock. It wasn't too late to call her mom as she didn't tend to go to bed much before midnight. She wouldn't have to do much talking, mostly just listen, and that would help get her mind off Dave and Kandy.

"Hi, Mom. It's me, Marcy."

"Hi, Sweetheart! I recognize your voice; you don't have to tell me your name, silly! I was just thinking about you, and was going to give you a call in the morning. I didn't know that you were still up or I would've called a few minutes ago."

"So what's new?"

Her mom was true to form and prattled on for the next half hour. Marcy stifled a yawn.

"Are you okay, Sweetie?"

"Yes, Mom, I'm fine. I'm just getting sleepy, that's all."

"Oh, I'm sorry. I forgot about the time. I'll let you go in a second; I just have one more thing to tell you. I saved the best until last!"

"What's that?"

"Mark gets a week off the end of next month. They're going to come and spend part of it over here. Isn't that just lovely? We'll all get to see the grandchildren for a few days! Oh, well you won't of course, because they're your nieces, you don't have any grandchildren yet." Her mom giggled. "Of course you don't have any grandchildren, you haven't even got children. When are you?"

"When am I what?"

"Going to have children, Sweetheart. Your dad and I would like more grandchildren, and you shouldn't leave it all up to Mark."

"I'm going to get married first, Mom. That's not a job I want to do by myself, you know."

"Of course not, Marcy! But are there any prospects?"

"When did you say they were coming up?"

"Who's coming up?"

"Mark and his family."

"Oh! The end of next month. I think it's the last week. That's only let's see," Marcy could hear her mom counting under her breath. "Yes, that's only six and a half weeks away! You should see if you can get a couple of days off so you can spend some time with them, too. You know I think that one of the kids has a birthday during that time."

"If one does, then they both do, Mom, or did you forget they were twins?"

"Oh, that's right. I don't know why I..." Mrs. Kelman twittered on for another ten minutes. By the time they said good-bye, Marcy's anger had diffused. She was tired and when she got in bed, she fell asleep quickly.

Marcy awoke to the telephone's insistent ringing. She reached groggily for the phone beside her bed glancing at the clock to see what time it was. 8:30 – who would be calling at this time of the morning?

"Hello?"

"Good morning." It was Dave's voice and it didn't sound to her like he really wanted her to have a good morning.

"Dave. Why are you calling so early?"

"You are scheduled to work this week end. You should have called if you weren't going to come in."

Marcy groaned, she had forgotten about the big circus sale going on and that she had been scheduled to work. She was given the choice to either work a register or help with the concession stand in the parking lot.

She had chosen the concession stand. It didn't open until 10:30, but there was a lot of setting up that had to be done.

"I'm sorry, Dave, I totally forgot. I'll be in as quick as I can."

Marcy felt harried by the time 10:30 rolled around. One of the stock boys had helped her to get the supplies and ready the stand. Dave lectured her about her tardiness, and lack of dependability and how it put everybody else out. She shouldn't expect to have special privileges just because they were friends. Her anger wanted to flare up and give him a piece of her mind, but there were other people around, and she despised making a scene in public. She was glad now that she had chosen to work the concessions, because she had to put on a clown outfit. That meant painting her face, which meant her smile could be painted on.

She also thought that it meant that she wouldn't have to see a very much of Dave, but she was wrong. It seemed like he took extra pains to be around the concession stand and make her miserable. It wasn't quite so bad when it was busy, because then he was too. Marcy was glad to see 4:00 finally roll around. Her replacement showed up and she was getting ready to check out when Dave appeared behind her.

"Where do you think you're going?"

Marcy turned to look at him. "Home. Its 4:00 and that is when I was scheduled to get off."

"You were scheduled to start at 8:00, too. But you were an hour late. You can get off at five."

Marcy clamped her lips shut and turned to go back to the concession stand. She clenched her fists. "Are you done?"

"That depends on you."

Marcy stood there for just a second to try to determine his meaning. Deciding it was a double-entendré, she walked on.

When she finally got off, she bought a newspaper. She hadn't thought that Dave was the kind of person to let his personal feelings affect his business relationships. Evidently she was wrong. If this was going to be the way Dave was going to treat her at work, then maybe it was time for her to consider a different job.

That evening, Kandy stopped by bearing cream puffs. She held the plate out to Marcy. "Will you forgive me?" Kandy had a cream puff reputation. They were the lightest, flakiest around and she often made several different fillings. Some were unusual, but none ever a flop. Whenever there was a party or dinner, Kandy was asked to bring her cream puffs. These were obviously a peace offering and probably filled with Marcy's favorite filling.

Marcy held open the door for her to enter, but didn't take the offering, nor did she say a word. Kandy would've had to been blind to miss the anger and hurt on Marcy's face. She set the cream puffs on the coffee table.

"Can we sit down?"

Marcy shrugged and sat in the recliner, she wasn't going to make it easy.

"I came to apologize and beg your forgiveness."

No response.

"Dave told me what happened last night, and that you were pretty upset."

Still no response.

"Marcy, you're my best friend. I never wanted to hurt you, please believe me. I don't want to lose your friendship."

"I told you how I felt. I asked you for help. You deceived me and betrayed me."

"I know," Kandy's eyes pleaded with Marcy for understanding. "I can see that now. At the time, I thought I was being your friend. I was wrong, please forgive me, Marcy."

"Why did you do it?"

"Dave seemed to care about you so much... I guess I thought maybe you didn't understand that. And he's such a great guy I couldn't see why anyone would not want him... Why don't you want him, Marcy?"

"What about Joe?"

"Joe? You mean Joe at work, Joe?"

"Yeah."

"What about him?"

"What if all of a sudden out of the clear blue sky, he came up to you and said that he thought that you two had been an item all along."

"Joe!?" Kandy guffawed, "You've got to be kidding! Joe's nice and we're friends and all, but as a boyfriend and possible mate? I don't think so. Besides, he has a girl."

"Exactly. It's not that there's anything wrong with him or that he's a bad person, he's just not for you. That's how I feel about Dave."

"Oh, Marcy, I'm sorry. I wouldn't want anyone to do that to me, and I didn't realize that's what I was doing. I guess I let my personal feelings get in the way." Kandy was truly contrite.

Marcy's anger dissolved. "You know, Kandy, sometimes I don't think that Dave really sees me in that way, either."

"What do you mean?"

"Well... I'm not sure exactly. It was just odd to me that after all the time we've known each other, the day that Jeanette... You remember Jeanette?" Kandy grimaced and nodded, "The day that Jeanette told him about Ryan Robinson being back in town, he came over to talk about our relationship. It came as a total shock to me, I had no idea. I know that sometimes I can be unobservant, but I would think that I would have picked up on *something* after all this time that would have given me a clue."

"Do you think Jeanette put ideas in his head?"

"I don't know. She could have. I know he told me that she said that Ryan and I were really good friends. Maybe she said other things, too. All I know is that he's been acting a lot differently than he had been before she said anything."

"How so?"

"It's like he's trying on different roles, and he tries to act like he thinks he should act in those roles. I'm not sure how to explain it. I think he's trying to get me to see him in a different way than friend. When he fixed breakfast, I think that he was in a husband fantasy. Last night I think that he was trying to be lover. I get the odd feeling..." Marcy drifted off.

"Like if he gets your approval, he'll stick to that role?"

"Yeah. The thing is I really like him in the role of a friend."

"Do you think that he really likes just being your friend, and Jeanette might have said something that made him feel he's supposed to be something more? Maybe he thought that he would lose your friendship if Ryan is around."

"Maybe. I don't know. All I know is that I'm thinking of quitting at the store. It's gotten to be pretty hard. Today was awful. I know that I hurt his feelings, but when I reach out to him and let him know that I still like him, he gets the wrong idea, and I end up hurting his feelings again."

"Do you think that you'll ever change your mind?"

Marcy shook her head, "No, I can't see it."

Kandy picked imaginary lint off her shorts. "Umm… would it bother you if I… well, if I 'set my cap' for him?" Kandy looked up at Marcy for approval, "I won't if it bothers you, but I'd like to get to know him better and wouldn't mind having his attentions."

Marcy's eyes lit up. "That would be great! Maybe you can get his thoughts off me! I'll even help if I can."

"Would we be doing the same thing to him, that you don't want done to you?"

Marcy paused. "I don't think so, because I don't think he sees you yet. We're just going to let him get to know you," Marcy giggled, "And help him form his own opinion."

Kandy and Marcy smiled conspiratorially at each other.

The phone rang, and Marcy answered it.

"Hello?"

"Hi dear! Am I calling at a bad time?"

"Hi, Mrs. Robinson. No, you're fine."

"I'm just calling to invite you to church with us in the morning and then to share lunch with us afterwards."

"Oh, I can't. I have to work at the store in the morning."

"Do you often work on Sunday's, dear?" Mrs. Robinson sounded concerned

"No, in fact I rarely do. We're just having a circus sale, and they needed extra people. I'm sorry."

"That's okay. We were looking forward to your company."

"Maybe another time?" asked Marcy.

"That would be wonderful. How about next week, maybe?"

"Yes… yes I think that I can."

"That's wonderful! We'll look forward to seeing you!" Mrs. Robinson sounded genuine.

"Me too. Thank you for the invitation."

"It's our pleasure. Good-bye, dear, and don't work too hard tomorrow."

"I won't. Good-bye." Marcy hung up.

"I'm nosey. Who's Mrs. Robinson? Is that good looking guy Ryan, married? And now you're chummy with his wife?"

Marcy giggled. "No, silly, Ryan's not married. Mrs. Robinson is Ryan's mother. So I guess that I am chummy with his family. They were like a second set of parents to me."

"So I assume that you're starting to pick up the relationship where it left off, huh."

"Well, I guess you could call it that." Marcy paused and sighed. "Now, he's someone that I could set my cap for."

"Who, Ryan?"

Marcy nodded. "I don't think he feels the same way, though. Besides, it feels funny. I've looked at him like a brother for so long, it almost feels wrong."

Kandy prodded for more details, but Marcy was unwilling to discuss her feelings, so the details she gave Kandy were scant. Marcy changed the subject quickly back to Dave and they plotted their plans while they ate cream puffs.

Chapter 9

SEAT SWAP

Marcy got up the next morning in a great mood. Talking to Kandy the night before gave her a fresh outlook. Now she didn't have to play a defensive position in the game with Dave. She had a plan and was now on the offense. She saw the newspaper on the kitchen table, still unopened. She picked it up and threw it away. She would not be quitting at the store yet. He'd have to fire her if he wanted her to leave before her mission there was accomplished. This morning, it hadn't been a necessity to paint on a smile for the concession stand.

Dave wasn't in quite the foul mood as he had been the day before. He still needled her, but Marcy wouldn't allow him to get her goat. She remained cheerful and friendly, and that got to Dave. By late morning, he didn't hang around the concession stand any more than necessary.

Kandy dropped by to check up on Marcy. They kept an eye out for Dave while they talked, then Kandy went in to the store to 'shop'. She didn't have to be anywhere so she took her time, hoping to see Dave. She did, and when they were done talking, he had accepted an invitation over to her house for dinner, to 'see what they could do about Marcy.'

When Kandy left the store there was a spring in her step and she gave Marcy a 'thumbs up' signal on the way to her car. Marcy smiled and signaled back. Yes indeed, things were looking up!

Monday saw Dave in a slightly better mood. He improved through the week. Marcy remained cheerful and friendly. On Friday, Marcy asked him if he wanted to come over to have homemade pizza with her and Kandy. He looked surprised.

"I don't hate you, Dave. On the contrary, I like you. But I like you as a friend."

"If you're sure that it's alright."

"Yes, it's alright, or I wouldn't have asked you, silly."

That evening, Kandy was already there when Dave showed up. Marcy thought that he looked a little uncomfortable when he came in. But Kandy and Marcy chatted and teased as they all pitched in to make the pizza, and soon he was relaxing. When they pushed themselves from the table, stuffed with pizza, Marcy looked at the clock.

"Say, listen, I have to go to Mrs. Kindle's to show her some samples of glazes. She ordered a pitcher, but she wanted to see what it looked like 'so it could tell her what kind of glaze and color it wanted to be'. I told her I'd be there at 7:00. It shouldn't take too long, and then we'll play some cards or something when I get back. Is that okay with you?"

"Sure, go on. Dave and I will clean up the dishes. He's pretty handy at that if I remember right."

"Uh, sure... Do you need a ride?" Dave asked.

"Naw, it's just a few houses down from here. You two go ahead and visit. It shouldn't take very long."

Marcy got the box with three pitchers in it and samples of glazes. The house was at the end of the block, to Marcy's left. But Marcy turned right and took the scenic route, walking around the entire block to get there. Mrs. Kindle was not known to make fast decisions, and Marcy encouraged her indecisiveness tonight by offering her a wide array of choices and three different pitchers. She then took the scenic route home.

Dave and Kandy were relaxing on the couch when Marcy came in. She offered no excuses for the length of time it took. Kandy needed none.

"Well, it might have taken longer than it needed to, but it was time well spent. It proved to be profitable as she decided to buy all three pitchers instead of just the one! Mrs. Kindle has a hard time making up her mind." Marcy took her box of stuff back into the studio and returned. "Well, who feels like getting walloped at a game of cards?"

Kandy looked at her watch, "I don't think that we have time for cards anymore, it's getting kind of late."

Marcy looked at the clock, surprised at the time. "Oh, gee, I didn't realize that it took that long! I'm sorry, guys!"

Dave stretched. "I couldn't stay late anyway; I've got to open in the morning. I'll need to leave in a minute."

"So do I," chimed in Kandy, "I work in the morning, too. You're the only one that gets to sleep in tomorrow morning."

Marcy's guests got up to leave.

"Where's your car, Kandy?" enquired Dave as he opened the door.

"I walked tonight."

"Well, I could give you a lift home if you'd like."

"That'd be great! Thanks!"

Kandy turned to Marcy as she walked out the door after Dave and winked. "Thanks, Marcy!" Marcy smiled at her in response.

Sunday morning Marcy overslept and was a few minutes late getting to the church. Mr. Robinson was waiting for her in the foyer.

"I'm sorry I'm late."

"That's okay, but you're stuck with just me, now." He grinned at her.

"What do you mean?"

"Marian teaches the first grade class like always, and they called Ryan last night to see if he could substitute for the seventh grade teacher. So that leaves you and me in the Adult Sunday School class. They will join us for service of course. I hope that doesn't disappoint you."

"You hope what doesn't disappoint me; that I'm stuck with you or that they will be joining us later?" Marcy twinkled at him.

Mr. Robinson wrapped his arm around Marcy's shoulders and gave her a squeeze. "That's my girl!" And he escorted her into the sanctuary where the adult class was being held with his arm still across her shoulder. It made Marcy feel loved and accepted.

The Adult Sunday School class was doing a study on the judges of the Old Testament. The story of Gideon and his band of 300 defeating an army with torches, trumpets and empty pitchers brought back pleasant memories of her Sunday School days.

The fourth grade teacher had taught this same story in a demonstrative way, which got Marcy to thinking about if her actions were pleasing to God, and decided that she should probably stop kicking. She had confided this to Ryan during church and asked him if he would help her to stop kicking like Purah helped Gideon overcome his fear. Since Ryan wasn't in the same class, he hadn't understood. Marcy's little-girl desperation to make him understand so he would help her, led to reprimands about disturbing others with their talking. It embarrassed Marcy when her behavior was such that it needed correcting, especially by the Robinson's. She always wanted to please them. So she was embarrassed, and Ryan knew, which made her angry. So she kicked him. As she looked back, it was funny – the one she had asked to help her overcome kicking, she had kicked.

She felt Mr. Robinson shift beside her. She glanced up and caught his questioning look. It was then that she realized she had been so caught up in her thoughts that she didn't know she had giggled out loud. She whispered her apologies and ducked her head, reliving the embarrassment of the childhood memory.

The class was soon over and people started filing in for the service. Mr. Robinson stayed at his seat, saying that the others would find them. He stood up to stretch and to talk with others around him. Marcy stood too, and watched the people come in. The church was quite a bit fuller this morning than the evening service had been. Marcy recognized several people but felt inexplicably shy. She stayed close to Mr. Robinson. As she watched the people, she caught a glance of Ryan coming through the back doors. Her breath caught in her throat. He was striking. She hadn't seen him in a suit and tie since his high-school graduation – he filled out his suit much better now.

Marcy went into a mild panic. She remembered the last time she sat next to Ryan and how her thoughts had run away with her and the guilty feelings she had experienced. How could she sit by him this morning?

Especially when he looked like that? Her knees felt like jelly. Her thoughts wanted to go in the wrong direction now, and he wasn't even next to her.

She would be expected to sit next to him, because that's how they had always sat, just like at the evening service. She couldn't; but where could she go? She couldn't just step out of the pew and go to another one after sitting with Mr. Robinson. Nor could she sit at the far end of this one, separated from the others. But if she stayed standing there, she would be expected to step down to let Mrs. Robinson and Ryan in. If she stepped out like Mr. Robinson did to let them in, then Ryan would just allow her to go in first.

Marcy turned around and sat down abruptly, leaving Mr. Robinson's seat open. Mr. Robinson stepped out to allow his son in. Marcy stayed seated and just tucked her feet back under the pew to allow him to pass. He turned and greeted her and saw his mother step in to take her seat. Marcy stayed put even though she knew that Mr. and Mrs. Robinson liked to sit together. Ryan, being the gentleman that he was, stepped down to allow room. Mrs. Robinson looked questioningly at Marcy.

"Would you like to sit next to Ryan, dear?"

Marcy played dumb. "Oh, that's okay, this seat is fine." Then she searched in her purse for something she could need. Anything would work, just as long as it would take her enough time to find. She would force Mr. and Mrs. Robinson to be her Purahs in the battle against her wayward feelings towards Ryan.

The service started. Mrs. Robinson sat where she was, next to Marcy with Ryan on the other side of her. Mr. Robinson sat in his seat without realizing who was sitting where. When he noticed it wasn't his wife, he looked for someone to answer his question about the seating arrangement. Marcy was still digging in her purse, pretending not to notice the others watching her. His eyes traveled to Mrs. Robinson, who, with a lift of her eyebrows and slight shake of her head said she didn't know. Ryan just shrugged and raised his eyebrows. He looked again to Marcy who seemed to have finally found what she was looking for and was now stashing her purse under her seat. He turned his attention back to the announcements that where being made, wondering what was going on.

Marcy had retrieved a stick of gum from her purse. She had no idea how long it had been there, but in her nervousness, she popped it into her mouth anyway. It was hard and crumbled when she bit into it. Some of the little pieces fell into the back of her throat causing her to want to cough. She tried to suppress the cough, making her eyes water. She tried to swallow, but that didn't work, and when she tried to clear her throat silently, the pieces tickled, making her eyes water worse and the urge to cough even greater. She retrieved her purse and found she didn't have a tissue or anything else to cough into. She stared into her lap trying to control what was going on in her mouth. A hand bearing a handkerchief appeared in her view. She gratefully took it and did what was necessary to regain control. She looked at Mr. Robinson, giving him a quick smile to show her appreciation. His eyes understood and he patted her hands that lay in her lap.

They stood for the song service and the same feelings of missing out on something swept over her again. The music was beautiful, and she enjoyed the singing, but could not rid herself of that feeling.

This time she had remembered to bring some money to put in the plate as it was passed. Proudly she put it in thinking it would help to dispel the feeling. It didn't.

When the message started, she realized other people had brought their Bibles. She wasn't even sure where hers was. Mr. and Mrs. Robinson usually shared with each other. This morning, Ryan shared with his mom and Marcy got to look on with Mr. Robinson. Once upon a time Marcy had received a reward in Vacation Bible School to be the first one in her class to memorize all the books of the Bible in order. Now Mr. Robinson turned the pages, because Marcy could no longer recall where any but the most familiar were.

Marcy's mind didn't wander as much this time, and caught a fair portion of the message. It was about King Solomon and how he had known God, but then turned to the world for pleasures. And the Book of Ecclesiastes was about his realization that the things that we seek to do apart from God are vanities – empty and futile.

About half way through the sermon, Mr. Robinson draped his arm across the back of the pew behind Marcy, as was his custom if it were his wife next to him instead of Marcy. As Marcy became more uncomfortable within herself as the message progressed, she unconsciously took shelter, leaning closer to the owner of that arm. It had provided the feeling of acceptance and love before, and her subconscious sought it now. Mr. Robinson looked at Marcy when he felt her wiggle in closer to his side.

The look on her face pulled at his heart. Her brows were pulled together and the look of concentration was one of someone who was struggling with an unpleasant problem.

With the hand that was still draped on the back of the pew, he tapped his wife's shoulder. Mrs. Robinson looked to see what he wanted, and he indicated Marcy. Marcy no longer was sitting straight, but was slouched slightly with her back pressed against the seat, leaning into Mr. Robinson. She looked like she was trying to hide in a corner. Her hands were twisting the handkerchief they held. Mrs. Robinson smiled at her husband and nodded letting him know that she saw what he did – a lost soul trying to find solace. Marcy was oblivious to her actions.

The message ended and the congregation stood up to sing a song during the alter call. Marcy fidgeted and was glad it was about over. Why did she say she'd come? She wasn't going to ever again. She didn't like feeling like she was missing something or that she was guilty of something she didn't know about. If they ever asked her again, she'd make excuses. She felt like plowing through all the people in the isle as they were leaving to get outside so she could breathe. But the people were friendly and talked to her, telling her they hoped she enjoyed the service and asking her to come back. She wanted to say no, she didn't enjoy the service and she was never coming back, but she just smiled instead.

She felt Ryan by her elbow, but she didn't turn to talk to him. Mr. and Mrs. Robinson were behind her. She didn't talk to them, either. Finally after shaking innumerable hands, she was outside. She took a big breath and let it out. She waited around quietly in the background for a little bit, then started for her car. Ryan went with her.

"Would you like me to ride with you so you don't get lost?" he teased as he opened her door.

Marcy smiled at his joke, but the smile didn't reach her eyes. She looked down at her shoes.

"Um... actually I... um, was thinking about begging to be excused from lunch." She twisted her purse strap.

Ryan's face filled with concern – first there was her odd behavior with the seating, and now wanting to get out of the lunch invitation. "Are you okay?"

Marcy didn't look up, just nodded. "I'm fine, it's just that..." she didn't know how to express what she was feeling. "I just... um... Could you tell your parents I'm sorry, maybe some other time? I hope your mom didn't go to a lot of trouble on my account."

"Are you sure you're fine?"

Marcy nodded, looked up at him and smiled weakly. "Yeah, I'm fine, really. I um... I'm sorry. 'Bye." Marcy hastily stepped into the car. Ryan shut the door, and Marcy pulled out.

Mr. and Mrs. Robinson watched the exchange. Although they couldn't hear what was said they guessed pretty accurately that she wasn't coming to lunch. All three watched her leave.

When Marcy got home, she changed her clothes and immersed herself in her work.

Chapter 10

CONFRONTATION AND
POTTERY LESSON

*R*yan took off from work a couple of hours early Monday afternoon. He pulled into his drive and skipped every other step to the porch. Calling to his mom that he was home, he headed up the stairs to his room. She came out of the kitchen stirring something in a bowl.

"Hi, Dear. You're home early, aren't you? Was anything wrong at work?"

"No, it's just that I thought I'd go see if Marcy would like to go out to dinner or something." He stopped a couple of steps above the landing to talk to her.

"Do you think she's ready?"

"I don't know. But I thought that I'd give it a shot." It'd been all he could do to stay away from Marcy's the evening before.

"Does this mean that I shouldn't set a place for you at the table?" she teased.

Ryan leaned over the banister and kissed his mom on the top of her head. "My, but you're perceptive tonight!" He smiled and headed up to his room to change clothes.

Marcy didn't work at the store on Monday; she spent the day producing pottery. She had loaded the kiln at the high school in the morning, and made trips back and forth checking on it. Ryan arrived in between one of these trips.

"Hi!" He grinned at her appearance as she opened the door. She had on cutoffs and T-shirt, both wet in patches and smudged with clay. Her hair was falling out of its clip and her cheek had a smear on it, too. "You must be working with your clay, again."

She looked down at her clothes to see what he saw, and smiled.

"Come on in. You're right I am working with *my clay*."

"I came by to see if you were hungry."

Marcy looked at the clock to see what time it was.

"If you're busy, I'll understand. I know that I didn't give you any warning."

"It's not that. I guess I am hungry, but I just was about to leave. I need to get my stuff from the school before 5:00. I have a load in the kiln right now that I need to check on. It should be cooling. There are also some of my wares filling some of their racks that I want to bring back. I hadn't even thought about eating, much less when to do it."

"Does it take long? Could I go with you and help?"

Marcy's heart warmed. "It doesn't take long. You could tag along if you want to. I was just going to come back here after and throw more pieces. But I don't have to."

"Good, then we could get something to eat!"

Marcy checked her clock again and nodded. "I'll change first, okay?"

Ryan smiled. "Then I'll wait."

It didn't take Marcy long to change and in just a few minutes they were in her station wagon headed to the high school. Ryan had offered to drive and Marcy had let him. It felt funny having Ryan drive her car, but comfortable at the same time. They didn't really talk on the way to the school, both of them caught up in their own thoughts. She pondered the reason that he had come over.

Marcy instructed Ryan where to park and got the keys out of her purse.

"They gave you keys to the school?"

"Yeah, amazing isn't it."

"Then why the time limit?"

"They didn't give me the alarm code."

"Ahh... they don't trust you that much!" Ryan teased.

"You got it! I can only be here when someone else is. I call to see if someone is going to be here and for how long, and let them know that I'm coming and when. That way I won't spook anybody and I won't accidentally set off the alarm. They usually keep the doors locked if there's not a school function going on. So they let me have a key to the door closest to the kiln so that I wouldn't have to try to find someone whenever I wanted to go in or out. They like to be out of the school by 5:00 during the summer. That's why the time limit tonight."

It didn't take Marcy long to check the kiln, then she and Ryan packed the fired wares into the boxes she brought. The janitor popped his head in as they were finishing.

"Hi, Marcy! Got yourself a helper tonight, I see."

"Yep! He works cheap, too!"

"Well, just be sure you get your money's worth out of him, anyway. You know how hired help can be these days!"

Marcy smiled at him, "We'll be out of your hair in just a minute, okay?"

"That's okay, no rush tonight, I'll be here late. Bernie said he wasn't feeling well and went home early, so it will take me a little longer to finish up." And with that he popped back out.

Lakeland Grove didn't have a very large selection of restaurants, and none were fancy, but they did have some good ones. Ryan took Marcy to a place that served great Chinese food. Inside it looked like any other restaurant, with the exception of pictures of China and Chinese art. The booths had very high backs and their own shaded light. Marcy always felt like she was in her own little room when she sat in one. They got there just before the supper rush so it wasn't busy, and they were waited on very quickly.

Marcy and Ryan carried on small talk until their food arrived. She picked up her fork to take a bite when she felt Ryan look at her. He had his hand extended on the table for her to take.

"Shall we give thanks, first?"

Marcy blushed, and laid her fork back down. She didn't take his hand but placed hers in her lap, tipped her head down and stared at the food on her plate. Ryan said a short prayer of thanksgiving for the food and Marcy's company, then picked up his fork and started eating. All of a sudden, she felt perverse. She hated how his praying made her feel – embarrassed. Guilty. She wanted to lash out and hurt him as if it were his fault that she felt that way.

Neither one said anything for a moment until Ryan commented on how good the food was. Marcy was silent. Ryan tried to make small talk while Marcy pushed the food around on her plate. He wondered about the change that came over her; she had seemed so relaxed just before he prayed. He took another bite of his food.

"How much did your dad pay to the University to keep you from getting expelled and your reputation unsullied?"

Ryan choked on the bite he had just put in his mouth. The question had come out of the thin air and surprised him.

"What?" he asked between fits of coughing.

"You heard me."

"I know I did. I just wasn't sure if I heard you correctly."

"I said, 'how much did your dad pay to the University to keep you from getting expelled and your reputation unsullied.'"

"I heard you right." He paused and took a drink of water.

Marcy saw the hurt look in his eyes that came from the accusation. It gave her a sense of victory, accompanied by more guilt. She knew what she had just said was mean and hurtful and that it was totally unlike her. But she didn't back down – she stubbornly looked at him with a challenge in her eyes. Was he going to lash back? That would make her feel better about herself.

Ryan searched her face, looking for answers to questions he wasn't sure how to ask. Marcy's eyes held steady, challenging him. Why, he didn't know. His dad had said Sunday that it appeared that there was a battle going on inside her and it confused her. He saw that now. It certainly would explain her sudden change in attitude. Her accusation no longer stung, nor did her hostility hurt. He wanted to help her win the battle.

Marcy saw the change in his eyes go from a hurt look, to one that asked questions, to one of compassion and understanding. The last look reached into her soul. She looked away and stabbed the food on her plate with her fork. She stuck it in her mouth but didn't taste it.

Ryan's voice was gentle as he answered Marcy's question. "Dad and Mom spent a lot to keep me from being expelled and my reputation unsullied."

Marcy looked up with a look that said, "Aha! I knew you weren't perfect, all along!" Ryan held her gaze and continued in his gentle voice. "But none of it went to the University to pay them off." He paused. Marcy looked at him questioningly, not quite believing or understanding. "They *spent* hours and hours praying for me. They *spent* a lot of money calling me long distance, trying to guide me into what was right and encouraging me when I needed it. They *spent* quite a bit on gas and hotel bills, coming to the University when my behavior needed it, and then to stand by me when I needed their encouragement and support. Not to mention the cost of the income Dad lost from being away from his work." Ryan paused, not knowing what to expect from Marcy.

Marcy looked down at her plate and started to push the food around again.

"Do you know what happened my sophomore year?"

Marcy shrugged. "I've heard bits and pieces of different things." Marcy was beginning to feel small, she had basically listened to rumors and gossip, a thing she detested, and even though she didn't think at the time they were true, doubt about the Robinson's had crept in.

"I heard that you had gotten wild and did something, I don't know what, to get you and a few others expelled. I heard that you were the only one that didn't get expelled and that it was because your dad paid off the University."

Ryan nodded. "Well, part of that's true. I did get wild. I joined a fraternity my sophomore year, with the idea that I had finally arrived. I was no longer subject to my parents' rules or standards of living. I didn't hate them, it's just that I was past eighteen and now independent. Mom had expressed her concern about joining the frat, but I didn't listen. In my mind she hadn't given me a good enough reason for not joining, so I didn't listen to her advice."

Ryan continued with his story of how his decision to join the fraternity had negatively affected his relationship with God, which led to more bad decisions. He began drinking with fraternity brothers and attending wild parties. Classes were skipped and grades fell. His personality changed for the worst and he got meaner. Parties got wilder and drinking got heavier. Things reached the lowest in his life when at one particularly wild drinking party, a frat brother they were picking on was almost killed when they dropped him while hanging him outside a window.

Ryan paused and leaned back in his seat. Marcy waited silently for him to go on. He glanced up at her then down at his fork. Marcy followed his gaze. His hands were shaking. Ryan laid his fork down and put his hands in his lap. He took a big breath and let it out.

"He almost died, it was a miracle he didn't. The cops came back and we were all arrested.

"They put all of us in the same cell. Most of us threw up on ourselves or whoever was next to us; too drunk to care. We slept it off in the cell. The school was notified and they notified our parents. Dad and Mom dropped everything and came running. When I woke up in the cell and saw the mess, the inside of me felt worse than my head.

"When I saw the look on Dad and Mom's face when they came to get me out of jail, I couldn't handle it. I saw the hurt and disappointment. They never condemned me, they loved me. Dad wrapped his arms around me, as badly as I smelled and as gross as I was. He said, 'If you're tired of this life and want to change, we'll help you. We love you, son.' I knew something had to change, and I knew it had to be me. I knew that I was guilty. Just as guilty as if I were the one that let go of the rope."

Ryan's voice broke and he stopped. He cleared his throat and took a drink. Marcy shifted in her seat and played with her napkin. Remorse for the painful memories she brought up had entered her heart. The stubborn hardness on her face had softened.

"You don't have to go on. I shouldn't have... I'm sorry."

Ryan looked up at her. "That's okay, it gets better." He paused, and she nodded for him to go on.

"Everyone was suspended for a week while they decided our fates. I came home. I took responsibility for my actions and did something that I hadn't done before. I told the Lord that I was messing up my life and couldn't handle the job. I asked Him to take over.

Ryan continued telling Marcy about the board's decision to expel all eleven that were involved in the incident and the hopelessness he felt about his future. He told her of his parent's support in appealing to the board for a second chance; the strict stipulations of the proposal that was set forth; and the struggles to hold to those stipulations.

Ryan looked at Marcy and smiled, trying to lighten the mood. "I graduated – with honors, even! That helped to land a very good paying job, so that I could pay off my debts. That good paying job was very instrumental in helping me to get a good position at *Krenshaw, Bixby, & Barnes*, which allowed me to move back home. Moving back home allowed me the privilege of scraping you off our tree once again."

Marcy giggled and caught Ryan's eyes twinkling into hers. She was drawn into them. His voiced softened, "And that allowed me to be sitting here, sharing lunch, and airing the skeletons in my closet with a lovely, lovely lady!"

Marcy blushed and dropped her eyes at his compliment. Not knowing what to do, she looked down at her watch, but didn't really see it.

Ryan looked at his watch, too. "Do you need to go?"

Marcy looked up, her face turning scarlet, bill-boarded surprised shock. She nodded and scooted out of the booth. Ryan started to get out too, wondering at her reaction. She had left her purse and was not going to the entrance. Ryan stopped and watched her walk away. A grin spread across the lower half of his face and a chuckle left his throat as he realized she was going to the ladies' room.

Ryan helped Marcy unload her car when they got back to her place. He sat the last box on her table and turned to her.

"Thanks for helping with my stuff and for supper. I'm sorry I ruined it for you. It was mean of me and I'm sorry."

"You're forgiven and you didn't ruin it. Not if it erased doubts about my family's character. Did it?"

Marcy nodded. "I shouldn't have doubted. I've known you all for so long. I just kept hearing things and it started to make me wonder. I haven't seen them for a while, you know. But then now that I've seen you again, I know I shouldn't have."

"You said you have to do more work yet, tonight?"

Marcy looked disappointed. "Yeah, I should."

"Would it bother you too much if I watched?"

Marcy's face lit up. "No, it won't bother me! I'd enjoy your company while I work!"

Marcy changed back into her work clothes and grabbed a chair. Ryan followed her through the kitchen to her studio. She sat and kicked the fly wheel to get it going once again. Ryan looked around at the studio and made comments. When Marcy was centering the clay, he sat, elbows planted on his knees, and watched. When she started pulling the sides up, he asked what it was going to be.

"A soup bowl."

Silence.

"Is it hard to do that?"

Marcy smiled. "Yes, very. In fact, it's impossible, and can't be done."

Ryan laughed at the absurdity of his question. Of course it wasn't hard for her, but to a novice it probably was quite a challenge.

"I'll tell you what..." Marcy pushed the sides back down to basically the same lump she had when she started.

"Why did you do that?! Was something wrong with it? It looked pretty good to me."

"Nothing was wrong with it. I just had an idea." Marcy left the wheel and went into her kitchen. She came back with an apron in her hand.

"I thought that I'd let you give it a spin. I need to mix some more clay anyway, and you can have a short lesson while I do."

Marcy coaxed Ryan into the potter's seat. He declined the apron; he didn't care if he got clay on himself. Marcy helped him get the wheel going to speed and showed him how to hold his hands to mold the clay. She went to the counter and started mixing a new batch. She watched as he tried to form the clay. They laughed and joked about his attempts. When Marcy was just finished mixing the new batch, Ryan gave up.

"I quit! This clay seems to have its own mind," he laughed, "I can't get it to be what I want. I guess I need to turn it over to an expert to make it into something recognizable!"

"You can't give up! Here, I'll help you." She stepped around beside him, and got the wheel up to speed. She wet down the clay, and guided his hands to push and pull the clay, coaxing the sides to form.

"That is great!" he beamed as it became something under his hands. Then Marcy changed the technique and it went back down to a lump.

"Hey!" he protested, "I was just starting to get the hang of it!"

"I know. So now do it yourself."

Ryan kicked the fly wheel to speed again and set to his task with a determined look. After a while his bowl came out lopsided, with thick sides, but recognizable. He stopped the wheel and looked at it proudly. Marcy removed it from the wheel.

"What are you doing?"

"I'm going to set it on the shelf to dry," she explained.

"Why? Aren't you going to smoosh it up and make something out of it again?"

"No. Something is already made out of it."

"But not good enough to keep."

"Yes it is. It's the product of your first lesson, and for your first thing, it's good! Besides," she teased him, "Think of how proud your mom will be when you bring it home and show her what you learned to do!"

Ryan swatted playfully at Marcy and got up from the wheel. "Okay, your turn. I want to watch you do something."

Marcy sat at the wheel again, centered a lump of clay, and sprinkled a little water on it. Ryan sat in front of her to watch. Within a few short minutes, her hands had pushed, pulled and coaxed that clay, the same substance with which he'd had a hard time working, into the soup bowl that it was intended to be.

Marcy glanced from the wheel to Ryan's face. As she was working, Ryan had become very quiet and something about him had changed. His focus was intent, his eyes were on her hands, but he wasn't seeing them. Marcy wished she knew what he was thinking. There was a look on his face that she couldn't describe. It was almost like he just had a brilliant idea, but not quite. His thoughts seemed miles from there. Wherever they were, it appeared to be a better place than here. Something inside of her wanted to be there, too.

Ryan spoke something barely loud enough to be heard, his eyes still focused unseeingly on Marcy's hands.

"What?"

Ryan came back from his reverie. "What?"

"That's what I said. You said something and I couldn't hear what it was so I said 'What.'"

Ryan nodded, and repeated what he must have said. "'But now, O Lord, You are our Father; we are the clay, and You our potter; and all we are the work of Your hand.' It's a verse that I'd read in my quiet time this morning. While I was watching you it suddenly became very real."

Marcy stopped the wheel, the bowl finished. Something inside her wanted to ask what he meant, wanted to know if that's what caused the look on his face. But another part told her not to ask. She examined the bowl that she just formed longer than necessary.

Ryan searched her face, trying to read her thoughts before he continued. "When I was trying to make something, it was like people trying to live their life without God. They don't know what they're doing, and at best it comes out clumsy and lopsided – some quality missing. When *you* work with the clay, it's like the people that yield their life to God. He knows what He's doing and it comes out right – beautiful and complete – like it's supposed to." Ryan stopped, waiting for a cue from Marcy.

Marcy didn't say anything. Ryan looked at his watch and stood up. She didn't want him to go on about God, but neither did she want him to leave.

"Are you leaving already?"

"Do you know what time it is?"

Marcy looked at her watch. She smiled at Ryan. "I guess that it is a bit late. The evening went so fast I didn't realize it."

"I hope that I didn't hinder your productivity too much."

"No, you didn't. I had to mix more clay anyway. Besides it was fun."

Marcy followed Ryan to the door. He stepped outside and turned around to say goodbye.

"Thanks for the supper, Ryan. I'm sor..." She started to apologize again, but Ryan put his finger against her lips, stopping her.

"We already went over that. You were already forgiven, and I enjoy being with you." His eyes twinkled. "Besides, I had fun tonight – I got to play with clay!"

Marcy's heart skipped a beat – he said he enjoys being with her! She wanted to tell him that she enjoyed being with him too, but she couldn't. "Thanks. I had fun too." Their eyes locked for a moment.

"Oh!" Marcy turned and rushed into the kitchen. She came back carrying his mom's baking dish. She giggled when she held it out to him. "I forgot to give this to you the other night."

Ryan chuckled. With one hand he took the dish, with the other reached up to her cheek where it lingered for a moment. Ryan was entranced with the emotions that flitted across Marcy's face. He felt her push her cheek against his hand ever so slightly. Her eyes became dark with emotion. He felt his heart begin to race again and warning bells went off. He patted her cheek then circled his hand to the back of her head and tipped it down. He planted a kiss on the top.

"'Night, Teach. Thanks for the lesson."

Chapter 11

MOVING

The next few weeks flew by for Marcy. She kept busy creating pottery and was pleased with how well her wares were selling. The new chain had increased her volume by almost twenty-five percent. If her pottery continued to sell as steadily, she could cut back her hours at the store. She might have to for the Holiday Season coming up, anyway.

Ryan called her a couple of times to chat. Mrs. Robinson and he issued invitations to attend church and Sunday dinner. She made excuses both weeks. She was determined not to go back to church: it was just too torturous. Of course she couldn't accept the Sunday dinner without going to church.

Things were getting back to an even keel with Dave. Kandy and she invited him to join the two of them for supper a few times. They alternated between Marcy's home and Kandy's apartment. Marcy was always careful to try and stay in the background and leave them alone as much as possible without being obvious. Kandy seemed thrilled with how things were progressing in her view. Dave started acting like the 'old' Dave with whom she had first become friends.

One evening Dave invited the two of them to see a movie with him. He had another friend with them when they met at his apartment. Dave briefly introduced Craig, but didn't explain his presence. Marcy and

Kandy gave each other sideways looks to ask if the other knew what was going on as they followed the two guys to the car. They both shrugged.

Marcy tried to keep herself paired with Craig for the evening. He seemed to be drawn to Kandy, who had eyes for Dave. It took a bit of skilled maneuvering on Marcy's part to sit between Kandy and Craig during the movie. Horrible thoughts of a triangle swept through Marcy's mind. When they went to dinner afterward, she maneuvered again to sit next to Craig in the booth. She worked hard to keep his attention from Kandy. Marcy caught Dave looking at her with a look of concern on his face a few times. They went back to Dave's place afterwards for a little bit. Marcy was glad when the evening was finally coming to a close. Marcy and Kandy left first. After they said their goodnights and started for the elevator, they heard Craig comment to Dave as the door was shutting. His voice was euphoric.

"Boy, that Kandy is something! Not only good looking, but great personality!" (Here he whistled.) "I don't know what you see in Marcy though. She's..." They didn't get to hear the rest of it because the door finally shut. They also didn't hear or see Dave's reaction. When Craig made the comment about Kandy, he took a second look at Kandy as the two headed for the elevator. He finished closing the door with a thoughtful look on his face.

When they got into the elevator and the doors were shut, they both let out school-girl giggles.

"Well you certainly hit it off, my friend!" Marcy teased. "Great personality, good looks... you've got it all!" Marcy imitated Craig's whistle. Kandy swatted at her playfully.

"What I want to know is what's wrong with you?"

"Oh, probably nothing, it's just you overwhelmed him with your dazzling beauty and personality. Next to you I appeared..." Marcy shrugged and made an exaggeratedly sad face. The two giggled again.

Kandy changed the subject. "Isn't Dave's apartment great? I love the decor! You didn't tell me he had such great tastes! Shame on you!"

Surprise flittered across Marcy's face. "Oversight, sorry."

Kandy rambled on. "I'd like to move. I don't like my place, it's so old fashioned. It makes me feel dreary. I've looked a little, but most places are beyond my means, or they're so far from work. Hey! Maybe we could rent a place together! Naw, you need a place for your pottery stuff. I know that's why you put up with where you are, because it gives you a studio to work in. Great apartments like these don't have back porches." Kandy sighed. "Oh, well, it was just a thought."

Marcy was surprised that Kandy didn't like her apartment. Marcy thought it was quaint and felt homey. True, it was old, but that didn't detract from it in Marcy's mind. She wondered if Kandy didn't like her house either, after the comment about 'putting up with it' because of the porch. Marcy smiled, it was funny that they had known each other all this time and she hadn't realized how Kandy's tastes ran.

Marcy let Kandy do all the talking on the way home. The evening had worn her out mentally. Kandy didn't seem to notice as she prattled on about Dave and how great he was until Marcy dropped her off at her door.

Dave shut the office door, and hesitated before heading to his desk. When he sat down he shuffled papers and tapped his pen several times. Marcy glanced up from her work. Dave usually dived right into his work. His face looked like he was trying to make a decision. He glanced up and caught her eye just then.

He hesitated. "Are you busy? Could I talk to you for a minute?"

Marcy laid down the pen and sat back in her chair. "Sure, what's up?"

"Well, it's about last night."

A sense of foreboding filled her mind. She didn't say anything, just waited for him to continue.

"I... You... I'm not sure how to start." He looked at her apologetically.

Marcy smiled at his struggle. "Just spit it out, we'll sort it out afterwards."

Dave took a big breath and let it out all at once. His words seem to tumble out on the tail end of the breath. "Craig isn't right for you." Marcy was taken aback and just stared wide-eyed at Dave. "He's not your type, Marcy. Besides, he seemed to be more enamored with Kandy. Not that I think that would be any better. I'm sorry if this came out badly, I didn't mean to hurt your feelings. I'm just concerned that you've fallen for him and I don't want you to get hurt."

Relief flooded through Marcy causing a laugh to start rolling deep inside and find its escape through the smile that taken over her mouth. Dave looked at her as if she just lost her marbles.

"Oh Dave, I'm sorry." Marcy settled down. "I didn't even like him that much."

Dave was confused. "But the way you threw yourself at him...?"

Gently, she said, "I thought that you were trying to set something up. And I didn't want you to get the wrong idea about me again, Dave." Marcy's voice perked up a bit. "His presence came as kind of a surprise, you know."

Dave nodded. "He was a surprise to me, too. He stopped by shortly before you came. He said that he was just in the neighborhood with nothing to do, so he thought that he would drop by. I didn't know how to politely get rid of him and I didn't think that it would hurt if he joined us. He's not a bad person really..."

"But you don't want to see your friends date him."

Dave grinned his affirmation. "You gave me a bit of a scare there. I've never seen you so forward or... or... pushy."

Marcy giggled. "I was pretty bad, huh?"

Dave smiled. "You could say that."

It was late when Marcy finally crawled into bed Thursday evening. She yawned as she reached over to turn out the light. Her hand never got to the light; instead it detoured to the phone. It was Ryan calling to ask if she wanted to see a play with him the next day. Someone where he worked had tickets that they could no longer use.

"Oh, I can't." her disappointment was evident in her voice. "I promised Kandy that I would help her move tomorrow. I've been helping her pack and clean for the last three evenings so she would be ready when everybody came tomorrow."

"Ah ha! That's why you've been so hard to reach!"

"You've tried to call before?"

"Since Tuesday evening. That's why I'm calling so late tonight. I've got dibs on the tickets and if I couldn't use them, someone else wants them. I needed to know in the morning. So I've been calling every fifteen minutes since 9:00."

"I'm sorry. If I'd known sooner..."

"That's okay. Is she going to move very far from here?"

"She's just moving about eight blocks from where she lives now. It's kind of neat, actually. It's in the same apartment building as Dave. She really hates her present apartment and about three weeks ago she saw Dave's. She thought it was great. When I told Dave what Kandy said, he told me that he heard that someone was moving out. She checked into it and found out that it was less than she was paying now. It never had a chance to get listed. It'll be even closer to where she works, not that it was very far to begin with. I'm happy for her," Marcy explained.

"Does your friend need any more help tomorrow? Or did she hire professional movers?"

"Nope, no professional movers. Just friends. I think that a friend of hers from work, Joe, is going to help. He's got a pick-up truck. Then there's Dave and me. I don't think that there is anyone else. She wanted to get the big stuff moved tomorrow, so that she would have time this weekend to sort through."

"What about her family?"

"She doesn't have any family around here."

"Well, since it doesn't look as if I'm going to be going to a play, do you think that she could use an extra pair of hands with the heavy stuff?" Ryan offered.

"I'm sure she would welcome the extra help, that's very kind of you."

Ryan showed up at Kandy's the following evening with more than a willingness to help. His parent's had come along and his dad had borrowed another pick-up truck. Marcy made introductions all around. Dave eyed them suspiciously, especially Ryan, but was cordial. The Robinson's showed they were eager workers, willing to take directions. With their friendliness and gracious manners, they were soon accepted even if they were strangers. It was with a sense of pride that she watched them win Dave over.

Kandy went back into the kitchen where Marcy and Mrs. Robinson were packing some last minute items. She was showing signs of stress as the two trucks were filled under her supervision. She had worked late into the night after Marcy left, and she wasn't able to get off work today as she had thought that she might. She looked exhausted. Mrs. Robinson saw her face and went over to her.

"Are you okay, dear?"

Kandy nodded. "I don't remember this much work the last time I moved. Of course that was quite a few years ago."

Mrs. Robinson wrapped her arm around Kandy's shoulder and gave it a squeeze. "It's amazing what we accumulate without realizing what we're doing, isn't it," she sympathized. "Is there some way I can better help you?"

"I don't know. I feel like I should be here finishing the last minute things and cleaning. And I feel like I should be over at the other place, or else it will probably all be put in the middle of the living room floor."

"May I make a suggestion?"

"Sure."

"Would you trust Marcy and me to finish up over here? We'll mark the boxes with great detail and then finish the cleaning. That way you can go over there and make sure things get put in the right rooms. Dave seems to be a good supervisor so he could oversee the loading on this end if you wanted to stay over there. It looks to me that with the two trucks and Marcy's station wagon, they'll be able to get everything in the next load."

Kandy thought that was a great idea.

By the time the trucks came back, Marcy and Mrs. Robinson had everything but the cleaning supplies ready to go. Mrs. Robinson had started washing down the kitchen shelves and Marcy was vacuuming the bedroom. Everything the two ladies could move was stacked neatly in the living room by the door. Kandy had come back with the trucks and her face lit up when she walked in the door.

"Wow! You two did a lot!"

"Nonsense, dear. We just organized it a bit. It looked overwhelming before because there were things all over. We just stuck them together." Mrs. Robinson smiled at her

The vehicles got loaded again and this time Marcy went with Kandy to help her make the bed and put the food away. They found and unpacked some of the boxes that had necessary things in it for her stay overnight. When Kandy went to lock up the now empty apartment, Mrs. Robinson had just about finished the cleaning.

Marcy was the last one to leave and waited for her friend to lock the door. Kandy had ridden over with someone, leaving her car in its new parking place. So Marcy gave her a ride home.

"Do you think that they would adopt me?" Kandy asked.

"Who?"

"Your second set of parents – Mr. and Mrs. Robinson."

Marcy chuckled. "I could ask them, if you'd like."

"Are they always like that?"

"Pretty much. They're not perfect, of course. They have their bad days like everyone, but it doesn't seem like they have as many bad days as I do. Even their bad days don't seem as bad."

"Are they always so physical?"

"What do you mean?" asked Marcy.

"You know, physical... touchy, huggy. Mrs. Robinson probably gave me three hugs this evening. I even got one from Mr. Robinson. He was carrying in a big box and couldn't see where he was going. I wasn't watching and came around a corner just as he was and we ran into each other. It was my fault, I made him drop his box, but *I* received a hug and an apology. I noticed that you got a lot from them, too."

Marcy smiled. "Yeah, they're like that all the time. You get a hug hello and a hug good-bye. Then if they think it's necessary, in-between, too."

"I'll have to take her up on her invitation to come and visit. I kind of like it. It makes you feel oozey inside."

"Oozey?" Marcy chuckled at Kandy's description.

"Yeah, you know, warm and... like you're special – oozey."

Marcy nodded in response. Kandy looked slyly over to her friend and a mischievous grin spread across her face. "Does it run in the family?"

Marcy glanced at her friend. "Does what run in the family?"

"You know very well what I mean, Marcy Kelman. Don't try to play dumb. But just in case you are: does Ryan give out hugs, too?"

Marcy blushed. "Kandy!"

"Well does he? I know you've seen him a number of times. Has he hugged you, too?"

"Yes. Like a brother."

"Ha! I'm sure! And has he kissed you like a brother, too?" Kandy chuckled.

"I'm serious; he treats me like his sister. I told you what our relationship was."

"He doesn't have a sister, so how would he know how to treat a sister?"

"Kandy." Marcy reproved.

"I don't think you know what your relationship is. I caught him looking at you tonight. And it wasn't like a brother, either."

"I think you're either making it up to tease or else you don't know what you're saying. Now stop or I'll stop. Then you'll have to get out and walk." Marcy's voice had a slight edge to it.

"Humph!"

They rode the rest of the way in silence. Kandy wasn't upset, but it appeared she hit a nerve with Marcy. She spent the last few blocks to her apartment trying to figure out Marcy. And Marcy spent the rest of the way to her house considering what Kandy had said.

Saturday evening, Mrs. Robinson stopped in on her way home from somewhere and invited Marcy to church and dinner afterwards. Marcy couldn't find an excuse this time and after all their hard work for her friend it was too hard to say no.

Sunday morning Marcy woke up feeling grouchy. She hadn't slept well, and she wished she could just go back to bed instead of to church. Her eyes were dark and puffy from lack of sleep. Then to top it off, her hair seemed to have a mind of its own. She finally gave up on it. Ryan showed up unexpectedly at her door to give her a ride to church. Thankfully, she had gotten up when the alarm went off and was almost ready when he arrived.

"Afraid I wouldn't show up? Or maybe that I would bolt afterwards?" Her voice was a bit dour as she held the door open for him to enter.

Ryan took in her circles under her eyes and smiled. "Nope, just couldn't wait to hear your warm welcome and see your smiling face."

"Humph." She turned around. "I just have to put my shoes on and I'll be ready." She spoke over her shoulder as she headed to get them. She scolded herself while in the bedroom.

Ryan was standing by her door with his hands in his pockets as she came out of the bedroom. Her heart did a flip flop. He was just as handsome as the last Sunday she went to church.

"Oh brother, not again!" She muttered at the conflict that started within her. She doubted very much if she could pull the same sitting situation again. She was glad that she had remembered yesterday to look for her Bible. At least she wouldn't be embarrassed that she didn't have it. It would also keep her from having to share with Ryan, thus avoiding more contact.

"Pardon?" He took in her scowl.

"Nothing. Just talking to myself."

"Is there something wrong?"

"No, I just didn't get much sleep. So I'm a grouch, I know... I'm sorry. I'm trying to snap out of it, really."

Ryan smiled and opened the door for her to leave.

"Aren't we going the wrong way?" Marcy asked as they headed in the opposite direction of the church.

"Nope. This is one of the reasons I picked you up this morning."

"What is?"

"Kandy is coming to church with us, and Mom thought that it would be nice if we picked her up since she hasn't been there before. I thought that she would be more comfortable if you were along."

This was news to Marcy. Kandy hadn't told her. Of course why should she? So Marcy just nodded a response.

Kandy was waiting for them when they pulled into the apartment parking lot. She looked perky and refreshed and happy to be going. She was practically in the car before Ryan could come to a complete stop.

"Good morning! Hi, Marcy! I didn't know you went to church, too. Isn't it a gorgeous day! Feels like it won't be quite as hot as it has been. Thank you for picking me up. I realize it is out of your way. But then maybe not too far out of your way if you pick up Marcy anyway. It was still sweet. Here, I didn't want to forget this." Kandy handed a casserole dish up to the front seat. "That was sweet of your mom to bring that over last night. I really appreciated it. It was delicious, too. I'm looking forward to the leftovers. Do you think that she'd give me the recipe?"

"She would be glad to give you the recipe. Asking her for it would be the best compliment you could give her," Ryan assured her.

Marcy should have let Kandy ride in the front seat, she chatted with Ryan all the way to church. And Marcy was glad to let her.

At church Marcy managed to get Kandy between Ryan and herself in the seating arrangement. The Adult Sunday School class was still studying the Old Testament judges. Marcy found it interesting and was able to keep her mind on the lesson fairly well. During the song service she watched Kandy to see how she was reacting. Kandy didn't appear to be uncomfortable at all. Neither did she seem that way during the message. In fact, it looked as if she was enjoying it. Marcy turned her attention back to the sermon wondering what was wrong with her. She caught a little bit of the message where the pastor was encouraging the people to be faithful to attend church and spend time reading their Bibles every day and why they should. The sermon seemed to be a lot shorter this Sunday.

Kandy was very friendly with all the people that greeted her after church. Marcy watched her happily visit while she, herself, hung back, envious that Kandy seemed to fit in when she didn't. Her face dared anyone to be friendly and she barely spoke to the ones that took the challenge. Ryan watched her carefully. When they got outside he nudged her arm.

"Why don't we go wait in the shade of that tree." He indicated a tree that was away from the crowd visiting outside. That was perfectly fine for Marcy. She didn't want to be in a crowd, anyway. Ryan stood with her for a while, not saying anything.

"Marcy," his voice was gentle, and she turned to look at him. He looked at her with hesitancy and concern. "To make friends, you should show yourself friendly."

Marcy scowled and snapped at him. "Are you saying I'm unfriendly?"

Ryan quickly looked down to hide the grin that tugged at his mouth. He struggled to keep the amusement out of his voice. "Not normally. You're usually very warm and friendly. But today..." He shook his head and looked up then and Marcy quickly turned away. But not before he caught sight of tears brimming her eyes and a quiver in her chin. He bit the corner of his lip deciding what to do. "I'll be right back."

Marcy didn't watch where Ryan went. She was mortified that her behavior was so reprehensible that he had felt the need to admonish her. He came back and escorted Marcy to the car.

"Kandy is going to ride home with Dad and Mom," he said in explanation as he started the car and backed out of the parking spot. "I saw Mrs. Malone start talking to them, so it will be a little while. Mrs. Malone likes to talk. Mom has to stop at the store afterwards, too. I thought that maybe you would like a little time away from the crowd before dinner... or did you want me to take you home?"

Marcy didn't reply – embarrassment and shame choked her. She stared out the window, her face turned from Ryan as they pulled out of the parking lot.

"Marcy, I know that it's more than just a lack of sleep bothering you. Although I think that just adds to what's wrong. Do you want to talk about it?"

"I'm fine." The lie was spoken in a clipped tone.

"Uh huh," was all Ryan said, but it clearly spoke his disbelief.

"Why don't you just take me home? I'm not very good company today."

"Hmmm," was his semi-guttural response, but the car didn't head in the direction of her house.

Marcy rolled her eyes. She could be stubborn, too. If they wanted a grouch for dinner then so be it. Her dour mood made her feel up to the clash-of-wills challenge set before her.

They rode in silence to the Robinson's but Ryan broke the silence as he opened the front door.

"Come on, Marcy, let's talk." He draped his arm across her shoulder and she let him lead her into the house. He didn't take her into the living room, but instead turned her into the front room and shut the French doors behind him. "I thought that it would be more private in here," he said in explanation as he laid his jacket on the nearest chair and loosened his tie.

"Okay, kiddo. What's up?" He asked as he sat down next to Marcy.

Some of the fight had left during the car ride. She shrugged and shook her head. "Really, I think I'm just over tired." *That and a little nut-so.* She hated the struggle with all the feelings she'd been having lately. And she wanted to be around the people that seemed to spark the feelings. Was she an emotional masochist? And why would she want to give someone else the chance to think that about her?

Ryan watched her twist a tissue into knots. When he spoke it was in low, soothing tones.

"You feel like there's a battle going on inside and it confuses you."

Surprised dismay settled in her eyes. "How did you know?"

Ryan smiled. "Your eyes and face have always been very expressive. Sometimes what you're thinking is clearly written there – you get that from your mom, you know. And today, if looks could kill, Kandy wouldn't be coming home for dinner with my parents. Do you want to tell me why? It's not like you, Marcy." His eyes probed hers and she had the feeling he could look right to the inside of her.

Marcy sat very still. Dread entered her heart and she willed a veil over her face, closing him off. She looked down at her hands then released the tortured tissue as if it somehow it could betray her feelings. She forced her hands to lie quietly in her lap. She didn't want him to see into her soul. She had already looked there and didn't like what she saw. She didn't want anyone else to know, especially not Ryan.

Ryan watched as the shutters closed and laid a hand on hers. "Marcy, please don't shut me out."

Her voice came out barely more than a whisper. "Please take me home."

"You used to talk to me about everything."

"I don't want you to know everything."

"Have we grown too far apart? Don't you trust me anymore?" Ryan gently probed.

"I can't."

"You can't trust me?"

"I can't tell you." Her eyes started to tear up.

"Why?" Ryan noticed she was on the brink of tears and handed her his handkerchief.

Marcy stabbed at her eyes, now angry at herself for being so emotional. "I don't know! Okay? I don't know!" Her words came out harsh with frustration she was feeling. She paused briefly while she stabbed at her eyes again. "I don't know... I felt angry because Kandy looked so happy and I felt so miserable... I feel irritated when... I don't know why... And when you... Then I... It makes me feel guilty."

Marcy paused in her incomplete explanation and Ryan, having no clues how to answer or even if he should, waited for her to continue. She let out a sigh that signaled her resignation to her plight and an end to the probing. Ryan sensed the change and waited for Marcy's direction.

"You all must think I'm an immature fruitcake."

Ryan chuckled, helping to lighten the mood. "Immature fruitcake? Do fruitcakes have to mature? Like wine?"

Marcy rolled her eyes.

Ryan chuckled again. "Nobody thinks you're a fruitcake. And we even doubt that you're a serial killer. Of course your face doesn't show *every-thing*." Marcy squinted her eyes and gave him a sarcastic smile. "You're just having confusing thoughts and don't know what to do with them, that's all. Everybody goes through that," he reassured her.

"You, your parents? The epitome of stability?"

Ryan chuckled. "Yes. We just learned Who to talk to. I fight some mighty fine battles myself every once in a while."

"Do you win?"

A looked crossed Ryan's face that Marcy couldn't read. His voice lowered more than it already was. "Not always right away."

Ryan shifted gears mentally and smiled. "So... Do you feel up to dining with us? Or do you still want me to take you home?"

Marcy searched his face while trying to decide. "Come on," he coaxed as he stood and helped her to her feet. "Please stay." He stepped to her side and gave her an avuncular squeeze.

When the others arrived, both of them were in the kitchen setting the table and chatting. Ryan joked with Marcy to help further dispel the cloud that had been hovering over her that morning. Both of them were laughing at an anecdote from work that Ryan had told.

Kandy was bubbly when they got to the Robinson's and stayed cheerful all through dinner. She gladly took Marcy's and Mr. Robinson's hands for the prayer and didn't look at all uncomfortable. She was absorbing being a part of their family.

"That's some church you go to! It's not like one I'd ever been to before. Everyone is so friendly and they seem so happy. Of course I've only been to funerals in a church. I was invited to a church wedding once but I wasn't able to go. I would hope that would have been happier!" she giggled.

"Didn't your parents take you?" Mr. Robinson asked.

"Heavens no! I don't even remember my dad, he left when I was just little. And my mom had to work a lot to raise us. I remember my older sister asking once to go to church. I guess one of her friends went all the time and she wanted to see what it was like. But Mom said no because that was the only day she could sleep in."

"How many brothers and sisters do you have?"

"Just one – Angie."

"Does your mom or sister live around here?"

"No, Angie's the closest. She's married and lives about four hours south of here. It's a little town and I forget the name of it. I've got her address at home, though. I don't see her very often – usually at Christmas. I don't know where Mom is. I haven't heard from her since she left."

"When was that, Dear?" asked Mrs. Robinson.

"Right after I graduated from high school. She said that Angie and I were old enough to take care of ourselves and she needed to live her own life now. She sent a letter to Angie once, but when we wrote to the address on the letter, it came back."

"I'm so sorry," Mrs. Robinson sympathized.

"Oh, don't worry about it, that's water under the bridge," Kandy waved it off. "Marcy said she would share you guys since you're kind of like a spare set of parents. Did she ask you yet if you would adopt me? She told me she would."

Kandy chirped on, she asked quite a few questions about church and things that were said that she didn't understand. The Robinsons were happy to answer questions and explain things to her. Marcy listened attentively. It made her feel better to have someone else ask the questions. In her mind she should have known the answers because she used to go to church.

Between Ryan and the cheerfulness that the Robinsons and Kandy brought in with them, by the end of dinner, Marcy was in a good mood and feeling like her old self again. She even lost gracefully at games they played all afternoon.

At 5:00 Kandy looked at her watch and sighed. "This has been great, but I really should be getting home. I still have more unpacking that I want to get done before tomorrow." She stood up to leave.

Mrs. Robinson scooted her chair back. "We'd love to have you stay longer, Kandy, but I understand and won't press you. Please know that you're welcome here anytime."

Marcy stood up to leave too. Ryan pulled the keys out of his pocket.

"I'll come with you, Dear. Mrs. Malone asked me for something, and we can just run it past on our way. Do you want to come too, George?"

Mr. Robinson smiled. "No, I'll stay here. There probably wouldn't be room, anyway. Besides, it will give me a chance to raid the 'fridge."

So Marcy and Kandy received good-by hugs from Mr. Robinson. They both went home feeling loved and accepted.

That evening she remembered what the pastor had said in his message about reading out of the Bible every day. She settled herself on the couch to read it. Maybe it would help straighten things out in her mind. Kandy had asked the Robinsons if they read their Bibles every day. Marcy knew the answer before they said it. Was that the secret to their... to their what? What was it that was different about them?

It wasn't that they were just 'good' people. Marcy was considered a 'good' person and so were Dave and Kandy. It wasn't that they had a stable family life, her family was considered stable, too. There was a different quality about them that she didn't have. Mr. and Mrs. Robinson had always had it, and Ryan had it now too. Marcy sighed. Maybe it was just something that was inherited that didn't show up until later in life, kind of like baldness. If reading the Bible helped them like they said it did, she would start to read hers everyday too.

Chapter 12

ICE CREAM AND FAMILY VISIT

arcy's phone rang Friday evening. Her heart beat a little faster. She hadn't heard from Ryan since Sunday and she was hoping it was he. It wasn't.

"Hello?"

"Hi!"

"Oh hi, Kandy."

"'Oh hi, Kandy?' Doesn't sound like you're very happy that I'm calling. Want me to hang up?"

"I'm sorry. I didn't mean to sound that way. Of course I don't want you to hang up."

"Maybe you were hoping it was someone else, is that it? Someone like maybe, let's see... hmmm... Ryan, perhaps?" Kandy giggled.

"You sound happy. What's up with you?" Marcy changed the subject.

"Oh, not much. I wanted to ask you a favor."

"Okay, shoot."

"Can I ride to church with you again on Sunday? That is if you and Ryan won't mind a third person. I know that three's a crowd."

"Uh... I didn't know I was going to church on Sunday. And Ryan doesn't always pick me up when I go, anyway."

"Why aren't you going? Don't you go every Sunday?"

"No... I'm not always invited." Marcy didn't want to tell her that she turned down a number of invitations, or she'd have to explain her reasons to Kandy.

"So? Mrs. Robinson told me to come whenever I wanted. She said that I didn't need a personal invitation and that I'd always be welcome. I can't imagine that wouldn't be true for you, too." Kandy paused and waited for Marcy to respond.

Marcy didn't respond, trying to think of a good excuse not to go, knowing what Kandy said was true.

"So can I ride to church with you or not?" Kandy asked again. "I'd feel funny going by myself."

Marcy sighed. "Sure. I'll pick you up."

"Thank you for being so enthusiastic about it." Kandy chided her.

"Sorry. So what's going on with you this week? I haven't heard from you since Sunday. Been keeping busy?" Marcy asked in a more enthusiastic tone, trying to make up for her ungraciousness.

Kandy was in high spirits. "I'll say! Did you know that Dave was a creature of habit? He does his laundry on the same day at the same time every week. He also checks his mail the same time every morning. Of course, that's if his work permits. He also uses the same elevator all the time!"

"How did you find all this out? You haven't even been there a week yet!"

Kandy giggled again. "Monday he invited me up for dinner. He said he thought that it would help me save time because I wouldn't have to stop to cook, I could just continue unpacking. I got there a tad early and caught him in the middle of folding his laundry. So I helped him. That led to a discussion about the laundry room and when was the best time to use it, etc. Through careful listening and a little prodding, I was able to deduce his laundry schedule. As for the mail, I ran into him once at the mail boxes. Figuring that if he did his laundry at the same time, all the time, maybe he was the same way about his mail. So I tried a little experiment, and I was right! This is really helpful information to have when you would like to be able to bump into someone."

"Kandy, you're quite a conniver!"

"Me! You gave me the idea! Besides, I get the feeling he doesn't mind running into me. Wednesday, there I am, minding my own business, unpacking my own things, when what happens? I get a knock on my door. It's Dave. He said that he wasn't doing anything and wondered if I could use a hand unpacking. Of course I found something for him to do!" Kandy giggled again.

"That probably explains it!"

"Explains what?"

"Well, Thursday, I needed to ask him something and found him in the produce aisle putting bananas on display. He didn't see me coming and I caught him with this funny grin on his face. When I got closer, he saw me and acted guilty."

"Do you think that he's attracted to me and feels like he's betraying you or something?"

"I don't know, but when he said something to me about my behavior with Craig, he said that he didn't think Craig was right for you either," Marcy encouraged her.

"Maybe, just maybe, what Craig said made him think twice!" Kandy sounded hopeful.

"Think twice about what? How great you were or what a dud I am?" Marcy teased. She was glad that Kandy was happy with how things were going with Dave. She listened contentedly to Kandy prattle on for the next half hour.

Five minutes after Kandy hung up, her phone rang again.

"My goodness, Sweetheart. You sure have been on the phone a long time!"

"Hi, Mom. I was talking to Kandy."

"That's nice, Sweetie. I just wanted to remind you that Mark and Janet are here this weekend. They got in this evening."

"I hadn't forgotten. I wasn't sure when they were getting in, but I planned on coming out tomorrow and spending most of the day."

"I hope you can come more than just tomorrow, Marcy! You haven't seen them in a long time!"

"I was planning on coming out Sunday, too, Mom."

"That's wonderful. Why don't you bring your pajamas and spend the night. We've got room; you can sleep on the couch. Then you won't miss a moment more of the weekend than you need too, and can visit all day Sunday, too."

"That'd be great, except that Kandy asked me to do something with her on Sunday morning, and I promised I would. I'll be there in time for dinner though. You'd probably all sleep late Sunday morning, anyway. So I won't miss that much."

Mrs. Kelman filled Marcy in on how cute the twins were and how much they'd grown since they saw them last along with all the other usual proud grandparent things. "Now, Sweetheart, I don't mean to push or even pry, but are you even looking for a husband, yet?"

"Mom!"

"I'm just thinking of you, Sweetie. I don't think that you realize what you're missing. Mark's kids are such a delight. I just don't want it to get too late and you miss the opportunity."

"I'm not that old, Mom. I still have several child-bearing years ahead of me."

"I know, but you don't even seem to be looking for a husband. It takes time, you know, and you're not getting any younger, you realize."

Thankfully Marcy heard her doorbell ring. "I have to go, Mom. Someone's at my door."

"Okay, Sweetie. We'll see you tomorrow. I love you!"

"'Bye, Mom. I love you, too."

Marcy went to the door to find out who was there. Almost anybody was a welcome relief from her mother's preoccupation about her childless state.

"I tried calling first, but your phone was busy." Ryan apologized as she opened the door.

Marcy smiled and motioned him in. A warm feeling spread over her. His presence was better than a phone call and he was definitely a welcomed relief.

"I was just wondering what you were doing this evening."

"Talking on the phone," she grinned, "What about you?"

"I had a craving for ice cream. There wasn't any at home. So I wondered if you have any here."

Marcy chuckled. "Sorry, freezer's empty."

"In that case, would you like to go for some with me?"

"Sure."

"Would you prefer to eat it here or eat it out?"

"If we eat it here, my phone will probably ring again," Marcy warned.

"I vote for out, in that case."

They drove to an ice cream parlor that boasted a wide variety of flavors. Marcy got two scoops of chocolate-marshmallow. Ryan got three scoops, each a different flavor. They weren't the more sedate flavor combinations either. The tamest one was Boysenberry Bump. Most of it was a lovely purple color, but she wasn't sure she wanted to know what the 'Bumps' were. They were green and dark brown. Marcy watched Ryan eat his choices while they talked about work and how their weeks had gone.

"You seem to be fascinated by my ice cream. Would you like to try a bite?"

Marcy shook her head.

"They're good."

"No, thank you."

"Are you sure? Yours looks pretty boring."

"I like boring."

Ryan laughed. "Chicken."

"I'm not chicken. I just happen to like mine quite well."

"You're chicken, and you know it."

Marcy reached over with her spoon and took a bit of the Boysenberry without any bumps, and stuck it in her mouth. "There. Satisfied?"

"That wasn't so bad was it?"

Marcy put on a haughty air. "It is not a requirement of proving one is not chicken, to say whether one likes it or not. The only requirement is to taste it."

"You liked it," Ryan stated confidently.

"I didn't say that."

"You didn't say that you didn't like it, either."

"That proves nothing."

"With you it does."

"Ha."

"Ha, yourself. I know you," he answered, smugly.

"Not as well as you think," she answered back, just as smugly.

"Better than you think."

"I doubt that."

"I'll prove it... I think that you would like to go on a picnic with me in the park tomorrow afternoon. Maybe take a canoe out on the lake or hike on the trails?"

Marcy's face fell. "I can't."

"But you would like to?"

"Yes, I would. That sounds like fun. Could I take a rain-check?"

"Maybe. That will depend on if your excuse for not going is good enough or not."

"Mark and Janet are here visiting for a week. I haven't seen them or the twins in quite a while. I'm going over to visit tomorrow morning. Mom wants me to spend to weekend over there. And so do I." She smiled. "Is that a good enough reason to warrant a rain-check?"

"Oh, I suppose so." If her mom wanted her to spend the weekend, then there would probably be no reason to invite her to church on Sunday morning. He smiled at her and she thought that he looked disappointed, too. "So how long is your brother going to be here?"

Marcy smiled back at him and they talked about Mark and his family while they finished the ice cream.

Ryan walked her to her door when he dropped her off.

"You have to come in."

"Why do I have to come in?"

"Because you have to finish what you started! Come on. I'll show you." Marcy led him into the kitchen where she had been glazing earlier that evening. "Here," she held out to him the bowl that he had thrown. "It's fired and ready for you to finish."

"Oh, no. I can't do that. I'm not artistic at all. You just paint it however you want. Or leave it like that. Why did you even fire it?"

"I thought that you would want to finish something that you started. It's your bowl, you know. If I finished it, it wouldn't say that it's yours. It's not hard. You don't have to make pictures on it – you could use one color to glaze the whole thing. Besides, think how proud your mom will be. She could put it on her refrigerator like she used to do with all your other artwork from school."

Ryan groaned and gave in. Marcy showed him all the different glazes he could use and handed him a brush. She sat beside him and worked on her own stuff. Ryan watched her for a little bit, then chose a glaze. He didn't stick with one. He applied several different ones in an abstract pattern. Marcy had the feeling that it was going to turn out a little like his ice cream choices.

Marcy was up bright and early the next morning. She was excited about seeing her brother and his family. She hadn't seen them since Christmas and here it was already autumn. Time had gone so fast and so slow at the same time. Marcy had felt close to Mark growing up and missed him when he had moved.

Marcy got to her parents a little after 8:30. Mark greeted her at the door with his finger to his lips, signaling to be quiet. He gave her a bear hug and ushered her into the living room. "Dad and Mom and the girls are still asleep. I don't care if Dad and Mom wake up, but it would be nice if the girls stayed sleeping!"

Janet came out of the kitchen with two cups of coffee. She handed one to Mark and sat the other on the coffee table so she could give Marcy a hug. Marcy refused the offer for coffee and sat across from Mark and Janet who snuggled on the love seat. Marcy reflected on how happy and contented they looked.

They wasted no time trying to catch up on each other's lives. Marcy wrote letters and talked on the phone to them once in a while, but some things were always better to talk about in person. It was particularly easier to talk about Christine and Elizabeth in person, especially while they were sleeping and not listening for their names. They would be turning four this week. Mark and Janet had a lot of funny stories to tell. Mark got a mischievous look on his face.

"So when are you going to start having children? You can't just leave it all up to Janet and me."

"Now don't you start, too!" Marcy scolded.

Janet elbowed her husband in the side. "Mark!"

Mark just laughed. "Sorry, Spitfire. Mom got started on that last night and I just couldn't resist saying something."

"That must have been right after she talked with me. She started with me on the phone and I had to cut her off in the middle because someone came to my door. I don't think that she had it out of her system, yet."

"You're right; it was just after she called you. I should have just told her to call you back! Let her vent her motherly frustration on the way-ward chick instead of us, the ones who already produced grandchildren for her. I don't think that's fair of you. You should have let the person at your door wait."

Marcy threw a pillow at her brother, who caught it and threw it back.

144

"As much as I hate to, I'll have to say one thing in his defense, though," Janet piped in on behalf of her husband. "He did stand up for you. He told her not to push because that getting the wrong mate is worse than staying single."

"Well, thank you, Mark! Do you think she'll listen and take your advice?"

He shrugged. "Seriously, sis, not to push; just out of curiosity... is there anybody special?"

"Mark, don't you think that's a bit nosey?" censured Janet.

"If she were a complete stranger it would be. But she's my sister and I care what's going on in her life. Besides, if she doesn't want to tell us anything, that's fine, too."

"There's nothing to tell. There's no boyfriend. There could have been one but he was not my choice."

"Would you care to satisfy my nosiness a little more and expound on that?" Mark probed. So Marcy told them about Dave. This of course led her to Kandy.

"...And that's fine with me if she wants to pursue him. He seems to like it, too. We're all three still friends. And not having to be on the defensive with Dave anymore makes work more pleasant."

"Speaking of work, how's your pottery business doing?"

"Great! I got into the *La CleAires* chain and it's really boosted my sales!"

"That's wonderful, Marcy! Do you think that you'll be getting enough business to take it on full time?" enquired Janet.

"Not quite yet. But I approached a few more stores and I'm waiting to hear back from them. One of the owners has four other stores. If he takes me that would be a big step."

"How does this affect renting the kiln at the high school?"

"That could be a problem. I think that I'm already using it more than they had thought that I would. It's getting to be harder to use it too, because I can't get in whenever I need to. I have to wait for someone to be there and I get backed up. And now that school has started again... I just hope that they don't study pottery before Christmas! That's one of the reasons I haven't been as aggressive in looking for outlets."

"How's your 'kiln fund' coming along?" Mark asked.

"Not too bad! I'm only lacking about five hundred to be able to buy one, but I'm not sure how much more I'll need to install it. My landlord gave me permission to put it in the basement, but he wants me to fire-proof the area first. If he approves what I do to it, then it will be fine. I think that he's a little scared of it. I figure that I should have the rest of the money in about nine more months, if everything stays like it is."

They had talked for almost an hour before they heard stirring upstairs and the sound of water running.

"Mom and Dad must be up," observed Marcy.

Pretty soon two pairs of small feet were heard padding down the stairs. Two little bodies, wrapped in towels and carrying bundles of clothes, came racing around the corner into the living room. Mark and Janet looked at them surprised. "What are you two up to?!"

"Gramma gave us a bath!"

"Yeah! Th'he told uth to be really quiet tho you wouldn't know."

"She said she wanted to, because she doesn't get to all the time. So we let her."

"Ith that okay? Th'he gives funner bathth than you do, Mommy."

"But Grampa woke up and then we had to get out..."

"... becauthe he needed in."

"We left him a lot of bubbles..."

"... and told him he could play with our toyth."

"Gramma helped us to get our clothes so that we wouldn't mess up the suitcase."

"Th'he said that you could help uth get drethed while th'he drethed herthelf."

It was then that they noticed Marcy. She had been sitting in the recliner with her back to them as they came into the living room. Their chatter ceased as they tried to figure out who she was.

"This is your Aunt Marcy. Do you remember her? You saw her last Christmas. She's the one that gave you the doll house for your dolls to live in."

Recognition dawned on their faces. Beth, as they called Elizabeth, was the bolder of the two. She went over to Marcy and wrapped her arms around her neck, pressing a wet head against her cheek.

"Thank you for the doll house. I play with it a lot."

Christine hung back, still a bit shy, but smiled at Marcy and nodded her head in agreement with her sister.

'Chrissie' and Beth weren't identical twins, and it was easy to tell them apart. They both had brown hair, but Beth's was naturally curly with big

146

loops and rings that usually fell in wild abandon about her face. Chrissie's was more on the straight side, with only a hint of curl and definitely more manageable. Chrissie looked more like her mother and Beth more like her father. Both of them were adorable.

Beth consented to let Marcy help her get dressed while Mark dressed Chrissie and Janet made their breakfasts. Mr. and Mrs. Kelman came down the stairs in the middle of this and got their breakfast, too. Mark and Marcy were still in the living room visiting.

"Grampa!" she heard Chrissie exclaim, "You and Grandma didn't tell Je'thuth thank you for your food! You need to tell Him thank you before you eat it!"

"Oversight on my part, Sugar," she heard her father respond. Then it was silent for just a moment before the chattering started again.

Marcy looked at Mark when she heard this, but it didn't appear that he was aware of the conversation in the kitchen. Soon everybody was done eating and ready to get on with the day.

It was beautiful out and they decided to go to Sheridan's small, but very nice, zoo. It was a part of a larger park complex that had nice playground equipment and picnic area among other things. The girls had a great time and Grampa, Gramma, and Marcy spoiled them. They got back to the Kelman's happy and tired. The girls didn't have their usual nap, so they were ready for bed early, leaving the evening free for uninterrupted visiting. It was ten o'clock before Marcy got up to leave.

Mark walked her to her car. "It's great to see you again, Sis."

"You, too, Mark."

"Will we see you tomorrow?"

"Sure! Didn't Mom tell you?"

"She said that she wanted you to spend the weekend and sleep on the couch, but you said you had something to do."

"Mothers!" she said shaking her head, exasperated. "I'm going to be here in time for lunch. Kandy asked me to go with her to church and I had told her I would." It was dark out and Marcy couldn't see Mark's eyes light up with interest.

"What church are you going to?" he asked casually.

"The one the Robinsons took us to when we were kids."

"Do you go very often?"

"Not normally," she said derisively. "But since Ryan's been back in town I seem to be going quite a bit. I wouldn't be going tomorrow, but the Robinsons offered an open invitation to Kandy last week and she took them up on it. She knew that I'd gone with the Robinsons a few times and asked me if I'd go with her because she said she'd feel funny going by herself."

"That sounds reasonable."

"I know. I just wish that..." Marcy finished her sentence with a shrug and sigh.

"You don't sound very happy about going. I thought that you use to like to go with them to church."

"I use to. Lately, I don't know. I do, but I don't, if that makes any sense. And tomorrow, I'd definitely prefer to spend time with you guys."

"Well... what if we came to church with you?"

Marcy squinted to better see Mark's face. She had not missed the girls insisting on prayers at meal times, and Mark seemed to be a little different, but she couldn't really put her finger on why. Janet seemed her same sweet self as the last several times she saw her. "Do you want to?"

"Sure. Mom and Dad will undoubtedly sleep in, so they won't really miss any time with us. Besides, they'll have us the rest of the time when you're working. This will give us a little more time together and I'll get to say hi to the Robinsons, too. I haven't seen them for a long time."

Marcy nodded and let her brother know what time Sunday School and church started.

Kandy was eagerly waiting again when Marcy picked her up the next morning.

She shook her head at her friend's eagerness. "Why do you like going to church so much?"

"Because... I don't know. It feels kind of like a family or something. I guess it just makes me feel good. Kind of..."

"Oozey?" Marcy finished for her.

Kandy chuckled. "Yeah, I guess. Why don't you like to?"

"Who said I didn't?"

"Your face. You're such a sourpuss."

"Thanks friend."

"Well really, Marcy. Look at yourself in the mirror. You should do like the song says and 'Put on a happy face.'" She sang the song snippet. "It would probably make you feel better. So why don't you like to go?"

"I do, and I don't. I can't explain why. And I am trying to figure it out. I started to read a chapter out of the Bible every day like the pastor said to last Sunday. I don't think that it's working though. I remember the stories from when I went to Sunday School as a kid, but the rest of it is either boring, or I don't understand it, which makes it boring."

"Maybe you just have to give it a little more time and it will grow on you."

"Maybe. I'm sorry for being a sourpuss. I'll try to 'put on a happy face' like you said. Ryan scolded me last week for my demeanor. I must be really bad."

"Ryan scolded you?!" Kandy giggled. "So that's why you left!"

"My brother, Mark and his family are going to be at church today." Marcy said a little loudly as she interrupted Kandy to change the subject. "You remember Mark and Janet from Christmas?"

"Sure I do! And their twins, too. So what are they doing here?"

"They had some vacation time and are spending a week at my folk's. They got here Friday evening. And they are leaving again early Saturday morning."

Marcy and Kandy got out of the car and headed to the church building. They heard a car give a short honk and turned to see where it was coming from. It was Mark and Janet just pulling into the parking lot. Kandy and Marcy waited for them to park and went to greet them at the car. The Robinsons were in the lobby when they all came in together and wasted no time in going over to welcome them. Marcy could tell that they were surprised and pleased at her appearance, even more so than at Kandy's being there. It was to her chagrin that she realized why this was and determined to 'put on a happy face' this morning.

The Robinson's had hugs for everyone, and after everyone had been thoroughly greeted, Mrs. Robinson showed Janet where the Sunday School Class was for Chrissie and Beth.

Marcy sat between Mark and Ryan with Kandy on the other side of Ryan. As she was struggling to not let his nearness affect her so, she saw Kandy out of the corner of her eye, leaning forward in her seat. When she turned her head to look at her more fully, Kandy was watching her, and pushed the corners of her mouth up into a smile with the tips of her index fingers. Since Ryan was in between the two, Kandy's actions caught his attention. Seeing

Kandy was motioning to Marcy, he turned his head to look at Marcy. He caught the displeased look she shot at Kandy and chuckled. Marcy looked up when she heard Ryan and caught his eye. She blushed and Kandy giggled. Marcy shot Kandy a withering look.

"Stop it!" she whispered across Ryan.

Kandy giggled again, and Mr. Robinson looked down the row. He leaned toward the three in mock seriousness. "If you children can't behave yourselves, I'll have to separate you." This sent Kandy into a spasm of giggles. Embarrassed, Marcy quickly sat up straight and faced forward, pressing herself into the back of the pew. This caught Mark's attention, who had previously been chatting with his wife about the children. He looked first at Marcy and saw her discomfiture, then to Kandy who was giggling, then to Mr. Robinson and Ryan who were grinning. He looked back at Marcy who was making plans to say a few words to Kandy after the message about her childish behavior in church. Mark leaned over and whispered in her ear.

"I don't know what you did, but if you smile, it will probably help you feel better."

Marcy's face flamed red. The leader had them turn to a scripture. Marcy did this with more effort than was needed. Then he asked everyone to read the passage together and gratefully the others' attention was turned elsewhere. Marcy pasted a small smile on her face and purposely determined to shut the others out by paying strict attention during the class. Her face might have looked attentive, but her mind wasn't so willing to obey.

Marcy didn't have to paste the smile on her face after class. She went with Janet to help her retrieve the twins for the service. They were happy and excited as they walked together to the sanctuary. They had to tell Marcy and their mom about what they did and what they learned. Their words tumbled out often crossing over each other and sometimes ending each other's sentences. Marcy was surprised how much they had absorbed. Apparently it was more than she did during her class.

Picking the girls up from their class and taking them to the restroom, took all the time and the service was just about to start when they got back to their seats.

"It's my turn to sit on Daddy's lap, and Chrissie's turn to sit on Mommy," Beth informed Marcy as she crawled into Mark's lap. "We take turns because that's fair."

Marcy smiled at her and watched her wiggle to get comfortable. Both the girls were very quiet during the announcements. When the song service started they stood between Mark and Janet holding hands. They apparently enjoyed the faster songs, for they 'danced', doing the little bouncing hops where their feet never leave the floor. It wasn't in time to the music, but they didn't care. They stood still and listened during the slower, more worshipful songs.

It was plain to see that the girls were used to going to Sunday School and Church. Evidently Mark and Janet attended regularly, too. She wondered when that had started. She glanced at Mark every now and then. He had that same... what... presence?... about him that the Robinsons had during the singing. She couldn't see Janet, but she knew without looking that Janet had it too. The girls didn't look like they felt left out. But of course, she reasoned, they were still little. She tried to see Kandy's face. It didn't have that look, but it certainly looked happy and content. It almost seemed like a conspiracy to make her feel the odd man out. What was wrong with her? Why couldn't she feel what they were feeling? Maybe Kandy was right. If she forced herself to act happier, maybe she would feel happier. She plastered the smile back on.

After the offering, Beth asked if she could sit on Marcy's lap. Mark looked at Marcy and she nodded.

"Okay Pumpkin, but you have to sit still and be quiet, okay?"

Beth agreed and climbed over to Marcy. Marcy put her Bible next to her on the pew and received Beth on her lap. She sat sideways with her back to her dad. Marcy wrapped her arms around Beth, who leaned against Marcy with her head resting against Marcy's shoulder.

Ryan watched and smiled at Beth. Beth smiled back. Ryan noticed that Marcy wasn't going to be able to follow along in her Bible very well. He handed his to Kandy, with whom he was going to share, and picked up Marcy's. He flipped it open to the passage and held it between them so Marcy could follow along.

Beth put her feet on Ryan, heels resting on his leg and toes pointing stiffly upward. Ryan looked at Beth, surprised at her friendly overture.

"My feet can help you hold it if it gets too heavy," she whispered.

"Thank you!" he whispered back.

Marcy followed along, but her mind wandered. It felt nice holding a child on her lap. Her curls tickled Marcy's chin and little fingers entwined themselves around hers. Beth sat very still, spending most of the time looking at Ryan, who would look back at her every once in a while and smile or wink. Half way through the message, she pulled Marcy's face down to hers.

"Do you like him?" she asked in a loud enough whisper that Ryan could hear.

"Yes, I do," Marcy whispered back.

"Good, because I do, too."

Ryan smiled at Beth again and she snuggled back down against Marcy. About five minutes later she was asleep.

After the service the Robinsons extended an invitation for lunch to everyone. Of course Mark and Janet couldn't go and neither could Marcy, since they were expected to go to the Kelman's.

"Are you coming over, Dear?" Mrs. Robinson asked Kandy.

"I rode with Marcy this morning." she responded, her voice sounding a bit disappointed.

"That doesn't matter," piped in Mr. Robinson, "You can ride with us and we can take you home whenever you want."

Kandy smiled, hopefully. "Really? That wouldn't be too much of a bother?"

"Of course not, Dear. We would love to have you and you'd never be a bother," Mrs. Robinson assured her. And Kandy gladly accepted.

They all said their good-byes with hugs all around. Mr. Robinson picked up Kandy's hand and placed it in the crook of his arm. He leaned down to her and whispered something in her ear. Kandy whispered something back and they both laughed.

"Now, George, what are you two up too?"

"Never mind, Marian. It's our secret. If we wanted everyone to know, we would have said it out loud," he teased. Kandy beamed.

Mrs. Robinson shook her head and took Ryan's arm. They all said a final good-bye and headed to their cars. Marcy smiled as she watched Kandy being escorted to the car by Mr. Robinson. She had taken her family for granted and had never thought how Kandy might feel, not having a close family relationship. It warmed her heart to be able to share the Robinsons with her. Kandy soaked up the love they offered.

Chapter 13

BIRTHDAY PARTY

arcy had a wonderful time at her parents' Sunday, and by Monday afternoon, she missed her brother's family, especially the twins. Mark and Janet had told them the good news that they would probably be moving into the area. The company was going to be expanding and the new branch was going to be located in Rossville. It was a town only about thirty minutes from Sheridan and twenty minutes from Lakeland Grove. They had assigned Mark the job of heading the project. This would mean several business trips to the area until it was further along, then the whole family would move.

Tuesday evening, her mom called. They were going to have a little birthday celebration for the girls Friday evening. Their birthday wasn't until Saturday, but since Mark and Janet were going to be leaving Saturday morning, Mrs. Kelman proposed they celebrate the evening before.

"At least it won't be so hard saying goodbye this time, knowing that they are going to be coming back before long. I hope that they will be moving to Sheridan, then... just a minute, Sweetheart." Mrs. Kelman laid the phone down and Marcy could hear two little voices in the background. Presently Mrs. Kelman got back to Marcy. "I'm sorry for the interruption. Mark and Janet went out for supper with someone and I offered to watch Chrissie and Beth. I'm feeding them just now and they insisted that I pray for their food." Mrs. Kelman seemed perturbed at that.

"Did you?"

"Yes. I should know how by now, I've certainly heard enough prayers. I think that Mark and Janet are going too far. They actually encourage the girls to pray as much as they do. They pray every time they eat and then they pray when they go to bed. Last night they wanted me to read them a bed time story. They didn't want the ones you and Mark heard growing up; they wanted one out of the Bible! And Mark! He wanted me to go to Church with him Sunday morning! I think that they go a lot now. He said they enjoy it. Can you believe that?"

"Well, they seem happy, Mom."

"Yes, I guess they do. I just hope that it doesn't go to their heads and they get too serious about it. He said that it was 'fulfilling', whatever that means. I thought that he was leading a rather 'full' life before he got into this religion stuff."

"Maybe he was doing a lot, but felt... I don't know... like he was lacking something and this fills whatever it was." Marcy sighed as she remembered how Mark had seemed to fit in at Church, and her voice got softer, "I know sometimes I do."

"Posh and nonsense, Marcy. He wasn't lacking a thing. He has a good family, a good job, nice home... If you feel like you're lacking something, it just because you're not married with a family."

"Mom, please don't start on that."

"Well, when are you going to listen to me? You need to go out more and meet more men. You work at the grocery store, and not even where you get to meet the public. You're stuck in the office. I think that you ought to ask your boss if you can change jobs."

"I don't want to change jobs, Mom, I..."

"It wouldn't be so bad if you didn't hole yourself up on your back porch..."

"Mom, please. I enjoy my pottery. I meet plenty of people. Now, please, is there anything that you want me to bring on Friday? Would you like me to bring the cake? They'll do a special one at our store's bakery. They have some cute designs."

"You changed the subject, Marcy." Mrs. Kelman sounded upset with her daughter.

"I know I did. I don't want to discuss the other one anymore. Now about the cake," Marcy persisted.

"I don't know what Mark and Janet were planning."

"Well, have one of them call me when they get in. Okay?"

"Fine."

"I'll talk to you later, okay? Love you, Mom."

"Love you, too."

Marcy sighed as she hung up the phone. Her mother was definitely not happy with her. Mark was the one that called her later that evening.

"Marcy, Marcy," he teased, "Can't we even go out once without you upsetting your mother?"

"She's still upset?"

"Not really, she just mentioned it. I think Dad must have worked his charm on her. So what was it about this time?"

"Guess."

"Same thing, huh."

"Yep."

"Stick to your guns on this one, Spitfire," he sympathized.

"I plan on it!"

"Good! So Mom said that you would get a cake?"

"The store has a very good bakery. I was thinking that I could get one from there," she informed him. They talked about the cake a little bit, with Mark consulting Janet about every other sentence. They decided on two small cakes, one for each of the girls.

"Say, Mark... could I ask you something?" Marcy hesitated.

"Sure, fire away!" Mark encouraged her. "Oh, sorry, hold your thought."

Marcy could hear little voices in the background calling for "Daddy!" Then she could hear Janet and Mrs. Kelman saying something, too. Marcy wanted to ask him about what her mom had said about Church being fulfilling. But she wasn't sure she wanted to over the phone, or with her mom able to overhear.

"Okay, I'm back," he said as he picked up the phone again. "I'm sorry about the interruption. Don't let me forget to ask you something. Now, what was it you wanted to ask?"

"Go ahead and ask your question first, mine can wait."

"You sure?"

"Yeah, it's not very important anyway."

"If you're sure."

"I'm sure. Go ahead," Marcy yielded.

"Janet thought that we could invite the Robinsons. Do you think they would come?"

"Ryan told me that his parents are going out of town on Thursday and won't be back until late Saturday evening."

"That's too bad. I'd like a chance to see them again. Why don't you invite Ryan over then? If he's going to be alone anyway, he might like to come over for dinner."

"Well, I could ask him, I guess."

"Great! That will help get rid of the cake!" Mark chuckled.

Mark got distracted again and Marcy let him go. She wasn't sure she wanted to ask her question over the phone anyway.

Thursday evening Ryan called to see if Marcy could call in her raincheck for the picnic. "Saturday is supposed to be a beautiful day. No rain, not too hot, not too cold."

"That sounds like I could hardly refuse," Marcy kidded. "Especially, since I'm dragging you out tomorrow."

"What do you mean you're 'dragging me out'?"

"Tomorrow evening, my nieces are going to be celebrating their fourth birthday. You've been invited to their party. Don't worry; it's not a big thing. There won't be a lot of children, just my parents, Mark, Janet and me. And you don't have to bring a present. They're going to have more than they know what to do with already. Your parents were going to be invited too, but I already told Mark that they were out of town. If you don't want to or already have other plans, they'll understand."

Marcy heard Ryan chuckle softly. "Marcy Kelman," he said in mock firmness, "Do you realize that this is the first time that you asked me to do anything with you in almost ten years? I was beginning to think that our friendship was all one-sided."

"Well, will you go or not?"

"Actually, I had lunch with Mark yesterday and he already asked me. I'm looking forward to going. I was thinking that I could pick you up about five, if you'll be off work in time, then we could ride together."

"You're cruel. You just wanted me to feel guilty. I'm getting off early tomorrow, so riding together would work fine. No sense in taking two cars when one will work just as well!"

"Humph! So it's a matter of conservation and not that you'd like my company, huh?"

"You know better."

"Well if my company is so desirable, would you like it tonight?" Ryan sounded hopeful.

"Yes, I would. But I have work to get done. And if I play tonight, I won't be able to play on Saturday. I'll have to work Saturday morning as it is."

"In that case, I'll leave you alone. Go get your work done, and I'll see you tomorrow!"

Ryan arrived early Friday evening, and Marcy was ready and waiting for him. Her day had gone exceedingly well. She got the work done extra fast at the store, and even had time to do a little work on her pottery. To top it off, it was payday and she found that she had received an unexpected raise.

"Ha! My chauffeur has finally arrived!" She said as she opened the door before he was able to ring the bell. She was in a good mood and the smile that spread from ear to ear, confirmed it.

"Hello yourself!" he grinned back at her. "Are you ready to go?" he asked as he stepped through the door.

"Sure am, but I could use your help." She handed him one of the cakes and picked up the other cake and a shopping bag containing presents.

"That's what chauffeurs are for! Two cakes?"

"Two girls with different tastes. It saves hurt feelings."

They had a delightful ride to Sheridan. Ryan remembered how Marcy liked to take scenic routes, so he took the river road instead of the highway.

When he turned onto the river road, they rode in companionable silence for a while. It wasn't the fastest route, but it was the prettiest. The road shared the same wooded areas as the river, and some of the trees were just beginning to change color. The lowering sun reflected off the water into the trees, making the trees glow as if they were giving off a light of their own. Marcy gave a happy, contented, little sigh.

Ryan looked at her. "And what prompted that?"

Marcy looked relaxed and serene.

"Oh, I don't know. Isn't this wonderful? It feels so tranquil, like time has slowed down." Her voice sounded wistful. "Don't you just wish it would stay like this and we could follow this road forever?"

"Dreamer," Ryan chuckled.

"Don't you dream?"

"Sure, but mine aren't monotonous."

"Mine aren't monotonous!" she protested.

"Sure they are! This road, staying just like this, following it forever?"

"This is nice!" she insisted.

"True, but my dreams are better," he teased.

"How so?"

"Mine have endings. They aren't just left up in the air. I could dream your dream; I'd just finish it, that's all."

"Okay, finish my dream."

Ryan smiled. "Time slows, and the road never ends... but we'd run out of gas and it would get dark and we'd have to walk miles and miles to the closest station. By the time we got there it would be closed, and we'd have to sit outside all night long on a hard bench, tired, cold and hungry, waiting for it to open in the morning. They wouldn't have anything that we could eat for breakfast, either, because it's one of those 'last chance' gas stations with just one pump and a cash register. The attendant is one of those old codgers with missing teeth that likes to 'chaw on his tobbaccy' and spit the juice at your feet, just missing your shoes. So we'd have to walk back to the car lugging a heavy gas can and with no appetite now, after seeing the tobacco juice that was squirted at us. By the time we got to the car, the sun would be at its zenith and we'd be tired and hot. And you would be cranky. It would be late when we got home, and we'd miss the picnic tomorrow, which would be really sad, because now we're hungry again. The road coming back would be just as long as going out, and there are no restaurants on this road, as you can tell."

Marcy groaned. "Oh, Ryan! That's not the way to dream! And why would I be cranky? Why wouldn't you be the cranky one?"

158

"Of course that's not the way to dream. That was your dream. I just finished it for you. And you would be the cranky one because it's your dream. I would be the guy in the dream – the dream guy – and you know that dream guys never get cranky!" He chuckled at his own joke at Marcy rolled her eyes in response.

"Now if it were my dream," he continued, "I would have made sure there was a spare tank of gas, so when it ran out the first time, we could switch over and then know it was time to head back. And it doesn't get dark, you see, until we get back. In my dream we would still be able to go on the picnic tomorrow," he grinned at her. "I just use a little forethought and planning when I dream. It works out much better that way."

Marcy didn't know how to respond to him, so she just smiled and shook her head. Ryan's eyes turned back to the road, but Marcy's eyes didn't leave his face. She loved sharing this time with him. A sudden feeling of emptiness stole over her. There was something lacking in her life. What, she didn't know, but she knew Ryan had the answer. But how could she ask when she didn't know what the question was? It was just a vague, wordless, achy, feeling deep inside her.

Something stirred within her then boiled up into an almost overwhelming urge to be close to him. She wanted his arm to reach out and pull her close to his side. She wanted to wrap her arms around his chest and lay her head on his shoulder, to hang on to him and for him to hold her. She wanted...

Marcy faced the front again and forced her mind back on the scenery. It didn't matter what she wanted.

As they pulled up to the security gate and gave their names, a horrible thought came over Marcy. What if her mother thought Ryan was her boyfriend and said something? That would be embarrassing for both of them. It sent a panicky feeling shooting through her.

"Oh, no!" she cried just barely audibly.

"Is something wrong?" Ryan asked as they waited for the security guard. "Don't tell me you forgot something and we have to go back for it!"

"Huh?" Marcy looked at him blankly. Thoughts jumbled through her mind, trying to find a remedy for what hadn't even happened yet.

The guard let them through.

"I asked what was wrong."

"Oh, nothing," she spoke out loud, "yet," she mumbled.

"You sure?" he asked, not convinced by her quiet exclamation.

She nodded her head, "I just thought of something, that's all." She pointed the way to her parents' home.

Marcy rang the doorbell and Janet was the one that greeted them. She took the cake from Marcy, and looked at the one in Ryan's hands, exclaiming how cute they were. Mark greeted them next. Then Mrs. Kelman came up. She was happy as always to see Marcy, but when she saw that a man had come in with her daughter, her face really lit up with hope.

Marcy and Mark saw it at the same time. Marcy felt rattled not knowing how to head off what she knew was coming. Mark caught the silent plea for help on Marcy's face and neatly stepped in.

"Mom, you remember Ryan Robinson, don't you? I had lunch with him on Wednesday and asked him over tonight. I thought it would give us a little chance to finish the catching-up we started Wednesday. We imposed on him further and had him pick up Marcy. No sense driving two cars out here when one would do just as nicely."

Mrs. Kelman's face looked disappointed, but she smiled and welcomed him warmly anyway. "Of course I remember Ryan. I wouldn't have recognized you though. It's been a long time, and you were just a teenager, then. I'm glad you could come over tonight."

Ryan caught the looks that Mark and Marcy had exchanged and watched the expression change on Mrs. Kelman's face. As Ryan followed Marcy into the living room, Marcy whispered "I owe you one," to Mark, to which he winked and responded "I'll remember."

When Mark took the presents from Marcy and moved ahead, Ryan leaned forward and whispered, "What was that all about?"

"You don't want to know, believe me."

Supper was soon ready to eat. Marcy watched Mark curiously as he asked the blessing on the food. Beth kept her eye on Ryan from her position across the table from him. Half way through supper, she piped up, looking at Marcy. "Is he the man we liked together in church?"

Ryan laughed. "I hope so!" he answered, "It was my leg you had your feet on!"

This satisfied Beth and she nodded, looking again at Marcy. "Do you still like him today?"

Marcy nodded, amused.

"So do I," Beth responded on a sigh and turned her attention to her potatoes.

Cake was served after the supper dishes were cleared. Two lusty rounds of "Happy Birthday to You" to each of the girls prompted them to want it sung to them again. But Grampa didn't think the candles would last that long, so they made much ado about blowing them out. When the cake was eaten, the presents were opened with great delight.

The adults drifted into the living room to visit, while the girls played with their toys on the floor. Soon both the girls were yawning and Janet had them tell everyone good night and took them off to bed.

"Your children sure are cute," Ryan commented to Mark as they watched them leave. "I bet their other grandparents are going to miss them when you move."

"Yes, they will. But they think that it's great that they'll get to know my parents better. And there will be plenty of trips, I'm sure, so they won't forget them."

"Do you have plans yet, about where you're going to be living when you move?"

Mrs. Kelman spoke up. "If I get my way, it will be in Sheridan. There seems to be units in this complex available fairly regularly. They could put their names in now. That would be perfect."

"Now, Mom, you know that we're thinking about living in Rossville." Mark addressed Ryan. "There's a new subdivision going up near where the new branch is, and we understand their school system is very good, too. If we didn't move there, our next choice would be Lakeland Grove, because it's smaller."

"In case you're interested, Albert Silvers is looking to sell his house. He's not listing it and the price he's asking is far below market value. He talked to Dad about buying it the other day. Dad's not interested right now, but Mr. Silvers asked if he would keep an ear out for a possible buyer. He said if he put it on the market, he'd have to get it shipshape, and he doesn't want to expend the energy."

"Is that the one on the corner of Cobblewood and Meadows?" Mark asked.

Ryan nodded.

"Now Mark, why would you even think about that monstrosity?" Mrs. Kelman interjected.

"Oh Mom!" Marcy interrupted, "That house isn't a monstrosity! It's gorgeous! I've always wanted to see the inside. I love the outside and the inside has to be just as great! I use to dream about living in that house! That'd be wonderful if they could get it! Then I could come over to visit and babysit all the time." Marcy's speech was passionate.

"If it's so great, Marcy, why is he selling it? You're just a romantic. It must be ready to fall apart by now," chided Mrs. Kelman.

Mr. Kelman spoke up. "It should be in pretty good shape, actually. He always took good care of it. He redid a lot of things not that long ago. He had just re-roofed it before we moved. He was in the process of rewiring. I know they added insulation, and replaced the siding and windows the summer before. It can't be in that bad of shape. Why's he letting it go for so little?"

Ryan agreed. "He said that he didn't need it anymore and that who-ever buys it might want to fix up the inside a little. He said he feels like he just rattles around in all that room since his wife died. He's eighty-three now and wants to move to the retirement complex. It's smaller and he wouldn't have the maintenance and upkeep. They didn't have any children, and there's no other family, so there's no one to leave it to when he dies."

"Will you consider it?" Marcy pressed her brother.

"Well, like I said, our first choice is to live in Rossville."

Marcy appealed to Janet, who had returned from putting the girls to bed. "It has a wonderful yard with nice trees. The back is fenced in. It's the best house in the neighborhood, probably the whole town. You should at least go look at it, you'd fall in love with it."

Janet smiled. "You sound like you already are in love with it. Wouldn't you feel like we're stealing your house if we bought it? Why don't you buy it?"

"I wish I could. Since I can't, the next best thing would be that someone I loved had it."

The conversation moved to different topics, and much too soon it was time to go home. It wasn't as hard saying goodbye this time, because Mark would be back on business trips before long and Janet and the girls might accompany him on some of the longer ones.

As Ryan pulled out of the drive, Marcy watched Mark and Janet as they stood with their arms around one another. They seemed so con-tent. She remembered last Christmas there were several tense moments between them. Mark had been moody and Janet, although still sweet, hadn't smiled as much either. There had been a sense of sadness in her eyes. They must have gotten everything worked out, because they seemed happier and more in love now than before. When Janet hugged her goodbye, she said she was sorry that they didn't get to spend more time with her alone, and that they were praying for her. It took Marcy aback, and wanted to know why, but she didn't ask. All that came out was the inane comment, "Thanks, I probably need it."

She had tried to get together with Mark and Janet this week, but time and schedules didn't permit. She had forgotten to ask Mark about church being fulfilling. There really wasn't a chance tonight. And now the opportunity was gone. Marcy sighed. Oh well, it would have to wait. At least he would be back before long.

"You must have a lot of those stored up inside of you."

"What?"

"A lot of sighs. You sigh a lot and each one must say something different, because they all sound different. Want to share what that one was about?"

She glanced at Ryan. Would he know what Mark meant? Undoubtedly, but could she ask him? She wasn't sure.

"I was just thinking about Mark and Janet. Mom made a comment the other day, and I wanted to ask Mark about it and I forgot." Marcy's voice softened, wistful. "They seem so happy."

Marcy felt Ryan looking at her. She turned to meet his gaze.

"Marcy?" He looked as if he were trying to decide whether to say something. He evidently decided against it. He shook his head, "Nothing," and put his attention on driving again.

"What! You can't just say 'Marcy?' then stop."

He looked at her again with the same look, and then a smile slowly crept across his face. "Oh, I was just thinking that you should have asked Chrissie if you could keep her barrettes. I thought the way she stuck all of them in your hair was brilliant. They did something for you."

Marcy could tell that wasn't what he was going to say, but he obviously didn't want to share it, so she wouldn't push it. "Yes, I know," she kidded back, "They made me 'bootiful.'"

Chapter 14

SATURDAY AT THE PARK

The weather forecasters had been right about Saturday morning. They had said it would be clear and sunny, with temperatures in the lower 70's. When Marcy had gotten up, there had been a nip in the air which promised to burn off by midmorning. It was going to be a beautiful day.

Marcy's 'outlook' matched the weather. She felt bright and sunny enough that even if there had been clouds, her disposition would drive them away. It was with eager anticipation that she went to work to get as much accomplished as she could. She knew that if she felt productive this morning, she wouldn't feel guilty picnicking this afternoon. And she didn't want anything to spoil the picnic.

And productive she was. Everything just seemed to be going right. She felt creative, and when she tried something, it worked out well. At eleven o'clock she stopped, looked at her work neatly arranged on the shelves, and felt that she had accomplished much.

It didn't take her long to clean up her work area, so she had plenty of time to clean herself up. She was waiting when Ryan rang the doorbell.

There were a lot of people that had the same idea as Ryan and Marcy. The main lot at the park was almost full. The picnic areas were crowded.

"Are you hungry?" Ryan asked.

"No, are you?"

"Not really. So what do you say to working up an appetite first? I thought maybe we could rent a boat for a while, if they're not all taken."

Marcy thought that sounded like fun, and they headed to the boat rental area. The row boats were taken, but there were still canoes and paddle boats. The canoes were the same ones that were for rent when Ryan and Marcy were kids and they looked like relics left over from an old theme park. They were painted when they needed it, but it was still the same colors – butter cream yellow, salmon pink, lime green, and a dull turquoise. The stern swooped up to about three feet above the sides then curled into a flattened out disc-shape that trailed slightly behind. Here, white numbers were hand-painted to identify the canoe.

They donned the life preservers and got into number fourteen, a salmon pink one, while an attendant steadied it. Ryan took up the paddle and Marcy followed suit. She had been in a canoe only a couple of times, and had left the propulsion of the canoe to the other two people with her. Now there were only the two of them, and she felt obliged to help. She was sitting in front of Ryan, and was concentrating hard on getting away from the most crowded part of the lake. She dipped and pulled her paddle hard, switching sides every little bit, but they didn't seem to be making very good progress. The canoe didn't seem to go in any direction for very long, or very fast.

"Marcy."

She turned her head to look at Ryan.

"What are you doing?"

"I'm trying to help you row."

He grinned. "A canoe is paddled, silly, not rowed. Where are you going?"

"I don't know. I thought the same place you were."

"Do you know where I was heading?"

"No."

"That might explain why we aren't going anywhere," he reflected. "Can two walk together unless they are agreed?"

Marcy looked back, past Ryan. She thought that she had expended enough energy to get half way across the lake, and they couldn't be more than fifty feet from the dock.

"Let's work together on this, shall we? Or did you want to stay in this spot?"

Marcy grinned sheepishly at him. "I haven't ever really done this before."

"I was beginning to wonder," he kidded. "Tell you what, why don't you do two strokes on your left, then switch and do two on your right. Then we'll start over with two on the left. Okay? Let's head over to that little island over there."

"Am I supposed to steer?"

"No, you just paddle. I'll 'steer.'"

Marcy nodded and dipped her paddle twice on the left, as Ryan called out 'stroke, stroke,' then switched. Or at least she tried to switch. She didn't get her paddle up far enough and knocked it against the canoe, throwing off her rhythm. So when he said 'stroke' for the other side, she felt that she was behind and had to make up for it. She wasn't fast enough, making her feel farther behind.

She turned to him, "Can you stroke slower?"

"Sure," he replied. "Stroke... stroke... switch."

Marcy turned back to paddling, still not mastering getting the paddle to the other side smoothly. She didn't see the laughter in Ryan's eyes. Marcy had always been willing to do her part in things and worked hard to do her share, but she was not known for coordination.

She turned to him again, "Do you think we could do maybe four strokes on a side before we switch?"

"Sure. Stroke... stroke... stroke... stroke... switch," he chanted, trying to help her get in rhythm.

Her strokes were uneven and when Marcy looked again, she was disappointed that they hadn't really gone that much farther. This time when she switched, she hit the paddle on the side of the canoe, and dislodged it from her grip. Ryan neatly caught it as they floated past it.

"You know, Marcy, sometimes you're a bit of a fruit loop."

She splashed water at him. "I'm trying!"

He chuckled. "I know you are. You've been working really hard at it. Why don't you take a break and just let me handle it for a while?"

"You can do it by yourself?"

"Well, I can take a shot at it, anyway."

"Okay." Marcy pulled her paddle in, and just relaxed a bit. "Could you pull over?"

"You mean like pulling a car to the side of the road?" he teased.

"Yes, silly. Pull to the edge of the water."

"Don't tell me... you need to get out because you didn't go before we left home, right?" He started heading to the edge of the lake.

Marcy laughed. "No, I just want to turn around. If I'm going to just sit, I might as well turn around so that we can talk."

"I don't need to go to the 'edge' for that, you can do it here."

"But won't I tip the canoe?"

"Not if you do it right." He told her how to do it and with much trepidation, she managed without capsizing the small craft.

Marcy enjoyed facing backward, talking to Ryan. She enjoyed watching the easy and graceful way his arms moved, his muscles seemed to hardly notice as he dipped and pulled the paddle. His strokes were even and powerful. The canoe moved through the water quietly and smoothly. She was surprised how far they had gone. They were moving much faster since she quit. She saw now that she had been more of a hindrance than a help.

"'Take a shot at it', my eye!" she huffed, "Where did you learn to handle a canoe?"

He grinned at her. "I started to get interested in camping and taking river trips my junior year at the university. That's what I like to do when I take vacations or long weekends. I just picked it up. Paddling a canoe in a calm lake doesn't require a great deal of skill. It's not all that hard, you know," he teased.

Marcy made a face at him and then watched the scenery silently for a while. She sat contentedly listening to the rhythm of the paddles dipping in the water, and the quiet song the water sang as the canoe parted it and glided through. The breeze, coupled with the gentle rocking, proved to be very relaxing.

Marcy turned her attention to Ryan's face. It too, was content, as he looked out across the lake. All was well with him. Peace and serenity were written not only on his face, but also in his very presence. This was both comforting and disquieting to Marcy. Ryan felt Marcy's eyes upon him and looked at her.

"Penny for your thoughts." Ryan kept his voice quiet in an effort to not interrupt the sweet tranquility he was feeling.

"They're not worth that much, I'm afraid." She gave a nervous half-chuckle and flipped her hand nonchalantly, "It's beautiful out here."

He nodded and smiled softly, then turned his attention back to what held it before. Marcy looked to where she thought Ryan was looking, to see if something out there was the reason for his state of mind. Nothing. There was nothing different than the scenery she had been looking at that she could see. Marcy was surprised to see how close they were to the island to which Ryan had said they were going. By looking at his eyes, one would think he was looking at something much further away.

Ryan had sensed the change in Marcy before he had met her eyes. She had seemed relaxed and carefree, and now there was a restlessness about her. He had caught her off guard when he looked at her. He caught her eyes intently searching his face, trying to find answers to silent questions. He saw the intent look leave and be replaced by embarrassment of being caught staring at him. She evidently didn't want to share what she had been thinking. He turned his attention away from her to give her back the space he had invaded. Marcy remained restless.

"Would you like to get out and stretch?"

Marcy looked around. They had neared the little island. She looked back at the shore from whence they had come, amazed at how far away it seemed. She nodded. Ryan paddled the canoe until the bow bumped up onto the shore. Marcy jumped out and held onto it until Ryan got out. He pulled it further up on the shore so it wouldn't float away.

Marcy worked the kinks out of her legs and thoughts as they explored the small piece of land. There was evidence that this had been someone's camping spot.

"We should have brought the picnic basket. We could have picnicked here," Ryan observed.

"I bet you're getting hungry, you've been doing all the work."

"A little, but I'll survive," he conceded. "Are your legs working again?"

"Sure. Want me to paddle back?"

"I'd like to eat sooner than that!" he teased. "I'll let you know if I get tired."

Marcy watched as Ryan pushed the canoe back out into the water with just the bow touching the land, and then in one fluid motion was in the boat. This action pushed the canoe further out into the water, and Ryan paddled it up again.

"Come on, your turn!" he urged her.

"I'm not sure that I can do that." Marcy responded looking doubtfully at the water and the bobbing craft's tenuous hold on the land. She had never learned to swim since being in water was not a favorite activity. Being dry in a boat *on* the water was okay, but she was afraid of being submerged. Being in the water with a life preserver on was too close to that for her comfort.

"Sure you can. I'll try to keep it close. Grab the edge where I did and pull it to you as you reach for it with your first foot. Then when that foot is established, push off with the other."

Marcy grabbed the canoe and pulled it to her as she reached out with her foot. The canoe wobbled, and her foot went back down onto the shore.

"That's okay, it'll rock, but it won't tip over. Try again."

Marcy tried again, and this time managed to get the foot in, but she was afraid to lift her other foot from the stable ground. Her first foot didn't feel at all stable and she didn't want the other one flailing around behind her, upsetting her balance. She found herself being pulled in two as the canoe was backing away from shore.

"Scoot it closer!"

"I'm trying, but you're pushing it away. Pull your other foot in."

Marcy's reach to the canoe was getting longer, causing her back leg to get closer to the water, and her center of gravity was starting to shift to the outside of the canoe. Something was going to have to give, and Marcy had the horrible feeling that she might not get out of this situation still dry. She shifted her weight and pulled her foot back out of the boat, putting it back on dry land. This left her hands on the edge of the canoe, bent in half, bridging land and canoe. Ryan paddled hard to push the canoe back to land. Marcy dug her toes in, bent her knees and torso, and with supreme effort pulled her upper body closer to her feet.

Ryan shook his head and laughed. "Why did you do that? You were almost in!"

"The only thing I felt 'almost in' was the water."

"Well you almost made it there getting back out! Come on, try again. This time go a little faster, you won't have as much time to think about falling in," he encouraged her.

Marcy looked at him in the boat, trying to figure another way in. "Can you get back out and hold it still while I get in?"

Ryan chuckled. "Yes I can, but you probably won't like having to change places, if you didn't like the way this felt."

"I'll take my chances. At least I'll be in the canoe."

Ryan climbed back out and held it steady for Marcy to climb in.

"You're going to have to move back so I can get in," he informed her as she sat where she stepped in. She stood up to move back and as she lifted her foot to take a step, the canoe rocked under her weight shift. She immediately sat back down.

"Can't you hold it still?"

"I was." Ryan chuckled. "Stay semi-squatted, keeping your center of gravity low. Keep your feet along the center as you move."

Marcy tried to obey Ryan's instructions and managed to get far enough back so Ryan could get in. She watched as once again, Ryan launched and entered the boat easily with agility and grace.

"Okay. Ready to trade places?"

Marcy nodded and listened to his instructions on how to change places safely. When she went to do it though, she found she was very reluctant to let go of the sides of the rocking canoe.

"It's not going to tip over, Marcy, just rock. You have to let go, or I'll have to step over you."

"I can't. I'm afraid I'll fall in."

"Why didn't you tell me you were afraid of boats? We didn't have to go canoeing," he sympathized.

"I'm not afraid of boats. I'm afraid of being in water. I didn't know that this was going to happen. I thought it was going to be a nice, dry ride."

"Well, so far it is, and I'm trying to keep it that way." He paused, considering what to do. "Why don't you scoot to the middle and hunker down. I'll step over you, okay? It will be pretty rocky, but you'll be able to hang onto the sides."

Marcy nodded and scooted forward, folding herself into as small of a bump as she could. She kept her head down and her eyes squeezed shut. The canoe rocked as she felt Ryan move closer. "Lean to your left, Marcy." She obeyed, not knowing how far to lean. She felt the canoe tip and water wet her fingers. She opened her eyes at this and was startled. The water was much closer to her face than she had anticipated. She jerked back to the center and upright, away from the water, blocking Ryan's movement in the process of crossing over.

Ryan fought to keep his balance. His front leg came down on the right side of her instead of behind her as planned. This tipped the canoe precariously to her right, and water sloshed into the boat. Marcy gave a stifled cry of fright as the water reached her. She flailed her right arm, knocking loose Ryan's hold of the side and leaned back to her left again. This undid Ryan's balance and his back knee hit the bottom of the canoe in front of Marcy. The bottom of the boat was now slippery from the water, and his front leg, losing its traction, shot straight out in front of him. He grabbed for the side again, but missed and fell on top of Marcy, flattening her in the bottom of the boat.

Water had now sloshed in from the other side. Marcy gave another cry of fright and grabbed onto Ryan's life jacket, certain the canoe was either going to tip over or sink. Ryan held still for a second, so the canoe could stabilize a bit and then raised himself up. He looked at Marcy's face, eyes squeeze tightly shut. She was holding her breath and her knuckles were white from her grip on his life jacket.

He spoke in soothing tones, "It's okay. You're safe. You're not going in the water."

Marcy tentatively opened her eyes to establish what Ryan had said was true. The canoe had stopped its pitching. She looked around and realized the boat was not half full of water as she suspected. She let out her breath.

"You can let go of me, now," he smiled.

It was then Marcy realized she was still clinging to his jacket, thereby, not allowing him to get up. She blushed and let go. His smile widened as he got up. Marcy started to get up and Ryan stopped her.

"Stay there a minute. I think that it will be safer," he teased. He moved easily to the stern where he had been headed in the first place. "Okay. Now you can move."

Marcy sat up and scooted to her spot and tried to regain her composure. "I'm sorry," she apologized, "I didn't mean to act like such a baby."

"That's okay. It'd be boring without little thrills every now and again. From now on I'll try to park by a dock for you, though."

Marcy busied herself with trying to scoop the little bit of water out of the boat and back into the lake where it belonged. By the time they got back to the rental dock, the sun had dried their damp clothes except for the parts on which they were sitting.

Marcy stretched when she got out at the dock, glad to be back on something stable. She was surprised that they had been out for as long as they were.

It was almost late afternoon and most of the picnickers were done eating, so there were plenty of open tables. But there were still a lot of people playing games and enjoying the afternoon in the larger picnic areas. Ryan drove to the smaller more remote areas. Most of them were near the lake. They chose a spot that had only two other families. Marcy declared that she was now 'starving' when they got the food out of the basket. Ryan prayed before they ate. Again. Marcy glanced sideways to see if anyone noticed. They didn't seem to.

They watched the other two families as they ate and chatted about unimportant things. Marcy now declared that she was stuffed and had eaten too much. She pushed her plate back and watched Ryan as he ate. Shortly Ryan pushed his plate away. "I think that I should have stopped when you did. Want to recline under that tree while the food settles?"

Marcy nodded. They watched three children, their dog and their father play Frisbee in a cleared area. After about fifteen minutes Marcy glanced at Ryan. He hadn't said anything for a few minutes. His head was tipped back and his eyes were closed. He looked asleep, his breathing had deepened. Marcy smiled at the sight and continued to watch the family play. After several minutes a stray Frisbee flew their direction. Marcy scrambled to her feet and retrieved it. Marcy's movement and the sound of children's voices woke Ryan up. He sat up as Marcy sat back down beside him.

"D'ja have a nice nap?" she grinned.

"I guess I did!" he said as he stretched. "I didn't mean too. Not real exciting company, am I?"

Marcy giggled, feeling in a silly and lighthearted mood, "I wouldn't say that! Watching you sleep was the most thrilling moment of my day!"

Ryan grinned back at her then looked at his watch. "Would you like to take a walk on a trail? We'll have enough time before it gets dark."

"Sure, that'd be fun! I haven't been on any trails since high-school."

"Unless of course, there's something about walking the trails that you're afraid of – in that case, let me know now so I can either avoid them or change my mind about going."

Marcy swatted him playfully and stood up.

They cleaned up the picnic things and stuck them back in the car. There were trails that started near where they were parked, so they didn't have to move the car. The trails seemed to be a popular place to be. There were a lot of people out walking around before it got dark. A couple of kids were upset that they had lost sight of their dog. It pulled out of their hands to give chase to some wild creature. Ryan and Marcy helped them find it. It hadn't gotten too far away before its leash got stuck on a fallen tree branch.

A couple of squirrels were playing in the trees overhead and they stopped to watch their antics for a while. Marcy saw some acorns in the path and picked them up. From then on she started collecting the nicest ones she came across. She had folded the bottom of her t-shirt to form a pouch and by the time they were starting to get near the parking area it was nearly full.

"Is there a reason you're collecting those?" Ryan inquired.

"Not really. I just think they're neat."

"Don't you feel guilty keeping those from the squirrels? Just think. Some poor squirrel might go hungry this winter because you took all his food."

"Ha! They forget where they hide the nuts most of the time anyway."

"That's true, but the ones they forget turn into trees, providing shelter and more food. Now you're depriving their children and grandchildren food and shelter!" he teased her.

Marcy giggled. "I'll take these home and plant them, and when they get bigger I'll bring them back here for your friends. Then they'll have lots of acorn trees to live in! Will that be acceptable to you?" she kidded back.

"Except for one thing."

"What's that?"

"They won't grow acorn trees," Ryan stated.

"Why not?"

"They'll grow oak trees."

"Same thing."

"Nope." Ryan shook his head. "There's no such thing as an acorn tree."

"There should be. Chestnuts grow on chestnut trees. Walnuts grow on walnut trees. Pecans grow on pecan trees. Acorns should grow on acorn trees. I think they ought to change 'oak trees' to 'acorn trees.'"

"It would confuse the squirrels to change the names now. You'd better leave well enough alone."

"I'd like to know how it can be any more confusing to them than having the tree by one name and the nut by another."

"They don't, though." his eyes twinkled with fun.

"What do you mean? Don't they know what kind of tree these come from?"

"They know that oak trees produce those little nuts, alright. They just think they're called oak nuts!" Ryan laughed at her.

"You're the oak nut, Ryan Robinson!"

"Better than being a fruit loop, Marcy Kelman!"

"I believe you're calling me a fruit loop for the second time today!"

"If the name fits..." he chuckled and shrugged.

"Oh!" She uttered the short offended sound and walked ahead a couple of steps. She turned around to face him, walking backwards. "When did you get to start calling names, anyway? I thought you were supposed to be a gentleman!"

"I started calling names the same time you did, my *lady* friend."

"Are you implying that I'm not a lady?" she bantered with him.

"Not at all. But on the other hand... hey! You better watch where you're going!" He reached out to stop her from tripping over an exposed tree root.

"You don't have to tell me how to walk, I know how!" She continued to walk backwards in front of him.

He chuckled to himself. She looked around to see if he saw something she didn't.

"Was that a private joke? Or are you going to let me in on it?"

"I'm not sure if I should." He chuckled again.

"Ryan Robinson, what's so funny?! Tell me!"

"Well, you told me not to tell you how to walk, that you knew how," he paused.

"Yeah," she prompted. "So?"

"I was just thinking that if you knew how to walk as well as you know how to ride your bike, it could be hazardous to your health," he laughed.

"Oh! You!" Marcy grabbed a handful of the acorns in her t-shirt and threw them at him.

"Hey! You asked!"

She grabbed more and continued to pelt him with the nuts. He quickened his pace to grab her throwing hand. She turned and ran, throwing more acorns over her shoulder. He put on some speed and she stopped throwing and turned her attention to running. Ryan gave chase. He could hear her laughing as she ran.

She felt like a kid again, when he used to chase her after she pulled a trick on him. She used to run to his mom or hers and they would protect her, not letting him retaliate. He would always tell her that he would get her later, but he never did. She never did find out what he would've done if he'd actually caught her. It was all a part of the game they played. But neither mom was here to run to now. This thought sent a rush through her as she ran.

When she got back to the picnic area she dodged behind the small pavilion and stopped. She was breathing hard from the run, but she tried to be still to hear where Ryan was. She waited for a bit and couldn't hear him. Maybe she had lost him. She doubted it. He hadn't been that far behind her. She edged to the corner of the building and peeked around. She didn't see him. She slid around that corner and looked back where she had come. Still no sight of him. She did the same thing at the next corner. Still no Ryan.

In fact, there was no Anybody. The other two families had left. Theirs was the only car in the small lot. And the sun's light was waning. It gave her a slightly eerie feeling. She shouldn't have gone behind the building. The suspense was too much. She stepped out away from the building and cautiously headed to where they had eaten their picnic. She knew now, he had to be hiding from her. She was sure he came out of the woods. She didn't call out his name, not wanting to give him the satisfaction of knowing that his game was getting the better of her. As she got closer to the picnic table, she decided that she was just going to sit there and wait him out. Two could play this game.

She didn't make it; he popped out in front of her from behind the closest tree, startling her.

"Ha!" he said as he tried to grab her. Marcy screeched and evaded his grasp. She ran down the lane that led to the lake this time instead of the building. The chase didn't last very long. When she got to the edge of the lake, she didn't know where to run to next. She heard him close behind her and shrieked as he caught her around her waist. She slipped out of his hold and flustered, ran out on the pier as if that would afford her some protection. She came to a sudden halt at the end realizing she was trapped. She turned around to see where he was. He was slowly walking towards her grinning like a cat that caught the canary.

"Now what are you going to do? I don't think that you can get around me. And we both know that you won't take to the water. You're trapped Marcy Kelman!" He was only a few feet in front of her and still slowly closing the distance.

"Ryan Robinson, you let me go! Or I'll..." Her eyes were bright from the thrill of the chase, her breath still coming hard.

"Or you'll what? Tell on me?" He had a sly look on his face. "Do you realize that this is the first time in all the years of chasing you that I ever caught you?" He was directly in front of her now. "It'd be silly to let you go, now wouldn't it?" His eyes were sparkling with mischievousness.

"Well, what are you going to do now that you caught me? You wouldn't do anything mean, so what use is there in not letting me go?" She smiled smugly at him.

Ryan hadn't considered that and searched her face. Marcy's eyes were dancing with fun. The breeze coming off the lake was blowing wisps of hair about her flushed cheeks. The setting sun was casting a soft glow and the water sparkled like jewels behind her. It almost took his breath away; she was beautiful.

Marcy saw the look in his eyes change from mischievousness to something else she hadn't seen there before. The smile slipped from her lips as she lost herself in his eyes' blue depths. He seemed to be examining every feature of her face. She stood transfixed as he raised his hand and gently pushed her hair back with his fingers. She started to tremble as she realized that he was going to kiss her. She was barely able to breathe as he slipped his hand behind her head and lowered his to her. It was a gentle kiss, hesitant, asking permission. Marcy's hands slipped up to his chest of their own volition, partly to steady herself. She felt like she was going to float away. He raised his head.

She opened her lips to say something, but no sound came out. She tried to swallow and couldn't. Her eyes were dark with emotion. They asked him questions. He could feel her hands trembling.

Ryan slipped his other hand around her waist and pulled her to him. His other arm moved down around her shoulders, and he lowered his head once again. Marcy slid her hands to the back of his neck. She relaxed in his arms and melted against him. Ryan shuddered and drew in a breath. He pulled her in tighter. She returned his ardor kiss for kiss.

He lifted his head to look at her again. Her face was soft, her eyes dewy. She wrapped her arms around his chest and nestled her head under his chin, not wanting to let go of him. He had kissed her. He was holding her. And not like a brother. When had his feelings for her changed? It felt good to be snuggled against him and she wanted to stay there.

"Marcy," he spoke gently and tried to look into her face.

"Please don't." Her voice was soft and shaky.

"Is something the matter? Talk to me… Please, Marcy?" He stood there, his chin resting against her soft hair, holding her close. She felt so good in his arms and he wanted to hold her like this forever. He waited for her to respond.

"Nothing's the matter, really. It's just that I didn't know… I thought I was wrong to feel this way about you… I tried not to, but I couldn't… You never gave any indication, always acting like my brother… I've felt so guilty… and now… I didn't know."

The words 'wrong to feel this way' screamed in Ryan's head when she said them. They called to him to resist the temptations at hand. The realization of what he had just done and what he still wanted to do dawned on him. Guilt washed over him and he closed his eyes. "Oh God, forgive me," he breathed.

He moved his hands to her shoulders. He had to get some space between them. Emotions were running too high. At least his were, and he was pretty sure Marcy's were, too. She was still clinging to his chest, talking to him like he had asked. 'Wrong to feel this way' kept echoing in his head.

Marcy sensed, rather than felt that there had been a change in Ryan and stopped speaking. A wall had gone up between them. She realized that she alone was now doing all the holding. She raised her head to look at his face. Gentle pressure on her shoulders caused her to release her hold. Ryan stepped back.

"We'd better go, it's getting late."

He kept his head down and did not look at her. He turned and stepped aside so she could pass. She hesitated, not knowing what just happened. When she stepped off the pier, he walked silently beside her to the car. He kept a space between them. When he opened the car door for her she hesitated before she got in and turned to face him.

"Ryan," her voice was uncertain. "Did I...? I didn't mean to, I'm sorry."

He looked into her eyes then and quickly looked away. He could see the hurt, self-doubt and confusion there. He sighed. "No Marcy, it wasn't you, it's me." He met her eyes briefly again. "I'm so sorry." The look in her eyes hadn't changed. He lowered his eyes again. She didn't understand. How could she? And he couldn't tell her right now.

She stood at the car door a bit longer trying to figure out what happened. The sinking sun caught her eye just before the last of it slipped out of the sky, taking its light with it. She felt like the light had just slipped out of her life with the sun. Only the sky had the sun all day long, and it would have it again tomorrow. She had hers for only a brief moment, and it didn't sound like there was going to be any tomorrow. She felt cheated.

The drive back was in strained silence. She tried to figure out what went wrong. Had she said too much? Revealed feelings he didn't want from her? He had said that it was him and not her. Then why did she feel like she was the one that wasn't good enough? He would say that because he was kind. Marcy looked to Ryan to see if there were any answers there. He looked straight ahead, his face unreadable. She turned back and looked out her side window. This drive seemed to never end, and she wanted it to, desperately.

Ryan pulled into her drive, but didn't shut off the engine as usual. When it became evident that he wasn't going to get out of the car, she opened her own door and started to get out. This would be the first time that he hadn't opened the car door for her or walked her to her house.

"Marcy."

She stopped and looked at him. He still didn't look at her. His voice was quiet, apologetic. "Thank you for a wonderful day."

She nodded, unable to speak. She got out of the car and closed its door by herself, then walked alone to her house.

He waited in the drive to make certain she could get in. She closed the house door behind her, not looking back. She did not want to watch him leave. She wanted to throw herself in her bed and go to sleep. She wanted to wake up in the morning and today just be a dream gone sour, never really happening. When she did wake up in the morning, she'd start the day over. Only she would learn from her dream and wouldn't let Ryan catch her.

Chapter 15

REGRETS

Ryan wanted to walk Marcy to her door. It was hard for him to sit and watch her go alone, but knew that he had better not take her. He watched until she had gone into her house and shut the door. He slumped, head resting on hands that gripped the steering wheel. Ryan felt weary. He took a deep breath, trying to release the tension. He slowly sat up and backed out of the drive. Slowly he drove home.

When he got home, he saw that his parents were still not back from their trip. He looked at his watch. It was only about an hour since the sunset. It felt like it was closer to midnight. He was grateful they were still gone. They would know something was the matter and he couldn't face them. He and his dad had just talked about putting oneself in compromising situations the other week. He knew that what he had done and the accompanying thoughts were just as wrong as if he had taken her to bed. She was not his to have. He knew that believers should not be yoked to unbelievers. And he knew that Marcy didn't believe as he did. He had been praying for her and now he felt like a hypocrite. He'd not only placed them both in a compromising situation, but he had left Marcy hurt and confused.

Ryan trudged up the stairs and showered. After he crawled into bed, he picked up his Bible. Within just a few minutes, he closed it with a sigh, laid it back down and turned out the light. He had read the same passage over four times and still didn't know what he had just read. Lying on his back, he stared into the darkness, waiting for sleep to come.

Marcy woke up tired and not well rested. She groaned. Sunday again; and Kandy had roped her into going to church again. She didn't used to dread Sundays. Why did she seem to lately? Because lately they caused her so much turmoil. *Now wait a minute,* she argued with herself, *that wasn't necessarily true.* There were a lot of things that happened on Sunday she liked. She enjoyed last Sunday. That was because her brother's family was here. What about the Sunday before? She did have a good time at the Robinson's after she snapped out of her bad mood.

The Sundays that she *hadn't* gone to church weren't anything to write home about. In fact, a couple of the Sundays that she hadn't gone to church, she was just as miserable. They had drug by because she was lonely and felt like she was missing something. See, it wasn't because it was Sunday, it was just her.

Kandy arrived at her door in the same disgusting, cheerful, perky mood.

"Good night, Marcy! You look like you're attending a funeral! Why are you wearing such somber colors?"

"Good morning to you, too."

"Well, why the drab outfit?"

"I don't know. I didn't really think about it. I was tired and felt ugly today. I just grabbed something to fit the way I feel I guess."

"Well, you did a good job, you look ugly!"

"Thanks, *friend.*"

"Oh, come on Marcy! Those colors are awful on you. I don't know why you bought them in the first place. They make you look pale and they accentuate the dark circles under your eyes, which really helps you look awful. And look at your hair! Did you even try to do anything with it?" Kandy looked at her watch. "Come on, we've got time." She took a hold of Marcy's arm and propelled her to the bedroom.

"Time to do what?"

"Change your clothes and fix you up. I'm not taking you to church looking like that!"

"Oh, Kandy."

"Don't you 'Oh, Kandy' me! You know as well as I do that how you look has a great deal to do with how you feel. So let's change the way you look and help you feel better!" She made a brief stop in the bathroom to turn on Marcy's curling iron. When she got to the bedroom she went to Marcy's closet and went through her clothes. Marcy sat on the bed and waited.

"Don't just sit there, girl! Peel! And while you're peeling, tell me where your accessories are."

Marcy indicated her bureau drawer, and Kandy started to go through that too. By the time Marcy had gotten out of her outfit, Kandy had another one picked out for her to put on. The blouse's bright colors not only looked more cheerful, but put color in Marcy's cheeks and brought out the beautiful colors in her eyes.

"Much better!" Kandy exclaimed. "Now, let's go fix your hair." Marcy found herself being dragged into the bathroom. Kandy made quick, efficient work of curling her hair and pronounced it easy to work with. She stepped back to look at Marcy. "The hair's much better but the face still needs something." She rummaged through Marcy's makeup.

"I don't normally wear makeup." Marcy complained.

"You don't normally need it." Kandy chirped back. "You want to put it on, or do you want me to?"

"I can do it!" Marcy snapped.

"Good!" Kandy grinned. "This will cover the dark circles and not too much eye shadow, just a hint. Use this color. And here," she handed Marcy a tube of lipstick. "Use this shade."

She grabbed the lipstick from Kandy. "I know how to put on makeup!"

Kandy smiled. "I remember I saw some earrings that should go well with the hair and outfit. I'll go get them," she said tactfully.

When she came back with the earrings, Marcy wasn't quite finished, so she stood in the doorway and watched her. When she was done, Kandy handed them to Marcy.

"Turn around and let me see," Kandy commanded. She looked Marcy over thoroughly. "Come with me."

She led her to the full length mirror in the bedroom. "There now, don't you look better than you looked earlier? And don't you feel better, too?"

Marcy had to admit that she definitely looked better and conceded reluctantly to the other, as well.

"Marcy, you are going to turn heads this morning, let me tell you!"

"Oh, Kandy, I'm not either, you're just saying that because you're my friend," Marcy smiled.

"I told you that you were ugly earlier," She grinned mischievously. "I bet there's at least one head you'd like to turn!"

The smile fell off Marcy's face. "Come on Kandy, we're going to be late."

Kandy drove a little fast, and they got to Church just before Sunday school started. Mr. Robinson and Ryan were already seated in the pew. Kandy reached them first and greeted them cheerfully. They stood up to let the girls in and Mr. Robinson gave them both hugs. Marcy glanced at Ryan, but avoided eye contact. They didn't have time to talk, so it was easy to avoid him. Marcy stepped in first, so that she wouldn't have to sit next to him. And since she was semi-interested in the Sunday School lesson, it helped keep her mind off him as well. When the class was over, Marcy slipped out of the pew, using the excuse of having to use the washroom. There was a line and she was grateful. As she left the washroom, she ran into Mrs. Robinson who was heading to the sanctuary.

"I'm so glad to see you this morning!" She greeted Marcy with the customary hug. "My, but you look especially nice today, Dear. Is there a special occasion?"

"No. Just Kandy," Marcy smiled at her. "She didn't like the outfit I was wearing when she picked me up this morning, so she made me change. She decided she didn't like the way I had my hair either, and fixed it, too."

"Well, I don't know that you could look bad if you tried, but you certainly look very nice this morning!"

"Thank you."

"Ryan said you went canoeing and on a picnic, yesterday. It certainly was a beautiful day for it. Did it wear you out like it did Ryan? He was already in bed when we got home."

Marcy didn't want to talk about yesterday. "Oh, that's right you were out of town, weren't you! How was your trip?"

"It was nice as far as business trips go. I always love to go with George when I can." Marcy kept her talking about her trip until they reached the others.

Mr. Robinson greeted his wife and turned to Marcy. "You know Marcy, I didn't get a chance to tell you this earlier, but you are a vision of loveliness today."

Marcy blushed. "That's very flattering and I'm sure you're exaggerating. But I thank you, anyway. You're very kind."

"Marcy, I do not lie, and I would not lie to you. Ryan," Mr. Robinson turned to his son who was talking to Kandy, "doesn't Marcy look lovely today?"

It embarrassed Marcy that he asked Ryan. She didn't want to look at him, but she was curious how he would respond, so she looked.

Ryan smiled a distant, polite smile as he looked at her. "Yes, she does." Then he turned back to Kandy.

"See, you have two opinions. Now do you believe me?"

Marcy smiled at him. Then it was time for the service to start and she slipped into the pew. Kandy stepped down, instead of letting her pass to where she had sat before. This annoyed Marcy, but she didn't say anything.

She didn't pay much attention to the announcements. Ryan's face stayed on her mind. When she had looked at him, she noticed that he looked especially tired today. She still felt a wall between them. Maybe it was just her imagination. Or maybe it was just her. She was still confused and hurt by what went on yesterday and that was affecting how she was reading Ryan. She made up her mind then to pretend everything was back to normal, as if yesterday didn't happen. She decided she was blowing things out of proportion.

During the song service, it didn't sound to Marcy that Ryan sang with as much fervor as he normally did. Marcy glanced sideways. His posture was as droopy as his voice. He usually stood with his head up and shoulders back. This morning his head was down and his shoulders sagged. His face didn't... didn't what? Marcy still couldn't think of a word that described how the Robinson's faces looked as they worshiped. Shine? Glow? Well, whatever it was, his face wasn't doing it today. Curious.

The message entitled *Walking Upright before God* kept Marcy's attention pretty well. At least the first half did, when he talked about how God's people in the Old Testament had to live by rules and regulations. He called it living under the Law. She got offended when the pastor started talking about how God expects us to uphold standards today. "*I'm not perfect, but neither am I a bad person,*" she reasoned, "*I don't sleep around, I don't cuss, I don't get drunk, I've never killed anyone, nor robbed a bank. And why would he tell that to this crowd, anyway. He should take this sermon into a prison or something!*" She missed most of the message after that. She had let a couple of sentences close her ears to a message that would have answered those questions she was struggling with, had she but listened. Instead, she let her mind wander to other things.

Everyone stood for the altar call. The pastor gave the usual invitation to those who wanted to get saved and to those who, like the Prodigal Son, had walked away from the Lord and wanted to return. This morning he also said that he was inviting anybody who, in any area of their life, was having trouble walking uprightly before God. He asked them to come, kneel at the altar and receive God's grace and forgiveness. She was amazed at how many people were leaving their seats. What amazed her even more was the fact that Ryan left his seat to kneel at the altar. She looked at Mr. and Mrs. Robinson. They didn't appear to be surprised or even concerned.

When the pastor dismissed the people, he asked everyone to please leave quietly out of respect to those who were still at the altar. Everybody stayed quiet, refraining from visiting until they got through the doors to the foyer. Ryan had been one of those that had stayed behind.

Mrs. Robinson extended the usual invitation for Sunday dinner. "Only today we're going out to eat. Since we were gone, I hadn't done the shopping yet. I was stewing over what to fix when George and Ryan said that they wanted to take me out for once."

Kandy and Marcy declined, saying they didn't want to intrude. Marcy wasn't sure she'd feel comfortable spending the afternoon in Ryan's presence.

"Nonsense!" spoke up Mr. Robinson, "If we ate in the dining room instead of the kitchen, would you feel like you were intruding?"

"No," Kandy giggled.

"Well, we're just changing tables, that's all. Only this one is a little farther away from our kitchen."

Kandy accepted and since Marcy rode with Kandy, she did, too. At least they could go home right after the meal instead of hanging around visiting like they usually did.

Ryan walked up just then. Marcy noticed that his posture was closer to what it normally was and not like it had been in church.

"Hi, Dear," his mom greeted him. "Kandy and Marcy are joining us for dinner today. Won't that be lovely?"

Ryan looked at Kandy and smiled. "Yes, it would. Will it ruin your barbeque later?" He spoke to Kandy.

"Nah, I'd eat anyway and Dave doesn't even get off until five."

"I was right, wasn't I?" Kandy gloated in the car, driving to the restaurant.

"Right about what?"

"How you look makes a difference on how you feel. You feel better now that you look better, don't you."

Marcy conceded that she did.

"So what's going on between you two?"

"What do you mean?"

"What's going on between you and Ryan?"

"Nothing, I already told you."

"Huh-uh," Kandy argued. "Things have changed since our last tête-à-tête about men. I would venture to guess through careful observation and my ingenious deductive reasoning that things changed yesterday. Am I right?"

"Has anybody ever told you that you're a snoop?"

"I thought so!" Kandy ignored the accusation. "What happened?"

"I never said anything happened, so what makes you think anything did?"

"You did just now by not answering my question. Besides, Ryan told me, too."

"Ryan told you what happened?! The cad!" Marcy was furious. How dare he speak of private things? At least she thought they were private. "So what was his story? The louse!"

"Hey! Whoa there! He didn't tell me with words, he told me with actions! He didn't mention a thing about yesterday."

"Kandy, you're awful! You tricked me on purpose, you sneak! How could you?" Hurt sprang into Marcy's eyes.

"I wasn't trying to trick you, Marcy, honestly. I am curious, true. But I wouldn't do something intentionally underhanded just to find out. We're best friends, Marcy. Can't we talk about things? Don't you trust me?"

Marcy nodded. "I'm sorry. I shouldn't have flown off the handle. So what did Ryan 'tell' you?"

"Well to begin with, he looked like he didn't sleep last night, either. Then when you slipped out to go to the washroom after Sunday School, he watched you until you were out of sight. There was definitely something in his eyes when he watched you, too. Not like he watched you before, mind you, there was a difference. Someone was talking to him and I don't think he heard what the man was saying until you were out the doors."

"Oh Kandy, you're imagining things."

"No, I'm not. I tried an experiment to see if I was right, and I was."

"I'm afraid to ask."

"Well, after the other man left, I got his attention and started asking him questions about the lesson. He answered me just fine, and we had a good little discussion going, even though he kept glancing at the doors. Then, viola! He changed. Sure enough, you were coming back and he didn't hear a word I said any more. I know because I said, 'well if that were true, then all men should wear miniskirts to church. Wouldn't that be right?' He said yes, he supposed so! When you got closer, he stopped watching you, but his mind still wasn't on what I said, but he was acting like he wasn't the least bit interested in you. Look at the way he commented when his dad asked him about how you looked. Polite, unenthusiastic. And just a bit ago after church? You almost might have not been there! He told me something all right." She paused and looked to Marcy. "So what happened? Did you two have a fight?"

"No, we didn't fight. And I'm not even sure what happened. We went out to the park for a picnic. We went canoeing and took some trails, it was a beautiful day. I enjoyed it immensely and he did too. Just before we left, he kissed me."

"I assume it was not a brotherly kiss?"

Marcy shook her head no.

"And is it safe to assume that you kissed him back?"

Marcy nodded.

"Did it go farther than that?"

Marcy shook her head, again. "No!"

"What's the problem, then?"

"His reaction."

"Marcy, for Pete's sake, will you just please spill it, and not make me drag it out of you piece by piece? We're not far from the restaurant, you know."

Marcy sighed. "After we kissed, he just held me. He told me to talk to him, I assumed about how I was feeling. And so I did. I guess I told him more than he wanted to know. A wall went up between us and that was it." Marcy took a shaky breath and willed the tears away that threatened. "He took me home. He hardly spoke to me. He said it wasn't me, that it was him. He thanked me for a lovely day, and didn't even open the car door or walk me to the house like he usually does. I don't even know what happened for sure." Marcy stared out the window for a moment. "I worked hard to keep my feelings inside. I've looked at him like a brother for so long I felt wrong when I started to get not-so-sisterly feelings for him. He kissed me like he... cared for me. I exposed my feelings and... and... I ruined a friendship." Marcy bit her lip. "I thought that I was imagining things this morning at church, but I guess I wasn't."

"I don't pretend to know what went on or why, but I don't think that he's happy about things either, judging from this morning."

"I guess that I'm a really bad judge of people. That's two strikes against me; first poor Dave, now Ryan."

They were coming to the restaurant. "Would you rather not go? I can run in and make an excuse."

Marcy pondered for a moment then sighed. "No, I enjoy the Robinsons and I don't want to offend them."

Kandy reached over and squeezed Marcy's arm. "Look at me." Marcy obeyed. "Your face is fine. So if you can manage to find a smile, put it on. Gather up the rest of your feelings and tuck them in your purse and they'll never know." Kandy turned into the parking lot and found a space as far from the entrance as she could to give Marcy more time to compose herself.

The dinner didn't go too badly. Marcy didn't really feel like talking, and Kandy, (bless her heart,) steered the conversation by asking a lot of questions about the message that morning. She wondered if she had heard the same sermon the rest of them had. The questions Kandy asked must have been about the part that she had tuned out. She watched Kandy's face. By all indications, she really wanted to know the answers and wasn't just making small talk. Listening to the conversation, Marcy began to wish that she had paid better attention in church.

Ryan was attentive to Kandy and polite to Marcy. Kandy observed Marcy and Ryan's behavior during dinner. Marcy was doing a good job of putting on a happy face. She didn't talk much, but she smiled and laughed. She glanced often at Ryan. Ryan avoided looking at Marcy altogether, much less making eye contact with her. The one time he did, his demeanor changed and he excused himself to use the washroom. Kandy thought that Mr. and Mrs. Robinson felt something was unusual, also. They seemed to watch Ryan's behavior with questions in their eyes.

Later that afternoon Mr. Robinson informed Ryan that Mr. Silvers had asked him if he would handle the transactions on his house.

"I was thinking about running over and talking to him, would you care to take a walk over there with me?"

"Did he find a buyer already?"

"No, there have been a few people looking though. I just need to talk to him about some preliminaries, and I thought that he would enjoy a bit of company today. He told me Sunday always seemed to be the longest day of the week for him. It's not that far and it would be a nice walk. Get a little stretch in after sitting around all afternoon."

Ryan smiled at his dad. "Sure, I'll go with you."

Ryan was curious what the inside of the Silvers house looked like, anyway. He'd never been in it, but like Marcy, he thought the outside looked interesting. The Silvers' house had been one of the things he had always teased her about while they were growing up. They always passed it going to and from school, and almost without fail she would look it over intently as they passed. About once a week she would say, "Someday I'm going to live in that house." He never let her know that he was almost as intrigued by it as she was. He had too much fun teasing her about her preoccupation with it. If her passionate defense of it the other night was any indication, she still felt the same way. Ryan smiled at the thought.

Mr. Silvers was glad to have them stop by. He was very chatty, and insisted on taking them to every room in the house. And with each room he reminisced about pleasant memories that room brought to mind. As they went along, he also told of each improvement that was made.

Ryan found himself thinking of how Marcy would see it. This house had a closed in back porch that was much larger than the one at her present home. It had been used as a utility room once upon a time and had a place for a sink.

It also had a large cellar lined with shelves that were used for storing canned food. Mr. Silvers had white washed it not long before his wife died. She had liked to preserve food from the garden, but didn't like dreary food cellars, so he painted everything white and put in more lights. Ryan pictured the shelves lined with Marcy's pottery. There were still ruffled yellow gingham curtains hanging in the little window. When the house was built the entrance had been outside. But when the previous owners had built on the back porch, they made sure that it surrounded the cellar doors and fixed the stairs leading to it.

They had a pleasant time with Mr. Silvers, and after two and a half hours, he was still reluctant to let them leave.

The next week lasted an eternity for Marcy. The flu was going around and Dave asked her if she would work extra hours at a cash register to help fill in for those that had caught it. She reluctantly agreed, knowing that even with her help they were still short workers. She worked over sixty hours that week. *"It'll make for a nice paycheck,"* she encouraged herself. She stayed up late at night to work on pottery so that she could keep building her inventory for Christmas. She usually started working on that right after Christmas, but this year, sales were good, and she kept depleting her stock. That put her behind for the holidays.

Saturday morning, Marcy woke up feeling like she had the last three mornings: like something the cat drug home. Only today she felt worse. For the last five nights she averaged only four hours of sleep a night and it had started to take its toll. She showed up at her appointed cash register just barely on time, and after just fifteen minutes her feet were hurting. Dave came by about ten-thirty, and did a double take when he saw her. No one was in her line at that moment.

"Good grief, Marcy! You look awful! Please don't tell me you're getting sick, too!" Dave had worked extra hours that week, also, but they had seen very little of each other, their schedules hadn't coincided very often.

"Thank you for the compliment, and no, I'm not getting sick."

"Good! So what's wrong?"

"Just tired. Between working all the hours here, and trying to keep up with my pottery demands, I'm working more than two full time jobs."

"I'll try not to use you as much this next week. It seems the flu is slowing down. I don't think there are too many people left to get it, at least in this store."

Marcy shifted from foot to foot as they talked, trying to relieve the ache.

"What time do you get off?"

"Five."

Dave nodded and looked down the line of cashiers. He looked at his watch and left without saying goodbye. She didn't have much time to notice, a lady with two small children started unloading her overflowing cart in Marcy's line. Thirty minutes and eight shopping carts later, Dave came back and told Marcy to close her line and take a break. She obeyed and when she started to head to the break room, Dave caught up with her and steered her towards the office.

"Here," he said, motioning to the old couch that was being 'stored' in there. "Put your feet up and rest. Fall asleep if you like. No one should disturb you. I'll get you in an hour."

"But my lunch is only half an hour."

"Not today," he smiled. He turned out the light and shut the door as he left.

"He's sweet," Marcy reflected as she scrunched down on the couch with her head resting on its arm. She fell asleep within five minutes.

Fifty minutes later, Dave woke her up and handed her a Styrofoam cup. Marcy pushed herself up on her elbow and blinked owlishly at Dave sitting on the edge of the couch. Having slept soundly and feeling disoriented, she was trying to figure out why Dave was waking her up and why he was handing her a cup. Dave grinned at her.

"It's orange juice. I thought that it would help you wake up."

Marcy sat up straighter, put her feet on the floor and took the cup from Dave. "Thank you, that's really nice of you."

"You sure were sawing logs a few minutes ago!"

"I don't snore!"

"Really?" Dave grinned at her.

"Really."

"Now tell me. How would you know? I believe you sleep alone."

"I don't *feel* like I snore."

Dave laughed outright at her. Marcy drank the orange juice.

"I changed your schedule. You can get off at three today. I looked over who was on and who was coming in and I think that we'll be able to handle it. You can go home and relax. Okay?"

"Thank you, Dave. You're so thoughtful."

"Kandy is coming up to my place at seven. We were going to watch a movie together. If you would like to, it'd be great if you could come, too. We haven't done anything together for a while."

Marcy smiled at him. "That sounds like fun, but may I let you know later? I had thought about working on some more pottery when I got home and then trying to get to bed at a decent time."

"I don't think that it would hurt you to take a break for a couple of hours. You wouldn't have to stay late."

"Okay. With one stipulation,"

"What's that?"

"If I fall asleep during the movie, you have to promise not to make cracks about snoring."

Marcy enjoyed the evening with Dave and Kandy. It was relaxing and she definitely needed the break. She smiled to herself when she noticed that Kandy certainly felt at home there.

Later that night when she crawled into her own bed, the thought struck her that Ryan hadn't called her all week. Of course she was too busy to care and maybe he had tried and she wasn't home. *"It wouldn't be the first time that he hadn't called her all week,"* she reasoned. *"Oh well, she'd see him in church in the morning."*

Just after she turned out her light, Ryan called. Rather than the warm greeting she had become used to from him, it was on the formal side. *"I might as well be a business acquaintance,"* she thought. The rest of the conversation wasn't any better.

"I'm sorry I called so late. I tried earlier but got no answer."

"I was out with Dave and Kandy."

"Oh. (pause) Mom wanted to invite you to church in the morning. Will you be there?"

"'Mom wanted to invite?' not 'I'd like you to come?'" Marcy thought to herself and then said out loud, "Yes, Kandy already asked if we could ride together."

"Okay. How are you doing?"

"'Okay?' What happened to 'I'm glad,' or even 'That's nice.' 'Okay?!'" "I'm doing fine, and you?"

"Fine." There was a long pause.

"Ryan," Marcy hesitated. She wanted to ask him about the park, but didn't know how. Ryan seemed to sense what she wanted to ask and cut in quickly.

"Well, it's been a long day. I guess that I should let you go."

"You just got me!" she wanted to scream. "Okay. Have a nice night."

"You too, goodbye."

Chapter 16

HOT DATE AND SEEDS OF JEALOUSY

Sunday morning the sky dawned bright and clear. Marcy woke up feeling rested and ready to tackle the day. She had a bright outlook. She picked Kandy up for church and decided that she was going to listen to the sermon this time. Ryan treated her with the same distant politeness. During church, the sky started getting cloudier. Marcy's outlook seemed to imitate the weather outside. By the time church was out, the beautiful bright blue had been over-taken and replaced almost completely.

They went to the Robinson's for their customary Sunday dinner. Marcy wondered silently if they ever got tired of having them over. They certainly didn't seem to. Right after they got there, Kandy's beeper sounded. She called the number and looked disappointed.

"They asked me to come in. Hospitals aren't immune to the flu. I was the fourth person they called. I told them I would."

Marcy started to put her sweater back on.

"Do you have to leave, too, Dear?" asked Mrs. Robinson.

"I drove."

"Well, how about this," piped in Mr. Robinson, "I'll drive Kandy home so she can change and get her car, and then you can stay and visit. Marian can fix a plate for her to take, so that she won't have to miss dinner. And I'll get to have the pleasure of her company longer than anybody else! How does that sound?"

Kandy and Marcy said that it sounded good to them, if it wasn't too much trouble, which of course they said that it wasn't. Mrs. Robinson put together a great lunch for Kandy, telling her that she was sorry that what they were having wasn't just quite ready. As Kandy was heading to the door, Ryan volunteered to drive her home. It clearly surprised Mr. and Mrs. Robinson and Kandy. Marcy felt hurt and turned quickly back to the job of setting the table.

"Oh, rats!" Kandy exclaimed as she started out the door, "It's beginning to sprinkle!"

Dinner was ready when Ryan got back and they all sat down. Marcy was placed between Ryan and Mr. Robinson, and when they took hands to pray over the food, Ryan seemed reluctant to take hers. Of course he did take it, but it wasn't the same warm embrace that nearly engulfed her hand for previous prayers over food. He just barely held the tips her fingers and didn't hold them a second longer than the prayer lasted. There was no warm friendly squeeze at the end. The conversation was pleasant and everybody participated. Marcy noticed that when Ryan spoke he addressed his parents and very rarely her. He spoke to her if she spoke to him first, then as if he were being polite to a stranger. Everyone helped clear away dinner as usual then they went into the family room to relax. Everyone except Ryan. Marcy noticed his parents communicating with looks married people often do. He didn't appear and after about an hour and a half of pleasant visiting with Mr. and Mrs. Robinson, Marcy decided to go home.

She stood up to get her sweater and purse. She heard Mr. Robinson call up the stairs to Ryan that Marcy was leaving. He came down as she was ready to walk out the door. She already received goodbye hugs from his parents; they had a sympathetic quality to them today, as if they felt her hurt. Mr. Robinson opened the door for her.

"Oh my, it's raining pretty hard out there." He looked at Marcy. "It's really coming down, why don't you stay until it clears up or at least lets up."

Marcy looked at Ryan for any sign of encouragement. He wasn't even looking at her.

She shook her head. "I've got work to get done."

Mrs. Robinson encouraged her to stay a while longer too. It would surely let up in a few minutes. She glanced again at Ryan and this time met his eyes and held them for a moment. He still said nothing. "No, I'm afraid it will get worse." Ryan quickly looked down to study his shoes and knew that she wasn't referring to the rain.

Mr. Robinson was going to go to the car to open the door for Marcy, but Marcy stopped him on the edge of the porch; there was no sense for him to get soaked. He saw the hurt in her eyes and it touched his heart. He wrapped her in another fatherly hug and planted a quick kiss on the top of her head.

Ryan headed up the stairs as soon as Marcy walked out the front door to avoid questions he was sure that would come from his parents – he saw their looks at dinner. He felt like a schmuck. He knew that he was hurting her, but wasn't sure what to do about it. He was surprised at the intensity of his feelings for her and he didn't trust himself until he could get a handle on them. He knew she deserved an explanation, but he didn't think she'd understand. He was concerned that at this point in time it would sour her on God. She and Kandy were very close, and he wasn't so sure that it wouldn't affect Kandy, too. He would rather both of them think that he was a jerk. Also, he didn't want Marcy to accept Christ so that they could have a relationship. She needed to accept Him because she saw a need for Christ in her life, not as a means to Ryan.

Ryan smacked his forehead with the palm of his hand. He should talk to his parents so at least they would understand his odd behavior and help him in his dilemma. But more than that, they could pray for him and maybe help Marcy as well. He headed back down the stairs and got there just as his dad came back in from seeing Marcy off.

Ryan felt much of the burden lift after the short talk he had with his parents.

"Uh, Dad?"

Mr. Robinson lowered the paper he had picked up to read. "Yes?"

"I'm thinking about buying Mr. Silvers' house."

Again Mr. Robinson raised his eyebrows in surprise. "Any particular reason?"

"I like the house, and I can't live with you and Mom forever. It would be a good investment, don't you think?"

"Anything else?"

"I'm not sure."

"I think that you ought to pray about it."

Ryan nodded.

The next week was much the same as the previous, only gloomier for Marcy. She felt depressed from Sunday, and the rain that lasted all week didn't help her spirits.

She had fewer hours at the store, but she put in more with her pottery. That week the art teacher started teaching pottery, and by the end of the week it was hard for Marcy to use the kiln. Of course the school had dibs on the kiln, but it still frustrated Marcy. She decided to cut back inventory in some of the stores where her wares weren't selling as well. She hated to drop them all together because of the holidays. Something was better than nothing.

That Sunday Ryan was friendlier, but still distant. He didn't spend more time than necessary near her. In fact, he and his dad had traded places in the pew. Marcy noted that he was still attentive to Kandy and seeds of jealousy were planted in her soul. They weren't invited to the Robinson's after church like usual.

The next week went on and Marcy was still unable to shake the blue mood. On Wednesday her car broke down and she had to dip into her precious 'kiln fund' to repair it. She went over to Kandy's on Thursday evening and Dave was there. Seeing them together made her feel even bluer and she left early.

Her mom called to chat Friday evening and to tell her Mark would be up the next week. She also mentioned that there was a nice looking eligible man in their complex and that she had taken the liberty of arranging a date with him for her for the next evening. Marcy was flabbergasted at her mom's audacity. Her mom defended herself by saying that she thought that she could help since Marcy didn't seem to be doing a very good job of it on her own. That struck a nerve with Marcy. She had to agree that it didn't seem like she was very good at choosing male friends. So she reluctantly agreed to go out with him, *one time*. What could it hurt?

Marcy drove to Sheridan the next evening so that he could pick her up at her parents' house. That struck a sour note with her right there. Maybe she was old fashioned in the dating game, but how badly did this guy want to date her if he couldn't even drive out to her home to pick her up? Why was she the one making the effort when she wasn't the one that really wanted to go out with him?

"Come on, Marcy, O girl. Maybe there's a good reason Mom told him he could pick me up over there. Maybe he's a really great guy and you're going to blow it going into it with a sour attitude." She gave herself a pep-talk as she approached her parent's home. "Maybe this will be a really great date. Just what you need."

The date was awful.

He might have been good looking but that was the only good about it. He took her to a bar to eat. Marcy never cared to go to bars, but she went in with him because he said that they served great food. When it became evident that he intended to spend the evening there, she requested that they go elsewhere. He looked at her like she was a spoil-sport at first. Then his look changed and a grin spread across his face. He drove to a liquor store and picked up a six-pack, then drove around town for a while.

When he headed out of town and stopped in a park that overlooked the river, Marcy got nervous. She didn't like the look on his face, nor the fact that he practically insisted she have a beer. "Come on, baby, it will help you forget your troubles, loosen you up a little." He then put his arms around her and pulled her next to him. She tried to push him away but he was stronger than she was.

She felt his breath on her neck and his hands started to follow the line of her collar bone as he whispered disgusting things in her ear. Marcy pushed at him harder, trying to get closer to the door.

"Stop it!" she hissed.

"Come on, relax! You'll like it."

"Take me home, now!" she demanded, as she reached up and pushed his face away from her. She was pinned against the door. She tried to reach for the handle.

"I've been told by several that I'm very good. You really should give me a chance."

Marcy made a disgusted sound in response.

He chuckled but didn't stop his pursuit. "Your mom said you were feisty. She was right." His hand reached for the buttons on her blouse.

Frantic thoughts rushed to her mind. A film she saw during a Sex-Ed class in high school popped into her mind. It was on self-defense. She applied one of the methods taught in a segment entitled, *"How to Cool Off a Hot Date."* She stuck her finger down her throat and threw up on him. Now he couldn't get rid of her fast enough and nearly shoved her out the door.

He took off; leaving her stranded and she had to walk nearly a mile to the nearest phone to call a taxi. She was still furious when she got back to her parents' and had the taxi driver go to the door with her. When her mom answered, Marcy pointed to her and announced to the driver, "This is the lady that will pay for the fare." With that she turned around and stomped to her car parked in the drive. She threw it in gear, screeched out of the drive and tore down the street.

She cried all the way home. When she got home her phone was ringing. She answered it angrily. It was her mom calling to see what was wrong. Marcy told her in no uncertain terms what a scoundrel the man was that she had picked out for her daughter.

Mrs. Kelman began defending herself by saying that he seemed so nice when they had talked a few times. "Besides, I thought that I was doing you a favor. You don't seem to be looking for anybody and you know how nice it was to have Mark's children here. Didn't it pull on your maternal instincts?"

Marcy lost her patience and blew up. "Mom, for crying out loud! What if I never want to get married? Are you going to reject me? Do you only love me because there's a chance that I'm going to get married and give you grandchildren? Thanks a lot!" Marcy practically threw the receiver back in its cradle.

She tried calling Kandy to vent her frustration and also tie up the phone so that her mom couldn't call her back. There was no answer at Kandy's. So she called Dave to see if she was over there. She wasn't.

"Oh. Did she get called in to work again?"

"No, she said that she was going somewhere. I forget where she said."

"Oh. Rats. I needed to talk to her."

"Something I can help you with?" he offered.

"No, that's okay. Thanks anyway."

Dave called back fifteen minutes later. "Hey, I remembered where Kandy was going. She went over to those friends of yours. The Robinsons. They probably won't mind if you call her there since you're all friends."

"Thanks, Dave." Marcy hung up. Feelings of jealousy welled up within her, compounded by the hurt she felt because she hadn't been invited. Maybe they didn't want her. A dark cloud settled around her as she went to bed.

Sunday morning Marcy went to church reluctantly. She picked up Kandy again this morning. Dave's car was in the shop, and Kandy had told him he could use hers. Marcy wouldn't have even gone to church, if Kandy had her own car to use.

Kandy was in her usual cheerful mood, and it took her a few minutes to realize that Marcy was unusually quiet and had barely said hi to her.

Kandy sighed, "Don't tell me you're in another bad mood! Marcy, I swear, I don't know what's gotten into you lately! You use to never be in bad moods, and now it seems like every Sunday you're a grouch!" She paused, waiting for Marcy to respond. When she didn't Kandy continued a little more gently.

"The Robinsons aren't the only nice people that go to that church. I've met several really nice people that I'm starting to become better acquainted with. I think that you would really like some of them, too. But how are you going to make friends there if you keep going with a sour face? You're going to scare people away, Marcy." Again, Kandy stopped, waiting for a response from Marcy. And again, there was none forthcoming. Kandy was frustrated.

"You know, I'm not sure that I want to keep riding to church with you if you're always going to be like this. I look forward to going. It's like a bright spot in my week for some reason. But your moods just put a damper on things!" She turned to face the front and the rest of the way to church was silent.

Marcy felt awful on the inside. She felt a perverse pleasure in thinking she might be dampening Kandy's mood, and exceedingly guilty for the same reason. They walked to the church together silently. Several people greeted them as they came in and made their way to 'their' pew. Marcy noticed that they greeted Kandy with warmth and enthusiasm. She got greeted with politeness. The only exception was Mr. and Mrs. Robinson. They greeted her the as always – with warm, loving hugs.

Marcy had put enough space between herself and Kandy for another person and a half to sit between them during the service.

At one point during the song service they were singing a song about the everlasting love of the Father. The words and music were sweet and tender, but Marcy, in her foul mood, thought it was boring. A movement caught her eye and she glanced in Kandy's direction. Ryan was handing her his handkerchief. When Marcy looked at Kandy's face, she saw tears.

This shocked Marcy. Kandy was not a person that someone could accuse of being insensitive or uncaring, but she had never seen Kandy cry, or even heard that she did. Kandy was always strong, handling everything that came her way. Kandy never cried over sad movies and poked fun at Marcy when she did. She had never seen Kandy cry when she was hurting, either physically or emotionally.

Kandy had a cat a few years ago, that Marcy accidentally ran over one summer. When she told Kandy, Marcy broke down and sobbed. Kandy went out to look at it. She pulled it away from the car and stroked it affectionately a few times, then went inside for some newspaper. When she came back out she gently laid it on the paper and wrapped it up. When she stood up, she sighed and did something that totally shocked Marcy. She walked to the garbage can, opened the lid and placed it inside. She looked up at the sun and said, "The garbage doesn't get picked up for a couple days, yet. I hope it doesn't smell too bad by then."

Marcy had come unglued, "How can you do that?! How can you throw that cat in the garbage like that!? I thought that you loved it!"

Kandy had looked at her levelly and said, "I did love it. But what am I supposed to do with it? There's no place here to bury it, and it's not like one of my fish that I can flush if it dies."

"But it seems so insensitive."

"I didn't *want* it to die, Marcy. But I can't bring it back to life, what's done is done. No use crying over spilt milk."

So why in the world was she crying now? She felt like reaching over to comfort Kandy, but Marcy wasn't ready to put aside the hurt and anger she felt about Kandy going over the Robinson's last night. Curiosity made her watch out of the corner of her eye. She wished she hadn't. Ryan gave Kandy a reassuring stroke on her back. Kandy looked up at him. Marcy watched as Ryan offered her a soft understanding smile.

Marcy snapped her eyes back to the words of the song, but she didn't see them. Jealousy pulled stronger at her heart. She bristled on the inside.

The message that morning was on the love God has for us, and how He loves us more than a good father would love their children. Marcy didn't hear most of it, but Kandy did.

The pastor gave examples of how fathers showed love to their children. Instructing them in ways that were right; providing for them, not just necessities, but things they knew their children would enjoy; and spending time with them, were just a few of the examples he gave and elaborated on. Kandy's mother had not been very nurturing, and she didn't even remember her father, much less know the tender love that the pastor was talking about. Other children would talk about their fathers and fathers would come to school activities to watch their children. Most of the birthday parties she went to had the father present. She remembered feelings of missing something, even when something negative was said about a father.

Kandy knew that a large reason she enjoyed the Robinsons so much was because she found some of what she had missed. She felt more like a part of a family with them than anything else she had ever known. Like last night: she had questions about things she was feeling and going through, and when she mentioned that she would like to talk to them sometime, she was promptly invited over that evening. They listened attentively as she opened her heart, and when she asked questions, Mr. Robinson got out his Bible and showed her what God had to say on the subject. She talked to them for quite a long while. They acted like they were truly pleased to be able to help her. She didn't just *feel* loved, she *knew* she was loved.

Kandy glanced at Mr. Robinson. She felt from him a fatherly love, more than she ever dreamed of knowing, but she knew when she watched him interact with Ryan, that his love for Ryan far surpassed his love for her. This didn't make her feel badly, it awed her. And yet, the pastor was saying that the Heavenly Father loves her more than a natural father could. More than Mr. Robinson could love Ryan. More than he could love her if she had been his own child. Her heart ached within her; she wanted to know that love. But how?

The pastor had them stand for the altar call. "You may be here today and never experienced the Father's love because you've never made Him your Father. Jesus said, 'I am the Way, the Truth, and the Life. No one comes to the Father except through Me'. We come to know the Father and His love by accepting the Son. If you would like to know the Father's love today, come down to the altar and I'll lead you to the Son."

Kandy didn't think twice. She knew beyond a shadow of a doubt that she wanted this more than anything.

Marcy was so taken up in her own dour thoughts that she didn't notice Kandy leave the pew. She noticed that there were three people that went to the front, but her thoughts were of getting out of there and going home. After the pastor prayed with them and welcomed them to the family of God with a hug, he introduced them to the congregation.

When Marcy heard Kandy's name, she looked up, shock written on her face. Kandy's face beamed. Marcy could clearly see that those were tears of joy running down her cheeks. The congregation was dismissed, and when Kandy got back to the pew where they were waiting for her, she was hugged and patted and hugged some more. Marcy could see tears of joy on Mrs. Robinson's face, too. Ryan reached past his mother and engulfed Kandy in a warm hug also.

Marcy could not feel happiness with Kandy's joy. The enemy of her soul was at work, building on lies and suspicions that he had previously laid there. If Marcy felt left out before, it was nothing compared to what she was feeling now. At that moment she loathed Kandy. She could clearly see that Kandy had just gotten what the Robinson's had. The thought never occurred to her that all she had to do was ask for it, too. Feelings obscured her reasoning.

The Robinsons were *her* friends, how dare Kandy be more a part of them than she was! She didn't want to be the only one without what they had! How dare Kandy leave her alone! And how dare she steal Ryan from her! She had already stolen Dave, the thief! Wasn't one boyfriend good enough for her? And the Robinsons, couldn't they see what she was doing? Worming her way into their lives, the sneak! And there they were loving her! She felt betrayed.

Ryan caught a glimpse of Marcy still standing in the pew at the place she had been sitting. She had not moved out into the aisle like everyone else had. He turned to encourage her to come with them. The look on her face momentarily eclipsed the joy in his heart. She was watching Kandy, stiff, unyielding, hands clenched into fists. He could see her whole body shaking. Anger, hatred and hurt poured out of her eyes. Her face was tight and hard, she didn't seem aware of the tears that had fallen from her eyes.

As Ryan stepped towards her, the movement caught her attention. The hatred left her eyes, but not the anger or the hurt. Something in her eyes stopped Ryan. They warned him not to come closer. She only held his gaze for a second, and then shuddered. She turned and walked swiftly out the other end of the pew. Ryan caught his mother's attention as Marcy was heading towards the side door, and motioned for her to follow her. Mrs. Robinson knew instinctively that something was wrong. She caught up with Marcy in the parking lot.

"Marcy," she called gently. Marcy stopped and turned around. Misery filled her eyes. "I can tell you're hurting. Would you like to talk, Dear?" she offered with much love, hoping that she would.

"There's nothing to talk about," Marcy replied stiffly.

"Is there anything I can do?"

"No. I don't feel well and I'm going home." She turned away from Mrs. Robinson and started for her car again. Mrs. Robinson watched her go, sadness filling her heart.

Ryan came up as Marcy was pulling away. Mrs. Robinson shook her head at Ryan's unspoken question. "We'll keep praying for her, Dear. The battle often seems the worse just before the victory is won, you know."

Marcy didn't lie when she said she didn't feel well. Not only did her head hurt, but she had never known she could feel such intense emotions as she was now, and they made her feel sick to her stomach. She hated the feelings that raged inside her. But mostly she hated herself.

Chapter 17

BLUE, BLUE, MY WORLD IS BLUE

M arcy's mom called Sunday evening to remind her that Mark was going to be there the next weekend and wanted to know if Marcy would come over.

"Marcy, I'm sorry about the date. I should have checked him out better before I let you go out with him." Mrs. Kelman sounded sincerely sorry.

"It's not all your fault, I should have said no."

Mrs. Kelman thought that Marcy sounded a bit despondent.

"Is everything all right, Sweetheart?"

"Yes, I'm just tired and have a headache."

"Okay, then. I'll let you go, so you can get to bed."

"Thanks. Goodbye."

Monday evening, Kandy called. Marcy didn't want to talk to her about anything and told her so. She felt mean and perverse when she hung up on her. Ten minutes after she hung up, the phone rang again. Marcy let it ring, and turned off the ringer so she wouldn't have to listen to it.

Marcy trudged through her week, doing things mechanically, feeling half numb. There was a horrible hurt in her heart and she didn't know how to get rid of it. Throwing herself into her pottery usually helped get her emotions under control, but not this time. There was no release in it for her. Not only that, nothing turned out the way she wanted. By Tuesday evening, she quit trying.

Wednesday she got to work late and did her work halfheartedly.

Thursday was her day off, and she stayed in bed, sleeping until well past noon. She didn't bother dressing, but slouched around the house in her kimono. She did finally dress about six, when she opened the refrigerator to discover nothing was in it except the three bottles of beer that had been part of the six-pack Dave had brought over. She really didn't have much of an appetite but had just looked because it was something to do. Maybe if she went out and got something to eat, it would help to shake off the feeling of lethargy. She did, but it didn't.

By eight o'clock, Marcy was getting ready to go back to bed. She didn't quite make it before the doorbell chimed. It was Ryan. Marcy opened the door just wide enough to stand in. Her hand never left the knob and she kept the edge in front of her shoulder.

"Hi, Marcy."

No reply.

"You haven't answered your phone all week. I drove by a couple of times, but you weren't home. I tried earlier this evening, and you still didn't answer so I thought I'd drive over to see if you were home and okay."

Still no reply.

"Marcy, I think that we need to talk. I know that I should have talked with you before now, but I didn't know how."

Marcy still stared at him, eyes cautious with pain. When she still said nothing, Ryan sighed a heavy sigh.

"Please, Marcy?"

"I'm listening."

Ryan hesitated and shifted his weight. "May I come in?"

Marcy stepped back and opened the door to allow him to enter. She turned and walked into the living room.

Ryan looked back at his car before stepping into the house. He had asked his dad to ride along with him and wait in the car. He knew his dad would pray for him, too. When he looked back, his dad was watching and gave him an encouraging smile. Ryan stepped in and shut the door.

Marcy had taken a seat in the recliner. Her feet were curled up in the seat with her and she had her arms wrapped around a large pillow. Ryan sat on the edge of the couch turned slightly to her. Marcy was silent.

"I want to apologize for what I did at the lake. That was wrong of me. I never should have kissed you. I know that I've hurt you, Marcy, and I've never wanted to do that. Please forgive me." He paused and searched her face. "I think not talking to you before this has hurt you more. I've handled this whole situation badly. Again, it's my fault, and I'm asking your forgiveness."

Again he paused. She sat immobile watching him. He heaved another sigh and drew a weary hand over his face. When he looked at her again, she was watching her hands pick fuzz off the pillow she was unconsciously using as a shield. She was not making this easy for him at all. Things did not seem to be cleared up, but he was at loss as to what to do next. He sat there for a couple of minutes, which seemed like hours, in silence. When he finally rose to leave, Marcy rose silently with him. He paused when he got to the door and turned to look at her. Her head was down.

"Marcy," He said softly. She did not lift her head to look at him, so he crooked his finger under her chin and lifted it. He looked into her eyes. "I'm so sorry. Please believe me."

Marcy met his eyes for just an instant, and then threw herself against him, wrapping her arms around him. Ryan could not hug her back, he knew that. He also knew that she was hurting and deliberated what to do for a second.

Marcy could not help herself when he tipped her chin up. Everything within her cried out to be held. She wanted to feel his arms around her sure that within them was an answer to her misery. When Marcy didn't feel her embrace returned, she pressed herself against him, in an effort to force him to respond and answer her need.

Ryan undid her grasp and held her away from himself.

"I can't do this. I can't have that kind of relationship with you, Marcy." The tenderness of his words reflected his heartache for her.

Her chin started to quiver. He had to leave. He opened the door and started to step through, his mind fighting a battle.

"Ryan."

He paused halfway through the door and looked at her. She took one step toward him and stopped, leaning slightly to him.

"Do you... do you like Kandy?" She could not force herself to say 'love Kandy.'"

Ryan looked puzzled. "Yes..." he replied, still battling his own emotions and not comprehending her meaning. "I like her very much."

Marcy dropped her head and nodded, not saying anything else. Ryan stepped outside and closed the door behind him.

Marcy burst into tears and sank onto the couch. The depression that had been moving in and hovering over her stepped in close now and pulled its heavy, smothering cape around her, enclosing her in its blackness.

Marcy never made it to bed that night, crying herself to sleep on the couch. The next day at work she was on the verge of tears all day long. Dave couldn't help but to notice. He stared at her as he sat at his desk and she at hers. He was concerned. This wasn't like Marcy. Duties had kept him from seeing very much of her at the beginning of the week, but she had seemed a bit down to him then, too. Kandy had mentioned that there was something wrong with Marcy, but didn't know what it was.

She looked up at him when she felt his eyes on her.

"Are you okay, Marcy?"

Tears welled up in her eyes, but she nodded yes. "I guess I just feel a little down today, that's all," she said as she dabbed her eyes with a tissue.

"Anything I can do to help?" he asked.

Marcy shook her head no.

"Do you want to talk about it?"

Fresh tears welled up and spilled over. Again, she shook her head. Dave didn't say anything for just a bit, and Marcy returned to her work.

"I have an idea. Why don't we go out? We could see what's happening in Sheridan. Kandy has to work, but that's okay. What do you say?"

Marcy gave him a weak smile. "Thanks Dave, but I don't think so."

"Come on, Marcy, we haven't done anything together in a long time. It'll be fun."

"No, I just don't feel like going out."

"Well, then let's not go out, let's stay in! Why don't you come over to my place tonight? I'll rent a movie, a comedy would be good, and we can pop some popcorn."

"Dave, that's sweet..."

"Good, I'm glad you like that idea!" he interrupted her. "And if you don't show up at my place at six tonight, I'll show up at yours! I'll cook supper."

Marcy nodded and gave in to his insistency. It would be better to go to his place as she could leave anytime she wanted. Dave returned to his task, pleased that he might be able to do something to help cheer up his friend.

Marcy showed up at his place at six like she was instructed. Maybe she *did* need this. Dave had fixed a delicious supper, but Marcy mostly played with her food, hardly tasting it. When Dave was done, Marcy still had over half of hers left on her plate. Dave took the plate from her, and stuck it in the refrigerator. When Marcy questioned him, he said, "Maybe you'll find your appetite, later." He didn't bother cleaning up the dishes and merely stacked them in the sink.

Dave had rented Marcy's favorite comedy, in hopes that would help brighten her mood. Half an hour into the movie, he got up and fetched a box of tissues.

"Sorry," she apologized when he handed them to her.

He smiled understandingly and offered her something to drink. Marcy hesitated.

"Do you have a beer?"

This surprised Dave, but he didn't show it. Marcy very rarely drank. If there was ever any alcohol in her house, it was what he supplied, and he was the one that drank it. She would have a little wine sometimes on special occasions. At the store's Christmas parties, she would nurse a drink all night. And then she probably took it more to escape the hassle of repeated offers and explaining why she turned it down. When he first got to know her, he had chided her about being a teetotaler. She explained that she just didn't care very much for the taste of it, and didn't see a need for it.

Dave retrieved one for each of them and sat next to her on the couch. He was even more surprised at how fast she drank it. *"She must have been thirsty,"* he mused to himself.

Halfway through the movie, Marcy was still teary-eyed. Dave looked at her, wondering what to do, this didn't seem to be helping. He draped his arm across her shoulders and pulled her closer, trying to provide some comfort. The tears came faster.

"This is the saddest comedy I've ever seen," he quipped lightly, trying to get a smile from her. It didn't work.

He picked up the remote with his free hand and turned the movie off. The TV stayed on, but he turned the sound quieter. Then he took the now empty bottle from her hands and replaced it with a fresh tissue. Marcy turned and pressed her face against his shoulder, still wiping at tears.

"Is there anything I can do, Marcy?" he asked, feeling frustrated that what he'd done so far hadn't worked.

"Could you just hold me for a little bit?" she asked hesitantly.

"Sure." Dave shifted positions and scooted down a bit, to better accommodate Marcy. He was glad that she told him something to do, relieved that it was as easy as that.

Marcy snuggled herself against his shoulder, her forehead nestling at his throat. Her hand holding the tissues, rested on his stomach. Dave wrapped both arms around her.

"I'm sorry I'm such a drag," she apologized again.

"That's okay." He gave her a squeeze. "I didn't have anything better to do tonight anyway."

They sat that way for a few minutes, Dave's thumb absentmindedly stroking her shoulder as he watched the TV. Marcy's tears seemed to subside. She shifted and sat up a bit straighter. He handed her another tissue and she blew her nose. Dave held up the waste basket that he had brought in with the box of tissues. She deposited the used ones in the basket and he handed her a fresh one.

This small act of caring touched Marcy. She stretched her face towards his and planted a kiss on his cheek. "Thanks, Dave," she whispered.

He returned the kiss to the top of her head and squeezed her shoulders. "You're welcome."

This brought tears to her eyes again. Maybe she was wrong in giving Dave up. Maybe she should have explored the possibilities of a more serious relationship with him. He certainly was kind and thoughtful and gentle. Her hand slid farther around his stomach and held him tighter. Dave pulled her closer, not knowing the thoughts that were running through her mind and turned his attention back to the TV.

Maybe he still had some feelings left for her, maybe it wasn't too late. She sat very still, pondering the possibilities. After a few minutes, Dave cocked his head to one side. "Hey, did you fall asleep?"

Marcy tipped her head back to better look at him. She scanned his face for a few seconds. Amused, he watched her. She sat up and slightly away from him, looking like she wanted to ask him something.

"Dave?"

"Yes?" he encouraged her to ask what was on her mind.

"Do you... can...?" She stopped and searched his face, unsure of herself. Then she tried again, "Is there... I'd like..." She faltered, not knowing how to ask what she was thinking. Dave sat quietly waiting, not knowing what she wanted to say. What she did next threw him totally off guard.

Marcy leaned into him and kissed him full on the mouth. It wasn't hesitant, or a 'thank you-for-being-so-kind' kiss, either. Dave sat there stunned at its implications. Her hands, which had rested on his chest, moved to around his neck. This movement called him to action. He reached up and pulled Marcy's hands back down, holding them in front of him. He sat up straighter himself. She sat back and looked at him questioningly. Dave took a big breath and let it rush out again through rounded lips.

"That was really nice, Marcy," he swallowed. "And if I wasn't seeing Kandy, I would love to continue."

"Kandy."

Dave spoke gently to her. "You knew I was seeing Kandy. You encouraged it. You didn't want that kind of a relationship with me, remember?"

Marcy nodded and studied his hands that still held hers. She looked back up, her eyes pleading, "What about just tonight?" she whispered.

Dave stood up, still holding her hands and pulled her up too, keeping a space between them. He shook his head, still speaking gently to her. "You're very beautiful, and that is an extremely tempting offer. Three months ago I would have taken you up on it. Not now, I can't. It wouldn't be fair to Kandy." Dave took another deep breath. "Besides, I don't think that is really what you want. And something tells me that isn't what you need, either. I don't know what you *do* need, but I don't think that spending the night with me is it."

Marcy was embarrassed and hurt at having offered and being refused. She jerked her hands out of his. "How do you know what I need?! You're not me!" She lashed out at him in her hurt. She grabbed her purse and jacket from the chair.

"Marcy, please don't take it that way."

Spitfire reared up. She delivered a hard kick to his shins then fled out the door. He limped after her, calling her name. He got to the elevator just as the doors closed behind her. Dave rested his head against the cool elevator doors wondering what he should do now. He had to agree with her on two accounts: It certainly had been time for her to go home, and he obviously didn't know what it was she needed. Dave hobbled back to his apartment, sank into the couch and turned the volume up on the TV set.

Marcy paced around in her house, tense with emotions and crying. Not only did she feel rejected and hurt, but now she felt like a wanton hussy. Whatever made her offer Dave what she did? What must he think of her? Those feelings just added to the ones that had been gathering inside her for the last several days.

She tried sitting and flipping through the channels on the TV, to get her mind onto something else, but that didn't help. So she got up and paced. She went into different rooms, opening drawers and closet doors, trying to find something – anything – to help her calm down. She closed them hard when they offered nothing within them as if it were their fault she was upset. She headed into the kitchen and started going through the cabinets. When she got to the refrigerator, she noticed the beers again. She reached for one.

Dave tried to pay attention to the TV, but couldn't get his thoughts off Marcy. What she had offered astounded him. It was totally unlike Marcy. Of course her behavior the whole day hadn't been like her. Look how fast she drank the beer. The longer he pondered her actions, the more he was concerned for her. She was pretty upset when she left.

An uneasy feeling crept up on the inside of him. He turned the TV off and went to the phone. He dialed her number, but there was no answer. Looking at his watch, he knew she should have been there by now. He remembered that Kandy had mentioned that she had tried calling her several times, and couldn't reach her. Could her phone be out of order? He hoped there was a problem with her phone.

Dave grabbed his jacket and keys and then headed for his car. He scanned the visitor parking spaces to see if by some chance, she were still there. He didn't see her car when pulling out of the lot and turned the direction to her house, keeping an eye out for her car just in case...

When he got to her house, her lights were on. He rang the doorbell and got no answer. He rang again and waited. Dave tried to peak in the window, but couldn't see anything. He pounded on the door and waited. He grabbed the door knob knowing Marcy didn't usually lock her doors until she went to bed. It was then that he noticed the door hadn't even been latched all the way and was surprised that it hadn't opened when he had pounded on it. Letting himself in, he called her name. There was no answer. He noticed two empty beer bottles on the coffee table. One was knocked over and there was a third one on the floor. He hurried to look in the other rooms of the house, but didn't see her. His uneasiness grew.

Dave listened for a dial tone on the phone. It seemed to be working. He checked the ringer, it had been turned off. He wondered how long it had been that way and turned it back on. Dave turned out the lights in Marcy's house and shut the door.

As he hurried outside, it was then that he noticed the garage door was open and her car gone. He closed the garage door, too. If she came back, it would be easy to tell as he drove up to the house. He had decided to look for her, checking back here every once in a while. He didn't know where to look. Judging by the empty beer bottles, he thought he should start with a place that sold liquor. There were two liquor stores in Lakeland Grove, and they were both about the same distance from Marcy's house in opposite directions from each other. There was no logical reason that she should go to one above the other, so he just picked one, keeping a watchful eye out for her car.

Neither one of the clerks at either liquor store remembered seeing her. He swung back by her house. It was just as he had left it. Where else could she have gone? What if she had gone into a bar and let someone pick her up? This thought made him feel awful. Maybe he should have tried to keep her at his apartment. No, that wouldn't work. He tried the bars, and no one remembered seeing her either. He swung back by her house again. Still no change. He headed out again, at a loss where to look next.

He drove up and down streets for a while just looking for her. The Robinsons! Maybe she went over there. He remembered they lived on Cobblewood and he was close to there now. He would swing by and look for Marcy's car. He turned onto Cobblewood and drove down the street. He didn't see anything that looked familiar. When he reached the end, he turned around. He passed the point at which he had started and soon thought he recognized Ryan's car. Dave wasn't sure in the dark. He didn't see Marcy's car, though. He looked at his watch. Just after ten-thirty. He pulled into the drive and looked for lights. The front part of the house was dark, but there was a light on upstairs. Someone must still be up. He debated whether to disturb them or not. But he had to know where Marcy was and these people might at least have an idea where to look if they didn't know. He hoped this was their house.

He rang the doorbell and waited a moment for someone to answer and was relieved when Ryan did. At least he got the right house. When Ryan opened the door, Dave could see that he was clearly surprised at his presence. He skipped the preliminaries and got right to the heart of why he was there.

"Has Marcy been here this evening?"

"No."

"Do you have any idea where she could be?" Worry was written all over Dave's face.

Ryan shook his head, beginning to grow concerned himself. "Is something wrong?" He held the door for Dave to come in.

"She was upset when she left my place. I tried calling her, but she had turned the ringer off. When she didn't answer, I drove over to her house. She wasn't there and it looked like she either left in a hurry, or just didn't care. I've been looking for her for over two hours. I didn't know where to look anymore. I was hoping she had come over here. Or at least maybe you have an idea where to look. I know that you're friends."

Ryan gave a short derisive chuckle at his last statement and stood still a moment, as if in thought. Dave watched him, wishing he would do something other than just stand there. Dave didn't know that Ryan *was* doing something. He was praying for Marcy and guidance where to look. Dave started to grow impatient.

Mr. and Mrs. Robinson's bedroom was at the top of the stairs, and sound traveled well. Mrs. Robinson had been in that moment between wakefulness and sleep, when she thought she had heard the doorbell, but wasn't sure. The sound of voices at the bottom of the stairs pulled her away from sleep. She could hear them talking, but could not understand what they were saying. She recognized Ryan's voice but not the other. Whoever the other voice belonged to was full of anxiety. She glanced at the clock on the nightstand then headed down the stairs.

"I'm really worried about her. Do you have any ideas at all?" Dave was talking when Mrs. Robinson appeared. He looked to her and she smiled. "Dave, isn't it?" She asked and held out her hand. He shook her hand and nodded. She stepped back and looked from Dave to Ryan. "Is something wrong?"

"We're not sure. Dave hasn't been able to find Marcy for the last two hours and she was pretty upset when he last saw her."

"Didn't you say Mark was getting into town this weekend? Maybe she went over there."

"That's a good idea, Mom." Ryan headed to the phone in the living room.

Dave followed him, thinking to himself that it was no wonder Kandy and Marcy like to come here; there was just something that felt nice about it.

Ryan looked up the Kelman's number and dialed. Dave felt hopeful.

"Hello, Mrs. Kelman? This is Ryan Robinson. I'm sorry I'm calling so late. Did I get you out of bed?... Good. I'm glad. Is Mark there?... I had something that I needed to ask him. May I speak with him?" Ryan didn't want to ask Mrs. Kelman. If Marcy wasn't there, she might get upset and then it would take twice as long to find out anything else. Mark got on the phone. "Mark, this is Ryan. I was looking for Marcy. Does she happen to be over there?... Well, was she over there earlier?... We don't know. She was over at a friend's house and left pretty upset. He's been looking for her, but hasn't been able to find her... Dave Lewis... About two hours... I don't know... Maybe it would be better if you stayed over there, in case she still comes... You could pray for her. We don't actually know that anything is wrong; we're just trying to find her... No, but that's a good idea... If she shows up there, call Mom. We'll let you know as soon as we know anything here... Thanks. 'Bye."

Dave's hopefulness dissolved during the conversation on the phone.

Mr. Robinson had joined the rest of them in the living room during the phone call, so they filled him in on what was going on. Mark had suggested calling the local hospital to see if she had to make another trip to the emergency room. Mr. Robinson suggested calling the police to see if there had been any accidents reported since she had left Dave's. They did both of these things, but neither one proved fruitful.

It was decided that Ryan would go out and help look. Mr. and Mrs. Robinson would stay there and wait for phone calls or if Marcy should still happen to show up. They called Marcy's house once more to see if she would answer the phone. There was still no answer.

Mr. Robinson suggested they pray before they left and Ryan moved to his dad and mom and took his dad's hand. Mrs. Robinson held hers out for Dave to join them. This was new and strange to him and he went hesitantly. Mrs. Robinson took one hand and Ryan took the other as they formed a circle. He wasn't sure what was expected of him, and felt uncomfortable standing with them. He did though. *"After all,"* he thought to himself, *"If God didn't know where she was, how are we supposed to ever find out? Maybe these people have some connections."*

"Heavenly Father," Mr. Robinson prayed, "We know that you love and care for Marcy more than any of us here ever could. We also know that you know exactly where she is, and what she is doing. We ask now in the Mighty Name of Your Son, Jesus, to show us where she is, and guide Dave and Ryan to her. We also ask that You send Your angels around her to protect her and keep her safe. We turn her over into Your more than capable hands, now, and ask Your peace to enter our hearts. We ask all of this in Jesus' name. Amen."

Everybody echoed the 'Amen'. The prayer wasn't fancy or long, but Dave could tell that Mr. Robinson had meant every word. Some dread had lifted from his heart, and he felt more optimistic. Dave searched their faces for something, he wasn't sure what. Possibly to see if the prayer had affected them in the same way as it had him. Did they pray like that every day? Somehow he felt like these were people that did.

Last Sunday, Kandy had tried to tell him what had happened to her at church, and he had listened politely, but inside he had scoffed. Through the week he had seen a change in Kandy. He liked the change, but it had made him uncomfortable. Just like these people made him feel uncomfortable. Did Marcy have what Kandy and the Robinsons had? He didn't think so. She seemed to be missing something. He searched for what it was. What had Kandy been missing and now had? What did these people seem to have that he didn't?... Peace!

These people had peace. Mr. Robinson had asked for it in his prayer, the rest of them seemed to already have it. You could see in their faces that they were concerned about Marcy, but they had peace that everything would be okay and that God was working. Maybe he had asked for it for Dave's benefit alone. His heart *had* felt lighter afterwards.

Dave pondered these thoughts as he walked back to the front door. As he waited for Ryan to get his socks and shoes, Mr. Robinson laid a hand on his shoulder. "She's going to be fine, Dave, you'll see."

Ryan came down the stairs with his jacket and keys.

"Have you finished packing, yet, Dear?" asked his mother.

"Not quite. I'll finish when we get back."

"May I finish it for you?" she offered.

Ryan thought for just a second. "That would be great. I think everything is on the bed that I need, I just have to put it in the suitcase. If you think I forgot something, just stick it in, too."

"Okay, Dear. You run along and find Marcy, and don't give a thought to the packing. I'll take care of it."

Ryan gave his mom a peck on the cheek and a quick squeeze. "Thanks, Mom."

Ryan asked Dave what he thought the best way would be to go about searching for Marcy as they headed for their cars.

"Uh... probably together... I have a feeling that one of us is going to have to drive her car back when we find her. We can take mine. Let's swing by Marcy's just in case."

This made Ryan curious, but waited for an explanation until they were in Dave's car. He didn't have to ask. Dave supplied the answer as they headed out.

"When I went over to her house, the lights were on and the door was open. When she didn't answer the door, I decided to go in. There were three empty beers in the living room."

"Those aren't all that potent," Ryan commented.

A sudden wave of guilt spread over him for having let Marcy have any alcohol, no matter how 'impotent' it was.

"I know, but she had another one at my place. It surprised me that she asked for one. She's not a drinker, you know. What surprised me even more was how fast she drank it. At the store Christmas parties, she could hang onto a drink all evening and not be half done with it when it was time to go. The beers were part of a six-pack that I had brought over when she fell off her bike. I know who drank the other three. I'm fairly certain that she didn't drink the last three before she came over tonight. In short, I think she's trying to get drunk."

Ryan understood Dave's concern, and thought that might be the case, too. "That doesn't sound like Marcy. Do you know why she would do that?"

"Well, yes and no." Dave squirmed a bit, feeling uncomfortable telling Ryan what happened. "She hasn't been herself all day. I haven't seen her very much this week, but when I did, I noticed that she was a bit down. I don't know why. This morning when she came in, she looked awful, her eyes were puffy... Anyway, she was on the verge of tears all day long. You didn't even have to look at her funny. I asked her what was wrong and she said 'Nothing, I'm just a little down, I guess.' I don't know what caused her to feel down, though."

Dave paused not wanting to go on. He glanced at Ryan when he stopped. Ryan tipped his head back on the head rest and scrunched his eyes shut. He then brought it up again and ran a hand over his face.

"I think I know why. At least part of it anyway." It was Ryan's turn to pause, not wanting to go on. "I went over to talk to her last night. Something had happened a few weeks ago that I handled very badly and hurt her. I wanted to apologize and try to explain. She... I ended up hurting her again," he said softly. "I know there are other things bothering her as well. It could be they were all piling up."

"That could explain her actions at my place." Dave segued into an account of the incident at his place." I didn't have the foggiest what was going through her head. I'm seeing Kandy, you know," he said, feeling he had to defend his actions and that would explain his motives.

Ryan nodded and smiled. "You're Kandy's favorite subject."

Dave smiled at the comment and continued. "Like I said, I didn't have the foggiest notion what was going through her head, I was watching TV. That's when she left." Dave reached down unconsciously and rubbed his shin at the memory. Ryan noticed this action.

"She kicked you in the shin?" It was more a statement than a question. Dave nodded and wondered how Ryan knew. "I got pretty good at dodging her foot when we were growing up. She hasn't done that in years." He almost chuckled.

They drove past Marcy's house and it was still as Dave left it.

Ryan asked Dave where he had already looked for Marcy. He told him. "I was afraid she would go to a bar and try to get picked up after what she had asked," feeling he had to explain. "But no one I talked to remembered seeing her."

They both sat silently for a while, trying to think of where she could have gone.

"Let's try the park," Ryan suggested.

"It's closed by this time," Dave said as he turned to head there.

"It might not have been when she got there, if she went."

The ride was silent again for a while, both of them watching for signs of Marcy on the way.

"Your mom mentioned that you were packing."

"Uh-huh. My job is sending me to New York for a month. There are four different week-long courses they want me to attend. It will mean a promotion and a big raise if I pass the courses."

"When are you leaving?"

Ryan chuckled, "There's an introduction session Sunday afternoon, so I'm leaving tomorrow. I have to get up at four to catch an early flight out of Sheridan."

"I hope you'll be able to sleep on the plane!"

"Me too."

The park was indeed closed when they got there, but the gate that shut them out was just a bar that dropped down across the road. Ryan got out and lifted it so Dave could go through. They drove first on the main road that wound its way through the park, taking them past the main picnic area. There were several side roads that went to the various more remote areas. They both agreed she would be more likely to gravitate to the lake instead of the woods.

Ryan had a hunch that if she were in the park, she would be either at the spot where they had often watched the sunset as kids, or the picnic area where he had kissed her. He suggested the first area to Dave. When she wasn't there, they checked the second.

They saw her car parked in the small lot. It looked like she had tried to park between the lines and missed. She had also run over the concrete curbs that were placed at each space to keep cars from pulling onto the grass. They parked next to her car and got out. Her purse was still in the car and the keys were in the ignition, but Marcy was not there. Ryan and Dave scanned the picnic area, looking for any sign of her. The full moon helped the single parking lot light brighten the picnic area, but it was still hard to see in the shadows cast by the big trees. Ryan zipped up his jacket. There was a breeze and the air was nippy. They both looked through the picnic area, around the pavilion and in the washrooms, calling her name as they went.

"Do you think that she went into the woods?" Dave asked.

"I don't think so. It would have been dark when she got here."

They looked around again as if the surroundings could lead them to her. Almost at the same time, their eyes fell on the gravel lane that cut through the trees leading to the lake. They looked at each other and as if by common consent took off running in that direction. Dave paled considerably; fear had just grabbed his insides and twisted them ruthlessly. Ryan silently prayed for Marcy's safety. This lane hadn't seemed nearly so long when he had chased her down it that Saturday. Now it seemed to stretch for miles. They both slowed as they approached the edge of the woods, and stopped when they reached it. Their eyes scanned the area. The moon's light was much more effective without the trees impeding it.

Marcy was hard to see. She was sitting on the far end of the pier, on the other side of one of the large wooden piles that stuck about four feet higher than the dock. Her feet were dangling over the edge.

Relief swept over both of the men when they spotted her. Dave felt weak. He realized that he had been holding his breath and let it out all at once.

"You okay?" Ryan asked.

Dave nodded. "Let's get her out of here."

Ryan nodded.

They approach the pier slowly, neither one of them sure how to handle the situation. They saw her raise something to her mouth. She was still drinking. Marcy felt the vibrations when they stepped onto the pier and looked over her shoulder at them.

"Go 'way an' leave me 'lone!" Her words came out thick and slurred.

Ryan spoke up. Dave was glad to let him, as he felt totally out of his element. "We came to take you home, Marcy," he spoke soothingly as they slowly approached her.

"I sssaid, go 'way an' leave me 'lone!"

"The park's closed, it's time to leave."

Marcy raised a bottle to her lips and took another drink. Dave tried to see how full it was, but couldn't tell.

"I don' care."

Ryan squatted down beside her. "Why are you doing this, Marcy?"

She didn't respond.

"Please turn around and talk to me. We want to help you."

"I don' wanna talk ta you."

"Why don't you want to talk to me?"

"B'caussse it hursss."

"What hurts?"

"I sssaid I don' wanna talk ta you."

"Will you talk to me then?" Dave asked.

Marcy looked at him like she just noticed he was there. "You ha' to come, too?"

"I was worried about you."

"Ha! You jusss' both came to laugh."

"Nobody's laughing at you, Marcy. We want to help you," assured Dave.

"I don' need your help." She belched and took another drink.

"Don't you think you had enough?" Ryan asked gently.

"No! I can ssstill feel. He sssaid that it wou' ma'e me forget my trouble and I ssstill can 'member."

"Who told you that?"

"Mom's date. I don' thin' I got the right stuff."

Dave and Ryan looked at each other wondering if the other knew what she was talking about. Both shook their heads. They noticed a white plastic grocery bag wedged between her and the pile. Dave was the closest to the plastic bag and reached for it. Marcy saw him.

"Tha'sss mine!" She tried to grab for it herself, but her coordination was off and her reaction time slowed. She missed. She hugged the bottle in her hand to herself as if to prevent them from taking it from her also.

Dave peered into the bag. There were two other bottles inside. Both of them had been opened and sampled. None of the three were the same. The sales slip was stuck to one of the bottles that he held up to examine. He couldn't make out what it said, but he could see that there were four items purchased.

"Where's the other bottle?" he asked, alarmed. How much had she been drinking, anyway?

Marcy pointed to the lake. "Tha'sss too bad too, 'cause it tasted the besss.'"

"How long have you been here?" Ryan asked.

Marcy shrugged and went to take another swallow.

"Come on, Marcy. Let us help you home." He took one arm, and Dave took the other as they stood. Marcy became belligerent as they pulled her to her feet.

"Le' go 'f me!" She struggled to get away from them. She swung her foot at Dave and landed a solid kick on his shin again. He dropped the bag with the liquor and at least one of the two bottles broke.

"Now look wha' you did! Thossse were mine! I ha'e you!" She tried to hit him with the bottle in her hand, but Ryan saw it coming and caught her forearm. Marcy didn't have a very good hold on it and it flew out of her grasp and into the lake. She made a motion as if she was going to go after it. They tightened their hold on her. Marcy wailed and struggled, telling them she hated them, calling them names. It took both of them to hold her. Her wild thrashing made it hard to keep their balance.

They decided it would be easier to carry her back to the car. As Ryan leaned over to grab her legs, she gave a mighty shove that sent him off balance. He lost his hold on her and she dropped to the ground, slipping out of Dave's grasp. Dave tried to grab her again, but she had leaned forward on her hands and knees. All he got a hold of was a piece of her jacket that slipped through his fingers as she tried to take off and run from them. Ryan and Dave lunged for her, but they were too late. Her balance was very poor and she veered into a pile. When Marcy hit the pile, she glanced off, causing her to spin around. She tried to catch herself, but she was moving backwards. Again, Dave and Ryan lunged for her. Ryan felt his fingers grab something, but it wasn't substantial enough to stop her. Her arms flailed and she fell off the pier backwards.

"I can't swim," Dave said instantly with apology and panic mixed together.

Ryan whipped off his jacket, hesitating only a second to see where she went in. Marcy bobbed to the surface, thrashing wildly. Ryan tried to jump in beside her before she went back under. He wouldn't be able to see in the black water. Thankfully the water wasn't as deep as he thought it might be. When he came up, Marcy was back under.

Dave shouted, "There!" and pointed to a spot just in front of him. He took a breath and went under again trying to feel for her. He felt something brush against his leg and grabbed for it. He couldn't tell what it was, maybe an arm, and he tried to pull it to the surface. He lost his grip on it, and tried to find it again, but couldn't. He felt disoriented not being able to see anything. Ryan surfaced for air and found himself facing the wrong direction. He turned around just in time to see Marcy going under again. She was still thrashing wildly.

He dove to where he saw her go under, searching wildly for her. This time he made solid contact with a leg. It was hard to hang onto it with her kicking, but he got a good grip of her pant leg. He struggled to the surface again, and managed to get a breath before Marcy's struggles pulled him back under. He felt something else hit him and grabbed for that with his free hand. He caught it. It was an arm. When he knew he had a good hold on her arm, her let go of her leg. He felt for, and found her head with his free hand. He wrapped his arm around her head and kicked to the surface. Marcy was still struggling but he could feel her weakening. He came up closer to the pier than he thought he would. Dave was waiting, anxious to help. As they got nearer, he laid down on his stomach to try and reach her. Ryan tried to push Marcy into Dave's grasp, but Dave couldn't reach her. Ryan pulled Marcy's arm up over his head. Dave stretched and made contact with her hand.

"I got her," he informed Ryan when he was sure he could hold her. Marcy had stopped struggling, but was now coughing and gasping for air. Ryan raised up her other arm and Dave grabbed that, too. He tried to pull her out of the water, but the angle was wrong. He laid there hanging onto her. Ryan had to swim to the shore to climb out. It was slippery with mud and he had a difficult time getting up the bank. When he finally got onto the pier, he sank down next to Dave to help pull Marcy from the water. Between the two of them, they managed to haul her onto the pier. Marcy was coughing up the water and starting to take decent breaths. Ryan sat back against a pile, worn out. He emptied his shoes of water, and watched as Dave took care of Marcy. He noticed Marcy's shoes were missing.

Marcy struggled, but only mildly, while Dave tried to take her coat off. The dip in the lake seemed to take most of the fight out of her.

"Ssstop it! Leave me 'lone!"

"Marcy, it's cold out here. I've got to get you out of this wet coat," he tried to explain. He did manage to get it off her, and when he was taking his off to give to her, she started to moan and hold her stomach. "What's the matter?"

"Ooooh, I feel sssick! Ooooh!"

Dave pulled back, repulsed, trying to anticipate where she might throw up. Marcy managed to get to her hands and knees, and Ryan helped her to the edge of the pier. He held her hair back while she rid herself of lake water and liquor. When Dave was confident that she was finished, he bundled her in his coat. Ryan reached for his own coat and put it on. He was shivering now from the cold and being wet.

They stood Marcy to her feet, but she was too drunk to walk. Dave hoisted her over his shoulder in a fireman carry. Ryan was grateful. It was hard for him to make himself get up and walk to the car, much less have to help carry someone. He picked up the sack and deposited it in a trash barrel placed next to the pier.

Marcy started crying and feeling sorry for herself. "You ha'e me."

"No, Marcy, we don't hate you," Dave responded indulgently.

"Yesss you do, you ha' to."

"No, we don't."

"You bo' came to laugh a' me." She tried to hold her head up while bobbing around on Dave's shoulders.

"No, we didn't. We came to take care of you."

"You thin' you're better tha' me."

"No, we don't."

Ryan cut in with a no-nonsense tone. "Marcy, we love you. Now be quiet and go to sleep."

"'kay."

Dave felt her relax. It made it a lot easier to carry her. By the time they got to the car, she was either asleep or passed out. Ryan went to open Marcy's car door and Dave stopped him.

"Let's put her in my car, the engine should still be warm. You'll get heat faster." Ryan nodded and opened the passenger side. Dave tipped sideways and dropped Marcy neatly onto the seat, while Ryan guarded her head. He swung her legs inside and shut the door. Retrieving the keys from his pocket, he handed them to Ryan. "You drive my car. I think that you need the heat, too."

"But you don't have a coat."

"If I'm out of the wind, I'll be okay. I'm not soaked like you are."

Ryan accepted the keys and smiled appreciatively. "Thanks."

"What are we going to do with her? We can't leave her alone at her house. I really don't feel like driving clear to Sheridan tonight and I'm not sure that would be the best anyway. I'd take her to mine, but that wouldn't be much better. I have to work in the morning. I'm sure Kandy would take her, but I'm not sure that she'd be able to handle her."

"Let's take her to my parents'. Mom and Dad will be there tomorrow. I'm sure they wouldn't mind, they wouldn't want her to stay alone either."

Dave nodded.

He got in and started the car then waited for Dave to get Marcy's car going and back over the curbstone. The engine was still warm enough to let the heater put out warm air. He turned the fan on high. It felt good since he was chilled to the bone. He reflected on Dave's thoughtfulness. He had to be cold, too. Ryan's bad impression of him was changing.

It was after one o'clock when they got back to the only house on Cobblewood with lights still on. Mr. and Mrs. Robinson heard them pull in and came out to meet them. It was harder to get her out than put her in – she was out cold and limp as a rag, so Ryan had to give Dave a hand.

"Is she all right?" asked Mrs. Robinson as Dave hoisted her onto his shoulders for the second time that night.

"If being soaking wet and stinking drunk is all right, she's fine." Dave answered wryly.

"We didn't want to leave her at home by herself," Ryan explained. "I thought maybe she could stay here. I have a feeling she'll sleep for quite a while. We don't know how much she had, but it was a lot more than she's used to, that's for sure. I don't think she's going to feel her best when she wakes up."

When they stepped into the house, Mr. Robinson noticed Ryan's appearance. "What happened to you?"

"We found her sitting on a pier at the lake. She didn't want to come home with us and fell in. Someone had to fish her out."

"Where would you like her?" Dave asked still carrying his burden.

224

"Oh, I'm sorry, Dear." Mrs. Robinson showed Dave where to deposit Marcy.

"I better call Mark," Ryan commented as he started to go to the phone. "He'll want to know what's going on."

"Mark has called here every half hour since his parents went to bed. He said he'll do that instead of having the phone ring late in the night and wake his folks."

Ryan nodded.

"Would you like some coffee? Ryan? Dave? It won't take long to make a fresh pot." asked Mrs. Robinson as she and Dave appeared again. Ryan shook his head no.

"Thanks, but no. I'd better go. It's pretty late," declined Dave. "Unless of course you need help with Marcy?"

"She'll be fine. We'll take care of her," Mr. Robinson assured him. "Thank you for all that you did. We really appreciate it."

"That's right," agreed Mrs. Robinson as she gave him a quick hug. "We're glad that Marcy has friends that care so much for her." She stepped back and looked into his eyes. "You know, Dave, you don't have to wait until the next crisis to come over. You're welcome here any time."

Dave could see in her eyes that she meant it. "Thank you. I might take you up on that."

Ryan extended his hand and Dave took it. No words were exchanged, but they both knew that their view of the other had changed and they had each made a new friend.

Chapter 18

SWEET SURRENDER

Marcy slept until nearly three o'clock the next afternoon. When she woke up, she felt worse than she had ever felt before. She lay in the bed for a while trying to figure out where she was and how she got where she was. Things were foggy. There was something about this room that was vaguely familiar, but she couldn't place it. She knew she wasn't at home or at her parents'.

She couldn't lie there any longer, nature was urgently calling. Marcy pushed back the covers and held her head. When it stopped pounding so violently, she pulled herself into a sitting position on the edge of the bed and held her head again. She noticed the nightgown that she had on. This was definitely not hers. She pulled out the front of the gown and looked inside. She wasn't wearing anything that was hers. A hot blush flamed across her cheeks. Who had dressed her? She might find the answer to that question when she found out where she was.

Marcy stood up and grabbed her head again, only this time she kept moving slowly to the door. Grasping the handle, she turned it as quietly as she could. She opened the door slowly and for the first time realized how dark it was in the room. The light on the other side of the door cut through her eyes and added a new dimension to the headache she already had. She recognized where she was now. The hallway she stepped into was on the Robinsons' second floor. She had been in the spare bedroom. The bathroom was next door and Marcy was glad.

As she came out of the bathroom, Mrs. Robinson was coming up the stairs. Marcy never realized how painful everyday noises could be.

"How are you feeling, Dear?" Mrs. Robinson asked quietly as Marcy gripped her head again.

"I'm not sure," Marcy whispered. "Do you know what I'm doing here?" When she opened her mouth to speak, she realized it tasted how she imagined sewage would taste. The thought repulsed her, but then, so did the taste in her mouth.

Mrs. Robinson smiled softly. "Recovering, I think. Dave Lewis and Ryan brought you here last night."

Marcy stood holding her head with her eyes closed, searching her befuddled mind. When she didn't reply, Mrs. Robinson continued. "Why don't you take a shower? It might help to clear some of those cobwebs. Your clothes are washed and on top of the bureau in the bedroom."

Marcy never opened her eyes as Mrs. Robinson guided her into the bathroom. She let Mrs. Robinson adjust the water temperature and lay out towels for her while she just stood there.

"Do you need help getting in, Dear?" she asked gently.

"No, I can manage... Uh... why did my clothes need washing?"

"They were wet and dirty from your fall in the lake," she explained, "You'll find a new toothbrush and some toothpaste in the top drawer on the right side of the sink, if you wish to use them. There's mouthwash inside the medicine cabinet," she offered as she was leaving. She closed the door gently behind her.

"My breath must smell as bad as it tastes," Marcy thought to herself as she slowly removed the nightgown.

The water felt good, she just wished it weren't so loud. While she showered she thought about the information she had gotten from Mrs. Robinson. Some things came back to her but not clearly. She remembered driving to the park and sitting on the pier. Dave and Ryan were there when she fell in the lake and pulled her out. And she remembered being carried somewhere. After that she remembered nothing. But before that...

Before that she remembered clearly. She remembered the whole depressing week. Correction: the whole depressing month. The evening Ryan came over and she had tried to get a response from him and how he rejected her, was very clear. And when she remembered how she had acted at Dave's... Marcy groaned. She wondered how abominably she had acted last night. She wanted to run away and not have to see anybody ever again. Getting drunk might have let her forget her troubles for a while, but it certainly didn't solve them. As far as she could tell, it made them worse.

Marcy found her clothes on top of the bureau just like Mrs. Robinson said. Not only were they clean, but pressed and neatly folded. It was clearly an act of caring.

Above the bureau, two framed prints caught her attention. They were pictures with scripture passages printed on them. The first one read:

"Search me O God, and know my heart:
Try me and know my thoughts:
And see if there be any wicked way in me,
And lead me in the way of everlasting."

"Humph!" Marcy thought, *"It doesn't take God to show me that I have 'wicked ways' in me."* Then the self-righteous thoughts that she had the Sunday before last came back to her. *"I don't sleep around, I don't cuss, I don't get drunk, and I've never killed anyone."* She felt sure of her goodness then. Indeed at that time, she wouldn't have imagined herself doing any of those things. Now look, two weeks later and she'd already gotten drunk. And it wasn't because of her 'goodness' that she hadn't slept with Dave.

The cussing? She couldn't even remember what she had said, so how could she know? She certainly thought cussing thoughts about Kandy, and if she had opened her mouth at the time, they probably would've slipped out.

And as far as the killing anyone, she knew that she probably shouldn't have been driving when she drove to the park. What if her impaired judgment would have caused her to hit someone? She shuddered at the thought.

Tears sprang to her eyes. Her life was a mess. Maybe not on the outside, but on the inside where it counted. And she couldn't seem to do anything about it. "O God," she breathed, "Don't search me or try me. I don't want You or anyone else to know my heart or my thoughts. I already know how ugly I am on the inside."

Her eyes slid down to the next picture. Its scripture read:

"The Lord will perfect that which concerns me. Psalm 138:8"

She sighed. She had gone to church so often with the Robinsons' when she was growing up and now she'd been going fairly regularly the last couple months. She'd even tried reading her Bible every day like she heard the pastor say. She was trying to do the right things, but she kept messing up. So when was this perfecting going to take place? She hoped it was soon.

Slowly, Marcy dressed, wishing she didn't have to go downstairs and face the Robinson's. She wondered briefly if there was a way of escape from the second floor. But according to what her dad had been fond of saying, she had made her bed and now she'd have to lie in it.

Marcy couldn't find her shoes in the room. As much as it pained her she knelt and looked under the bed. Still no shoes. Holding her head as she got up, she painfully made her way downstairs. Each step jarred her head. She wished that she could hang onto it with both hands, but she felt the need to hold onto the banister also.

Mr. Robinson stood up from his place on the couch as Marcy entered the living room. Mark was sitting opposite of him, with his back to the doorway. When Mr. Robinson looked at Marcy and stood, Mark twisted in his seat then stood too. Both men were at loss for words, neither one had seen her looking so wan before. She stood awkwardly in the doorway. Mark's presence surprised and dismayed her. How many other people knew of her idiotic behavior? She was thankful that Ryan wasn't there. She hoped she could get out of the house without seeing him at all.

Mrs. Robinson broke the ice. "Are you feeling a little better, Dear?" she asked quietly.

Marcy wasn't sure what to answer. Her breath did, and maybe her head a little, but she felt worse on the inside. So she shrugged indecisively, embarrassed by the whole situation.

"I kept some lunch for you, if you would like."

"Lunch?" Marcy said in a normal tone then winced at the loudness of her voice. "What time is it?" she whispered.

"It's a little after three-thirty. Would you like something to eat?"

Marcy, shocked at the time, gave her head a tiny shake at the offer of food. She stayed in the doorway, unwilling to enter the room.

"I, um, want to apologize for my, um, behavior and, um, for putting you to so much trouble. I'm sorry," she faltered, unable to look them in the eyes. "Thank you for, putting me up, and, um, putting up with me." She stopped, not sure what to do next.

Mr. Robinson walked over to her and wrapped her in a fatherly hug. "We don't 'put up with' you, Marcy. We love you."

Tears started to run down Marcy's face, and she stepped away from him. His kindness made her feel even worse. She deserved a scolding at the very least.

"I think I'll go home, now," she whispered and turned to leave.

"I'll take you." Mark spoke up.

Marcy looked back at him and nodded. It dawned on her that she didn't know where her car or her purse was. Maybe she did something to her car. She headed for the front door. Mrs. Robinson held out her purse and a jacket for her to take. The jacket wasn't hers, and Marcy looked at it questioningly. Mrs. Robinson held up a bulging plastic grocery sack.

"Yours is in here. It has to be dry-cleaned. You can borrow this one for now."

Marcy nodded and accepted the jacket. "Thanks."

Mrs. Robinson gave her a hug. "Marcy, if you ever want to talk about anything, please know that we're here for you."

Marcy nodded, more tears fell. She turned to go out the door that Mark was holding open for her, then stopped and turned back.

"Um... I couldn't find my shoes upstairs."

"You weren't wearing any when they brought you in last night."

Marcy nodded again and walked out the door. She groaned and put her arm up immediately to shield her eyes. The house lights were dim in comparison to the sun, and so was the pain they inflicted. Mark took her arm, and Marcy blindly followed his leading as he guided her down the steps and into his car. He reached across her to retrieve the sunglasses from the dashboard and dropped them in her lap. "Here, these might help."

Marcy picked them up and gratefully put them on. "Thanks," she whispered.

She noticed her car parked in the drive as they were backing out. "My car is here." She stated simply.

"You can get it later. I didn't think that you would feel like driving home. Was I right?"

Marcy looked down and nodded. "How did you find out?"

"They were worried last night when they couldn't find you, so they called me to see if I knew where you were."

"Do Mom and Dad know?"

"No."

The rest of the ride home was silent.

When they got in Marcy's house, Marcy collapsed on her couch. Mark went into the kitchen and fixed an ice pack for her head.

"Here, this might help," he said as he handed it to her. "Your refrigerator is empty and so are your cupboards. I'm going out to get some groceries. Is there anything in particular you might want?"

Mark left and she was alone in her misery. But only for about half an hour. The doorbell rang, and it was so loud it made her jump. She got up to answer the door, it was Dave. Marcy groaned. She knew she had to face people, but did she have to face them all today, when she was feeling so miserable already?

"I called the Robinsons to see how you were and they said that you were home. I was just getting off work, so I thought I'd swing by and check up on you. I was wondering if you made it, I didn't see your car. You don't look very good, Marcy," Dave said as Marcy let him in.

"Mark brought me home. I don't feel very good," she said, still pressing the ice-pack to her head. She walked back over to the couch and sat down. Dave took the recliner.

"I won't stay long. I've been hung-over before, although probably not as bad as you are. You were pretty bombed last night." He paused to examine her features. He continued quietly. "You gave me quite a scare, Marcy."

Marcy was embarrassed. "Dave... about at your place... I, um... I'm sorry. I don't know what got into me."

"I think I do. Ryan told me about when he saw you Thursday evening..."

"He told you?!" Marcy almost squeaked in anger, then winced, and started over in a whisper. "He told you about Thursday evening? Did you two have fun laughing at me together?" She was humiliated and hurt.

"We didn't laugh at you, Marcy. It wasn't like that. He didn't tell me any details. I figure that you probably felt rejected by him and were looking for acceptance elsewhere, that's all."

"So why did he say anything at all?"

"Marcy, please listen and try to understand. When you left my place, I got worried, so I tried to call. You never answered your phone, so I came over. When you weren't here and I saw those," he motioned to the empty bottles still on the coffee table, "I got really worried. I drove around for two hours looking for you. I finally went over to the Robinsons' to see if you might have gone over there or if they might have an idea where you were. I told Ryan that I thought we ought to go together because I had a feeling you might be drinking. He asked me if I knew why you were acting so out of character. So I told him what I knew. He just filled in a piece of the puzzle." Marcy groaned with the shame, and Dave hurried on. "It wasn't like that, it wasn't locker-room talk. We were concerned about you, Marcy."

Marcy sat silently, wishing she could just sink into the couch and not be seen or heard of again.

"You've fallen for him, haven't you." It was a statement, not a question. Marcy looked into Dave's eyes and could see he already knew the answer. She nodded. "I can see why. He's a great guy, and his family is great, too."

"I didn't mean to. The feelings aren't mutual." She looked at Dave. Did she put him through the same thing? "Dave... I'm so sorry I hurt you, I didn't know."

Dave's smile was forgiving. "That's okay. Live and learn, I guess." He stood up then. "Your place is a mess."

"I know. I haven't done much of anything for a while."

Dave scooped up the bottles and threw them away. "Have you eaten yet?"

"No, but I'm not hungry."

"You should eat anyway. It'd probably help you feel better. How 'bout I fix you something?" Marcy heard him open the refrigerator then close it. He started to go through her cupboards looking for something to fix. He went and stood in front of her, arms crossed. He examined her for a minute. He thought she looked like she had dropped a couple of pounds. "You have virtually nothing to eat in this house. Why not?"

"I haven't really felt like eating, so I didn't bother shopping."

"I'll go get something."

"You don't have to. Mark's out shopping now."

"When do you expect him back?"

"Anytime now."

Dave nodded. He'd stick around to make sure. "Why don't you go lie down on your bed? You'd be more comfortable. I'll wait for Mark."

Marcy nodded and went obediently to her room. She could hear him doing something, but couldn't tell what. Pretty soon she heard the vacuum. He was cleaning. She groaned but didn't get up. Her ice pack was no longer an ice pack, so she removed it and stuck a pillow over her head.

She must have dozed off, because the next thing she knew, she heard talking and could smell food cooking in the kitchen. She got up and noticed her head was feeling a little better. She went to the bathroom to freshen up. The bathroom was cleaner. As she made her way to the kitchen, she noticed that Dave had done a pretty thorough job of cleaning. He had picked up, dusted, and vacuumed. Even the pillows on her couch were plumped and neatly arranged. In the kitchen, Dave had cleaned too. In fact, he was still cleaning. He had one of her aprons on, washing dishes. Mark was cooking, also wearing one of her aprons. They were visiting and didn't notice Marcy right away. Marcy chuckled. They looked up when they heard her.

"You two make a cute couple," she teased. "I thought you weren't going to stay long, Dave. You cleaned my house."

He shrugged. "I was going to stay to make sure you got something to eat, anyway. And I had to do something while I was waiting."

Marcy rolled her eyes and shook her head.

"You got up just in time. Supper's just finishing." Mark put in.

Dave left after supper, and Mark and Marcy sat on the couch.

"Dave's a nice guy." Mark said. "Apparently he was pretty worried about you last night."

Marcy could tell he didn't say what he just said, just to make conversation, he had something on his mind. She looked at him warily. "I already told you how I feel about Dave. He's just a friend. A good friend, but still just a friend. And besides, he's seeing Kandy," she replied testily.

Mark chuckled. "I wasn't even thinking about that, so don't get bent out of shape... What I want to know is, why... Why did you do it, Marcy? It's not like you."

Tears threatened again. She picked up the big throw pillow and wrapped her arms around it. She studied the fringe and shrugged.

"I don't know," she said. "I just felt so miserable, I couldn't handle it."

"Did it help?"

"No," Marcy shook her head. Tears started to slowly course down her cheeks. "Now I feel even worse. Not just my head, but on the inside, too." She paused, tying and retying the pillow's fringe into knots. Tears came in earnest now. "I guess I just fell apart. I feel so ashamed..."

Mark scooted closer to her. "Come here." He pulled her next to him and took the pillow. He wrapped a brotherly arm around her. "Chrissie says that my shoulder is the best one to cry on. I don't think that she'll mind if you use it."

Marcy tried it out for the next ten minutes. When her tears subsided, she sat up, leaving a big wet spot on his shirt.

"Sorry," she said sheepishly. "I've cried so much these last few days I didn't think that there were any tears left."

"Do you want to tell me about it?" Mark offered sincerely.

Marcy hesitated, she could talk to Mark, she knew, but she didn't want to let even him know what a horrible sister he had.

"Marcy, this is me, Mark. Your brother. I'm not here to judge you, I'm here to help. Won't you let me?"

She started from when she heard Ryan was back in town, because that seemed to be when her troubles started. She told him how she felt confused around him, and the feelings she felt guilty having. She told him about the Saturday at the lake.

"I thought from his kiss that he was feeling the same thing for me, he seemed to care. I guess I was wrong. A wall went up, and I felt like I had lost my best friend. Thursday he came over to apologize for kissing me at the lake, and I threw myself at him. He told me that he couldn't have that kind of relationship with me. I had suspected that he was beginning to be interested in Kandy, so I asked him point blank if he liked Kandy. He said yes very much."

Mark had talked with the Robinsons while waiting for Marcy to wake up that afternoon. They had told him about what they thought was happening and how Ryan felt about Marcy, so he knew that this was not true. He also knew that he couldn't say anything about it. "Marcy, are you sure? That doesn't seem right. I thought that you said Kandy and Dave were seeing each other. And Dave seems to think that their relationship is pretty secure. There must be a misunderstanding about Kandy and Ryan."

"Maybe Kandy doesn't return his feelings. It's happened, you know."

Mark shook his head, "I can't help to feel you're mistaken."

Marcy shrugged and went on. She wasn't able to look at him when she told him what she had done at Dave's. If any of this shocked Mark he didn't let on. Marcy paused. She had taken up the pillow again and resumed tying the fringe in knots.

Mark hadn't been a Christian very long, and he had never personally led anybody to the Lord. He and Janet had wanted to get together with her the last time they were up and share with her then, but schedules didn't work out. He and Janet had prayed that God would make an opening during this visit, and that the Lord would give him wisdom for saying the right words. Mark looked like he was paying attention to his pant knees when Marcy paused, and didn't speak right away. He was praying silently for wisdom to help Marcy. He was turning over in his mind how to bring up the subject when Marcy spoke.

"Mark, can I ask you something?"

"Sure," he said, almost disappointed that he hadn't spoken sooner. He prayed that he hadn't lost the chance. What Marcy said next brought joy to his heart.

"Mom said something the last time you and Janet were here and I was going to ask you about it, but there never seemed to be a good time." She looked at him then and searched his eyes, "She said that you said going to church was fulfilling. Is it to you?"

Mark smiled broadly at that, and Marcy could see before he answered that it was. "Yes it is. Why?"

"It's not to me," she paused. Mark waited for her to go on. "I've gone to church with the Robinsons and I'm pretty sure they feel the same way about it as you do. I watched their faces, and when you came that Sunday, yours was the same way.

"I feel like I'm the only one who isn't enjoying it, or doesn't get what's going on, or doesn't understand what's so special or something. I feel really left out. When I go I feel agitated and I don't know why. It's hard to pay attention. Kandy's told me that I'm always a grump on Sundays. And I feel guilty about the way I feel. I guess I feel like I'm missing something. I tried to start reading my Bible. It's hard and I don't understand what I read most of the time. So what makes it fulfilling to you?"

Mark smiled but didn't answer right away. "I think, Marcy that it's not so much that going to church in and of itself is fulfilling, it's the reason I go."

"What do you mean?"

"When I go to church, I go to worship God with other Christians, and learn more about Him and the Bible, His Word to us. I became a Christian and made Jesus Christ my Lord and that is what's fulfilling."

"When did you do that?"

"Last February."

Marcy nodded, "I knew there was something different about you this time. Is Janet a Christian?"

Mark smiled and nodded. "She was a Christian when we got married, only she was backslidden."

"I've heard that term, but I don't know what it means."

"It means that she had gotten saved, or become a Christian, but had quit serving the Lord like she should."

Marcy nodded. "So why did you become Christian?"

"Because basically my life was falling apart, and I couldn't seem to get it back together. I was unhappy on the inside and when I tried to do things to make me feel better, it ended up hurting either me or someone I loved. I felt trapped and guilty. Do you remember last Christmas and how there where 'tense moments'?"

Marcy nodded.

"Janet and I were going through a rocky time in our marriage. We almost got a divorce. Janet had rededicated her life to the Lord about a year before that. I thought it was just a phase she was going through, and didn't listen to her when she tried to tell me. She would invite me to church with her and I would go on occasion. But when I went, I would feel something akin to jealousy. It was fulfilling a need in her life and I wanted to be the one to do that. I realized that I couldn't, but I still wanted to. I guess that I felt threatened, like what she had was going to come between us. She had an inner strength, and I wanted to be the strong one. She seemed to have a joy and a peace that I was missing. She got pleasure in attending church. Janet would read her Bible, and teach the girls Bible stories. They would ask me something about the Bible stories and I couldn't answer their questions, but Janet could. I felt inadequate.

"I started to give her a hard time. About November, I had decided that maybe what I needed to do was to make her jealous, to show her that I could be happy without her. So I started to look around. I didn't try to hide it from her, because how could she be jealous if she didn't know? It didn't drive her away from the Lord, she got closer. She got the Ladies' Bible Study Group and a bunch of her friends from church to start praying for me. Janet still loved me and she never seemed to lose her peace or joy. Well, maybe she did on occasion, but she would go to the bedroom and when she came out, she would have it back again. The whole time, I was miserable. I felt guilty and I could see that I was hurting her and the girls.

"In February, I just got to the end of my rope. I told her I was leaving and wanted a divorce. That was a Saturday night. She begged me to come to church with her one last time the next morning. I said okay because I knew it was the last time.

"A man gave a testimony how the Lord had saved his marriage. He said he'd been trying to fix it himself and it didn't work, but since he turned it over to the Lord, it had gotten better than it had ever been before. That's when something happened. I realized that it was like the man said, I'd been trying to do it all myself and I'd proven that I couldn't do it. I didn't really want to leave Janet and the girls: I loved them. So I laid down my pride and surrender my life to the Lord."

Marcy wasn't looking at him and she looked stricken. "The potter," she whispered.

Mark wasn't sure he heard her correctly, if he did, he didn't understand. "What?"

"The potter," Marcy said louder. "That's what Ryan said. He said he was messing up his life, so he gave it over to the Lord. I didn't understand what he meant. Later when he was watching me work on the wheel, he told me that when I was working with the clay, it was like when people yield their life to God, it comes out right. And when they try to do it themselves, it turns out messed up, like when he tried to do it." She looked at Mark, her eyes large. "The scripture in their spare bedroom said that the Lord would perfect what concerns me. When will He do that?"

Mark smiled. "The Lord is a gentleman, Marcy. He waits for people to ask Him. Are you His?"

"I guess that I thought I was a Christian, because I went to church with the Robinsons quite a bit. And I always tried to be good."

Mark chuckled. "Going to church doesn't make you a Christian any more than sitting in a garage makes you a car. And being good doesn't make one a Christian. Do you have your Bible handy?"

Marcy nodded and went to get it. He prayed while she was gone.

Mark turned to Romans 5:19. "None of us can be good enough for God on our own because of Adam's fall. See here? 'For as by one man's disobedience many were made sinners'" Then he pointed to Romans 3:23. "It says right here 'for all have sinned and fall short of the glory of God.' We can't do it on our own; we'll always slip up and fail. We deserve death." Mark turned to Romans 6:23. "'For the wages of sin is death.'"

"I know I sin. Two weeks ago I prided myself on being good. I've blown it royally just this week. And I feel so guilty all the time." Marcy interjected.

"Marcy, God knew that we couldn't live up to His perfection on our own. But He loves us and doesn't want us to die. He loves us so much He sent Jesus to die in our place. Look here at Romans 5:8. 'But God demonstrates His own love toward us, in that while we were still sinners, Christ died for us.' And I know you've heard John 3:16: 'For God so loved the world that He gave His only begotten Son, that whoever believes in Him should not perish but have everlasting life.'"

Mark turned to 2 Corinthians 5:21, and showed Marcy. "'For He made Him who knew no sin to be sin for us, that we might become the righteousness of God in Him.' Look at the rest of verse 19 in Romans 5: 'so also by one Man's obedience many will be made righteous.' That's why He sent His Son Jesus. He was the only One that never sinned. Jesus' perfection allowed Him to be the sacrifice that it took to cover all our sins. But Jesus didn't stay dead. God raised Him from death. He conquered sin and death.

"I know what you mean about feeling the guilt and shame. I felt tons of it. I didn't think that I could ever hold my head up or look those that I loved in the face again. I found out something, though. Romans 8:1 says, 'There is therefore now no condemnation to those who are in Christ Jesus.' I didn't have to feel guilty again about what I'd done to Janet and the girls. Do you know why?"

Marcy shook her head.

"Because when you become His, He doesn't just merely forgive you, He makes you a brand new person. 'Therefore, if anyone is in Christ, he is a new creation; old things are passed away; behold, all things have become new.' The person that did those ugly things is gone. You're not your same old self. You're brand new."

Mark looked at Marcy who looked like she was thinking these things over very hard. She looked at Mark with eyes full of longing. "I've grown to hate me. I'd like to be able to start over and be new. How do I become His?"

Mark's heart was thumping with excitement. "It says right here," he showed her Romans 10:9 and 10. "... 'that if you confess with your mouth the Lord Jesus and believe in your heart that God had raised Him from the dead, you will be saved. For with the heart one believes to righteousness, and with the mouth confession is made to salvation.' 'Believe' means to trust from the heart, not just mentally assent to. Do you believe that Jesus was the Son of God and that He died for your sins? And that God raised Him from the dead?"

Marcy nodded.

"'Lord' means like a master, or boss, someone to be obeyed. Do you want Him to be your Lord? Are you willing to surrender to Him the running of your own life and doing things on your own?"

"You did that?"

Mark smiled. "Yes I did. And I haven't been sorry for a moment. He's doing a much better job than I ever did. At first, I thought that He would make me do things that I'd hate, or couldn't stand to do.

"I'm Chrissie and Beth's boss. I like to see them happy and enjoy things because I love them. Sometimes I make them do things they don't like, like eating their vegetables and going to bed, not because I'm mean, but because I know that it will be the best for them. They might not know it now, but they will when they get older.

"God's the same way. He's my Heavenly Father and He loves me. He likes to see me happy, and He likes to help me through the rough places, just like I do for my girls."

Marcy nodded. "I'm certainly not doing a good job of running my life.... I'm willing to surrender it to Him."

"Then all that is left is to call on the name of the Lord. Romans 10:13 says, 'For whoever calls upon the name of the Lord shall be saved.'"

"I don't know how."

"How about if I lead you in a prayer? You can repeat after me, if you agree with what I just said."

Again Marcy nodded. Mark held her hand and led her in prayer. Marcy felt like a heavy burden lifted off her when she turned her life over to God. She felt peace, unlike she'd ever known, flood her soul. Tears started to stream down her cheeks again, but this time they were tears of happiness and joy. Marcy covered her face and wept into her hands, so great was her relief.

Mark pulled her into a hug. His eyes were teary with joy, also.

"I have a feeling that you aren't going to feel left out at church tomorrow morning. Before you weren't a part of the family of God, now you are. Before it would have been like if you went to Janet's family reunion and tried to fit in. The people would be nice to you, but when they started talking about family things, you wouldn't know what they were talking about, you'd feel left out.

"But now you are a part of the family. It will feel entirely different. Now when you read your Bible every day, it will start to make sense to you. When you sing the songs at church, they'll have new meaning. At least I know that it happened that way for me, and I'm sure it will for you, too.

"God is going to start doing His perfecting work in you. Perfecting doesn't happen overnight, you'll still have problems, but at least now you'll know that you don't have to handle them alone. Take them to your Father and He'll guide you through them."

They talked for quite a while and Marcy asked several questions. Mark knew the answers to some, but wrote the others down so that he could find out later for her. It was quite late by the time they were ready to say good-night. With a promise from Mark to pick her up in the morning, Marcy went to bed looking with a new outlook and slept a sweet, peaceful sleep.

Chapter 19

Confusing Signals

Marcy woke up happy and was looking forward to the day. She was finally glad that it was Sunday. She woke up before her alarm clock, and almost two hours before Mark was due to pick her up. Mark arrived about a half an hour early with the idea to call Janet and share the good news with her.

They still got to church early, arriving before the Robinsons did. Marcy felt like a little kid, unable to wait to share a secret. Mark smiled to himself as he watched her. She constantly went to the front door to see if they were coming yet, then would pace back to where Mark was.

There was a definite difference in her. One couldn't help but to see it on her face. She greeted people that she recognized who had tried to extend friendship to her in the past. They were surprised at her warm and friendly greeting, and studied her a second before they returned her greeting.

Marcy was engaged in an animated conversation when the Robinsons arrived. They saw her through the glass doors before they got into the building.

"I think that our prayers have been answered, George." Mrs. Robinson confided happily to her husband.

"I think you're right, Marian." He gave his wife's shoulders a happy squeeze.

When Marcy noticed them coming, she suddenly felt shy and awkward about telling them. Mark noticed her hesitancy, so he laid a hand on her back in support.

"Marcy has some great news!" he said, smiling when they reached them.

"I think I can guess what it is," beamed Mr. Robinson. He engulfed her in a big hug. "Welcome to the family, Marcy. We've waited a long time for this."

Mrs. Robinson hugged her with tears in her eyes. "I think that you already know that we've been praying for you. We're so happy for you!"

They talked a little bit and Marcy wondered where Ryan was. Kandy wasn't there, yet, either, maybe he was going to bring her.

Marcy was apprehensive about seeing Kandy. She had said some ugly and mean things to her on the phone earlier that week. She had talked to Mark about Kandy last night. He told her that she needed to get things right with her. He relayed what the Robinsons had told him about Kandy getting saved. Marcy shook her head. She hadn't even realized that was what had taken place the Sunday before. She understood now, why Kandy had been crying and why everyone was so happy for her. She had received the same warm welcome this morning.

"Now, you're not only friends, but you're sisters in the Lord. You're part of the same family, and you're going to spend eternity together," Mark had explained.

Kandy was clearly surprised to see Marcy at church. Marcy went over to her as she came in the door, uncertain how to approach her.

"Kandy," she hesitated, not sure how to go on. Then she threw her arms around Kandy's neck. "I'm so sorry! Please forgive me!"

Kandy hugged her back. "I was worried about you all week. Yesterday, Dave told me what happened on Friday night. I'm surprised you're here today." She stepped back and looked at Marcy.

"Do you forgive me then?"

"Of course I forgive you! Are you all right?" Kandy asked, searching Marcy's face. The others had joined them by that time.

"Marcy's more than just all right, Kandy," Mrs. Robinson put in, and Marcy nodded eagerly. They shared Marcy's good news with her. Kandy squealed and threw her arms around Marcy. "I thought there was something different!"

Mark had been right about the service. The songs took on new meaning and so did the sermon. Marcy was eager to learn, hungry for knowledge.

She had been curious about Ryan's presence, or rather, lack of it, but unwilling to ask. It wasn't until after the service that she found out that he had left early Saturday morning and wouldn't be back for a month. This both relieved her and disappointed her. It relieved her, because she wouldn't have to face him. She still had feelings for him and didn't want to see any disgust for her and her actions on his face. It disappointed her because she wanted him to know about her salvation.

They were invited to the Robinsons' for Sunday dinner as usual. The mood was festive in celebration for both of 'their girls' as Mr. Robinson put it. They spent a good part of the afternoon discussing questions that both Kandy and Marcy had.

The weekend after Ryan left, he called home just to chat.

"Dad, has anyone bought the Silvers' house yet?"

"There've been a few people that have looked at it, but no one has come forward to buy it yet."

"Well, I've been praying about it, and I think I'd like to go ahead and buy it."

"If you've been praying about it, then I think that's a good idea, Son."

Ryan was slightly surprised at his dad's response. Had he been able to see his dad's face, he would have been more than slightly surprised. It was hard to keep this secret. Nobody had told him about Marcy, waiting so that Marcy could tell him, herself. Mr. Robinson's large grin, would have made him suspicious, and probably given it away.

"Well, could you start the ball rolling over there? I'd like to get started on it as soon as possible."

"I think that would suit Mr. Silvers just fine. He told me he was hoping to be in the retirement complex by Thanksgiving, but he couldn't do that unless the house sold. I think that he's looking forward to the people for the holidays. I guess they plan activities together. He's gone over there and already started to become acquainted."

"Find out how much he would like for a down payment, and I'll wire the bank and have them transfer the money to you. And when you talk to him, don't let him know that it's me that wants to buy it. I don't want him to feel like he needs to give me any special deals just because I'm your son and you're handling it. I want to be fair."

Marcy worked hard to catch up with the pottery demands. She cut back her time at the store so she would have extra time at home. It was still hard to use the kiln at the school because the art students were still studying pottery. She checked with the Junior College about using their kiln. They gave her permission, but the times she was allowed were restricted and not very convenient. They also wanted quite a bit of money, which would take a big bite out of her profits. The upside though was that their kiln was much larger and she could fire more pieces at once. It was only nine weeks until Christmas, so she figured that she could manage for that long. She wanted to make sure that she had enough of her wares out there for the Christmas shoppers. It was for her like it was for other manufacturers – Christmas was the biggest season.

Two weeks later, the school called her, and said that the new art teacher had complained about Marcy's use of the kiln. And considering that it was at the art department's discretion, they were going to have to ask her to not use the kiln any longer. Marcy told them about Christmas and they consented to let her use it until the Christmas break, but not after.

Marcy told Mr. and Mrs. Robinson and they prayed with her about it. They reassured her saying that God had plenty of time to work things out.

Ryan got back from New York on a Sunday evening. When he arrived home, the usual Sunday company had left already. He had a good talk with his parents. They were naturally interested in how his month had been, and asked him many questions.

His dad brought him up to date on the Silvers' house. Everything had gone well and there were just a few formalities left. Everything should be completed by the end of the week and Mr. Silvers was thrilled; he'd get to be in the retirement complex by Thanksgiving. He scolded Mr. Robinson when he found out that it was Ryan who wanted to buy the house. "I would have given him a break, if I'd known!"

Ryan chuckled when his Dad told him.

He had spent four weeks trying not to think about Marcy and was surprised that he had passed the courses with such good scores. He had been concerned and asked about her when he had called after he had arrived in New York. That was Saturday evening and they had told him what they knew. He forced himself not to ask about her each time he called. The couple of times he did ask, their answer was much the same. "She's fine," with a couple of minor news items thrown in. He hadn't found their information very satisfying. He resisted the urge to drive over to see her that evening.

It wasn't until Thursday evening that he saw her. He accidentally ran into her at the mall, while picking up something for his mom.

"Hi, Marcy," he said quietly coming up behind her.

He had startled her and she jumped. She turned around to see who had spoken to her, and when she saw Ryan, her cheeks grew hot.

"H-hi," she stammered. She had been nervous about meeting him. He had been the only one she hadn't faced since that night and she wasn't prepared for this encounter. "You startled me."

"Sorry. I wasn't trying to," he smiled at her. He wasn't feeling very confident himself, not sure what to say to her. "How are you?"

"Fine. And you?"

"I'm fine."

"H-how was your trip?"

"It was long. But other than that it was fine."

"Did your courses go well?"

"Yes. I passed with higher scores than I had expected."

"That's great."

There was an uncomfortable silence that followed the inane conversation. They stood nervously for a bit, Ryan looking openly at Marcy, Marcy shifting uneasily trying not to look at Ryan. Finally Marcy looked at her watch, for something to do. She knew she had to say something so she might as well just blurt it out.

"Ryan... I'm sorry about that Thursday evening. I behaved very badly. What I did wasn't right. I had no right to expect you to, um... And Friday night. I know that what I did put you to a lot of trouble, especially since you were leaving early the next morning. I know you didn't have to. It was very kind of you. I appreciate it. Really." Marcy let the rest of her breath out on a rush and licked her lips nervously. She shifted to the other foot. Again she looked at her watch for something to do.

Ryan didn't respond immediately, he wanted to talk to her, ask her questions and tell her things. He had caught the joy that had come into her eyes when she first saw him, but it was fleeting and left almost instantly. It was replaced by nervousness and a little sadness.

"Marcy," Ryan pulled her attention to him gently. "Would you go for a cup of coffee with me?" He had been fighting the battle of wanting to be with her and knowing he should leave. She looked like she was going to bolt. Even if he couldn't spend much time, the space for a cup of coffee would extend the precious minutes.

Marcy dropped her eyes and shook her head. She couldn't, her attraction for him was still too strong. She had prayed and asked the Lord to be in charge of her feelings for Ryan, and thought that she was doing pretty well in that department, but she hadn't seen him in person, yet. Maybe she would have been able to if she would've had time to prepare herself, but this unexpected meeting threw her off guard. It would probably be better to try to avoid seeing him alone as much as possible. Had she looked at him, she would have seen the disappointment on his face.

"Marcy," he was going to ask her again, she knew it.

"I can't," she interrupted. She looked at him briefly and gave him a quick, apologetic smile. He nodded and she turned and left. Ryan stood watching her walk away. He sighed a heavy sigh then went to get what he had come for.

Marcy was in the parking lot when she realized that she had forgotten to ask Ryan if he knew she had gotten saved. Even though she hadn't asked the Robinsons not to tell him, she was pretty sure they hadn't. He didn't mention anything just now, so he probably didn't know yet. Oh well, she could tell him Sunday.

Saturday had been rainy, but the wind in the night had pushed the clouds away. So Sunday morning dawned bright and clear. Marcy woke up refreshed and humming a song from church. She giggled to herself, remembering how Kandy's cheerful attitude on Sunday used to irk her. She had gotten a lot accomplished this last week and she felt like she could give herself a break today. She purposely closed the door to her back porch. She wasn't going to even think about the pottery.

As she was closing the door, she spotted the bowl Ryan had made. It had been ready for quite a while, and she kept forgetting to give it to him. She retrieved it from the shelf; she could take it to him at church.

Marcy's car was outside instead of parked in the garage like normal. She had gone out yesterday and when she had gotten back, it was raining hard, so she parked close to the door. This morning her car was covered with soggy, brown leaves. It was her turn to drive this morning, so she had to clean the leaves off her windshield. Kandy pulled into her drive behind her.

"Hi!" she greeted her friend, "I thought that I was driving this week."

"You are. I got called into work so I won't be able to go to church. I tried calling you earlier, but you must have been in the shower or something. I'm on my way in now."

That meant she would be going alone. Dave was working, too, so he wouldn't be going. He had gone with them on the Sundays that he didn't work. Marcy suspected that it was partially so he could spend more time with Kandy. He seemed pretty smitten with her the last several weeks.

Marcy was disappointed. She enjoyed riding with Kandy and Dave when he went. Not only that, but she hoped that Kandy's presence would be a shield and help keep her thoughts in line. She didn't let that put a damper on her good spirits, though. She sent up a prayer for help along that line and continued humming the song from church.

That is until her engine sputtered to a stop.

"Oh, no!" she groaned, "I didn't."

She looked at her gas gage and confirmed her suspicions.

"I did," she groaned again.

She had forgotten to put gas in her car. She shoved the gear shift into neutral to coast down a small hill then pulled to the side of the road. She was going to be late to Sunday School. It was almost ten blocks to the nearest gas station. Sighing, she got out of the car and locked her doors.

"Lord, could You perfect my memory, too, while You're working on the rest of me? Thank You," She sent up the plea as she started walking to get gas. The wind was cold and she pulled her coat tighter around her, but it didn't prevent the wind from swirling around her legs under the flapping bottom edge. By the time she got to the gas station, she felt frozen and her feet hurt. The gas attendant was surly and insisted that she purchase the can before she filled it up with gas.

"Don't want you takin' off with it, without paying for it."

"I'm in high heels; I don't think I could run very fast."

"Them's my rules. If you don't like it then go somewhere else."

"Would you fill it for me, please?" she asked, "I don't want to get gasoline on my clothes."

"This is self-serve. I only take money."

Marcy sighed. On her walk to the station, she had thought briefly that maybe there would be someone available to give her a ride back. She didn't even bother asking. She could hear his retort, *"I ain't a taxi service; I only take money."* She looked at her watch and sighed. Sunday School was almost over by now. As she was filling her can, she prayed.

"Father, I don't want to miss church, too. I don't see how, but could you please make a way so that I don't have too?"

Marcy had to stand in line to pay for the gas. As she did, the can grew heavier in her hands. She dreaded the thought of having to lug it back to the car. Not only that, but she had spilled some on the outside of the can, and she was trying to hold it away from her so it wouldn't get on her. When it was her turn to pay, she noticed a taxi pull into the station. Her eyes lit up with delight. Maybe God answered her prayer already!

She waited until the taxi driver came into pay and then approached him.

"Is your cab for hire?"

"Yep."

"Good! I'd like to hire you!"

The cab driver looked her over and at the gas can in her hand.

"Okay."

"Talkative sort, aren't you," Marcy mused to herself. The cab driver put Marcy's can in the trunk while she got in the cab. She told him approximately where her car was then looked at her watch. He started to pull out of the station and Marcy stopped him.

"No wait. Take me instead to..." and she told him the address of the church. If she went to take care of her car now, she would miss a good deal of the service, too. She could go directly to the church and take a taxi afterwards. The driver sat there a second.

When Marcy looked at him to see why he wasn't moving, he said, "Sure?"

"Yep."

A few blocks from the church Marcy got curious. "I didn't think that taxis filled up at gas stations. I thought that the company had its own pump."

"That's right."

"Then, if you don't mind me asking, why did you get gas at that station?"

"Was low and didn't know if I could make it back," then added almost as an afterthought, "Don't know why I didn't remember to check before I went out this morning."

Marcy smiled. She knew why.

Marcy put the gas can behind some bushes near the entrance of the church building. She couldn't very well take it in with her and she didn't know what else to do with it.

Service had started already, but she didn't hear singing as she entered the foyer. They must be still making announcements. She raced to the washroom to try and get the gas smell off her hands and quickly run a brush through her hair. She hung her coat up hastily and hurried to the sanctuary. The people were standing to sing. She felt rushed as she debated whether to just sit in the back or go up and sit with the Robinsons. An usher told her it was okay to go on up, so she did.

They just started the first song when she stepped past Mr. and Mrs. Robinson. Ryan stepped down and Marcy stood next to Mrs. Robinson.

"We were getting worried about you, Dear," she whispered.

"I ran out of gas," Marcy whispered back.

"Where's Kandy?"

"She got called into work."

"Well I'm glad that you made it."

Marcy nodded in response then joined the singing.

Marcy felt herself relax and thanked the Lord silently that Ryan's presence wasn't unnerving her. She got caught up in the worship and didn't notice the side glances Ryan gave her periodically during the song service. She also didn't notice how he watched her during the sermon. Today, Ryan was the one that had a hard time keeping his mind on the service.

After the service, Ryan stayed at her elbow while people visited with her. He found himself feeling impatient with the people that greeted him and wanted to ask him about his trip. Today, he was the one that wanted to hurry and get out the door. Finally, they were out.

Mr. Robinson extended the usual invitation for dinner.

"I don't think that I should today. I really should work on my inventory." Marcy declined. Sitting in church with Ryan was one thing, but to have to spend the afternoon with him was another thing entirely, especially without Dave or Kandy there. *So much for not thinking about pottery today.*

"Are you sure you don't want a break? You've been working awfully hard lately."

"I'd love a break. But the holidays are going to be over before you know it, and I'll get plenty of breaks then." She smiled warmly at them and thanked them again for their invitation. She looked at her watch. "I'd better call a taxi, or I won't get home until late, anyway," she smiled.

"Why do you need a taxi, Dear?"

"I left my car where I ran out of gas. Oh, I didn't tell you, did I?" and she recounted briefly how God had answered her prayer.

"You don't need to call a cab, I'll take you." Those were the first words that Ryan had spoken to her.

Marcy looked at him, not very comfortable with the idea. "That's okay, really. You don't need to go to the trouble," she smiled, but he saw the uncertainty in her eyes.

"It's no trouble," he pressed. He didn't want her to get away this time.

"I, um... okay," she gave in reluctantly.

Ryan had ridden to church with his parents, so they went to their house first. Mrs. Robinson asked Marcy if she wouldn't consider staying for dinner and getting her car afterwards, but Marcy stayed firm. Mrs. Robinson fixed her a plate anyway, while Ryan quickly changed his clothes.

"Don't wait dinner on me," he whispered to his mom as he headed out the door. She saw a light in his eyes as he spoke and she noticed a spring in his step as he went to his car.

Marcy was quiet as they drove down Cobblewood. She watched as they passed the Silvers' house. She had heard that it had sold. She was a little disappointed. She knew that she couldn't afford it herself, but she had been hoping that Mark and Janet would have bought it. Then it would've at least been in the family. She kept forgetting to ask who bought it. Maybe Ryan knew. She glanced at Ryan. No, she'd just try to remember to ask Mr. Robinson the next time she saw him. Marcy felt nervous being with Ryan.

"Why didn't you tell me?" Ryan spoke softly.

Marcy looked at him wondering what he meant. He smiled at her, and then she knew.

"I wondered if your parents had told you," she stated.

"They didn't. I think they thought that maybe you would want to."

Marcy nodded.

"So when did this happen?" he prodded.

"The Saturday that you left. Mark picked me up from your parents' and took me home. We had a long talk about... things. He shared with me what happened to him and then verses out of the Bible."

Ryan's heart sang with joy as they talked about her experience. Marcy could hear the joy in his voice and felt herself relax a little. She didn't feel like he was keeping a wall between them today. She kept her distance, though. *"I can't have that kind of relationship with you,"* kept resounding in her head. She was not going to allow herself to get carried away and thus get hurt again.

Ryan felt Marcy distancing herself from him. As she was talking with him, she skirted personal questions and kept the conversation on a surface level. He could hear the joy in her voice, but it was almost as if she was trying to hold it back for some reason.

They reached her car much too soon for him and not soon enough for Marcy. He took the gas from his trunk and poured it into her tank, then stood by to make sure that it would start.

"Thank you. I appreciate your help," she said. Her words sounded formal even to her ears. Ryan's eyebrows quirked a little at her words. She didn't know how to make them sound friendlier without sounding like an idiot, so she said nothing else.

"Do you really have to get right home?"

"The holiday season is the busiest. I got pretty far behind this year." *'That wasn't a lie, I just didn't answer his question,'* she reasoned to herself.

"We could grab a bite at the burger joint. That would be pretty fast. You need to eat," he persisted.

"Your mom fixed a plate for me."

251

"You can save it for your supper."

"I can't." There, that was honest.

"Well, could you schedule some time to go to dinner this week?" he asked hopefully.

Marcy's brows knit together trying to figure him out.

"I'll have to see. I'm pretty busy." She certainly didn't encourage him.

"I'll call you."

Marcy nodded and turned to put her car in gear. Ryan didn't move. "Marcy..."

"Oh, I almost forgot," she cut him off. She picked up his bowl from the seat beside her and handed it to him through the open window.

"What's this?"

"It's your bowl. Don't you recognize it?"

"Ah, yes, my bowl. It looks different."

"Glaze changes a lot when fired. I'm sorry I didn't get it to you sooner."

Ryan nodded. Neither one said anything for a moment. Marcy studied the bowl. Somehow she was reluctant to give it to him. Maybe that was why she had forgotten all this time. It was a piece of him and if she gave it back she would have nothing.

Ryan studied Marcy's face. He saw a kind of sadness come into her eyes and wondered at it.

"Would you like to keep it?" he asked her gently.

Marcy was surprised by his question. Could he tell what she had been thinking? *"No,"* she told herself, *"You turned it over to God, and you can't just keep hanging on."*

She shook her head. Her voice was quiet when she spoke. "What you said about yielding to the potter helped, you know."

Somehow he did know. He smiled gently at her. "I'm glad."

She rolled up her window and pulled away from the curb.

Ryan called her three times the next week. Each time she made an excuse not to see him. Sunday, Dave and Kandy were both at church and they all went over to the Robinsons' afterwards. Marcy kept her distance from Ryan, physically as well as emotionally. She joined in conversations and was friendly, but avoided looking at him. She could feel his eyes upon her a number of different times as if he were willing her to look at him. She didn't want to make eye contact with him.

He called her the next evening. She kept the phone conversation light, unimportant and short. She was glad that she was busy. When he asked her if she had free time that week, she said no.

"It's a short week because of Thanksgiving, you know."

"So will you be taking the weekend off?" he asked hopefully.

"Yes. I'm going to be spending it at my parents'. Mark and Janet are going to be here. I want to spend as much time as I can with them because they won't be here for Christmas."

"Oh," His voice was disappointed.

"I need to get back to work. I'll probably see you in church."

Ryan conceded, feeling disappointment and frustration when they hung up. She was definitely holding him at arm's length. It didn't occur to him that she thought he wanted it that way. No one had told her differently.

"I just don't understand him!" she confided to Mark when they got a free minute to talk alone.

It was Saturday afternoon and something was needed at the grocery store. Mark volunteered to go and Marcy volunteered to help him. He had asked her how things were going for her, and the subject had gotten around to Ryan. "He told me that he didn't want that kind of relationship, and yet he's constantly asking me to do things with him. I can't do that. I don't feel like I can just be his buddy anymore. I thought he would understand that. I guess that I just have to tell him plainly. I didn't want to; I hoped that he would get the message when I kept putting him off. But pretty soon the holidays are going to be over, and I'll run out of excuses."

Marcy was quiet for a while. Mark was pondering what she had just told him. Mr. Robinson had told him how Ryan had felt. He didn't think that Ryan had changed his mind about Marcy, especially in light of what Marcy had said about his persistence. It didn't look like anyone had told Marcy. What could he say without breaking confidences?

Marcy spoke again. This time instead of frustration, it carried a hint of sadness. "I guess I'll just have to say 'Look, Ryan. I'm sorry but I can't be your buddy because that's not how I feel about you. I love you, and it hurts too much to be around you.' I just have to lay my heart on the line and hope he doesn't step on it too hard," Her voice broke and she turned her face to the window.

Mark felt he had to say something. He was sure he was right; he just hoped he wouldn't say too much.

"Marcy, did he say he *couldn't* have that kind of relationship, or that he *didn't want* to?"

"Couldn't. What difference does that make?"

"A big difference. When did he tell you this?"

"That Thursday before that awful Friday. Two days before I got saved."

"Do you know what 2 Corinthians 6:14 says?"

"No. What?"

"I'm not going to tell you, because I think that you should look it up for yourself. Then think about the questions I asked you."

Marcy forgot to look up the verse that Mark told her until the next morning in church. They were sitting in the pew behind the Robinsons, and she was studying the back of Ryan's head when she remembered. Then she couldn't remember which one to look up. Mark was too far away to ask. Janet was in between them and Chrissie was sitting on her lap this morning, so she wouldn't be able to until after church anyway.

She had Sunday dinner at her parents'. Mark and Janet had to leave right after they ate. It was going to be late when they got back home as it was.

When Marcy got home that evening she looked up the verse and tried to read it in light of the questions Mark had asked. Hope sprang up in her heart. This verse said to not be unequally yoked. It was a direct command, not an option. Before she was a Christian, Ryan had told her that he couldn't have that kind of relationship with her. Maybe he *did* have feelings for her and because she hadn't been a Christian it was wrong for him. But she was a Christian now, and he knew it.

Marcy wanted to jump and shout. But wounded feelings held her in check. *"What about Kandy? He told you that he liked Kandy."* Marcy thought that over for a bit. Possibly, but why would he be seeking her company instead of Kandy's? *"Go cautiously,"* her head said, *"Maybe there was another reason, altogether."*

Ryan called her Monday afternoon from work and asked if she would like to go out to eat. She honestly couldn't that evening as she had both kilns scheduled to load and fire. He sounded disappointed.

"Well, Miss Kelman, do you have any idea when you might have a free moment in your busy schedule to pencil in a few minutes with an old friend?"

"I'm running my route tomorrow," she said hesitantly, "if you would like to meet for lunch."

Marcy couldn't help but to notice the tenor in Ryan's voice change. A broad smile came to her face as they made plans. *"Caution,"* her heart warned again.

Ryan was surprised that she suggested it. He was prepared for another one of her standard 'I-don't-know-I'll-have-to-see' answers. He wished they could have a leisurely dinner together, along with a long talk. But that was not to be. He only had a short time for lunch, and the place Marcy picked was usually crowded. The service was fast and the food good, but the ambiance left something to be desired.

The next day at lunch she purposed to keep a distance. The conversation remained light and impersonal. She was just testing the waters, she told herself. After all, she didn't want to get burned.

On Thursday, Ryan stopped by after work just as Marcy was getting ready to leave.

"I'm sorry that you stopped by for nothing," she said.

"Maybe it isn't for nothing," he responded, not to be put off so easily. "Where are you going?"

"I have to go unload the kilns that I fired yesterday then reload them. I got a break at the junior college this week, and have unlimited access to it. I need to take advantage while I can."

"Well, see, there's something I can help you with. It'll save you time if I go and help. And with the time you save, you'll have time to grab a quick bite to eat with me. I didn't stop 'for nothing' after all," He wormed his way into her day. She knew that she couldn't get out of it without sounding ungracious.

"Okay," she resigned herself. "I've got to load my car first."

Ryan backed his car out of the drive then helped Marcy load hers. They headed first to the high school. When they got there, the art teacher was still there.

"I unloaded your stuff already. I need the kiln tomorrow morning." The teacher was in a cantankerous mood, her voice cross. "I'm sorry you felt you had to do that," Marcy apologized, "Didn't you get my note telling you I'd be here this evening?"

"Notes mean very little to me. You'll find your stuff over there," She pointed to a corner where Marcy's 'stuff' was stacked. It didn't look like much care was taken. Two pieces were broken and she found another one that was chipped.

"Those aren't so badly broken that you can't glue them together." She stated simply, when she saw Marcy examining them. Her voice didn't hold even a hint of an apology in it. Marcy didn't respond. Even if they could be glued together, they wouldn't be sellable and the teacher knew it. This kind of thing had been happening ever since the school said that she could finish out the holiday season. The art teacher took it upon herself to make Marcy sorry she hadn't quit earlier like she had wanted her to do.

She talked to Ryan about the situation on the way to the Junior College.

"I don't have enough money for my own kiln, yet. My lease is up the end of February, and my landlord doesn't want me to get the basement ready to put one in before my lease is up, even if I had the money. I think that he's getting cold feet. Your mom and dad prayed with me about it, so I'll leave it in God's hands. It's hard though. I want to know how things are going to work out in advance."

Ryan chuckled, "Don't we all?!"

They weren't able to park very close to the door, and Marcy had several boxes of pottery loaded in her station wagon. They each took a box into the college.

"Why don't you start unloading the kiln? I'll go fetch the rest of the stuff from the car. I think that will save time," Ryan suggested.

Marcy wasn't sure after a little bit. It seemed to take him an awfully long time to make one trip. She had the kiln unloaded and was starting to load it again by the time Ryan got back. But when he did get back he had the rest of the boxes from the car with him.

He grinned broadly at her when he saw the look on her face. "Thought I got lost, didn't you?"

"Where'd you get that?" she asked about the cart he was pulling.

"I'm not telling, let's just say I'm resourceful," he teased.

Marcy smiled back at him, and started loading again. The cart saved many trips back and forth to the car.

Ryan took her for pizza on the way home. Marcy felt herself relaxing a little in his presence. She still kept her distance, but it was closer than it had been. Ryan could feel the difference, too.

When they got back to Marcy's, he dropped her off. She didn't invite him in and he didn't ask. He had pushed enough for one day.

Marcy's work was slowing down. She had been able to get enough of her wares out and store owners didn't want too much left on their shelves after Christmas. Ryan pushed to see her a few times over the next couple of weeks and she didn't have a convenient excuse. The distance between them was waning, her head said to keep her distance and her heart said something entirely different. Although to Marcy, her heart seemed to be winning. As hard as it was for her, she still kept time with him short and impersonal.

Had Ryan but known the battle going on within Marcy, he wouldn't have felt frustrated. Even though Marcy was spending more time with him, it still seemed on the stiff side. He would have been happy to get it back to the easy friendship they had when he had first gotten back to Lakeland Grove. Maybe that kiss had ruined their friendship altogether.

Chapter 20

CHRISTMAS

 week before Christmas Marcy got her store work schedule. "Oh, no! Dave, I won't be able to spend Christmas with my family!"

"I know. I'm sorry Marcy. You know that I would like to play favorites if I could. But those that had to work the Thanksgiving weekend get the first considerations and full time employees were next. You weren't in either one of those groups. I'm going to be shorthanded the way it is."

Marcy could tell that he was truly sorry. "I know. I'm just disappointed that's all. Mom and Dad are going to Mark and Janet's, so they won't even be here."

"If it makes you feel any better, I have to work, too. We can both wish we were somewhere else together," he teased her.

"Well at least the store closes at 1:00 on Christmas Eve."

"I can't see my family either, this year. I know Kandy is by herself. Maybe we can do something together."

Marcy smiled at him. She knew that he would rather it be just Kandy and himself. "We'll see."

The Sunday before Christmas, Mr. and Mrs. Robinson found out that their 'other three children' weren't going to be with family over Christmas and promptly invited them to spend Christmas Eve with them.

"We'll have a holiday meal, and then attend the Candlelight service and we can enjoy eggnog while we open presents!" Mrs. Robinson had been an only child and so had her husband. She had always wanted a big family, and the desire was always heightened around the holidays. Here, an opportunity was presenting itself and her hope and enthusiasm was evident in her voice. No one turned down her offer. Marcy, Kandy and Mrs. Robinson made their plans that Sunday afternoon.

That evening, Ryan was surprised to get a phone call from Mark. Mark engaged Ryan in small talk for a few minutes, but Ryan was sure that wasn't why he called. Presently, Mark got to the real reason.

"I probably should have talked to you sooner, I just wasn't sure if I was meddling or not. You probably already know that your parents filled me in on some things when I came to get Marcy from their house that Saturday afternoon."

"Yes, I knew they had."

"I just wanted to let you know that Marcy and I had a talk over the Thanksgiving weekend." Mark paused not knowing how to continue. Ryan waited. "I know it's none of my business, but are your feelings for Marcy still the same?"

"Yes," he admitted, "And I thought that she felt the same. But I'm not sure lately."

"Have you told her how you felt?"

"No, I haven't been able to. She closes me off when I try to get personal. I think that she avoids spending time with me. The last few times when I've been able to see her it hasn't been quite as bad, but everything is still surface."

"She isn't sure how to relate to you anymore, Ryan. She's afraid that she's lost her best friend and doesn't want to get hurt," Mark paused. "I don't know if I over stepped the bounds or not. I didn't want to break confidences, and I tried not to, but I also want to help my sister. I asked her some pointed questions and told her to look up 2 Corinthians 6:14. I'm sure she didn't know about not being unequally yoked... Someone needs to tell her, Ryan," Mark said pointedly.

Ryan knew Mark was right, and he told him so. Of course Marcy wouldn't know what she meant to him if no one had told her. She needed to know the reason behind his actions, and if she still wanted to keep him at a distance, well at least she would know his heart.

Ryan's heart sang with Mark's next words. "She loves you, she told me she did."

Marcy's mood all that week was festive. She wasn't the only one, Kandy and Dave seemed to be looking forward to Christmas Eve, also. The three of them went shopping together to get something for Mr. and Mrs. Robinson. They had asked Ryan what his parents might like and he gave them several ideas.

Marcy felt a little like a fifth wheel with Kandy and Dave. Her mind wandered to Ryan every little bit. She had wanted to let down her guard with him over the past weeks. She could feel herself slip a little more each time she was with him. Her head kept warning her to be careful. She hadn't seen him this week, but she had talked to him on the telephone a couple of times. Their conversations weren't long, he said that he was very busy this week and didn't have a lot of time. Marcy didn't ask; she assumed that it was just because it was Christmas. She felt disappointed at not having seen him.

Christmas Eve finally arrived. Marcy could hardly wait to get off work and Dave teased her when she kept looking at the clock. She didn't care. Time just seemed to go so slow today. She wasn't sure why she was so excited; she hadn't felt this way about Christmas since she was a child. It had lost something as she had grown up. Maybe because this year she knew the real meaning of Christmas, it was fresh and exciting like it had been when she was a girl.

Marcy and Kandy arrived early to help with the dinner preparations. Mrs. Robinson had decorated the house beautifully. It was a quiet, stately elegance. There was nothing gaudy or cheaply done. The decorations continued in a theme throughout the house. She had even gotten three matching holiday aprons. They could tell that she was just as excited about having them help her as they were to be doing it.

Kandy was thoroughly enjoying preparing for the 'family get-together'. At one point when Mrs. Robinson bossed her on something, Kandy replied, "Yes, Mom."

Mrs. Robinson looked at her seriously. "You know, Kandy. I rather liked the sound of that. I always wanted daughters as well as sons and wouldn't mind if you just wanted to keep it up."

Kandy threw her arms around Mrs. Robinson's neck, unable to say anything. From that point on, she was 'Mom' the rest of the night to Kandy. Dave said something about it to her during dinner.

"I can call her that if I want. She adopted me today. Maybe if you're good, she'll adopt you too."

Mrs. Robinson turned to her husband. "You know, George, if she's my daughter, then she's yours, too."

Mr. Robinson looked over the top of his glasses at Kandy. "Well, then, I guess I'll just have to get use to a female voice calling me 'Dad.'"

Kandy beamed. They had given her the best Christmas present she could have received from them.

They ate in the dining room, which had been decorated with extra care. Candles were burning on the table and buffet, and with the chandelier lights turned low, and it gave a cozy, intimate atmosphere. Mr. Robinson's prayer was especially heartfelt and brought tears to Marcy's eyes. Everyone seemed to want to linger over the meal, unwilling to break the mood.

The Candlelight Service was beautiful and stirring. The pastor gave a moving message on God's love toward us. Kandy nudged Marcy toward the end of it, and motioned for her to look at Dave. Marcy looked at him, trying not to be obvious. She saw what Kandy had seen. His face showed that the message had spoken to his heart. He didn't go forward at the altar call, but he was especially quiet and thoughtful after the service. They knew that God was working on him. "Soon!" Kandy whispered to Marcy. Marcy nodded and smiled back at her friend.

Ryan pulled Kandy behind as they left the church to talk to her. Marcy noticed they were lagging and was going to go hurry them up, but Mr. Robinson started talking to her and took her arm to escort her to the car. Dave had gotten in the habit of escorting when he was around them, and had taken Mrs. Robinson's arm. Marcy noticed they were talking about something, and she figured that it was about the service. She hadn't noticed that Mrs. Robinson was the one that had taken Dave's arm and shooed her husband back to get Marcy's. Mr. and Mrs. Robinson had ridden to church separately, since everybody wouldn't fit in the same car. Marcy got deposited in the back seat of Dave's car. Dave got in behind the wheel. Ryan finally got Kandy to the car, and Marcy noticed the quick hug he gave her. Kandy got in the back seat with Marcy, insisting that it would be more comfortable for him in the front since his legs were longer. *"Thanks, Kandy,"* Marcy thought sarcastically to herself.

Dave missed a turn on the way back to the house, and they came down Cobblewood from the opposite direction. Everybody's eyes had been drawn to the Christmas lights along the way. The drive had been hushed by the snow that was falling. It had started earlier in the evening and there was some already accumulated on the ground. All the houses were lit up and most were decorated with outside lights. All, that is, except the Silvers' house. Marcy watched it sadly as they drove by. It looked lonesome to her. She didn't see Kandy's broad grin as she watched Marcy watch the house.

When they got back to the house, Mr. and Mrs. Robinson were already home and had glasses of eggnog poured. Opening the presents was the next thing on the agenda. Mr. Robinson made a great show of passing out presents, enjoying dragging the time out. He insisted that only one person at a time got a present and that everybody got to see what it was before the next person got theirs. There was much laughter and teasing.

After presents, there was pie, more eggnog and a lot more talking. Kandy started talking about all the houses with lights on in the neighborhood.

"So what's with that house on that one corner? It looked deserted."

"That's the Silvers' house. No one is living in it right now," said Mrs. Robinson.

"Why not?" Kandy asked.

"The new owner's haven't moved in yet." That was Mr. Robinson.

"Who are the new owners?" asked Marcy.

"So why haven't they moved in yet?" cut in Kandy.

"They didn't buy it that long ago. You know how it is around the holidays. Everybody is busy," supplied Mrs. Robinson. Marcy's question never got answered, she decided to try again. But before she could open her mouth, Dave stood up and stretched.

"All this pie and eggnog have made me drowsy. I feel like taking a walk. Kandy, you want to come?" Kandy didn't answer immediately but Ryan did.

"I think I would like to, too," and he stood up and stretched.

Kandy got up. "Sure, I think I'll go, too. I could use a stretch. It'll be nice to see the lights again."

Marcy stood up. A walk would be nice. "Are you coming, too?" she asked Mr. and Mrs. Robinson.

"No, Dear, I don't think I want to. I'll stay here and keep the house warm," smiled Mrs. Robinson.

"I don't think I will, either. I'll stay and keep Marian warm," he winked at his wife. "But I have an idea. I have the key to the Silvers' house. You use to always moon over that house when you were young. Would you like to see inside? Or don't you moon over it anymore?"

"Of course she still moons over it," Kandy put in. "You should have seen her on the way home from church. And if she doesn't want to, I know I would like to!"

"I thought you didn't like old houses, Kandy?" Marcy questioned.

"I don't like living in them, but I don't mind looking around inside them."

Mr. Robinson got the keys out of the office while everybody got their hats and coats.

"Are you sure the new owners won't mind?" asked Marcy.

"I'm sure that it will be okay just this once," he said as he handed the keys to Ryan.

"So who are the new..." Marcy didn't get to finish her sentence. Kandy was pulling on her arm, trying to drag her out the door.

"Come on, Marcy. What does it matter anyway? Hurry up before it stops snowing! Christmas lights need to be seen in the snow and they're even better if the snow is still coming down."

Kandy kept up a constant prattle for a while. Dave could hardly get a word in, and neither could Marcy. It didn't seem like Ryan even tried. A couple of blocks from the house, Ryan pulled on Marcy's sleeve and letting her know to slow down so Dave and Kandy could go ahead a little. She questioned him with her eyes.

"I just feel like a leisurely stroll and didn't want to walk alone. Besides, the night is too beautiful. It needs to be strolled though in quietness."

Marcy agreed. The big lazy flakes were taking their time joining those already on the ground. There was no wind to ruffle and tease them. They brought a peaceful hush to the neighborhood. Even Kandy must have sensed their request for silence, for soon she had stopped talking and was just strolling hand in hand with Dave.

Marcy watched them as they walked together. She felt a twinge of envy. They looked so comfortable together. Every once in a while they would playfully swing their hands in a big arc or one of them would pull the other closer and share a private thought. She and Ryan were walking with their hands in their pockets. She wanted to reach out and hold his hand. She knew she couldn't though. She still had some reserve within her.

They watched as Kandy slipped on some ice and Dave caught her. Kandy turned around and cautioned them. When Ryan and Marcy approached the same spot, Ryan took his hand out of his pocket.

"Here," he said as he offered his arm. "I don't want to spend the rest of the evening in the emergency room."

He chuckled as Marcy made a face at him. She gladly took his arm and he placed his other hand on top of hers. He didn't let go of her hand afterwards. Her head told her to remove her hand but her heart said leave it; after all he made the first move. Shouldn't she trust her heart more? It felt nice there; comfortable, safe, as if it belonged and she wanted to enjoy it for a few minutes more, so she didn't pull hers away.

They were soon at the Silvers' house. Kandy and Dave were already at the door, waiting. Kandy started talking again, and pulled Dave through the door as Ryan opened it. Ryan felt around the wall for a light switch. Marcy looked around in silence. The entry was better than she had imagined. Kandy pulled Dave from room to room. Marcy felt almost annoyed. How could she just flippantly look and walk out? These rooms need to be taken in and appreciated. She started to follow, feeling like they were supposed to stay together. Ryan pulled on her sleeve again.

"Let them go. You don't have to rush just because they are. They aren't the ones that dreamed about this house since they were little. Enjoy it while you have the chance."

She was grateful he felt that way. She felt a little apprehensive at the thought of being alone with him. But she didn't want this chance ruined, she had dreamed about this house for too long to rush through it. Kandy and Dave had started upstairs first and they followed suit, only a lot more slowly. Marcy ran her hand long the banister feeling the smoothness of the wood.

"So if this were your house, what would you do with it?" Ryan asked.

Suddenly Marcy didn't want to know the name of the new owners. What did it matter anyway? Just for the time being, she could pretend that she was the one that was going to be moving in.

Ryan encouraged her in each room to tell him what that room would be used for and how she would furnish it. He joined in with her telling how he saw it. Marcy was surprised at how close their opinions matched. Dave and Kandy had been through the whole house before they got through three of the rooms upstairs. They heard them tromping back up the stairs.

"Hey, you slow pokes!" called Kandy, "You still upstairs? What's taking so long? There's nothing up here except a bunch of empty bedrooms! Do you mind if we head on back? I'm starting to get cold."

"No. That's fine." Ryan said. "I'm sure we can find our way home without you leading us."

Kandy started to say something and this time Dave pulled her along. They could hear them going back down the stairs, laughing as they headed to the front door.

"Kandy sure is wound-up tonight. I think this is one of the best Christmases she's had," Marcy commented.

Ryan smiled and agreed with Marcy. They turned back to daydreaming their 'what-ifs'. Marcy wanted this time to last.

"Are the people that are moving in, older?" she wondered. Maybe there was still hope that someday in the distant future...

"They're a younger couple."

Marcy nodded. She was silent as she looked out the window of the fourth bedroom. It overlooked the back yard. A street lamp, enhanced by the snow, provided just enough light to see. Ryan watched her. "Do they have children?"

"Not yet, I think they want to have some, though."

"That's good."

"Why?"

"Because that's the perfect yard for children. I always wanted to play in it when I was little. I always thought that it was sad that there never were any children for it. One time I thought that I would ask the people that lived here if they would like to hire me to play in their yard. I told Mark, and he told Mom. She wouldn't let me. I was mad at Mark for a week."

Ryan chuckled and they moved to the down stairs.

"Do you know them very well?"

"Pretty well. I know him, better than her. She seems like a person I would enjoy getting to know better, though."

They saw the kitchen next and then Marcy spotted the door to the back porch. She went quickly over to it. She stood in the doorway and took in the new cabinets and sink. "O-o-oh!" was all she said then headed down to the cellar. Again "O-o-oh!" was her only comment. She headed back up quickly and left the porch.

"We probably should leave," she said.

"Why? What's the matter?"

"I love this house. It's the perfect house, just like I knew it would be."

"So why do you want to leave?"

"Because I find myself being envious of the people that get to live here." She didn't see Ryan smile. "Do you think that they'll change this house much?"

"Maybe some minor things, but I think that they'll leave it pretty much the same. They both love it like it is."

"That's good. If they change something, don't tell me. I won't want to know." Ryan smiled again.

"What are they like?"

"Well, he's very nice. She's, well... she takes some getting used to."

Marcy looked at him strangely. "I thought that you said that she seemed like someone you would enjoy getting to know?"

Ryan smiled and shrugged. "One more room, then I'll let you go if you don't want to see any more. This one is my favorite."

They moved into a cozy room that had no ceiling light to turn on. The only light came in through the doors of the adjoining rooms. There was a fireplace on one end and Marcy went to stand in front of it. Ryan walked over and stood next to her. He didn't say anything. Marcy was looking at the room, Ryan was looking at Marcy.

"Oh," she said dreamily. "What a wonderful room! Can't you just imagine a fire in here? A couch there," she pointed, "Facing the fireplace with chairs turned in on each side." Marcy felt Ryan's eyes on her and she turned to look at him. The way he was watching her made her nervous.

"Don't you think a couch there would be perfect?" she asked trying to keep her composure. He nodded, his eyes never leaving her face. Her eyes flitted away then back again.

"And bookshelves against that wall." Her hand gestured, but her eyes locked with his. "This room would need lamps, of course." She kept talking, trying to keep her heart in one piece and herself from doing something foolish. "There's no ceiling light, but then, lamps are nice." Her eyes would try to quit looking at him, but couldn't stay away. "They wouldn't over-power the fire's light the way a ceiling light can. They can also be very nice for reading. I would..."

Ryan took a step toward her and put his finger to her lips. She stopped talking and swallowed, trying to calm her racing heart. She took a step back, away from him. "Ryan, I can't do this... It's too hard." Her voice came out barely above a whisper.

His eyes caressed her face. He reached his hand up, and she stepped back again, avoiding his touch. He saw a hurt look cross her face. She forced herself to turn away from him. "I think it's time to go," she said flatly as she started to walk away.

He followed and caught her arm. "Please, don't leave," he begged gently. She stopped but didn't turn around. His voice was a soft caress. "I love you, Marcy." She turned to face him, not sure if she heard right. He stepped closer to her, again. "I love you," he repeated, a tender light in his eyes. "I realized I loved you in high school. And when you fell back into my life in front of the house – I wanted to spend every moment with you." He reached up and stroked her cheek with his finger, his eyes drinking in her face. "It was agony not being able to tell you. But I couldn't until... And then I handled every-thing so badly. I thought I had ruined everything. Have I, Marcy? Please, please say you love me, too."

Tears filled Marcy's eyes. Her heart won, doubts being erased from her mind. "I do love you. I tried not to, but I couldn't help it."

He pulled her into his arms and kissed her. "I've wanted to do that for a long time," he said when he lifted his head. Marcy snuggled into him, and he held her tightly.

"There's something for you on the mantle," he whispered. Marcy tipped her head back to look at him.

"You'll have to let go of me if you want it," he chuckled. She reluctantly stepped out of his embrace and he pulled her back to the fireplace. There was a flat box about two inches square, sitting in the middle of the mantle. Marcy wondered why she hadn't seen it earlier, but more, she wondered what it was. It looked like the kind of box a department store would put a brooch in. She looked at Ryan questioningly. He smiled at her, watching her face.

"What is it?" she asked, as she reached hesitantly for it.

"I hope that it's an engagement ring.... Will you marry me?"

Her hand never made it to the box. It stopped in midair. "Oh Ryan!" she sobbed as she threw herself against him. He hugged her.

"Does that mean yes?"

She was crying and couldn't answer, but he felt her head nodding against his shoulder. He held her tighter. Finally, she could speak. "I love you" was all that would come out. He pushed her back after another minute.

"Don't you want to see your ring? I picked it out myself. I hope you like it." His voice sounded cheery. Marcy looked at the box. It was a strange one for an engagement ring. "Did you wrap it yourself, too?" She smiled at him.

"Yep," he nodded, grinning from ear to ear.

Marcy lifted the lid on the box and removed the top layer of cotton. She looked puzzled. There was what looked like a simple brass-colored key ring inside that was definitely too big for her finger.

"It was the closest I could get to gold," he explained.

She looked up at him, still puzzled.

"Don't you like it?" he asked.

"Uh, yes, it's nice," she said, not sure what to say.

Slowly he took her left hand in his and turned it palm up. His eyes never leaving her face. She watched, still puzzled, as his other hand reached into his pocket, pulled something out and deposited that 'something' into her upturned palm.

"I thought that it would fit this perfectly." He removed his hand. Her face changed from puzzlement to joy as she recognized the key he had used to unlock the front door.

"You bought this house?" she asked incredulously.

"Merry Christmas, Marcy," he smiled. "It comes wired for a kiln."

Marcy wrapped her arms around his neck and pulled his face to hers. She didn't know if she could hold any more joy. Something he said came back to her and she pushed him away.

"Wait a minute!" she frowned, "What do you mean I take some getting used to?!"

Ryan chuckled and pulled her back to finish the kiss.

A Note from the Author

There was a time in my life that I identified with Marcy. I was raised going to church, but had never been told (or perhaps I wasn't listening) that I needed to make a personal choice for Jesus. I attended a Christian college and found that my life started to spiral out of control. I felt like I didn't fit in anywhere and the people that I most admired definitely had something I didn't. (Perhaps that's why I admired them?) I thank God that He sent a very patient person into my life who explained it all to me and led me to the Lord. I found the acceptance and peace that I was so looking for and have never regretted making the decision for Jesus. He patiently helps me to grow: revealing the character of His love and giving peace and answers in trying situations.

Perhaps you also identify with Marcy, or maybe Kandy, who had never known a father's love. Or maybe you identify with Mark who was trying to 'fix' things by himself and just made it worse. Whatever the case, Jesus is waiting with out-stretched arms saying, "Come, I'm here waiting for you. I've been waiting all along for you to let me help you. Won't you give me your life?"

If you would like to make a decision to let Jesus be the Lord of your life pray this prayer below. Then tell somebody you know that has already done the same thing.

"Dear God in Heaven, I come to you in the name of Jesus. I acknowledge that I am a sinner and I am sorry for my sins. I need forgiveness. I believe that Your only begotten son, Jesus Christ, shed His precious blood on the cross

and died to redeem me from my sins. I am now willing to turn from my sin. You said in Your Holy Word in Romans 10:9 that if I confess the Lord Jesus and believe in my heart that God raised Jesus from the dead, I shall be saved.

Right now I confess Jesus as Lord. I believe that You raised Jesus from the dead. Right now I invite you, Jesus, to become the Lord of my life, to rule and reign in my heart from this day forward. Jesus, I accept you as my own personal Savior, and according to the Bible, I am saved.

Thank you God, that I can now call You 'Father' and that I am Your child! Thank You for loving me! Thank you, Jesus for dying for me and giving me eternal life! Amen!

If you are not currently going to church, find one to go to. Going to church is necessary to your new life in Christ. They will be able to pray for you, help you with Bible study, and give you the Christian fellowship you need to grow in the things of God

About the Author

Sharon Manea is a wife to a wonderful husband for over 36 years and mother of three children (two grown and a late-in-life surprise.) She stays active in her church by being on the ministry prayer team, teaching Sunday School, helping with Vacation Bible School and various other activities. She also teaches cooking related classes. She enjoys keeping busy with vegetable gardening and preserving the harvest of her gardens. Sharon maintains that when she grows up she wants to build a new 'old' house, complete with plenty of nooks and crannies, a huge wrap-around porch, lots of gingerbread, and one creaky step.